WICKED DESCENT

WICKED DESCENT

SCARLETT KOL

The characters in this book are fictitious. Any similarity to real persons, living or dead, places, or events is coincidental and not intended by author.

*To anyone who has ever doubted their dreams
but followed them anyway.*

"This thing of darkness, I acknowledge mine."

- William Shakespeare,
The Tempest

ONE

Seventeen Years Ago

Boom ... boom ... boom.

A fist rattled the front door in its frame. The hollow sound, heavy and angry, rumbled through the wooden panels and echoed through her skull, piercing the darkest depths of her mind.

She stood rooted at the foot of the stairs with her fingers gripped knuckle-white on the oak banister. It was time. He was here.

Stay calm.

She closed her eyes and released a wavering breath, her lungs deflating around her anxious heart.

This is my last chance to make things right. If only I hadn't waited so long.

She descended the last step, leaving only inches between her and the pounding fist of rage. Dropping to her knees, she laced a ribbon around the doorknob and tugged roughly on the knot. A clear glass ornament dangled from the end, gleaming in the dusky rays of sunlight from the living room window. Fragile hope hanging on a satin string.

One last hope.

Boom ... boom ... boom.

The glass ball clinked against the vibrating door. She rose on unsteady legs, smoothed her curls, and slowly opened the door.

He charged in, throwing her sideways.

"Where is she?" His dark-eyed gaze darted around the foyer, empty but for well-worn shoes and a gilded mirror. He stormed toward the kitchen and struck his open palm on the floral wallpaper.

"Lizzie," he shouted. "Let's go."

No answer. No footsteps creaking down the stairs. No faces appearing in the kitchen doorway. Just empty silence.

His frown hardened. "Lizzie!"

His ringing demand died into silence.

The woman turned the knob and edged the door closed, clicking the deadbolt in place. She drew a deep breath, steadfast in her resolve. "She's not here, Nick."

He halted at the end of the hall and threw a fiery stare that threatened to burn her to a crisp from the soul out. "Tell me where she is."

"I can't do that." She fought the quiver in her limbs and straightened her stance, feet wide and shoulders back, matching his stare, hate for hate. Her throat tightened.

He scowled and charged past her, knocking her roughly into the banister. As he reached for the front door, she blinked twice, and he rose into the air as if pulled by invisible strings.

He gasped.

She whipped her arm to the left. He hurtled backward down the hall and crashed on the floor.

Blood pounded beneath her skin as she scrambled into position between him and the door. There would be no escape for him. Not this time.

As he crouched on the floor, a lock of dark hair flopped across his brow, and his arrogant snarl dissolved into innocent, wide-eyed surprise, diffusing his dangerous edge. With high tops and ripped jeans, he gave the impression of a typical teenage boy. Except it wasn't real. She knew the truth. He wasn't human. Wicked lies wrapped in handsome flesh.

She forced herself to see past his counterfeit face. "I know what you are."

A crooked smile grazed his lips. "I wondered if you did."

"I won't let you destroy my family."

"That's not your choice." He laughed. "I honestly didn't think you could wield any real power, but I guess we both have our secrets, don't we?" His smile widened as he pressed his hands to the floor and pushed himself up, focused, steady, like a wolf ready to attack.

Her muscles tensed.

He can't get to his feet.

She blinked once. Before she could blink a second time, he sprang up and turned his face to the ceiling, spreading his arms open wide. A fierce wind radiated from his core and ripped down the hall toward her, smashing pictures into the hardwood and slamming her back against the door.

He leaped forward and wedged his arm under her chin, pressing her into the door and squeezing her windpipe. "I could've done this the easy way, but it's been a while since I've killed someone with my own hands."

She slid her arm along the door until her hand brushed the doorknob. She entwined her fingers in the satin ribbon attached to the glass ball and held tight.

Please, just let me finish this.

With that singular desperate thought, a familiar pain slowly stretched from the back of her skull and spidered across her brain, aching behind her eyes.

His grip around her throat tightened. "I would've killed you eventually, but I wanted you to see her suffer first."

He pressed his face so close to hers that she could taste his sulphuric breath. All traces of his humanity blurred in and out of focus until she saw nothing but the red fiery glow ringing his dark ember eyes.

She bit her cheek and tasted copper. Pain and power battled, melding in her blood. Hot tears burned her cheeks and blinding white flashed behind her eyelids. He pressed harder. Her limbs flopped loose and heavy like doll parts. Pain exploded in her head and rippled through her body.

She drew one last haggard breath and screamed, "*Protego, admoderor, defende.*"

He let go.

Fresh air rushed back into her lungs. She sputtered, struggling to lift her eyelids. The world was cloudy, but the boy was gone.

She slumped to the floor with her fingers still tangled in the ribbon, her arm twisted at an awkward angle above her head. She gazed up at the glass ball dangling from the doorknob. Dark-purple shadows danced inside.

She smiled. Safe. At least for now.

Closing her eyes, she pictured her daughter's face. She'd be furious for a while, but maybe one day she'd understand.

"Forgive me," she whispered, but no one was there to hear it.

The ache in her head pulsed. Once ... twice ... darkness.

Two

"Just humor me, Avery," Mom said with one of those condescending looks only she could give. Her unnatural half-squint was supposed to mean anger, disappointment, embarrassment, or any combination of those emotions rolled into one convenient scowl. A rare, underappreciated talent.

She called it her evil eye, the only thing she claimed she inherited from my grandmother, but she'd perfected it over the years until it became distinctly hers—and it looked ridiculous every time she used it.

"Seriously, Mom. More decorations? Aren't we done yet?" I laughed as I slid the last of the golden bells on a tree branch and chucked the empty decoration box into the plastic storage bin.

"We'll be done when we're done. Right now, that front hall still looks terribly barren, but those evergreen garlands will liven it up." She put her hands on her hips and stared from the foyer to the living room, huffing at the stray hairs dangling in her face. "Besides, I thought you said you wanted to help."

Wanted to. Had to. Didn't matter. They amounted to the same thing: three hours of blissful Sunday slacking I'd never get back.

I headed for the stairs. "Fine, but I still think you're completely insane."

Insane? I winced and glanced over my shoulder. The word

just slipped out. So stupid. You were never supposed to call someone that, especially to their face when they hadn't exactly been stable lately. Fortunately, instead of running to her bedroom, Mom continued stringing lights around the living room as though she hadn't heard a thing. *Phew!*

It wasn't like she was truly clinical, just temporarily out of sorts. All the crying. So hard to watch, especially knowing I couldn't help her, couldn't make her pain stop. And even though she'd improved, she still wasn't herself, not like she was before Grandma died. Maybe she'd never be the same again.

I climbed the last few stairs to the second floor and pulled the attic ladder down from the hall ceiling. It seemed odd to have a ladder right in the middle of a hallway, but nothing in this forgotten little town made sense. At least not to me. As I stepped onto the first rung, a cold nose nuzzled against my foot and a soft purr vibrated against my skin.

"C'mon, Whiskers." I tapped my thigh and called to the gray ball of fluff on the floor.

She sat down and tilted her head, but continued meowing up at me.

"Lazy kitty." I scooped her into my arm and headed up the ladder again. A few steps up, she tensed and clawed at my shoulder.

"Easy girl."

She hissed and jumped out of my arms, scrambling down the hallway. I shook my head and kept climbing. *Guess it'll be a while before Whiskers feels comfortable in this house too.*

I flopped down on the dusty attic floor and inhaled the stale air.

Muted pink shards of sunset shone through a high dirty window and cut stripes across my jeans, warming my legs and sending a toasty tingle up my back. Exposed wooden rafters peaked around the room, creating shadowed alcoves and secret corners. The whole charming space lifted the heaviness in my chest, like when I stood on the roof of our apartment in the city. On that roof, the noise of the world fell away. Up there, I wasn't boring Avery Belmont, but someone more. Someone hovering above a bustling city waiting for life to start. Up there, the future pulsed in my fingertips and prickled my spine, bigger than Detroit, and definitely bigger than Shady Creek. My own special place above the world.

With some cleaning, this could be my new place to get away. It wouldn't be the same without the hum of the city and the glow of the moon over the skyline, but it could work. If the chaos of my first few weeks in Shady Creek continued, I'd need it. Maybe I could string lights through the rafters and get rid of some of the boxes stealing all the space. What was even in them all? Half ours, half Grandma's. Probably all junk. Stuff that didn't really have a place.

Like me.

I closed my eyes. Over the past month, the world had spun too fast for my brain to catch up. Two weeks ago, we left the hospital. Dingy white hallways reeking of bleach and human fluids swirled into a dizzying tornado of funeral plans and moving boxes, then—poof—I landed in Shady Creek, Nowhere. But clicking my heels wouldn't send me home. Grandma was gone, and so was everything I'd ever known.

Even worse, I didn't know how I was supposed to feel. Everyone seemed to expect me to grieve, to cry. After all, that was the normal thing to do, but I never really knew my grandmother. It was always just Mom and me. And being in this house—Grandma's house—felt awkward. Like I was a fraud who didn't deserve to be here. Not that I wanted to be here anyway.

And poor Mom. During Grandma's last days, she lived at the hospital. They hadn't talked more than five minutes in years, but as the color in Grandma's cheeks faded, so did all the bad stuff that had kept them apart. One day, they even laughed and whispered like best friends. Like Mom and I used to do before everything exploded. At least they finally put whatever was broken behind them. If only they'd done it sooner, we could've been a real family.

I pulled my shirt sleeves over my hands and dug my fingers into the cuffs. My throat swelled.

No more unhappy thoughts. I couldn't change things anyway.

I stood up and brushed the dust off my jeans. Okay, where to start? I rummaged through boxes of old afghans and ugly knickknacks but couldn't find another box of decorations. Too much stuff. Too much dust.

Achoo!

I covered my mouth with my arm and sneezed again. When I looked up, a box marked *Evergreens* screamed at me from its high shelf in the left corner, wedged under a wooden beam. Of course, I'd miss the most obvious, boldly labeled box in the whole space.

Shifting a pile of other containers out of the way, I created a narrow path to the shelf and grabbed onto the top cardboard flap. I pulled, but the box refused to budge from under the beam. I caught my breath and yanked harder. This time, it gave way and knocked me back onto a pile of old magazines, and then it landed square on my chest.

Stupid box.

I pushed it off and struggled to my feet, kicking the box across the floor toward the ladder. I looked up. Some kind of reflection danced across the ceiling. It wasn't there before. I turned and followed the light back to the top shelf and stood on tiptoe, running my hand over the surface. Something must've caused that reflection. My fingertips brushed against a round, hard object that was hidden behind the evergreen box.

I stretched taller and grabbed, but the object rolled away and slipped over the edge of the shelf. Glass! I gasped and lunged for it, but missed. I cringed, waiting for it to shatter, but it simply hit the ground, rolled into the wall, and stopped.

With a massive sigh, I picked it up by the ivory satin ribbon strung on one end and swung it in front of my face. Detailed pewter end caps wrapped around a glass ball like icy silver fingers, clutching it between metal palms. It looked expensive, and I was thankful there were no cracks. Mom would likely slaughter me if I broke this one.

I turned the ornament over in my hands and stared at a purple gas-like substance swirling inside. Hypnotized, I tapped my fingernail on the glass. The purple stuff changed direction and pulled away from my finger.

I blinked. Fascinating.

"Avery!" Mom called from downstairs.

I jumped and the ribbon slipped from my fingers. Not again! I snapped my hand out and caught the ball a split second before it would've smashed on the floor.

"What?" I yelled, slipping the ribbon around my wrist.

"Did you get lost up there?"

"No. I'm coming."

I dropped the box of garland out the attic hatch and climbed down the ladder, the glass ball dangling from my arm. At the bottom of the stairs, I lowered the box and held the ornament up for Mom to see. "This one's pretty."

"Sure is. Where did you get it?"

"In the attic. Behind a bunch of boxes."

"It's beautiful." She grabbed the bottom of the ornament and studied the swirling contents, as if in a trance. "I've never seen this one before."

"Do you know what the purple stuff is?"

"Not sure." Mom twisted the ball on its ribbon and shook her head as it spun. She filled her arms with evergreen boughs. "Go put it on the tree and then come help me with these."

In the living room, the Christmas tree glistened with Grandma's shiny collection of ornaments. No handmade pipe cleaner reindeer or cotton ball snowmen, just dozens of beautiful red and gold balls hung between glittery organza ribbons. Spending Christmases here and opening presents under this tree probably would've been perfect for any kid. Picturesque. Like some old black and white movie. Maybe that was what sparked Mom's mid-November decorating mission. Way too early to put up a Christmas tree, if you asked me. Maybe she was searching for a happy memory to chase away the sad ones.

I held up the ornament again. It didn't match the others, but I slid the ribbon over a thick branch right in front anyway, then carefully pulled my hand away. The glass ball bobbed gently but securely, the ribbon tucked safely between tufts of pine needles.

Past the tree and out the front window, chest-high snow banks edged the sidewalks. Tall enough to trap you like an icy jail cell. A shiver jolted through me. I hated winter and the chill that froze me to the core, never really thawing until spring. Dark cloudy days. Wind, ice, and of course, snow. Cold, depressing, snow. In the city, we didn't have snow like this, just a light dusting on the streets.

Mom crept up behind me and pulled back the gauzy curtain. "What are you looking at?"

"Nothing." I crossed my arms and leaned against her chest, my head falling between her neck and shoulder. "Just wondering what everyone back home is doing, I guess."

She rubbed my arms, coaxing warmth through them. Her heavy sigh rustled my hair as she curled against me. "We've been through this. Moving here will help us out in a huge way. No more worrying about rent, no hour-long commutes, and no public transportation fees."

I grinned. I wouldn't miss the special smell of body odor and wet dog reserved for city buses. Not enough reason to leave, though.

"It's a blessing that your grandmother left us this place. I know you aren't happy, but trust me, it'll be a good thing. Just give it a chance."

"But can't I wait to start school in January? I could help out around the house."

"No." Mom pulled away from me. "I'm starting work tomorrow, and I don't want you to be home alone."

"Why? Afraid I'll get into some kind of trouble? What trouble could I possibly get into here?" I spun around and threw my arms out to the side. "Besides, since I transferred so late, I still have to take the exams from my old school to get credit for this semester. What's four weeks of independent study going to hurt?"

"My answer's final. You're going to school. It's your senior year, and the faster you make new friends, the faster you'll get used to this place."

"I already have friends," I muttered under my breath.

"Please, can you just do this for me?"

"Fine," I huffed and pulled her into a hug.

She let go and placed her hands on my cheeks, pulling my face to meet her gaze. Her eyes were glassy. I braced for tears, but instead of crying, she swept the hair off my shoulders and smoothed it down my back. "Now, are you going to help me with this naked banister or not?"

"Sure." I forced a smile. She nodded and headed upstairs.

All right. Enough already. I rubbed my eyes with the heels of my hands and tried to shake off the gloom setting in. I wasn't going to change her mind, so I might as well get over it. I stumbled into the foyer and fixed my hair in front of the tacky gold mirror.

The doorbell rang.

I yanked open the front door, and clouds of icy air billowed in around an older woman standing on the doorstep. She was all bundled up in a winter coat, hat, and scarf. I couldn't exactly recognize her, but she looked familiar.

"Hello dear," she said softly. "Is your mother home?"

"Mom," I called.

Mom raced down the stairs. "Why, hello, Alice."

Right. Alice Abernathy, the lady next door.

"Elizabeth." Mrs. Abernathy thrust a tinfoil-covered casserole into Mom's hands. "I'm so sorry for your loss."

"Thank you. That's very kind. I know my mother meant a lot to you too." Mom leaned in to hug the old woman while carefully balancing the dish in one hand.

"Yes." Mrs. Abernathy swallowed and looked toward the ceiling, the lines on her face creating a dark shadow over her expression. "She really was a remarkable woman."

"Let me put this in the kitchen," Mom said. "Avery, please invite our guest inside. It's freezing out there."

I opened the door wider and stepped back to give Mrs. Abernathy more room.

"Thank you, dear, but I can't stay." She entered the foyer anyway. "I have my book club to attend to."

"No problem. I..." What was I supposed to say? *I don't really know you, and your friend just passed away and we're living in her house, but how's the weather out there?* I didn't want to be insensitive and say the wrong thing, yet not speaking seemed to be just as rude, if not more so.

"You don't know who I am, do you?" Mrs. Abernathy asked.

"Um, of course, I do. You live right next door."

"You know, when you were a little girl, you climbed up that big tree out front and said you were a fairy princess and were going to live in the tree forever." Mrs. Abernathy chuckled. "Your grandmother waited for you to come down all day. Such a spirited child you were."

My cheeks flared and I glanced out to the shadow of the tree in the yard. "Sorry, but I don't remember." Maybe it was some other little girl.

"She loved you very much." Mrs. Abernathy locked eyes with mine.

"Thanks," I said politely, taking a small step backward. Her stare creeped me out. A little too comfortable, as if she knew me, but she definitely did not.

"You two must've shared something special," she continued. "She was very ... unique, you know. Are you unique too?"

"Um ... I guess so..." I glanced at the floor, studying the lines between the wood slats, feeling her eyes watch me and hoping the conversation would end. "I'm not sure what you mean."

Mom returned to the foyer and I sighed. Finally.

"Can I take your coat?" Mom asked.

"Thank you, but I must go." Mrs. Abernathy winked at me, opened the door, and stepped back into the night. "Come by for tea sometime, and we can talk more if you'd like."

"Sure." I took a deep breath and closed the door behind her.

"It was sweet of her to bring us dinner, don't you think?" Mom asked.

"Yeah." The old woman's comment repeated in my head. Unique? What did that even mean? "Mrs. Abernathy seems nice, but is there anything wrong—"

Smash!

Mom and I glanced at each other and raced toward the

living room, stopping short in the doorway. Chunks of broken glass sparkled across the dark hardwood floor.

"I'll get a broom." Mom shook her head and headed back into the kitchen.

I tiptoed around the fragments to the tree, crouching to see which ornament had broken. On the far side of the room lay a familiar ivory ribbon, still attached to a pewter claw. I frowned. I swore that branch was strong enough for the weight, but maybe it wasn't. Or maybe after three falls today, its time was up.

Mom swept while I collected the larger pieces. The glass was perfectly clear with no trace of whatever had given it that purple swirly effect.

Bang!

I jumped and twirled around, dropping the glass pieces and shattering them further. Wintry wind blew the front door wide open and gusted through the hall. Snowflakes whirled through the air.

I leaped over the rest of the broken glass, landing just short of the foyer. Sharp pain ripped through my foot.

"Shit. Ow. Dammit." I hopped to the door on my good foot, slammed it shut, and locked the deadbolt. I collapsed against the door and winced, my foot throbbing. Could nothing go right today?

I limped to the stairs. Sure enough, a dime-sized piece of glass had cut through my sock and wedged into the fleshy ball of my foot. I tensed and yanked out the glass, but there was no blood, not even a scratch. I sighed. My foot throbbed as though it were sliced wide open. Maybe I was thick skinned. I rubbed the spot and the pain faded a little.

Mom peeked out from the living room. "I think we've had enough decorating for one day. How's about dinner in front of some chick flick, then call it a night?"

"Sure." I smiled. Anything to get out of décor duty and off my sore foot.

"And Avery," Mom said as she walked back into the living room, "I'm sure it hurts, but watch your mouth."

I shook my head and rubbed my aching foot again. The faster tomorrow came, the faster I could start over. Things had to get better, right?

THREE

I stood outside my third-period history class—fifteen minutes late—with my hand hovering over the doorknob. Registering took way longer than expected, and I didn't get to slip into the back of the classroom unnoticed before the bell. Instead, I'd have to march right in and disrupt everyone. Nothing like calling attention.

Through the tiny window in the door, I scanned the room. Rows of students faced forward, listening attentively to the teacher, or at least faking it well. They looked like the students in my old school, except they weren't. They belonged here and I didn't. Back home, I'd successfully navigated through three years of high school, falling right in the middle of the social food chain. I didn't have the pressure of perfectionism like the popular girls, but I managed to keep above the reject line and all the torture that came along with it. I was just me, and that was fine. But now, being an outsider, who knew where I'd end up? Mom had always hated Shady Creek. She never said why, but she repeated it so many times that I started hating it for her. How was I supposed to just forget that?

But maybe Mom was wrong. Things had probably changed since she went to school here, and no one in the classroom looked awful. Besides, surviving the next seven months between now and graduation meant dealing with whatever came, even if this place was as horrible as Mom remembered.

It's going to be all right... It's going to be all right...

I adjusted my sweater and rubbed my palms across my thighs, then knocked on the door and turned the handle.

"So can anyone tell me what year World War II finally..." The history teacher peeked up from her textbook and gave me a bright, almost too enthusiastic smile. "Can I help you?" She was much younger than the stodgy teacher at my old school who'd probably lived through most of the historical events she taught, and already this one seemed way less grouchy. That was a plus.

I smiled back, trying to trick myself into happiness and stop the churning in my gut. "I just transferred here. Sorry I'm late."

"No worries, c'mon in," the teacher said with a slight drawl. She ran her index finger across a paper on her desk. "It's Avery, right? Avery Belmont."

I nodded.

"I'm Miss Bradley." She tilted her head and pointed to the center of the room. "There's an open desk there. Come see me after class for your textbook."

"Thanks." I stared at the floor and headed toward the one empty seat in the middle of the room. Questioning stares fell heavy on my shoulders. I fought the urge to pull my hands into my sleeves and remembered to take deep breaths—but not too deep to be weird.

"And where exactly are you from, Avery?" Miss Bradley asked as I walked away.

"Detroit. For most of my life." I glanced back at her. "But here originally."

Whispers erupted around me as if a gossip bomb had exploded and I was standing at ground zero. I could've sworn my name tumbled through the room in a wave of muffled voices, but maybe it was just my own paranoia. Either way, I sped up, trying to make this introduction end.

Then I tripped.

My hands smacked the linoleum, and a jolt ran up my arms.

I rolled onto my side to find my foot tangled up in a backpack strap, and some guy with slicked-back blond hair staring down at me.

Heat rose up my neck and burned my cheeks. "H-hi," I said.

He raised an eyebrow and laughed in an "okay, freak" kind of way.

I untangled my foot and stood. Any chance people weren't staring and whispering about me disappeared as the chorus of voices increased in volume. I scurried to my desk, eyes down. I slumped into my seat and fought the urge to put my head down on the desk and hide.

Miss Bradley clapped her hands twice. "All right, everyone, enough chitchat."

The room silenced and Miss Bradley continued talking about World War II, but her words sounded quiet and far away. A few lingering whispers still whirled around me. I cringed. Today looked about as promising as yesterday had.

As soon as the bell rang, I bolted from my desk and charged for the door.

"Avery," Miss Bradley called. "Your textbook?"

Right. I struggled against everyone pushing their way out of the room, grabbed the ratty copy of *Our History, Our World* that Miss Bradley held out to me, and tucked it into my bag.

"Nice entrance, by the way." Her mouth twitched.

I turned my eyes down and tapped my fingers on the edge of the desk. "Saw that, huh?"

"Couldn't really miss it."

I looked up and she gave me a reassuring nod. "Also, I wanted to tell you that I'm administering the exam from your old school. Once I receive it, we'll set up a time to write. Okay?"

"Sounds good." I tucked my thumb underneath the strap of my messenger bag and turned to leave.

"Avery."

I stopped and met her eyes.

Her smile fell into a frown of concern. "Things will get easier."

"Sure." I tugged at the cuffs of my sweater, a big knot forming in my throat. I rushed out the door and around the corner of the main hallway, trying to put distance between me and that classroom.

"Hey, Belmont."

I skidded to a halt and the messenger bag banged against my hip. Two girls leaned against the wall across the hallway, watching me nearly fall over my own feet. Again. One looked a lot like me—average height, chocolate-brown hair—but the other was tall, blonde, and far better dressed. Every piece of clothing clung to her body as if it was made just for her, but the designer logos stitched on the hem said otherwise.

The tall girl peeled off the wall and stepped in front of me. The soft scent of exotic flowers and coconuts swirled around her. "Hi, Avery. I'm Lily Price."

"Hey," I responded cautiously. Back home, new kids were considered to be diseased and avoided until proven otherwise. What did they want from me? "Uh ... can I help you?"

The Lily girl laughed. The other girl joined in.

I didn't get the joke.

"No, no. We wanted to help you," Lily said. "We figured since you're new and all, you might want to have lunch with us."

I stepped back and warily looked up and down the hallway. Was this some kind of practical joke? "What's the catch?"

Lily's eyebrows furrowed. She glanced back at her friend and shrugged. "No catch. We were just trying to be nice."

"Oh." Was she for real?

"We don't get a lot of new people here. You're kind of a celebrity."

A celebrity? Me? Not quite. But with these two, I could avoid sitting at some cafeteria table all by myself like a loser. "Then sure. Thanks."

"Fantastic." Lily clapped her hands together while her dark-haired friend nodded in approval.

Uh oh, what did I just agree to?

Lily's friend stepped toward me. "I'm Taylor, by the way."

"Hi," I said and started walking down the hall.

"Where are you going?" Lily's voice echoed behind me.

I turned around, puzzled. "The secretary told me the cafeteria was this way. Isn't it lunchtime yet?" My stomach rumbled.

Lily caught up to me and linked her arm in mine. "Avery, no one ever eats at school. The food's lousy and the cafeteria has terrible lighting. Trust me. Don't do it."

"Then what do you do for food, exactly?"

"Usually we go to someone's house, but lucky for you, we've decided to go to Java Nation today." Lily patted my shoulder, barely breaking stride as we sped down the hallway. "But don't worry, it's not just coffee. They have sandwiches and things."

We headed out the school's front doors, and a cold breeze rushed at us. I shivered and pulled my arms close. My cheeks burned against the chill. "Can't we get in trouble for going off campus? At my old school, we weren't allowed to leave during the day."

"Trouble? No way." Lily scrunched her face into a frown, still looking far too pretty. "If you haven't noticed, nothing ever happens here, so we can do whatever we want."

"Nice." Freedom was definitely a worthwhile perk. "But don't you find it boring?"

"Sure, but it's easier if you hang out with the right people.

Non-boring ones." Taylor smiled. "That's why we invited you to lunch."

"Thanks." I cast my gaze down toward my feet. "How come you're all so nice?"

Lily shrugged. "I dunno. Local charm, I guess. So what brings you to Shady Creek?"

"My grandma died and left us her place. My mom thought it would be easier to move into it than sell it."

Taylor raced in front of us and walked backward down the sidewalk. She plunged her hands into her pockets. "Your grandmother was Wilomena Edwards, right?"

"I-I think so... Why?" I'd never heard anyone refer to Grandma using her maiden name before. Even though Grandpa left when Mom was little, I didn't think she ever went back to it.

"Well—" Taylor began.

Lily shook her head. "No reason."

Taylor snapped her mouth closed.

"Everyone knows everyone around here," Lily continued. "Small towns never forget anything, you know."

"Yeah, I've heard." I turned my head and stared at the cute little shops lining the street. Brightly colored awnings dripped with icicles, and frosty front windows held meticulously detailed displays of things no one really needed. "My mom never talked about Shady Creek much, but when she did, it was usually pretty harsh."

"Makes sense, considering her family history and all." Lily's nose scrunched up and her eyes narrowed. "Besides if I ever got out of here, there is no way I'd ever come back."

"What history? Do you mean about my dad?" Of course, everyone else would know more about him than I did. He bolted on my mom while she was pregnant—probably a huge scandal around here.

"Yeah, your dad." Lily cast Taylor a piercing stare.

"It's fine. I don't think I've missed much without him around."

Both girls looked at each other, then at the ground, and then at anything that wasn't me.

"Really, guys, it's okay." I raised my eyebrows. "Is that what everyone was whispering about in history class? I thought I heard people talking about me."

"Maybe," Taylor said. "Or maybe—"

Lily sped forward and grabbed Taylor's hand. She pulled her toward a small brick building on the corner. The sign hanging above the door swung in the wind, the words "Java Nation" and a picture of a steaming cup of coffee emblazoned across it.

"We're here." Lily yanked the door open wide and stepped inside.

Taylor shrugged at me. She grabbed the door before it slammed shut and ushered me in.

It was an unusual kind of place. On the left, a diner, with everything bright white and stark. On the right was a typical coffeehouse with muted colors, cozy couches, and a hint of acoustic music wafting in the air. I followed Lily and Taylor to the diner side where a bunch of students were gathered around tables pushed together in the corner.

"Hey, guys." Lily stood before the group. "This is Avery. Avery, this is everyone."

I stood beside her and raised my hand in a hesitant wave. The collective stared at me for a moment, and then everyone went back to their conversations as if I didn't exist.

At least they weren't whispering.

Lily motioned to an empty chair beside her and I sat down. Taylor sat at the other end of the table, wrapping her arms around some big athletic-looking guy with spiky brown hair.

The weight of the day dragged on my limbs and mind, but I tried to pay attention as Lily pointed out every person on her long list of friends. There was Taylor's boyfriend, Justin, a girl with corkscrew curls named Katie, a skater guy named Max wearing a backward cap, and a girl at the end of the table with blue eyes, dark hair, and severe bangs, Nora. I lost track of names after that—fuel for embarrassment later—but I did register an invitation to a hockey game tomorrow night, which sounded all right. If my head didn't explode first.

"So." Lily tapped her perfectly manicured fingernails on the table and leaned closer. "Tell me everything about living in Detroit. It must be way better than growing up in this sleepy town."

I laughed. At least I wasn't the only one who felt that way. This girl might just keep me from going crazy before graduation. "It's really great. Actually, it's better than great. It's awesome. So many cool places to go, so many concerts and things going on. I loved it. I'd do anything to go back."

Lily propped her elbow on the table and rested her chin on her hand, her pale-green eyes drifting dreamily toward the ceiling. "One day." She sighed. "I can't wait to get out of here next year and get a real life."

"Maybe you could come with me the next time I go back. I could show you a few places to go."

"Really?" She put her hand on my arm. "That would be amazing."

I looked down at her hand on my arm and fought the eye roll coming on with a smile so wide that the dimple in my cheek pulled my skin tight. "No problem."

A gray-hooded figure snuck up behind Lily. A guy. He held his finger across his lips in a shushing gesture and stared at me. His deep-green eyes twinkled with trouble.

"Uh, Lily?"

Before she could turn around, he mussed her blonde hair across her face.

She whirled around and punched the guy in the shoulder. "Jerk."

The guy shrugged and dropped into the chair beside her, grinning, and spread his lunch across the table.

Lily smoothed her hair back into place and shot a scowl at her assailant. "Avery, this is my baby brother Bennett."

"Isn't that I'm-one-minute-older-than-you garbage ever going to get old?" Bennett ripped off his hood and unwrapped his sandwich. "No one cares."

"Whatever. Ben, this is Avery Belmont, the new girl everyone's talking about."

Great. I wasn't imagining things. People *were* talking about me.

Bennett jutted his chin toward me and smiled. "Hey."

He had a great smile. Light and easy, as if it was his birthday and Christmas and the first hot day of summer all rolled into one. Pure happiness mixed with a touch of mystery that made me want to know exactly what he was thinking in that moment.

"You must be starving," Lily said.

"Sorry. What?" I dragged my eyes from Bennett's lips to Lily's face.

"You must be hungry watching everyone else eat. I'll go grab you something."

My stomach rumbled in agreement.

Lily raised an eyebrow and jumped up from the table. I reached into my bag, fumbling around the bottom for some cash.

Lily flipped her hand toward me. "Don't worry about it. My treat."

"Are you sure?"

"Of course. You can owe me one." She winked and turned

to Bennett, her expression turning from sweet to sour. "Be nice to my new friend, okay?"

"Sure thing, boss." Bennett gave Lily a small salute.

She shook her head, and as she walked away, I glanced at Bennett, struggling to see the resemblance between him and Lily. At best they could be cousins, but definitely not twins. The only things they seemed to share were green eyes and blond hair, but the shades didn't match. But then, Lily's hair color might've been more related to peroxide than genetics.

"Are you and Lily seriously twins?" I asked.

"Yeah." He laughed and shook his head. "At least that's what our parents keep telling us. How did you end up here with her, anyway?"

I shrugged. "She found me after class and invited me to come."

"Sounds like Lily. Always looking for a new project."

"Oh." And there it was, finally. The real reason she'd invited me along. I grabbed my bag off the floor and stood.

"Wait!" Bennett waved his hands and stared over my shoulder in Lily's direction. "That's not what I meant. Lily's always meeting people and doing something new. It's her thing."

I crossed my arms.

"Trust me, you're lucky Lily picked you. Being on her good side will make everything a lot easier here."

I stared at him for a moment and then sat back down. "If she's the good one, are you the evil twin?"

He laughed again. "I said she had a good side. I never said she was good. You've met her, right?"

"So far she's not that—"

A hand slapped down in front of me and shook the table. Long fingers and knobby knuckles—a boy's hand. A guy in a plaid shirt stood at the end of the table to my right. He leaned forward, his flannel-clad torso inches from my face, its blue and gray squares making a curtain between Bennett and me.

What the hell?

He spun around and sat on the tabletop between us, completely cutting me off from Bennett. I shifted to the left and tried to peer around him, but he angled back, blocking my view. I pivoted right and table guy shadowed me again. Enough! I slammed my hands into the table, pushed back my chair, and stood to escape the body parts in my way.

The stranger looked up at me, and I shivered.

He was even more annoying face-to-face but in a different way. The kind of way that made your knees shake and your mouth go dry. His sharp, angular jaw carried a smirk that whispered all kinds of bad things, and his stare ripped through me and came out the other side. His eyes were the deepest brown— like charred wood or the strongest espresso—intense and dark with a hint of something burning underneath. Equal parts intriguing and absolutely intimidating.

"Hey, New Girl." He thrust a hand at me. "Drew Montgomery."

I stepped back. "Avery."

"Yeah, I know." He leaned forward and thrust out his hand again.

Not sure what else to do, I took it. His palm was warm and his grip so tight that it pinched my fingers. His touch felt strangely familiar, like a song that was stuck in your head, but you didn't know the words.

A song I would've changed the station to avoid.

I yanked my hand away and slid it into my back pocket. "If you know my name, why call me New Girl?"

His deep-red lips twisted into a devious grin. "Because I can."

In one smooth motion, he pushed off the tabletop and

planted his feet on the ground. He glanced at me again and then walked away, waving over his shoulder. "Later, New Girl."

"Nice to meet you too, buddy," Bennett muttered.

What was that all about? I locked my stare on the exit, half expecting him to come back and explain what just happened, but he didn't. An uneasy feeling twisted in my stomach. I pulled my hand out of my pocket, still tender where he'd squeezed.

"Okay, who was that?" Lily tossed a chicken wrap on the table in front of me and dropped into her chair, staring at the door.

I shook my head and sat down. "You don't know him? I figured you knew everyone."

"He must be new too," she replied, still watching the vacant door. "And I bet he has one hell of a body underneath that ugly shirt."

"Yeah, so that's my hint to get out of here." Bennett stood and nodded at me. "See you around, Avery."

"Sure. Whatever." Lily dismissed him with a fluttering hand. "Now, who was that guy?"

I ripped the waxy paper off my wrap and picked at the corner. "I have no idea."

Lily leaned back in her chair, resting her arm across the back, a sly smile spreading across her face. "Don't worry. I'll find out."

FOUR

The walk home from school was colder than expected. The wind whipped my cheeks as the fading sun dropped behind the skinny two-story houses flanking the narrow road back to Grandma's house.

Mrs. Abernathy stood in her front window, watching me. I pulled my jacket collar closer around my neck and waved as I passed. She closed the drapes. The same thing she'd done when I walked by on the way to school.

But it didn't bother me. Day one was over and I survived, thanks to Lily. I could worry about my strange neighbor another time.

I pushed open the front door.

"Avery, is that you?" Mom called from the kitchen.

"No, it's a burglar."

I shed my coat and boots and padded down the hall, trying to stomp out the last bit of chill in my bones.

Mom sat at the table looking, over some paperwork, still in her pale-pink scrubs, a Shady Creek General Hospital badge dangling from her hip.

"How was your day?" She signed her name across a page and flipped it over.

"All right, I guess." I shrugged and deposited myself in the chair across from her.

"Just all right?" She looked up and her lips pulled into a tight line. "Did something happen?"

"Not really. Went to class. Met a few people. Came home."

"Met some new friends, maybe?"

"We'll see." I raised an eyebrow and squinted at her, my tone flat. No reason to get her hopes up when I wasn't totally sure about Lily and her crew yet. "But they invited me to go to some hockey game tomorrow night, if that's okay? The school team is playing."

"Sure." She nodded slowly, then winced.

I looked her over and frowned. "How was your first day?"

"Busy." She sighed and sank back into her chair. The pen dropped from her fingers and rolled off the table. She didn't bother picking it up. "No matter how many jobs I've had, there's always so much to learn. My head is pounding." She rubbed her temples and clenched her eyes for a moment. Pain scrunched her brow and drew lines across her pale face.

"Maybe the universe is telling us we shouldn't have moved. We could still pack up and go back," I joked. Half-joked.

"Enough with this attitude, Avery," Mom barked. "We're staying and that's final." She grabbed her temples and curled forward.

Whoa. Where did that come from? "Attitude? I was just making a joke."

Mom winced again as her voice rose. "No, you weren't. I know you're not happy about this move, but it happened and you need to start dealing with it."

"Why? It's not like anyone asked me if I wanted to move. I got dragged away from my friends, my school ... everything. That wasn't my choice."

She massaged the sides of her head harder as if she were trying to burrow into her brain tissue.

I sighed. Then I grabbed a bottle of ibuprofen and a glass of water and placed them in front of her.

She opened the bottle with quivering hands. "I'm sorry for snapping at you, but you have no idea how hard this is for me."

She shook a couple of pills onto her hand. "Coming back and dredging up all these memories. Dealing with all the things your grandmother left behind. Things you just wouldn't understand."

I opened my mouth to tell her I knew it wasn't easy on her either, but that didn't change how miserable I felt about the whole thing. Instead, I snapped my mouth shut again, plucked a granola bar from the cupboard, and marched out of the kitchen.

"Avery," Mom called after me. "What about dinner?"

"I'm not hungry." I grabbed my schoolbag and pounded up the stairs to my room.

I toppled onto the bed and polished off the granola bar in three angry bites. Mom's crazy mood swings were getting tedious. Sad. Happy. Angry. Ever since we'd arrived in Shady Creek, I didn't know what to expect from her. Our relationship used to be so much easier. Just us versus the world.

This new dynamic sucked.

I lay back and stared at the ceiling. My stomach growled, but I didn't want to go back down to the kitchen, so essentially, I was trapped in my room for the rest of the night. I flipped through my cell. No emails. No texts. No sign of life of any kind. My old friends seemed too busy to keep in touch.

I felt numb. The world wouldn't stop because I changed area codes, but at least I could hope. I missed everyone so much that my heart hurt, but they had lives I wasn't a part of anymore.

I tiptoed into the hall. Voices hummed from the TV downstairs. Any other night, Mom would've locked herself in her room by now, especially with a headache. Why did she choose tonight to keep lurking around? It was probably on purpose, waiting for me to come down, but that wasn't going to happen. I crept back into my room.

Leaning against the closed door, I slid down to the carpet, knees to my chest. Being trapped made the room seem smaller, but if today was any indication of the next year, I'd be spending a lot of time in my room.

If only I knew how to make it feel like home. It needed a ton of work. The loft-style ceilings were fun, but painting the stifling eggshell walls had to wait until I could open a window without freezing my butt off. And the hideous retro curtains with their tiny yellow and green flowered fabric went far beyond vintage and firmly planted them in the realm of ugly. Seriously, who picked those?

But it didn't matter. This place was only a pit stop on the way to the rest of my life. Next year, I'd be in college, and all this would be a hazy memory.

A few unpacked boxes sat in the corner. I hoisted one of them onto my bed and pulled it open. Random stuff. Things I didn't need, but couldn't bring myself to throw away—pictures, teddy bears, the purple elephant blanket I'd had since I was a baby, the spelling bee medal I won when I was nine.

I scanned the room, trying to find places for everything, but none of it belonged. I chucked everything back into the box and tried to wedge it under the bed. Far too big. The attic? Nope. No way I'd risk another encounter with Mom tonight. The closet? That would do—at least until I found a better place to stash it.

I shoved the box onto the top shelf and it jammed in place at an angle, the left half hanging over the edge. Gritting my teeth, I pushed again, but it wouldn't budge. Knowing my luck, if I left it hanging off the shelf even a little, it'd fall on my head one day.

I grabbed my desk chair and climbed on it for a better look. Squeezing my arm between the box and the wall, my fingers brushed against a hard, flat edge. I pushed up on my toes and pulled out a dusty book. Brown cover. No title. Old. I flung it on my bed and fit the box into place. Nothing could just be easy, could it?

The next box had books, another held clothes, and one had movie posters—color for the dull walls. Finally, I ran out of stuff to unpack. I ran my sleeve across my forehead and yawned.

Still fully clothed and exhausted from the first real day in my new life, I flopped down on the bed. A sharp pain dug into my spine. I reached under my back and pulled out the old book I'd found in the closet. I rolled onto my side and tossed it onto the floor, and something glittered along its edge.

I rolled and leaned over the mattress. A chain with a gold heart stuck out of the cover like a fancy bookmark. Interesting. Didn't notice that earlier. I thumbed through the pages. Handwriting was scrawled across lined sheets of paper. I stopped on a random page.

September 3

Senior year, finally! Less than twelve months and I'll be out of this hell hole. I still have no idea where I'm going, but I'm never ever coming back to Shady Creek.

I laughed. Mom's diary. Things clearly hadn't worked out as she'd planned.

But I did meet a new guy today. He's such a hottie. He's got these really deep cocoa eyes that

I could stare at all day and a great smile with the most perfect teeth.

Perfect teeth? I snickered. Out of all the things she could look for in a guy, this was what she found attractive. Maybe I should try to hook her up with a dentist. If she had a boyfriend, maybe she'd ease up.

I've seen him around, but I totally ran him over in the hallway today and my books went flying. He picked them up for me and I almost screamed when we brushed hands. I'm such a tool. Maybe he'll be at Becky's party next week. I hope so.

I closed the book and held it to my chest, chuckling. Mom had to see this. I jumped up but stopped at the door. I'd forgotten how late it was, and if Mom's headache hadn't subsided, she'd probably gone to sleep. Besides, a bit of leftover anger still niggled at the back of my brain. Mom could wait.

I propped my pillow against the wall and leaned back on the bed. What other kinds of scandalous stuff had Mom written? I flipped to the last page. August 4th. Right before I was born. She must have written this while she was pregnant with me. And the hottie with the great teeth—was that my dad? Mom said they met in high school. Maybe she'd written about him in here too.

I used to dream my dad would come back, but he never did. After a while, I stopped hoping. Maybe these pages would tell me why he left us.

Turning back to September, I read a few more passages. Nothing more about the guy.

I yawned, my eyes heavy. Enough for tonight. As I slid the book under my mattress, I closed my eyes and tried to picture what my dad looked like. If he looked anything like me. Maybe I could ask Mom when I told her about the diary. And I would tell her—just not yet.

FIVE

"Don't worry about it. Nora said she'd give me a ride to the game." I hurried to keep pace with Lily and Taylor as they rushed toward the school for their yearbook meeting. I could've stayed at Katie's house instead of coming back from lunch early with them, but I would've felt strange without Lily there. Only day two, and she'd already drawn me into her orbit. A speck of cosmic dust hovering around this galaxy's brightest star.

"Just remember to take your shoes off before getting in her car." Taylor snickered.

Lily elbowed her in the ribs.

"Huh?" I asked.

Lily stopped short and we almost piled on top of her. She pointed toward the parking lot. "Anything out there look different to you?"

I scanned the rows of cars. All colors. All models. Nothing unusual, except one shiny black car attitude-parked across two stalls in the far back row. The sleek side panels and hood emblem belonged to those super expensive cars you'd see outside fancy restaurants in the city, except this one seemed immune to any speck of dirt or snow. Its sparkly paint gleamed in the midday sun.

I couldn't stop staring. "That's Nora's car?"

"Yep. A pity present from her dad after he had an affair last year," Taylor explained. "But if you like that, you should see the one her mom got."

"Does nothing stay secret around here?" I asked.

We hurried across the parking lot, burst through the front door, and booked it down the hall. The metallic whine of an electric guitar echoed off the ceiling.

"No." Lily clamped her hands over her ears. "Not again."

The music wasn't terrible—just raw—but the closer we got to it, the angrier Lily's face twisted.

"Where's that coming from?" I asked, stripping off my coat and tucking it over the top of my bag.

"The music room. Bennett probably. Mr. Fort lets him mess around when there's no choir practice." Lily rolled her eyes. "Keeps him for playing at home, though. He's so loud and his taste in music sucks."

Taylor grabbed Lily's arm and tugged her farther up the hall. "C'mon, we're going to be late. See you later, Avery."

I waved as they raced away. Chucking my bag on the floor, I leaned against the wall and slid down to sit. I pulled out my history notebook and tried to read my scribbles from last semester in Detroit. Exams would come sooner than I'd expect. They always did.

I tapped my pencil on the edge of the notebook, and the words on the page jumbled and swirled before me. My gaze darted from the page to the posters on the walls. Bright winter light spilled through the windows onto the yellowish, early-1970s flooring covering the empty hallway. Back home, the halls would be packed at lunchtime. The place to be seen. But here, they could've held a parade and no one would know.

The distant whine of the guitar paused for a moment, the absence of sound somehow louder than the music. Then the notes of a familiar song drifted toward me.

I gathered up my things and followed the rhythm to the music room in the next corridor, and peeked inside. A set of wide carpeted stairs led to the center of the room and held every type of instrument I'd ever seen, while clusters of chairs and music stands punctuated the empty spaces in between.

Bennett sat on a stool near the percussion section, leaning down and concentrating on his fingers, bright blue headphones covering his ears. He tapped his foot and bobbed his head in rhythm with the chords, his jaw clenched so tightly that tension rippled in his cheeks.

I leaned against a metal bookshelf beside the door and listened, soaking up all of his amateur rockstar charm. I hadn't heard this song in forever. Sad and angsty and beautiful, and Bennett was killing it.

"Whoa!" The music halted and Bennett jerked forward, whipping his headphones down around his neck. "Didn't know anyone was in here."

I stepped back, my ears burning. "Sorry, I didn't mean to scare you. I just heard you playing from the hall and stopped to listen. You're pretty good."

"I don't know about 'good,' but thanks." He pulled the guitar over his head and placed it on a stand.

"My mom used to play that song when she went on one of her throwback Brit rock binges. Oasis, right?"

He beamed. "Not bad. Most people don't recognize it. Do you play?"

"No." I stared down at the flat gray carpet, noticing pulled fibers and bits of dirt. "My mom works a lot, so I usually have to help out at home. Not too much time for other things."

"You didn't do anything at your old school?" His voice dripped with pity. Not what I wanted. I should've kept quiet.

"Nothing really interesting." I tapped my finger along the cymbal of a nearby drum set, the dull tinny sound vibrating against my fingernail. "Are you going to the hockey game tonight?"

"I think so."

The other doors opened and students filed in, finding their places and gawking at me, a stranger in their space.

I caught his gaze. "Good."

Bennett smiled, and I glanced out the door I'd come in through to hide my own goofy grin. The hallway had filled up with bodies whipping by on their way to class. I rushed toward the door.

"Avery! Look out!" Bennett shouted.

I stopped and turned. The dark shadow of the bookshelf teetered toward me. I leaped sideways, but not fast enough. The top metal corner stabbed my upper right arm and carved a line through my sweater all the way down to my wrist. Pain exploded under my skin, hard and searing.

I curled my injured arm into my chest and attempted to right the bookshelf with my left hand. Bennett bounded up the steps, grabbed the other side of the shelf, and help me put it back into place.

"Are you okay?"

"I think so." I cradled my injured arm and restacked a pile of scattered sheet music.

He scooped up a mound of books and shoved them into haphazard rows on the shelves.

The other students stared and whispered. My ears warmed. I thrust the last few books onto the bottom shelf and slipped back toward the door, my arm still throbbing against my chest.

"Maybe I'll see you later," Bennett said, keeping hold of the bookshelf, far away from me.

Probably safer. I might knock him over too.

"Yeah, see you later." I bolted toward the exit with my head down and slammed into a shoulder. I glanced up. The weird hot guy I met in Java yesterday stood in the doorway, glaring down at me as if I'd ruined his entire day. "Sorry," I mumbled and sprinted toward my locker.

I leaned against the bank of lockers and held out my arm to look at my injury. My sweater sleeve was split down the middle like a hotdog overcooked on a campfire, but otherwise, the skin beneath looked untouched without even a drop of blood. I yanked the sweater over my head and twisted my arm in front of me, wincing as pain burned in my veins. Not a mark. Not a scratch. Not even a small indent where the bookshelf first hit and pain pulsed the hardest. This didn't make sense.

"Do things like that always happen to you?" The dark-eyed guy appeared in front of me. His stare stayed fixed on my arm and crept along my skin.

"If you mean random objects falling on me, then no. Not usually." I tucked my injured arm behind my back and used the other one to open my locker and stuff the torn sweater inside. "You're ... Drew, right?"

His face contorted into a mean scrunch. "Less than a week and already causing a scene. Destroying the music room may not be the best strategy to get people to take notice, you know." He maneuvered himself between me and my open locker door.

A little too close for comfort.

I slid away from him. "Thanks for the advice. I'm glad you figured out this whole moving to a new town thing so fast. Lucky for you."

"I'm not new here." He paused and stared at the floor. "I mean, I'm not new to town like you. I was shipped off to boarding school for years, but I've always been from Shady."

"Sounds like the trend around here."

"But not for you." He laughed and squinted, long black lashes casting shadows across his pale cheeks. "And that's actually why I came to talk to you. I thought I could show you around. The secret life of Shady Creek tour."

"I thought no one had secrets around here. Not ones that haven't been told, anyway."

"Oh, there are still secrets. You just need to know where to look." He winked and crossed his arms over his chest.

I shivered. "Interesting." Or weird. Probably just weird. Besides, the thought of being anywhere alone with this guy creeped me out. "But I'm already going to the hockey game tonight. Sorry."

"Really?" He tilted his head to the side, his eyebrows knitted together. "Sounds boring. But if you want to hang around the pathetic people in this town, that's where they'll be." He shrugged, his expression flat.

"Wow, a little judgmental, don't you think?"

He leaned closer, his dark-eyed stare almost too intense, borderline starving, like a big bad wolf. "No, just a keen observation. You should really put more thought into who you spend time with. You wouldn't want to catch their mediocrity, would you?"

"Thanks for the advice. I'll see you around." I pushed my locker door closed, almost catching Drew's t-shirt sleeve before he jumped out of the way.

He narrowed his eyes and snorted. "Have fun at your game. I guess."

I watched him swagger away, entranced by his audacity. What was wrong with him? One thing was for sure, though— they didn't teach social skills at boarding school.

SIX

I PEELED BACK THE FRONT WINDOW CURTAIN AND peeked out to the street. Snow swirled in thick white spirals, growing heavier by the minute. Still no Nora. I slid my cell phone out of my pocket. Ten minutes late. Maybe she'd forgotten about me. My shoulders sank. I'd even washed the soles of my boots to keep her fancy car clean, just in case.

"Don't worry. She'll get here," Mom said, almost telepathically.

Maybe my pacing had tipped her off.

"I can drive you if you want."

"Uh, no thanks."

"Right. You're too cool to have your mom drive you." She laughed. "Just take the car yourself then."

"Maybe, but if Nora ditched me for a reason, I don't want to just show up there and look like a loser."

"Avery, you're being ridiculous. There's no reason for anyone to ditch you. Why would you ever think that?"

"I don't know. I just think some people at school might be saying things about me."

"Oh." Her smile faded, and she put down the old leather bound book she'd been reading. "I'm sure it's nothing. It's just because you're new. It'll pass." She walked into the foyer and looked out the small window in the front door. "Besides, I think you'll do just fine."

The hollow *thunk* of a car door echoed from outside. I ran into the foyer and yanked on my boots. "Thanks, Mom."

"Have fun." She rummaged through her purse and pulled out two twenty-dollar bills. "Buy your friends some hot chocolate or something."

"I don't need the money, Mom. Really."

"Please take it. Everything's going to be okay here. I promise." She took the money and stuffed it in my coat pocket. "Now, go have fun."

I bolted out the door and ran into Taylor on the front step.

"Whoa, I was just going to knock," she said, regaining her balance.

"Sorry. I didn't want to make you wait. I thought Nora was picking me up."

"Change of plans. Nora's not coming." Taylor chuckled. "She said something came up, but honestly"—she lowered her voice as if someone might hear—"I think she didn't want to bring her car out in this weather."

~

By the time we arrived, the snow fell harder. My boots slid through the loose powder as Taylor and I ran through the parking lot.

"Who's all coming?" I hurried to keep pace with Taylor, who tore through the snow as if it were dry pavement.

"Me, you, Lily, maybe Katie."

"Is Bennett coming?" I tried to keep my voice from lifting —tougher than expected as I huffed and puffed from running.

"Yep. Maybe he'll bring his girlfriend too."

"Oh." I slowed to a walk, my throat tightening.

"I'm just screwing with you." Taylor laughed and circled back, putting her arm over my shoulders. "So you like him or what?"

"Well, maybe..." My palms started to sweat in my mittens. "Or maybe not."

Taylor laughed again and squeezed my arm. "All right, but he's single, and I think you should totally go for it."

"Are you sure? He's Lily's brother."

Lily. She'd been so nice to me. What would she do if she knew I had a thing for her twin brother? I didn't want her mad at me and besides, I wasn't even sure if I liked him yet. But lately, snow and Bennett both gave me goosebumps.

She shrugged. "It'll be fine."

We followed the crowd through the arena door and into the cramped lobby. A large green and gold banner that read *Go Shady Sharks* hung across a display case of trophies along the far wall.

"Finally!" Lily bolted toward us, Katie and Bennett racing to keep up with her. "We thought you were never going to show."

"Sorry. The weather keeps getting worse," Taylor said.

I shoved my hands into my pockets and tried to look at anyone but Bennett, except Taylor's words kept rolling around in my head, making it impossible not to stare directly at him. He caught my gaze and nodded, and I snapped my eyes away like an idiot.

Thanks a lot, Taylor.

"Hopefully we can still get some decent seats." Lily trudged off through the lobby crowd and into the arena, with everyone following quickly behind.

I'd expected the rink to be dingy and cold with uncomfortable wooden bench seats like at my old school, but this looked professional. The heaters worked, and everything appeared clean and freshly painted—at least sometime within this decade. Three tiers of brightly colored seats led to a wide concrete walkway around the upper level with ads lining the walls. Music pumped through the speakers, and above center ice hung a massive scoreboard with video screens, probably as big as the one in a professional arena. Maybe bigger.

"You'd think Shady Creek had its own NHL team with a rink this nice. And where did all these people come from? It's like three full towns are crammed in here." My head swiveled from one side to the other so I could take everything in.

Taylor spun around in the middle of the aisle and stopped, almost knocking me over. "It's probably more than three towns. Hockey's kind of a big deal around here."

Lily marched on ahead of us, stopping in front of a string of empty seats several rows behind the visitor's bench.

"Uh, ladies first, Bennett." Taylor reached past me and Katie, tugging on his arm.

Bennett shrugged and then backed up on the stair, letting us into the seats first. In the commotion, Taylor pushed her way in front of me, winking as she passed.

I gulped and sat next to Bennett, hoping no one noticed her blatant setup.

Lily stood on her tiptoes, craning her neck to see the players' bench below. One of the players glanced up. She crouched slightly and stood back up when he turned away.

"What are you doing?" I asked, wrenching my focus away from the end of the row and my unexpected proximity to Bennett.

"She's looking for Vaughan. He's the captain of the Raiders. Number nine. Second from the left." Katie pointed, much less concerned with being noticed than Lily was. "Lily's kind of obsessed with him."

"I am not." Lily locked her stare on Vaughan again. "I just have an appreciation for guys who are brutally gorgeous. Don't you think he's gorgeous?"

"All I can see is the back of his head," I replied. "It's a nice head, though."

Bennett snickered and Lily narrowed her eyes to slits so sharp they might carve the flesh off his face.

"It'd never work, anyway. He lives four towns over and has a ton of girls chasing after him. I just like to look." She finally sat down, still staring but less obviously. "Besides, I think I might try my chances with that new guy."

"Drew?" I asked, surprised.

"Yeah, Drew Montgomery. Apparently, he got kicked out of some fancy boarding school in Boston and moved back here to live with his mom who hasn't been seen outside her creepy old house in forever. He's a Pisces, hates girls with facial piercings, and has a thing for really old books. Rumor has it, his family goes back to the first mayor of Shady Creek, but I haven't been able to confirm that yet. No girlfriend and he's a bit of a loner, but those problems are fixable." She lifted her chin and flashed a smile.

"Do you know his shoe size too?" Taylor shook her head and smirked.

Lily blinked a few times, her perfectly trimmed eyebrows drawing together. "No, that's all the info I could find."

"He is pretty cute," Katie said. "I have no problem staring at him in class."

Lily cocked her head to the side and clasped her hands in her lap. "I know. We'd look so great together, and—"

The teams skated out on the ice. Lily settled back in her seat and her mouth snapped closed.

"Thank God," Bennett whispered.

We stood for the national anthem, and then the game started. The ref dropped the puck and the opposing captain scooped it up off the faceoff, deked out the defensemen, and popped in a goal off the crossbar in less than twenty seconds.

That set the tone. The game got rougher as the Raiders fought to keep their lead.

Taylor gasped as a winger rocked Justin into the boards and he went down somewhere around the five-minute mark, but he shook it off and kept skating. Penalty minutes lit up the scoreboard faster than goals.

Bennett tapped me on the shoulder. "Are you having fun?"

"Yeah, I think I am," I replied, noticing that I'd slid to the edge of my seat.

"Too bad we're losing." He grimaced as the Raiders scored again. "These guys are first place in the league and we just can't beat them, but normally we don't suck this much."

"Back home, our team never won a game. Even losing, these guys are a thousand times better." I smiled. "How come you don't play?"

"Not really my thing." Bennett's face blanked and red crept over his cheeks. "Plus, I kind of got cut first round."

"Ouch." I winced. "Don't worry. I didn't play any sports at my old school either."

"Right. With your mom working and stuff." He glanced at the scoreboard and shook his head. "So no music and no sports. What did you do back in Detroit?"

"You say that as if I'm hopeless. Maybe I'm just not athletic. Or musical." I shrugged and turned my gaze toward the roof. "Or ... maybe I ran with a gang and hotwired cars instead."

"Right. Don't think so." He laughed. "I guess I'll just have to get you out skating or give you some guitar lessons or something."

"Is that a threat?"

"No, a promise." He nudged me with his shoulder. I fought an elated smile, which probably came off as a weird smirk.

"And I forgot to ask, how's your arm? That bookshelf fall looked nasty."

"Oh, that." I slid my arm slightly behind me as if he could see through my jacket and notice the perfectly intact skin. "It's fine. No big deal."

A rumble filtered through the crowd and Bennett looked back to the game. Number nine raced down the ice on a break-away, the Sharks too far behind to stop him. He wound up just past the blue line and rifled a slap shot into the net.

"No!" Bennett yelled along with the crowd, pressing his hands into the sides of his head. Our disappointed team shook their heads and slammed their sticks on the ice.

The play continued. Bennett leaned forward, resting his elbows on his knees. I watched him watch everything else. The way he fidgeted with the small silver ring on his thumb. The way his jaw muscles clenched as he concentrated on the action. The way the ends of dark-blond hair curled at his neck. I wanted to reach out and tangle my fingers in it. It was probably super soft. It'd look great a little longer too.

Whoa. Get it together, Avery.

I shook my head, pushing my thoughts down, then covered the side of my face with my hand, shifting my focus back to the game, but I couldn't concentrate.

I tilted toward him and whispered, "Can you keep a secret?"

He turned toward me and smirked. "Of course."

"But you can't tell anyone. Not even Lily."

He nodded. "I promise."

"I was on the academic quiz team."

His eyebrows furrowed, then he erupted in laughter. "What did you say?"

I tugged at my sleeves. Why did I open my mouth? I'm such an idiot. "You asked what I did in Detroit. I was on the academic quiz team."

He stopped laughing, his eyes wide. "Whoa. That means you're—"

"A complete super geek." I shrank down in my seat. "That's why you can't tell."

His eyebrow arched. "I was going to say smart. We don't have a team here, but I'm guessing you'd need to be really smart to do something like that."

"Yeah. I do okay."

"I'm going to have to tell Lily though." He leaned away from me, and a broad smile spread across his face. "I think there's a maximum GPA requirement to be her friend. If you're over that, she'll have to kick you to the curb."

"Thanks." I crossed my arms and glanced at the girls sitting beside me.

"I'm kidding." He rolled his eyes. "Katie's a genius and Nora's going to go to some fancy film school next year. Being around you might make Lily look good."

"Maybe you are the evil twin." I glared at him, fighting the grin tugging at my lips.

"Maybe I am." He laughed and mimicked my squinty stare, inching closer to my face.

The scoreboard buzzer squawked the end of the period and our conversation. Lily's crush had racked up six goals, and the Sharks were getting slaughtered. I pulled out the money Mom had slipped me.

"Does anyone want a hot chocolate? It's on me."

"Thanks, Avery. That would be great," Lily said.

Taylor and Katie nodded in agreement.

Bennett stood up to let me pass. "Why don't I come help you?"

"Thanks." I smiled and then backed up a step to let him lead the way. Taylor made a tiny squeal and my stomach somersaulted. I was ridiculous.

Tightly packed bodies and the hum of voices created chaos

in the lobby. A low rumbling noise tumbled through the crowd and vibrated in my chest.

"What's that sound?" I shouted, leaning into Bennett.

He pointed upward. "Storm's getting worse. Might be ice hitting the roof."

Ice? They didn't just have regular fluffy snow here—they had ice. I peered at the wall of glass behind us. Thick white curtains of snow blocked the view outside the windows.

The lineup at the counter thinned, and Bennett pushed me forward. His hand lingered on the small of my back, and I shivered. I hoped he didn't notice.

"Thanks," Bennett shouted as the concession worker filled our cups. "You didn't need to buy for everyone."

"It's okay. I wanted to." I smiled and dared to sneak another sideways glance at him. The sweet scent of wintergreen mint rolled off his jacket and I resisted the urge to lean closer. Maybe this town did have some potential.

As Bennett carefully placed four of the cups in a cardboard tray, a hand waved in the crowd to the left. I leaned back and scanned through the faces. The hand belonged to Drew.

What was he doing here? Hockey games were beneath him. I waved back. Drew motioned for me to come toward him. I shook my head. He nodded and waved harder. I shook my head again. He held his hands in a prayer position, and his dark eyes seemed to probe inside my brain, almost as if he were trying to drag me over. He started moving toward me. I blinked and forced myself to look away, hoping he'd get the hint that I wasn't interested in whatever he had to say.

A hand tugged on my arm. "I need to talk to you. It's important." Drew's voice hissed in my ear, ruffling the small hairs on the back of my neck. "Or do you want me to come sit with you?"

Hell no. I whirled around, but Drew was already slithering through the crowd and motioning for me to follow.

Bennett handed me a cup and grabbed the tray off the counter. "Let's go."

He pushed through the crowd and I followed, with Drew's stare bearing down on me. He couldn't sit with us. Lily might be fine with it, but I wasn't going to blow my chance with Bennett because some prep school jerk decided to get all stalker-like. Besides, what if he started being rude to everyone like he was with me? It'd be my fault.

"Wait," I said to Bennett. "I need to call my mom. She worries. Why don't you go ahead without me?"

"I can wait," Bennett replied.

Why did he have to be so nice? "I don't want the drinks to get cold. I'll just be a minute."

Bennett shrugged but obeyed. The crowd swarmed in between us, swallowing him whole.

I pushed my way over to Drew and gritted my teeth. "What do you want?"

"Hello to you, too." The smirk on his face didn't match his words. He probably enjoyed getting under my skin.

"I thought you said you weren't coming. Too boring for you or something."

"I thought by now you'd want to get away from these losers."

"No, Drew, I don't. I'm having a great time with my friends. And my friends are waiting for their hot chocolate which is getting cold while I stand here talking to you."

"Honestly, why you would want to spend time with these people, let alone serve them? Don't you think you're better than that?" He motioned at the cup in my hand.

"Unlike you, these people are nice to me. Maybe if you weren't such a jerk people might actually want to be around you." It just slipped out. Maybe it was out of line, but I didn't care. He seemed to go out of his way to annoy me. Why was I so special?

His eyebrows dipped as if I'd thrown a cup of hot chocolate on him. I considered apologizing but decided against it. Besides, he deserved it. Drew opened his mouth as if to say something, but closed it again and threw his head back, staring at the ceiling instead. The lights flickered, as the storm outside picked up. Pellets of ice pounded against the windows like thousands of pebbles being thrown at the glass. Drew lowered his head. He donned a mischievous smirk and glared at me again, his dark-brown eyes almost black under the fluorescent lights.

"I'm going back. Don't follow me." I spun around and walked away. His hand brushed my arm, but I shrugged it off. He wasn't going to ruin this night for me.

The buzzer sounded, signaling the start of the second period, and the lobby crowd thinned. A few people lingered around the windows, watching the storm. Ice pounded against the glass so loudly that I swore one of the windows would break before it was over. I couldn't remember a storm this bad in Detroit, but that was what happened when you moved into the wilderness.

Heading back toward the stands, I growled, frustrated for wasting time with Drew. I stopped beside the boards, garnering angry stares from the people in the front row, and scanned the crowd until I spotted Lily's bright pink scarf behind the visitor's bench. Relieved, I bounded up the narrow flight of stairs.

Then the lights went out.

SEVEN

I tripped up the stairs and fell forward, and I yelped as my cup of hot chocolate dumped down the front of my jacket. Searing liquid soaked through my jeans and burned my thighs. Fantastic.

As if to mock me, the lights surged back on.

I pulled a mitten out of my pocket and brushed at the spill, but I couldn't soak it all up. Now I had a wet mitt too. I took a deep breath and continued back to my seat. Halfway up the steps, the lights went off again. Determined not to trip, I stood still until they came back on. Ten seconds ... thirty ... sixty ... nothing happened. Emergency lights around the outer walls kicked on, casting an orange glow without making it easier to see. I swallowed hard. I kept reaching for something to hold onto, but the stairway left me exposed.

Ice pellets pounded harder on the roof, rumbling like thunder, like the hammering pulse in my ears. My knees shook. I squinted, stupidly hoping it would help me see better in the dark.

The rumbling grew louder. I covered my ears.

It's going to be all right... It's going to be all right...

I couldn't panic now. Panic would lead to mayhem.

With a deafening smash, the far window burst inward, spraying glass over the end of the rink. Someone screamed. Ice and snow poured in the open hole, and the cold air burned my lungs.

People rustled in their seats. I pulled my jacket tighter and turned to find my way back down the stairs in the dark. Why hadn't I just gone back to my seat with Bennett?

A gust of wind swept through the building, and the giant scoreboard's shadow swayed in front of me. Its support chains jangled and then let out an ear-splitting groan as they let go.

A gush of air radiated from the falling board, forcing me backward, rippling through my body. I lurched forward, trying to regain my balance. Sparks and debris exploded from the ice. Scoreboard shrapnel fired against the rink boards with loud cannon-like booms, the Plexiglas wobbling like gelatin.

More screams. A blur of dark faces rushed toward me. I headed back down the stairs, bumping back and forth against the panicked hoard. Sweat and stale beer assaulted my nose. My foot caught the edge of a stair in the darkness, and my stomach slammed into my throat as I fell.

I flailed my arms, trying to catch a hold of something— anything—but only air slipped through my hands. I closed my eyes, waiting for the pain, but I didn't hit ground.

"This way." A hand gripped my bicep and pulled me through the dark, off the stairs, and into the seats, away from the rush of bodies. It dragged me, stumbling, over rows of seats toward the top of the arena, my knees and elbows bashing against the hard plastic. It didn't make sense to go up while the crowd ran down, but even though I struggled against the hand, it wouldn't let go.

As we cleared the last row of seats, Drew's face appeared under the eerie orange glow of emergency lights. He released my arm and took my hand. We raced toward a light—a door, slightly ajar—and clambered down slippery metal steps to the parking lot below. Drew squeezed my hand and kept running until we were midway through the lot. Then he finally let go.

I grabbed the tops of my knees and bent over, trying to

catch my breath. Cars and people passed us in a blur of color and sound. "Thank you," I whispered between gasps.

The storm had passed, but for a few flakes of snow floating silently through the night sky. I looked up. How could everything change so quickly?

Drew watched me, his head tilted to the side. "Are you gonna live?"

"Yeah. I'll be fine. How did you find me in there?"

"You stormed off before I was finished, so I followed you. I saw you fall and thought you might need help."

"Oh." My stomach rolled into a huge knot. He still had the decency to rescue me, even though I'd been super mean to him. "Sorry about that."

I struggled to find something profound to say but my brain couldn't seem to function. Sirens blared toward us, and I focused on the ambulances and police cars trying to maneuver around the gridlock of cars trying to escape. Nothing about tonight made sense.

"We should get you out of here." Drew stepped closer, drawing my attention away from the chaos. "Are you hungry? I could take you somewhere to eat."

His face took on a different shape. Gentler, as if he was really worried about me. His pitch-dark eyes softened, and the signature smirk fell from his lips. The knot in my stomach tightened as a second wave of guilt struck. Maybe I was wrong about him.

"Avery!" A clamor of voices shouted from behind. I turned. Lily, Katie, and Bennett ran toward us through the snow.

"Are you okay? We were so worried when you didn't come back." Lily grabbed me by the shoulders and looked me over. "Your clothes ... they're wet and dirty. What happened?"

"I fell. But Drew helped me get out of there."

"That was nice of you." Lily shamelessly batted her

eyelashes at Drew and slid past me. "Avery is pretty lucky you were there."

I looked at Katie and Bennett, ignoring Lily's blatant flirting. "Where's Taylor?"

"She went to see if Justin was all right," Katie explained. "She asked us to take you home."

"You don't need to. We were just going to grab something to eat." Drew pushed past Lily and rejoined our conversation.

"I really just want to go home." The adrenaline from running had faded, and my feet were freezing from the hot chocolate in my socks. I craved a hot shower and my warm bed.

Drew stepped closer to me and turned his back to everyone else. He lowered his forehead. "Are you sure?"

"We can go with you if Avery wants to leave." Lily tugged Drew's arm and broke his weirdly intense gaze.

I exhaled and shook the sudden cloud of dizziness from my head. Probably just all the excitement.

Bennett clasped Lily's wrist and guided her closer to Katie. "Why don't you two check on Taylor, and I will take Avery home." He placed his hand on my back.

Katie linked arms with Lily and pulled her toward the arena.

"What's the rush?" Lily asked.

"My car's over here." Bennett shuffled me in the direction of the main parking lot and waved at Drew. "See you around."

I glanced back. Drew stood with his hands in his pockets, watching us. Part of me wanted to run back. We weren't friends. I wasn't even sure I liked him that much, but I did owe him.

Maybe I'd take him up on that tour idea.

Bennett led me to a silver Civic that looked stock. All the guys in my old school would've spent every cent they had changing and upgrading all the features of their cars. Maybe modding up was just a city thing, but Bennett definitely wasn't a city thing. He opened the door and I fell into the car, finally realizing the full extent of my exhaustion. My feet were officially frozen solid and my fingers tingled. That might've been my first and last Shady Creek hockey game.

"Did you get a hold of your mom?" Bennett asked as the car slipped out of the lot.

In the dark, it was possible he couldn't see my burning cheeks. I'd forgotten I'd lied to him. A lie that wasn't worth it. "Oh yeah. In the lobby. I forgot."

"I'm sorry I didn't wait for you. I would've felt really bad if you got hurt."

And if I hadn't sent him away so I could talk to another guy, it wouldn't have happened either. "Don't worry about it," I said. "I tripped, but Drew caught up before I got trampled." Guilt about ditching Drew crept back. My conscience was working overtime.

"Everybody seems to love that guy, don't they?" Bennett said.

"What's that supposed to mean?"

"Nothing." His tone softened and he glanced at me. "I'm just happy you're okay."

"Thanks." I didn't want him to worry. It was my fault for lying. If only I'd told Bennett I was going to talk to Drew, or better yet, ignored Drew ... but if I'd ignored him, I might be on my way to the hospital right now. Except without him, I wouldn't have been on the stairs in the first place. Stupid Drew! I twisted my hands together in my lap. First, he was an arrogant jerk, then five minutes later he was downright chivalrous. I didn't get it. He'd crawled under my skin like a parasite and infected my life. Worst of all, I owed him for helping me out. I should've just walked away.

Bennett stared at the road, jaw tight and lips held in a tight line. Hazy streetlights washed over his face and brought out the gold strands in his hair.

What was I doing? We were finally alone, and I was blowing it. Lying, talking about another guy. What was wrong with me?

All too soon we pulled up in front of my house. I unclipped my seat belt and reached for the door. I needed to say something. Anything. "I really did have fun. All things considered." Not fantastic, but at least they were words.

He sighed. "Just hang on. I'll walk you up."

He got out of the car, came around to my side, and opened the door.

I dragged myself out of the car and stepped onto the sidewalk, my left foot landing on a patch of ice. That too familiar weightless feeling rose in my stomach. I was going down—again. For the second time that night, a tight grip on my arm kept me from crashing to the ground.

"You are having a rough night." Bennett laughed as he helped me stand upright.

I nodded. "Or maybe it's just dangerous hanging out with you."

He laughed again and shot me that carefree smile. The cloud hanging over us in the car lifted under the stars.

"Nights like this don't happen here all the time. Maybe you're the dangerous one."

I joined his laughter. Me? Dangerous? "Highly doubtful."

"I hope all of this didn't turn you off hockey though. It'd be fun if you came with us again sometime." He ran his hand through his hair. Tiny snowflakes shook loose and drifted down onto his shoulders.

"I'd really like that."

I tilted my head to the side and gazed up at him. His face tinged pink, but it could have been the cold night breeze. Or maybe I was being hopeful. The air between us thickened. It weighed down on my shoulders and kept me rooted to the spot with a feeling, warm and heavy, almost tangible, as if I could grab a fistful of it and keep it in my pocket to remember this later.

Bennett looked at his feet, the muscles in his jaw tensing as he shifted his weight from side to side. He glanced back up, his eyes locking on mine.

"Avery." A voice filtered into my periphery from somewhere in the distance.

I ignored it. Bennett and this moment were all that mattered. I trembled as I stared back at him, coaxing my eyes to say all the things my mouth couldn't form into coherent words.

"Avery." The voice, louder this time, rang in my ears and disrupted my concentration. I snapped my head toward the front steps.

Mom stood in the doorway, her hands on her hips "Say goodnight and get in the house."

The sensation building between Bennett and me fell to the sidewalk and shattered like glass. A sudden chill descended over us. "Thanks again," I croaked, as I finally found my voice.

"No problem. See you tomorrow." Bennett flashed me an awkward smile and headed back to his car.

I watched him drive away and sighed.

"And who was that?" Mom barked the second the door clicked closed behind me.

"Bennett. Lily's brother. He drove me home."

"Where's that Nora girl who picked you up?" She crossed her arms and stared.

"That was Taylor. Nora couldn't make it."

The detail change seemed to feed her anger as her nostrils flared and she let out an exaggerated huff. "And where is Taylor now?"

"There was an accident at the arena. She stayed to make sure everyone was okay. That's why I needed a ride home."

"An accident?" Mom shook her head, as her seething became muddled with confusion.

"The storm blew out some of the arena windows, and the scoreboard fell and smashed onto the ice. People were screaming and running for the exits. It was freaky."

She stared at me and blinked as if I spoke a foreign language. "What storm?"

"The huge ice storm ... you know, the one that happened about an hour ago."

"What are you talking about?"

Now I was confused. The scoreboard story may sound farfetched, but there was no way she missed that storm. "You're kidding. The ice pounded the roof so loud I thought it would split open. How did you not hear it?"

"Avery, I sat right here reading all night and there wasn't a sound beyond the wind, and that died down just after you left. Maybe you're being a bit dramatic."

"Dramatic? The scoreboard didn't fall down by itself. I'm not making this up."

"I never said you were, but this doesn't change the fact that you lied about going on a date with that ... that boy." She jabbed her finger toward the closed door and wrinkled her nose as though she was talking about some sort of criminal.

"You're so overreacting. I didn't lie. I went with a bunch of people, and he happened to drive me home." I yanked out my cell phone and thrust it toward her. "Go ahead and call him. Call anyone, they'll tell you."

"Enough." Mom threw her hands in the air. "Just go to bed."

Giving her my nastiest scowl, I thumped up the stairs, changed my wet clothes, and flopped down on my bed. What was her problem? Even if I'd been on a date, what did it matter? I wouldn't have lied about it. Why would I? I was seventeen. Even she'd had a boyfriend at my age. Why couldn't I? She didn't make any sense these days.

I growled, grabbed a fistful of my hair, and tugged it, then rolled over and pulled the old diary from underneath the mattress. My eyes drooped, but Mom had me too wound up to sleep.

October 1

He asked me out!! I was walking home from school and I saw him heading down the other side of the street, watching me and smiling. Then all of a sudden, it started to rain. He ran over and held his jacket over my head, and we went to hide under the awnings of city hall until it stopped. He was so sexy, the way his dark wet hair flopped around his face. Then for some reason, he asked me to a movie. Me. I have a date with Nick.

EIGHT

I STUMBLED INTO CALCULUS AND COLLAPSED INTO MY desk. Only the first class of the day, and already I couldn't wait to go home. I must have slept. The last thing I remembered before the alarm screamed in my ear was chucking Mom's diary beside my bed, but this morning, exhaustion still weighed heavy on my limbs.

I leaned back and let my eyelids close, just for a second, but flashes of tumbling down the arena stairs and the faint echo of the scoreboard crashing forced them back open. Coupled with the acidic burn of guilt in my throat from Mom's clear disappointment in me, my productivity would be off today. But at least last night wasn't a total social disaster, even after everything that happened.

"Yeah, my dad said he hasn't seen anything weird like that happen in years. His buddy is on the arena committee, and he said the scoreboard's chains are tested at least four times a year. Plus, there's a set of beams holding it in place, and they just snapped like toothpicks," said a guy sitting across the aisle from me. Jonah, maybe?

"What do they think happened then?" Another male voice, slightly farther away.

I leaned over and faked the world's slowest search for my textbook, waiting for an answer that never came. My gaze flitted up and Jonah's eyes locked on mine with laser-sharp precision, cutting just as deep.

Busted.

Heat rose up my neck and pricked the top of my ears. Jonah rolled his eyes and leaned toward his friend, his voice fading to a whisper. Hoping to save some dignity, I grabbed a notebook and flipped randomly through the pages. Jonah's hushed voice disappeared in the babel of whispers that had erupted around me. I spun around and the voices stopped, replaced with glares and quickly shifting glances.

What was going on? It was like my first day all over again, but twice as awkward.

I turned back to my book, and the whispers started to build again. Indistinguishable mumbles floated past my ears, but I kept my gaze glued on the page, flicking the pen in my hand. They probably weren't talking about me, anyway. Lack of sleep had probably just sparked paranoia.

"Hey." Nora appeared in the doorway and settled into the desk beside mine.

I sighed and loosened the death grip on my pen. The din of voices faded to a minor irritation, along with the tension in my shoulders. Definitely all in my head.

Nora swept her severely straightened hair behind her shoulders. "Sorry about yesterday. I had a thing to go to last night, but I'm assuming Taylor made it there for you."

"Don't worry about it." I chuckled at her vagueness, remembering Taylor's joke about Nora not wanting to drive in the snow because it would mess up her car. "It's best you weren't there anyway. It was pretty chaotic."

"I heard. It's all everyone is talking about." She turned and faced forward.

The whispers started again, louder, whistling a pitch above the normal level. This time, I swore I heard my name. I tapped my pen on my desk, trying to drown it out, but it wasn't enough.

I leaned toward Nora. "Is everyone staring at me ... or am I completely insane?"

"Everyone thinks you smashed the scoreboard last night," she said matter-of-factly.

I slammed my hand on my desk and lurched the rest of the way across the aisle, nearly falling out of my seat. "What?" I blurted, then dropped my voice to an irritated hiss. "How is that possible? Do they think I shimmied up the side of the building and cut it down? That's ridiculous."

"Not yourself. With, you know, your witch powers and stuff." Another flat response.

I glanced around the room, expecting this to be a joke, but no one was laughing. "Witch powers? Are you kidding me?"

"No. Everyone thinks your grandma was a witch, so you must be one, too. Personally, I don't care." She heaved her bag on top of her desk and rummaged through her books as if she hadn't just sent me spiraling into a loop of analyzing every conversation, every interaction I'd had since arriving in this irrelevant, nothing little town.

"You think I'm a witch?" I asked.

"I don't know, but if you are, whatever."

Did she seriously not hear herself speaking? I stared forward, my fists so tight they vibrated. I'd been worried about saying or doing the wrong thing when I didn't know I was already blacklisted. And for being a witch? Come on.

It took every ounce of my strength not to jump up from my desk and throttle the first person I could find. Instead, I scribbled angry circles across my notebook—faster, darker—until the pen tip tore through the paper. I ripped the page out and crumpled it in my fist. "When exactly did everyone decide this?"

"No one decided anything. It's just an old rumor about your family. When you and your mom came back, it started up again. That scoreboard thing only added fuel." She shrugged. "Small-town life."

Small town, indeed. Stupid, ignorant, small-minded town life.

"Does everyone believe I'm a ..." I couldn't say it out loud. "... you know?"

"Beats me. When the next exciting thing comes along, people will forget about it." She settled back in her chair and yawned, twirling a purple pen between her fingers. "Unless more bizarre drama happens around you. Then it'll probably get worse."

Nora was probably the least empathetic person I'd ever met, but she had no problem telling me the truth. It was about time someone did. That was why everyone was so interested in me on my first day. They thought Grandma was a witch and I was one too. Idiots.

Mr. Brockington closed the door, and the walls seemed suddenly closer, thicker, suffocating me. Anger boiled and bubbled through my veins. A witch? Really? How dare they?

I closed my eyes, but the whispering grew louder. How could people be so mean? Was Lily just being nice to me because she thought I was some kind of freak show? A cool new accessory to show off, like the latest cell phone? And Nora said this rumor had been around for years. Did Mom know? Is that the real reason she moved to Detroit all those years ago?

I wanted to run out of the room and all the way home, but that would probably draw more unwanted attention. I gripped the edges of my seat, my knuckles white as bone, and focused on the clock slowly ticking at the front of the room. When the buzzer rang at the end of class, I raced out, refusing to look at anyone. I whipped my locker open with all my might and it slammed into the one next to mine. The loud clang of metal banging on metal gave me slight relief.

I slammed the door again.

"Someone's having a bad day."

I turned. Bennett stood behind me, which normally would've made me happy, but right now, it made me feel worse. Had he heard all the stupid rumors too?

"What did your locker do to you?" He laughed.

"Nothing. It's not talking to me, which makes it one of my only friends right now."

"Ouch." He cringed. "What happened?"

"Nothing. Just stupid people making stupid comments over things they know nothing about. Pretty normal high school stuff, really." I tried to sound calm, but my voice shook with anger. Embarrassment and anger.

Bennett's brow furrowed. "Don't worry about it. People around here need to get to know you, and when they do, I'm sure it'll be fine. You need to make some more friends, that's all."

I forced a smile.

"And," he said, as he crossed his arms and leaned against the bank of lockers, a wide smile bursting through his concern, "I think I have the solution to your problem. My parents are going to New York for the weekend, so Lil and I are throwing a party Friday night. You should come and let some of these mean old country kids get to know you. Besides, Justin should be out of the hospital by then, so it's a bit of a celebration."

"Justin's in the hospital? Is he okay?"

"Minor cuts and bruises. When the scoreboard shattered, a big panel flew out and hit him. They're keeping him for observation, but they say he'll be fine."

"Was anyone else hurt?"

"Everyone at ice level got banged up, but only a few ended up at the hospital. Justin's the only one who hasn't been released yet."

"That's good, I guess." My stomach churned. I wrapped an arm around my waist and stared at the blur of students streaming by. They all thought I'd done this. That I'd actually tried to hurt people. That I really was a—

"So." Bennett waved his hand in front of my face.

I blinked.

"Are you coming? I would—"

"Of course she's coming." Lily marched up to us and linked my arm with hers. "Everyone we know will be there and maybe even some we don't." She winked.

"Now." She pulled me down the hallway and away from Bennett. "I need to talk to you about something."

I'd have to fight her off to get away. I glanced over my shoulder. Bennett shook his head and walked away.

Why couldn't anyone let us finish a conversation?

"First thing, though, I need to know if you're into Drew. Do you like him?"

"What?" I stared at her to see if she might be joking, but she wasn't laughing, only biting her lip. "Hell no."

She dropped my arm. "Oh ... okay. Then could you ask him to come to my party for me? I can't exactly ask him myself. Way too obvious."

I shuddered. "Why me? I'm sure you have a ton of friends who'd be thrilled to—"

"Yeah, I know, but you're the only one he seems to talk to. I figured if you asked him, then maybe he might show up, and I can take it from there."

"If I have to," I grumbled under my breath. I didn't want to do this. Although I needed to thank Drew for last night, I didn't want to play matchmaker for him.

"Please?" She grinned so hard it probably hurt. "Pretty please."

I sighed. "Fine."

Lily squealed. "Thank you, thank you, thank you. I'll make it up to you. Promise." She squeezed my arm and hurried down the hallway.

The bell rang for my next class but I hadn't had a chance to grab my books. It was turning out to be another great day.

~

Out of breath, I slid into a desk in the back row in English class, hoping I wouldn't be noticed for coming in late.

"Page ninety-eight, Miss Belmont," Mrs. Sharp said.

I sighed. So much for going unnoticed. I flipped through my book as Drew appeared in the doorway, oblivious that class had already started. He swaggered in and plunked himself into the empty desk beside me.

"Hey," Drew whispered as he leaned forward on his elbows. "You okay today?"

"I'm fine," I whispered back. "You?"

"Do you have anything to say, Miss Belmont?" Mrs. Sharp asked with an accusatory stare.

A few whispers erupted around the edges of the room.

"No." I sat up straighter in my chair.

"I didn't think so." She turned back to her lesson.

I faced forward.

"Avery," Drew whispered.

My head twitched to turn, but I forced myself to stare straight ahead at Mrs. Sharp. She paced in front of the class, flinging her arms about as she spoke a little too passionately about Shakespeare.

"Avery," Drew whispered again, louder this time. "Hey!"

"Later," I hissed back.

Mrs. Sharp paused and glared at me for a moment. I stared

back, and then she continued. "After Alonzo has arrived on the island with..."

I didn't understand Drew. How could someone be so totally abrasive one minute and borderline considerate the next? Maybe he needed medication. With his hair hanging in his face and his jaw clenched, he was apparently concentrating hard on something—a drawing. As though he felt me staring, he slowly raised his head and glared back, unblinking. Then he smirked.

I trembled and faced forward again.

Why was Lily so infatuated with him? Sure, he had a certain tall, dark thing going on, but he was totally unpredictable. He was a secret code that needed to be decrypted, but I wasn't sure I wanted to know what the code unlocked. It bothered me to be intrigued and wary of him all at the same time—as if my brain had its signals crossed between curiosity and condemnation and messed with my better instincts.

But why? That was the part I hadn't figured out yet.

Finally, the bell rang. I quickly gathered my things and bolted out of the classroom. A stare seared the back of my neck as I rushed into the hall. I turned. Drew, following way too close behind me.

"Sorry for getting you in trouble back there. I just wanted to see how you were."

"Thanks. And I'm fine." I tucked my hair behind my ear, barely believing I'd heard him apologize for something. So confusing. "Actually, I was hoping I'd see you today."

"Really?" He grinned.

"I felt bad about leaving after you helped me. I really did appreciate it. Thank you."

"No big deal. But you owe me one." He pointed at me, his eyes narrowing. "Wonder Boy get you home safe?"

Wonder Boy? "Oh. Bennett. Yeah."

"He's kind of a boy scout, don't you think? Unless you like that sort of thing."

"And what if I do?" At least I thought I did.

"Do you?" He rubbed his hand across the back of his neck, mussing up his hair. "Sorry. I heard what you said about acting like a jerk. And I am trying to stop. At least with you."

"It wouldn't kill you to be a bit nicer."

"I actually think it might." He laughed as if it was some sort of inside joke.

So weird.

He stepped forward and I stepped back, pinning myself between him and the wall. My pulse quickened. I pulled my books close to my chest. "Are you going to Lily and Bennett's party on Friday?"

He stared down at me intently. "I don't think I was invited."

"It's not really an invite-only thing." I looked away, trying to avoid his eyes. "Besides, Lily said she wanted you to come."

"Are you going? It seems like a real waste of time. I mean, I can think of far better things to do on a Friday night."

"Probably. But you're definitely not going, right?"

"Definitely not," he snarled.

So much for trying to be nicer. "Okay then. That's fine. See you around. Thanks again," I said, sidling away. I turned around and sped off, not stopping until I reached my locker. I rested my forehead on the cold metal as my heartbeat thrummed in my ears. Why did he have to stare as if he might bite me or something? I was glad he'd declined Lily's invitation. Things seemed more complicated with him around. Besides, his intensity was exhausting.

Someone tapped my shoulder and I jumped.

"I saw you with Drew. How did it go?" Lily clasped her hands in front of her.

"He's not coming." I tried to sound disappointed.

"He's not?" Her bottom lip protruded in a sullen pout. "How strange. Did he say why?"

"Nope. Sorry."

"Thanks anyway." Her shoulders slumped and her smile faded. "But you're still coming, right?"

"Of course."

"Good." She nodded approvingly.

"Lily, I wouldn't bother with him. He seems like a bit of an ass."

She frowned for a moment and then her smile reappeared. "Well, that's generally my type. I love a challenge." She turned on her heel and charged off.

~

The rest of the day passed uneventfully. A few people still whispered as I walked past, but it seemed as though the novelty had worn off. Anyway, I couldn't wait to get home. Out of the cold snow and the even colder halls of high school.

I waved at Mrs. Abernathy, who was standing guard in her window like always, and opened the front door to a blast of warmth and the scent of garlic. My stomach growled its approval.

"Hi, honey." Mom stood behind the door, buttoning up her coat. "How was your day?"

"Fine, I guess." I gave her a quick hug and rested my head on her shoulder.

She patted my hair and kissed the top of my head. "What's wrong?"

"Nothing." I sighed but reconsidered. I might as well ask. "Some people were saying things at school today. About Grandma. About us."

"Like what?" Mom pulled away and looked into my eyes. Worry lines creased her forehead. "Don't tell me they still haven't stopped with all that nonsense."

I raised an eyebrow. "Huh?"

"When I was in school, they said all sorts of terrible things about our family. Some even said we were witches."

"Exactly. That's what they were saying."

"Unfortunately, as nice as small towns are, they never forget."

"Never forget what? Are you saying it's true?"

She wrinkled her nose and pursed her lips into a sour expression. "Once you get a reputation in a small town, it's hard to get rid of. Even if you don't deserve it." She leaned forward and swept my hair over my shoulder. "Don't let them get to you."

I nodded.

"I hate to leave you like this, but I have to work the night shift. I left supper in the kitchen." She pulled a pair of blue stretchy mitts from her pocket and slipped them on. "I'm off on Friday though. Why don't we do something fun? Make it a girl's night."

I chucked my schoolbag on the floor and slid out of my jacket, hanging it on a hook. "Sorry, Mom, I already have plans. Lily and Bennett are having a party."

"Bennett?" She pointed toward the front door as if he were still standing outside on the sidewalk. "The boy who brought you home last night?"

"Yes."

"But you just met him."

"So? He just drove me home. What's wrong with that?"

Mom's face set in a grim line. "We've barely been here a week. You don't want to get a reputation. Isn't the witch thing enough?"

"Are you kidding me? I needed a ride home. He gave me one. That's it."

"Boys are trouble, Avery. You don't need that right now."

"You're being paranoid."

"No, I'm not. I'm looking out for you. Keeping you safe. This world ... this town ... there's so much you don't understand yet, so much." She blinked. "You're not going to that party."

"But—"

"Enough. I have to go. We can talk about this later." She slammed the door on her way out as if to make sure I knew she was serious.

Grrr! I kicked my schoolbag down the hall, smashing my toe against a textbook. *Ow!* Grabbing my foot, I leaned against the wall. I couldn't even get angry without something bad happening. Whiskers padded into the hall and nuzzled my leg, meowing loudly.

"Yeah, I know. She's insane." I petted her soft furry head. "C'mon, girl. Let's eat."

I filled Whiskers's bowl and grabbed the plate of chicken parmesan off the counter. Of course, she'd made my favorite when I wanted to be mad. I balanced the plate on my hand, scooped up my schoolbag off the floor, and settled onto the couch. Resting the plate on my cross-legged lap, I flicked on the TV and flipped through the New Releases guide.

Cover images of movies and shows cycled by until I'd checked all the menus at least three times. I turned the TV off and tossed the remote onto the coffee table next to the leather-bound book Mom had been reading last night. How was I going to tell Lily that I wasn't coming to her party? Mom wanted me to make friends—that was all she'd talked about since we got here—then when I finally did, she forbade me to see them. How was that fair? Especially since she never told me about the rumors. Didn't she think to mention, oh yeah, by the way, people might think you're a witch? I already needed to work extra hard here. Why did she have to make it tougher?

I leaned back and pushed the chicken around the plate with my fork. It looked great, but my hunger had disappeared. Maybe I was under some diet spell or something. I snickered. That was about as likely as Lily wearing sweatpants to school. Me, a witch? Seriously?

Whiskers curled up in my lap, her purr vibrating against my leg. I ran my fingers along her back and down her tail. "At least I've got you."

Reaching around Whiskers, I pulled Mom's diary out from under my chemistry book. I'd planned on sneaking in some pages during Physics, but I'd been too distracted by all the deafening whispers to concentrate.

October 10

I hate my mother right now. I absolutely hate her. Does she not want me to be happy, ever? Things were going so well too. Nick is even better than I'd imagined. He's smart, sweet and so hot. And I think he might really like me, or he did until he met my mother. She waited at the door for me and then lectured him for twenty minutes about keeping me out too late. It wasn't even midnight! No wonder she has a bad name in this stupid town. She needs to get a life and stay out of mine.

NINE

As I walked in the front door after school on Friday, Mom was walking out.

"Hey." I stomped the snow off my boots on the small brown foyer rug. "Are we going out for dinner? I thought we were ordering Chinese?"

Mom's lips pinched. "I'm sorry, honey. I know, but Georgina called in sick and I have to cover her shift. Next week maybe?"

Mom gone. The whole night. My life just improved tenfold.

After dinner, I'd planned to beg her to let me go to the party. Now, I didn't have to. I wasn't going to get into any trouble, and besides, she'd probably really like Bennett if she met him. I'd just go to the party for a few hours and be home in bed before she got back.

I forced down a smile. "Sure. Do what you've gotta do. I'll be fine."

"I love you, you know that?" She kissed my forehead. "I should be home by 12:30."

She scampered down the street and left me standing alone in the doorway. My stomach twinged. Mom and I didn't have many secrets, and I'd never outright betrayed her before, but lately she'd been so unreasonable. I wasn't a bad kid. What was she so afraid of?

I changed into a cute top with cut-outs in the back—nice, but not trying too hard—and waited by the phone for Mom's regular late shift check-in call. Just after 9:30, I hung up and sprinted for the door. I had to be back by midnight—glass slippers and all.

Mrs. Abernathy stood in her front window again, all spy and shadow, watching me speed past her house. She probably wouldn't tell Mom, but the possibility that she might nagged at me.

I ran the last four blocks to the Price house and took a deep breath before knocking on the door. Some guy in a backward cap and jeans answered.

"Hey, girl-I-don't-know. Coats upstairs, drinks in the kitchen." He held up his palm and gave me a poorly-timed high five, nearly hitting me in the face.

I squeezed through the door and tried not to laugh as he stumbled off into the house. I checked my phone. 9:45. All right, I had a tight schedule, but if I focused, I could pull it off. I raced upstairs, chucked my coat in one of the bedrooms, and weaved my way through the maze of people on the stairs back down to the main floor.

"Avery," Lily shouted as I stepped off the last stair. She wrapped her arms around me, hanging on tight while holding her half-full drink away from me. "You made it."

"Of course. I said I'd be here." Although it was sheer dumb luck that I'd made it.

"Come with me." She grabbed my hand and twisted it up over our heads, dragging me behind her as she jumped and shimmied through the crowd.

Body heat fogged the windows and made the air hot and sticky. People lined every room, on couches and chairs or leaning against the walls. More people than the entire high school. More than the parties I went to in the city. Lily must be more popular than I'd thought.

Music blared and the tiny hairs on my neck vibrated to the bass. Lily introduced me around. I couldn't hear names, so I just smiled and nodded. The house looked as if it came from a magazine, but it might not look so great in a few hours. Empty beer cans already bordered the back wall, and the likelihood of a fancy vase or expensive knickknack getting broken increased with every person who staggered down the hall. If I lived here, I'd be terrified right now.

"Hey Lily," I shouted. "I'm going to go get a drink. You want one?"

"You're so nice, Avery Belmont." She smothered me in another unexpected hug, tight enough to squeeze the air from my lungs, then pressed her forehead against mine. Her breath was sweet and strong, like a drunken pineapple. "I've had lots, but find me later, okay?"

I nodded and walked toward the archway into the kitchen. Dirty looks and spilled drinks marked my path as I jostled through bodies, like fighting my way up the arena stairs, waiting to fall. I shuddered. At least here there were lights. Finally, I emerged in the kitchen. The crowd was thinner in this room and I breathed deeply.

I pushed past a few more people, heading toward the far counter by the sink. It was surrounded by stacks of red cups, a gigantic camping cooler, and a mass of liquor bottles in every color imaginable.

Taylor stood by the cooler, a tight white sweater accentuating her flushed cheeks. I stepped back, but she'd already seen me. "When did you get here?" she asked, her voice friendly. Maybe she didn't hate me for almost squashing her boyfriend with a scoreboard the other night. Even though I didn't actually do it.

"A few minutes ago." I hesitated but decided to test the waters. "Where's Justin?"

"He's in the basement. By the way, sorry for ditching you at the arena, but I heard Bennett took you home." She gave me a wink. "How did that go?"

"Fine, I guess." I sighed.

"Ouch. Well, give it some time. Or keep looking. There's a ton of hot guys here." She scooped a bunch of beer bottles from the cooler and rested them on the counter, then laced the necks precariously through her fingers. "You should come downstairs later. They are playing some stupid drinking games down there. It's pretty funny."

"Yeah. Maybe I will."

~

11:26. Just enough time to grab my coat and get home. I pounded back the last few sips of my exotic berry cooler and dropped the empty cup in the garbage. Pushing my way down the hall toward the front stairs, I took one last look for either Lily or Bennett. No luck. Probably better anyway. I didn't have any time left.

Bang! My shoulder slammed into someone's chest. A red cup flew into the air and tumbled to the floor.

"I'm so sorry." I dropped to my knees and scrambled to pick it up.

"Lucky for you, that one was empty."

I glanced up. Bennett stood above me, his hand outstretched, and a shy smile across his lips. "So you did make it."

"Told you I would." I took his hand and shivered as his skin brushed against mine. Flesh to flesh. I didn't want him to let go. Maybe he didn't want to either. His fingers lingered on mine once I was safely on two feet again.

"I tried to find you, but it was too crowded in here," I

admitted, hoping to sound more sincere than obsessive. "Thanks for inviting me."

"No problem. I was hoping you'd come."

"Really?" I fought the urge to squeal with excitement. *Deep breath.* "Besides, I should get out and meet people, like you said, since I have no friends."

Oh. My. God. Did I just say that out loud?

He raised an eyebrow. "That's not what I meant."

"I know, I..." Words wouldn't come. I shook my head and stared at the floor, wishing I could disappear.

"It's okay." He placed his hand on my chin and gently raised my head. As we locked eyes, he yanked his hand away. "I wanted to ask if maybe sometime..." He stepped closer.

Goosebumps spread up my arms.

He leaned toward me until his warm breath fell on my cheek and whispered, "You might want—"

"Hey, Benny!" Someone yelled and grabbed Bennett's arm, pulling him away from me. "This is your place, right, man?"

Drew, of course. Always when I least expected him.

I shrank back against the wall, trying to steady myself. Why couldn't anyone let me talk to Bennett? First my mom, then Lily, now Drew. Seriously?

"Somebody started a fire out back. I threw some snow on it, but it's too high." Drew pointed toward the backyard.

Bennett bolted down the hall toward the kitchen. "Sorry, Avery," he called over his shoulder. "We'll talk later."

I frowned. I didn't have a later.

"Let's get out of here." Drew wrapped his arm over my shoulders and guided me away from Bennett. I tried to shrug him off, but he clamped my shoulder tighter and ushered me toward the front door.

"Wait! Where are we going? I have to get my coat." I twisted my body out of his grip.

"No time." He whipped off his own coat. "Take mine."

Caught up in the panic of the unknown, I followed him outside to the porch. He sped down the front walk, but I stopped, my mind finally catching up with my feet.

"Wait a second. Why do we have to leave? And who says I'm going to go anywhere with you?"

He stopped and turned back, hands in his pockets, arms tight to his body, shivering. "I'm taking you home. Would you like to sit around and discuss this, or would you like to get gone before firetrucks and police descend to break up this party, and you're taken home in a squad car for drinking underage?"

Good point. I pulled on his coat and scurried down the front steps. Being here was already risky. Getting arrested wouldn't make things better.

We rushed along in silence, except for my grumbling as I tripped through the snow. My lungs ached from gulping the icy air, but getting caught would hurt much worse. Finally, we turned the corner of the street and I stopped to catch my breath.

A thin trail of smoke rose behind the Price house. A wailing siren pierced the air. I turned and watched the red and blue lights dance across the snow banks, a sense of calm tingling through my limbs. Far too close.

Drew tugged on my arm. "See. Told you."

"I guess you were right." I hugged Drew's jacket closer to my body, inhaling its scent, heavy like dark things—black licorice and leather. Leaving the party just a few minutes later would've created a monsoon of trouble. He'd saved my butt again. "Thanks."

I shook my head and followed Drew. As he walked under the glow of the streetlight, I noticed the tiny hairs on his arms sticking straight out, and realized he wore nothing more than a short-sleeved t-shirt. "Aren't you freezing? You can have your jacket back."

"I'll be all right. Besides we're almost at your house."

"How do you know where I live?"

"It's a small town. I know where everyone lives."

"Oh." Of course he did. Everyone knew everything about everyone around here. "So how come you changed your mind about coming tonight?"

"I decided to see what all the fuss was about."

"And?"

"Definitely a waste of time." His words dripped with disgust.

We walked silently the rest of the way, Drew always a few steps ahead. I wasn't sure what to say after he'd come to my rescue again. My own jackass in shining armor.

"This is me." I pointed up the front walk to the door. "Thanks."

"Can I come in to warm up for a minute? Since you're still wearing my jacket."

I looked at him shivering and bare-armed, on his way to hypothermia. "Sure, but only a few minutes. My mom will be home soon and she'll kill me if she sees you in the house."

"Not big on guys, is she?" He raised an eyebrow.

"She isn't a big fan of anything these days." I opened the door and crossed my arms, standing with just enough space for him to enter, but not get too comfortable. I shouldn't be letting him in, but he'd kept me from being grounded for the next millennia, so it was the least I could do.

Whiskers darted up to me and puttered around my feet, nuzzling her nose into my legs.

"Nice kitty." Drew reached down to pet her.

Whiskers hissed and sprinted under the living room couch.

"I guess she doesn't like visitors either." He shrugged. His gaze darted around. "This place looks as if it hasn't changed in years. The wallpaper screams old lady house."

"We haven't had much time to redecorate, but I'm sure we will." Drew was right, the wallpaper was hideous, but did he need to say it? I glanced at the hall clock. It was 11:46.

I slid out of Drew's jacket and handed it to him. "Thanks for keeping me out of jail."

"Someone needs to look out for you, otherwise who knows what trouble you might get into." He flashed me a devious smile and chuckled. He might have been charming if he wasn't so caustic.

"Very funny." I opened the front door, giving him his cue to leave. "See you Monday."

"Sure." He took my hint and headed out. "By the way." He stopped and leaned against the doorjamb. "This awesome band is playing in the city tomorrow. Want to come?"

"Oh." I shifted my stare to the floor. "Maybe you should ask Lily to go."

He squinted and his mouth tightened into an ugly expression. "Lily? Why would I ask Lily?" His frown dissolved and he chuckled. "You thought I was asking you on a date? Uh no. I thought you might need a friend and maybe do something cool for once. Never mind. Forget I asked."

He gave me a dismissive wave and marched down the front steps and into the night.

"I'm sorry," I blurted. "I'd love to go." Dammit! Why did I say that?

He turned mid-way through the yard and grinned slyly. "If you're sure you want to go with me."

I blushed. No, but I couldn't take it back now.

"Okay then. Pick me up outside school at ten."

"Wait. I have to drive?"

"Would you rather I sit down and chat with your mother before we go?"

"Fine. I'll drive," I mumbled, picturing the disaster of Drew and Mom in the same room.

"On that note, I should go before your mother gets home and finds you unchaperoned with a male visitor." He winked at me and continued toward the sidewalk.

I shuddered. "Wait, Drew," I called after him. "How did you know the cops would come so quickly?"

"Easy." He shrugged his jacket onto his shoulders. "I called them."

I stood frozen on the doorstep. *He* called them?

Still facing the street, Drew flipped his hand over his shoulder and waved. "Good night, New Girl."

TEN

RAYS OF MORNING SUN REFLECTED OFF THE SNOW IN A blinding sheet of light, and I squinted as I signaled, then turned into the school parking lot. I found Drew waiting, just as he'd promised, perched on top of a picnic table in the courtyard. He rested back on his hands, his legs stretched out so that his sneakered feet hung over the edge, and his head tipped up between his shoulder blades, staring at the sky. I leaned forward and looked up, seeing miles of clear blue but nothing unusual. Maybe he was just enjoying the quiet. Ten was still pretty early for a Saturday, and from the lack of traffic, it seemed as though the whole town had been told to sleep in.

Except for Mom. She'd awoken just before dawn, cleaning and rearranging furniture in the living room. I'd thought she'd demand I help, but instead, she hurried me off, almost too eager to have an Avery-free day. Maybe she needed a break from me for a while. I knew I needed one from her.

I hadn't told her about Drew, though. She'd been so anti-guy lately, I couldn't risk another lecture about my reputation. I'd told her I was seeing a band with a friend—I just hadn't said which one. Besides, it wasn't a total lie, she had all the vital information. The bigger lie was referring to Drew as my friend.

Drew opened the door and jumped in the passenger's side.

"Morning, New Girl," he chirped as he settled into the seat of our rusty old Corolla. "Nice wheels."

"Very funny." Sure, the car was old, but at least it was still running. "It's better than walking."

"Not by much." He rolled his eyes and changed the radio station to something louder and angrier. "At least the music's better now. How can you stand that happy, happy dance stuff?"

I shook my head. Which was worse—that I'd agreed to spend the day with him, or that I'd gotten used to his obnoxious behavior?

As I pulled out onto the street, he drummed on his thigh and bobbed his head to the music.

"How come I had to pick you up here?" I turned down the radio. "Don't you spend enough time at school during the week?"

"I'm not the only one who had to lie to get out today." He smirked.

"You think I lied?" I peered through the side window, trying to hide the guilt likely spreading across my face. Even though I did lie, I didn't appreciate it being a foregone conclusion. "Maybe my mom trusts me more than your parents trust you."

"First off—parent, not parents. Second, no one trusts me. And I'm not really sure they should."

I cringed and he smiled, probably getting the exact reaction he wanted. Did he say things like that to everyone, or did he only enjoy seeing me squirm?

"Do you live with your mom or your dad?" I asked.

"My mother. Dad left when I was young."

"I guess we have something in common then. Mine left before I was born. Do you remember him—your father?"

"No. Not like I care to anyway." He shrugged, no emotion in his tone or his expression.

"Yeah, me neither."

"Unexpected." He sat up straight in his seat and looked at me. It was a good thing I had to keep my eyes on the road or his stare would have been awkward. One of those looks you didn't need to see to feel. "I figured you'd be one of those daddy-issue type girls."

"Uh, no. I've never even met him."

"Doesn't mean he doesn't impact your life. He's still your family."

"I've been fine without him so far. And besides, I don't know a thing about him. There are no pictures or reminders of him anywhere. It's like I was born through immaculate conception or something. What's to miss?"

"Sounds a little bitter to me."

"Not bitter, just practical. Besides, didn't you say you didn't give a damn about your father either? Why do you think I would be any different than you?"

"Because at least I know who my father was. You don't know anything at all. Maybe he was a good guy."

"And maybe he was a total loser. Fact is, my mom doesn't talk about him and I've never asked. It's not that I wouldn't want to know about him." An understatement, considering the way I binge read Mom's teenage diary, searching for clues about him. "I just haven't bothered to look. Like I said, I've been fine without him this far. And it's pointless. He obviously wants nothing to do with me."

"Maybe he would if he knew you." Drew's voice softened. Hushed. Eerie. I pulled my eyes away from the road to look at him. He still had his cocky grin, but it didn't curl up as much at the edges, and his eyes were big and wide, almost lost—so different from his usual arrogance and smart mouth. He seemed different. He seemed ... well ... human.

"Thanks, but I'm really okay." I gave him a brief smile and tried to change the subject, yet again. I would need to stay on my toes to survive the day. "What band did you say we were going to again?"

"I didn't. They're called The Razorbacks."

"Never heard of them."

"I didn't think so. Not quite your thing."

"Then why would you invite me if I'm not going to like them?" His confusing behavior made my head hurt.

"You never asked me who we were going to see. If you wanted to know, you would have asked. Is it my fault you jumped at the chance to hang out with me?" He reclined back in the seat and tucked his palms behind his head.

I gritted my teeth and clenched the wheel tighter. My cheeks warmed. I didn't remember things going down that way. I remembered mistakenly thinking he was asking me out, then frantically agreeing to anything to avoid feeling like an idiot. But right now, who knew what I really agreed to?

"They aren't death metal, are they?"

"No. Rock. Kinda punk."

"Good." The chaotic pound of death metal mixed with Drew's unpredictability might push me over the edge.

"You should take the next left turn up here." Drew thrust his arm in front of my face and pointed out the window.

"I don't think so. We have to stay on the interstate. Trust me. I know where I'm going."

"So do I," he barked. "And I'm telling you to take the next left. It's a shortcut."

"A shortcut?"

"Yes, shortcut. The venue is east. The interstate will take us in from the north. Don't you ever listen to anybody?"

"Sure I do." I turned the wheel sharp to the left. The faster we got there, the faster I could get out of the car. "I just don't like taking risks."

"It's a shortcut, not life or death. Wow, are you uptight." Drew settled back into his seat.

"And you're being a jerk again."

Drew opened his mouth as if to say something but turned to stare out the car window instead. Smart move.

Traffic on the side road was nonexistent, and except for a few rough patches, driving conditions were better than expected. We passed large empty fields dotted with small bluffs of old naked trees that reminded me how cold it was outside. I shivered and nuzzled my chin down into the collar of my spring jacket, regretting leaving my winter one at Lily's last night. If this road did prove faster than the main highway, maybe I'd take it again one day. Maybe in the summer when thick leaves covered the trees and the fields stretched out green under the blue sky. But I'd never give Drew the warped satisfaction of telling him he was right.

"So you don't like risks," Drew said, still gazing out at the horizon. "How boring is your life if you never take risks?"

"I take some risks. I'm spending the day with you, aren't I?"

"That's a risk to you?" He snorted and shifted his attention back to me. "Do you think I'm evil or something?"

I chuckled. "Not sure yet, but I doubt it."

"Oh Avery, I wouldn't be so sure."

Was he joking? With his twisted sense of humor, probably. "I'm conscientious. That means I'm careful about what risks I take. Is that a bad thing?"

He glanced up at the roof of the car. "There's just so much out there to experience. I wouldn't want to sell myself short is all."

"And I'm sure I'll experience enough in my lifetime. We're still young, you know."

"But what if you died tomorrow?"

I squirmed in my seat. "I don't think that way. Besides, I don't take risks, so I will probably live forever."

"I'll bet living forever isn't quite as fun as you might think," Drew said.

"I guess you'll never know."

"Don't play any sports either, do you?" he continued.

"Sure, I do." Was I that obviously unathletic, or had he been eavesdropping on my conversations with Bennett? I didn't look that pathetic, did I?

"What? Like croquet?" He chuckled.

"No. I'm not a total jock, but I'm not a complete shut-in either."

"Ever been seriously hurt? Broken any bones?"

"What does that have to do with anything?" My voice rose. I gripped the steering wheel tighter, and the flesh on my knuckles whitened.

"Easy. Most kids get hurt over the years. Unless they don't live very hard, that is."

"Live hard? What does that even mean? Do you 'live hard,' Drew?"

"Of course. Why wouldn't I?"

I rolled my eyes.

"I'm guessing you're not a bleeder either then?"

"You are completely messed up, you know that?" I blurted. What was his problem? I surveyed the snowy road ahead for a turnoff. Enough of this 'trying to be nice' thing. We were heading back to Shady Creek. Now. Drew could find someone else to torment. "No, Drew. I'm not accident-prone, I've never broken bones, and I'm not a bleeder. Anything else you need to know before I leave you here on the side of the highway?"

"Just one more thing," he said calmly. He flashed me a wide smile. "Watch this."

He grabbed the steering wheel and jerked the car left into the oncoming lane.

"What are you doing?" I screamed, clenching the wheel tighter. I turned hard to the right.

Drew yanked the wheel again, his grip too strong to fight. The car hit a patch of ice and slid toward the ditch on the left side of the road.

I smashed my foot on the brake and tried to turn again, but the wheels locked up. I wasn't in control, and neither was Drew. The back end of the car twisted sharply and we began to spin, rising into the air, gliding. Then the car pitched, slamming us against our seats.

An engine revving.

Screaming—my voice, but very far away.

Color and light twisting and blurring in front of me, my stomach swirling. I closed my eyes.

I was going to puke.

The top of the car smashed into the ground. Glass shattered and metal groaned. We rolled over and over, hair floating around me, tears streaming down my face. Then the car teetered one last time and crashed to a halt.

The air lay still and eerily quiet, save the distant hiss of the battered engine. I guessed this was what it was like to be dead. Dead on the side of the highway. Silent and surprisingly cold.

All the plans I had for my life, all my dreams ... just gone. Mom would be a wreck when the police told her they found my body. I ached to hug her right now. Feel her hold me and tell me everything was going to be okay. But it wouldn't be okay. It'd never be okay again.

Tears poured down my face, and my lungs burned from the pressure of forgetting to exhale. But wait. If I was dead, I wouldn't need to breathe. My eyes fluttered open. I was still in the driver's seat facing the windshield, the remaining glass splintered into a spider web of cracks. Fragments of the car lay in my lap. My nostrils burned from the smell of gas, but I could wiggle my toes in my boots, move my hands, and turn my head side to side.

I wasn't dead, but I hurt all over.

The strange heavy weight of a stare fell over me. I suddenly remembered I wasn't alone and glanced at Drew, who watched me with a mixture of curiosity and fascination in his eyes. He seemed as unscathed as I was. As I caught his gaze, he tossed his head back and burst out laughing. "Quite a ride, huh?"

Hot saliva burned the back of my throat and my hands curled into fists. "You insane, sadistic, sociopath," I sputtered. "You tried to kill me!"

I fumbled with my seat belt clip, slamming my fingers against the release button over and over again, but it wouldn't let go, the thick straps crushing down on my lungs.

Drew stopped laughing and grabbed the belt running across my lap. I flinched against his touch and pressed my legs down into my seat. He reached into his back pocket and pulled out a small object, flipping it in his hand to expose a large steel blade.

A knife!

"Don't move." He leaned over.

I gulped.

As he brought the blade closer, I tensed. He locked eyes with me as if to ask for permission, and then he sliced through the seat belt as if it were a thin piece of thread.

As soon as the belt fell away, I crawled over what was left of the dashboard and pushed my way through an opening in the windshield. I clambered onto the mangled hood, glass crunching below me, and I slipped, tumbling into a snow bank.

Drew followed me out and jumped gracefully to the ground. He offered me his hand. "Here."

I ignored him and struggled to my feet, heading off toward the highway. I didn't care about the wet snow in my shoes or the ridiculously cold chill burrowing under my skin. I needed to get as far away from him as possible.

"Avery, where are you going?"

Refusing to look back, I kicked one of the plastic car trim pieces that littered the ground. It flew onto the pavement and splintered.

"You're going to freeze," he taunted as I walked farther and farther away.

"Avery," he called. "I'm serious. You shouldn't be going off alone in the cold. Calm down and come back here."

Calm down? Who did he think he was, telling me to calm down? He just tried to wipe me out. It was smarter to keep walking away, but rage coursed through my veins, thick as blood, compelling me to run him down.

I turned and raced back. "What the hell did you think you were doing?" I slammed all my weight squarely into Drew's chest and knocked him to the ground.

He started laughing again.

"Do you think this is funny?" I kicked his shoe as hard as I could, sending a jolt of pain through my foot. "What is your problem? You hijacked my car and tried to kill me."

He opened his mouth to speak, but I continued. "This isn't a joke. You should be dead right now. I should be dead right now."

"Yeah, you should be," he replied, matter-of-factly.

"What?" I shook my head.

"You're right. You should be dead right now, but you haven't got as much as a broken nail. Why do you think that is?"

"Errrgh!" I couldn't form words.

"Any thoughts?" he asked.

"Enough." I pressed the tips of my fingers to my temples, my head murky from his nonsense. "You're screwed up."

Cold air choked my lungs as I charged away again. How did I let myself get trapped inside the carnage of a Corolla with a psycho? And what did he mean, I wasn't hurt? He's lucky I survived. This way, it was only attempted murder, not full-blown manslaughter.

"I'm sorry," Drew shouted. "I just needed to know."

I kept walking.

"There was no other way."

No other way? No other way for what? To see how much I could bleed? He seemed quite interested in that. "You're sick," I screamed, without bothering to turn around. "Leave me alone."

"I can't. I've spent most of my life searching for you."

I clamped my hand over my mouth and tried not to gag. Did that freak show think violence was some sort of turn-on? He obviously found the wrong girl. My brain screamed *run!* but my horrified body wouldn't respond. I scanned the horizon for a farmhouse, a gas station— anything within walking distance—but the road was desolate. I fumbled through my pockets, but no cell phone. My heart sank. I must've left it in the car.

"I know about your father, Avery."

I stopped. My father?

"He's not who you think he is, but I needed to know for sure before I told you."

I didn't want to take the bait. Probably some cruel joke anyway. But for my entire life, everyone avoided talking about my father. "Needed to know what?"

"Come back here and I'll tell you."

Not good enough. I kept walking.

"Fine," he said. "I needed to know if you were indestructible."

"Indestructible? Seriously, Drew. Go mess with someone else's head for a while."

"It's true," he shouted. "Any normal person would have died in that crash, but you're perfectly fine. Can you please just trust me on this?"

"Trust you?" I screamed. "After what you did to me, why would I ever trust you?"

"Because I'm your brother."

Eleven

I stood in the middle of nowhere, paralyzed in confusion, staring vacantly into the cold, snowy distance. My thin jacket did little to keep the howling wind away. Drew—my brother?

No way. "I don't have a brother." I refused to face him. Looking at him might make this nonsense believable.

"Fine. Half-brother."

"You're lying," I screamed into the empty frigid air.

"Don't you always wonder why he was never there? Why you never had a father? There is so much I can tell you about him. So much you need to know."

My ears throbbed as the cold settled into my skin. There was no way he could be my brother. It wasn't impossible for my dad to have had another life—one without me and Mom—but why Drew?

"C'mon, Avery. Just get back here and I'll tell you everything I know."

"How do I know I can trust you? You tried to kill me."

"I've been trying to talk to you for a week now, but you wouldn't listen. I needed to get your attention."

He definitely had my attention now.

"I don't want to hurt you. Just come back. If you still don't believe me, I'll leave you alone and you'll never see me again. I promise."

What choice did I have? Keep walking to who knew where —potentially freezing off several body parts—or go back and hear what he had to say? If he'd wanted to kill me, he could've done it so many times already. And I sure wasn't "indestructible."

Did he really know anything? I summoned all my courage to turn around. "What if I don't come back?"

"Then I guess you will spend the rest of your life not knowing who you really are, which won't be long as you'll probably freeze to death out here."

I stood quietly, fists balled at my sides, trying to absorb everything that was happening and plan my next move.

"No one knows the things I know," he continued. "This is your one chance to find out where you came from."

I couldn't clearly see his face for the distance between us, but he did sound sincere. There was none of the sarcasm or disdain that I'd come to expect. Either he was finally being honest, or he was a great actor.

"Prove it," I dared, but refused to move any closer. "Tell me something."

He hung his head for a moment, then looked up again. "His name was Nicholas, Nick for short. He met your mom at Shady Creek High, and she had you when she was barely eighteen."

"Everyone knows that."

Footsteps crunched over the snow toward me. "Your dad never left you because he's never even seen you. He took off hours before you were born, but left you a fuzzy pink blanket with purple elephants on it. He's not even on your birth certificate."

I couldn't speak. He was right. I'd carried that blanket everywhere until I was five. I didn't know who it was from, it was just a blanket, my favorite blanket. And I'd never told anyone about my birth certificate. I didn't even know where Mom kept it, but I knew she was the only parent listed. Question was, did Drew really know these things from knowing my father, or was the collective small-town memory making details accessible to psychos like him?

I looked down the desolate highway. Not a lot of options left without proper winter clothes. I sighed and my head dropped to my chest. If I wanted to survive, I needed to get my phone.

The steam from my breath trembled in the air as I trudged back to the corpse of Mom's car. I tried to visualize a plan for escape, but my thoughts kept blurring. What if Drew wasn't lying? Did he really know my dad?

Drew stood by the driver's door and waited, smart enough not to approach, letting me come to him. He rubbed his hands together, blowing into his palms to keep them warm, watching my careful steps.

"Thank you," he said, his voice low and calm.

I stopped, out of arm's reach, and stared at the crumpled car, wishing he'd move so I could get closer.

"I'm not saying I believe you, but I'll listen. This better be good." I crossed my arms and tried to keep my voice from wavering.

"I'll tell you everything you want to know, but first we should get you somewhere warm. I don't want you to get sick." He moved slowly toward me, and I backed up. "I'm serious, you could die out here. We need to get you inside."

"Aren't I 'indestructible'?" I sneered.

"I can't hurt you from the outside, but you can still freeze to death inside. You can still get sick." He slid forward a step. "Let's go somewhere to talk and I'll explain."

"How exactly are we going to do that? You totaled my car, or don't you remember?" My heart thumped painfully in my ears, echoing in the still, icy air.

"I can take care of the car, but you need to step back."

I shuffled backward, refusing to take my eyes off Drew.

"A little more." He waved me back.

I obeyed.

Drew placed his hands on the car hood, almost like a criminal before a police officer pat down. I wondered how many times he'd been in that position before. He closed his eyes. Everything went deathly quiet. Even the wind stopped howling through the open field.

My knees shook, the silence more unnerving than Drew's chatter.

Bang!

I dropped to the ground and scrambled toward the highway. What the hell was that?

Bang!

I flattened my face into the cold snow. Were those gunshots? I squeezed my eyes closed, expecting pain as I pushed up on my hands and crawled forward. I knew I should've kept walking. Now I would die out here.

More heavy bangs exploded behind me. My stomach hollowed at each blast, but nothing touched me. Winded, I peeked back over my shoulder. Drew's eyes were shut tight, and both of his hands were still on the hood.

The car clanged and groaned. Dents and dings smoothed away as the entire vehicle took on its former shape as if someone were filling a car-sized balloon.

I gasped and scrambled to my feet. How was that possible?

The sunken roof popped up, and the metal shrieked as it stretched back into place. Tiny shards of glass tinkled, rising into the air around me and hanging suspended as if on invisible strings, shimmering like sugar crystals in the sunlight. I reached out to touch them, but they flew away from me and toward the empty window slots, neatly filling each space like intricately patterned puzzle pieces.

Drew groaned loudly and the shards fused together, melting

into perfectly clear sheets of glass. He ripped his hands from the hood and staggered backward, his face anguished, his breathing heavy.

My legs wobbled out from under me. As I dropped to the ground, Drew reached out and pulled me up.

"Not bad, huh?" he asked with a mischievous grin.

"How did you? I mean ... what did you? I mean ... what are you...?" I managed to say over the fear gripping my chest.

"I told you. I'll explain everything, but first, we need to thaw you out."

Speechless, I stared at the car, then at Drew, and back again. Save some pieces of plastic trim and side mirror scattered in the snow, the car resembled its former un-smashed self.

It couldn't be real.

"I'll drive. I think you might be a little too shaken up." Drew extended an open palm. "Keys?"

I stepped back and clenched my sweaty palms.

"I promise I won't hurt you." He put his hands up in surrender. "Believe me, I have so many things to tell you that I couldn't think of doing anything to lose you now."

There were too many questions to walk away. And even if I did, deep down I knew running away was pointless. I didn't know who—or what—I was up against.

I searched my pockets for the keys, but they were nowhere to be found.

Drew whipped open the driver's side door and dove inside. He came out dangling my "I HEART DETROIT" key chain on his index finger. "Now the real test. Let's see if she runs." The engine spurted and coughed, but eventually turned over and growled as if it hadn't smashed into the ground.

"Perfect." He flashed a satisfied grin. "Let's go."

Drew approached one careful step at a time, likely trying

not the shatter me into a billion pieces. Slowly, he extended his hand.

My head told me to fight, but my shaky limbs no longer responded to my brain. I took his hand. We moved toward the passenger door. Jagged scratches carved the paint, but the huge dents that had covered the side panels were gone.

Drew opened the door, eased me into the seat, and buckled me in. My hands trembled in my lap. I closed my eyes, aching to know more about his secrets, yet terrified of what they might reveal. But the most frightening part was knowing that I was inextricably connected to him—like it or not.

TWELVE

"Hot chocolate, extra hot." Drew approached the cushy burgundy couch by the window in Java Nation and handed me a paper cup.

"Thanks." My first word to him since standing on the side of the highway. I wrapped my icy hands around the cup. It burned, close to the point of scalding, but in this moment, I didn't care. Any pain reminded me that I was here and this—whatever this was—was real. I let out a low, labored breath, thankful Java wasn't busy today, and none of my new friends were hanging around. What would I say to Lily if she saw me here with Drew?

We stared at each other for a few minutes, and I tried to figure out what he was thinking, unsure of where to start on the massive list of questions in my brain.

I opted for the vague but blunt line of interrogation. "So ... what the hell was that back there?"

He laughed and then took a sip from his own steaming paper cup. "Would you care to be more specific?"

"Specific?" I hissed. "I don't think I need to be specific. There is a whole lot of stuff you need to explain."

He slid closer. "If you want me to explain, you need to take it easy, all right?" He stared at me for a moment and then leaned in even closer. "All right?"

"All right, but you'd better start talking."

"I'm not like everyone else." He tilted his head toward me.

"Really? I would have never guessed."

"If you want to know, try to be nice."

He was lecturing me on being pleasant? I held my tongue.

"I was born with special abilities that allow me to manipulate the elements."

"When you say manipulate, you mean...?"

"Control." His brow furrowed. "Earth, air, water, and fire. I can make them do anything I want."

"Anything?" I rubbed my forehead. Thoughts whirled around my brain, causing a sharp sting behind my eyes. Like waking up from a bad dream, or being hit in the head with a rock, or maybe both at once.

"There are limits. I can only use so much power at a time. It's pretty exhausting until you get used to it."

"Is that why you stumbled after fixing the car?"

"Yeah. That was a bit of a stretch, but I'm fine."

"A car really isn't an element though."

"Parts of it are. Glass is made up of sand, and metal is well ... metal. The less pure the element is in an object, the harder it is to work with."

"Oh."

"But I can explain all the details to you later. Not in public."

I frowned. I wanted to know more now. "Where did these powers come from?"

"How else do people get all messed up—it runs in the family. Or at least I think so."

"You don't know for sure?" I shivered. What if others like him were out there?

"The powers seem to run on my dad's side, but he's not around anymore. Remember?"

"Right." A lump grew in my throat. I'd hoped Drew would be able to introduce me to my dad, but I guessed that wasn't happening. Seemed he wasn't interested in sticking around for any of his children.

"Turns out Dad left me something to hate him by. A legacy of trouble."

I slid closer to the arm of the couch and away from Drew. "Trouble?"

"Yeah, all sorts of trouble, until I learned to control it. But we can get to that later."

Again with the "later." How could he throw this on me then expect me to wait? "Okay, so why do you think these powers came from your father?"

"I tracked him back and found he was a descendant of the first mayor of Shady Creek."

My chest tightened. Mom never talked about my dad, so if it weren't for biology, I wouldn't have known I even had one. At least Drew knew something about him. "What does that mean?"

Drew continued. "When the mayor's son was about seventeen, he fell through the ice out on the lake. Someone fished him out, but by the time the doctor saw him, it was too late. The mayor was so upset about losing his only son that he turned to a very powerful witch in town and asked him to save the boy. That witch did some kind of dark magic, and the kid survived, but he was never quite the same. He was moody and angry and started fights. Plus, wherever he went, bad things happened. Fire, water, and wind damage, and other accidents. It was as if he turned into a human wrecking ball." Drew leaned in, lowering his voice. "Some people said that when he came back from the dead, he lost his mind. But others say something else came back from the dead with him."

I wrapped my hands tighter around my cup and shivered—and not because of the cold this time. "How did you find out all of this?"

"The accident was in the newspaper archives, but I found

out the rest by talking to people. Folks around here really keep up with their ancestry. Small towns never forget."

"And you actually believe all of it?"

"I know it sounds insane. I didn't believe it at first either." His voice dropped to a whisper. "But did you not just see me put your car back together simply by willing it to? Your definition of reality changes when you see the things I've seen."

I took a deep breath. None of this was logical, but so far, not much had made sense to me today. "How do you know you are distantly related to this guy?"

"Birth and death records. And that's where you come in."

I sipped my hot chocolate and coughed at the unexpected chill. It had cooled to the wrong side of lukewarm.

"Too hot?" he asked.

"No. Too cold."

Drew took the cup from me and wrapped his hand around it. He closed his eyes, fluttering his dark lashes. His eyes snapped open again and he handed the cup back.

"Here. Try again."

I took a sip and the soothing warmth of chocolate rushed over my lips. "How did you do that?"

"I have elemental powers, remember? I can heat things." He shrugged and glanced at the floor.

"Good point." Blood rushed to my cheeks. It was hard to keep all the twisted details straight. "Go on."

"So when I looked into my father, I found out that he'd gotten some other girl pregnant." He shifted in his spot. "Wilomena Edwards also had a granddaughter who was short a male parent.

"Edwards?" Grandma's maiden name again.

"Sorry, Belmont. Not important. Anyway, it was hush-hush, but it wasn't hard to dig around for the truth. That's when I knew there was someone else out there, someone who might be like me." Drew beamed, and he looked happier than I'd ever seen him. "I've waited years to finally find you."

"If you knew about me, why didn't you try to find me back then? Why now?"

"I was kind of stuck. My mother sent me to boarding school the first chance she got. Hard to talk to someone when you're halfway across the country."

I raised one eyebrow and glared at him. "They have phones in boarding school, don't they?"

"And say what? 'Hi, I'm the brother you didn't know you had. Oh, and by the way can you control the forces of nature with your mind?' Real productive."

I smirked at his sarcasm, but he had a point. I would have hung up and had his number blocked.

"Besides, I needed to know for sure that you were really like me."

"But I don't think I am. I can't control the elements and all that."

"Maybe you just don't know how yet, but I have a feeling you can. I know it."

"You know? How?"

"I'm getting there. You're impatient."

"And you're too dramatic."

"Something we have in common, no?"

I grumbled. He was so great at irritating me that he might actually be my brother.

"As I was saying, as soon as I heard you'd moved to town, I knew I had to get back here and find out the truth. So I left school."

"You just left?"

He looked away and flipped his hand in the air. "Left school, got kicked out. Details really."

"So that rumor is true."

"Sort of. I didn't steal the headmaster's car and leave it in the swimming pool though."

"I hadn't heard that one. I heard you cheated on a test."

"Where's the glory in that?" He sneered. "I set the chem lab on fire."

I gasped.

"Started an argument with my teacher, then went back at night and set the lab on fire, hoping they would think it was me. Plan worked perfectly. Goodbye prison, hello public school."

"A little reckless, don't you think?"

"I made sure no one was around. Besides, I needed something good if I was going to get kicked out for sure."

"Well, you could have gotten hurt." Or maybe killed a bunch of people. I pictured his not-so-little pocket knife and quivered.

"I don't need to be that close to start a fire. Besides, nothing can hurt me either."

"Right, the indestructible thing. What's that about?"

"It seems to be some sort of protection from our own abilities. Can't start ourselves on fire or anything."

"Does that mean we can't die?" I asked in amazement. "Assuming I am like you, of course."

"Oh, you can die. I said indestructible, not immortal, but death would have to come from more natural causes—getting sick, getting old, those kinds of things. Besides, if you were immortal, you wouldn't get any older."

"And you tried to kill me to see if you could?" I'd forgotten I was almost in the bottom of a body bag. The crash flickered in front of my eyes. Crushing, snapping metal. Breaking glass. Weightlessness and waiting to die. I closed my eyes and the image of the accident played in my thoughts. I grabbed the arm of the couch, digging my nails into the velvety fabric.

"I knew you'd be fine." Drew's voice sounded far away.

A few deep breaths until the car stopped tumbling and the world drifted back into focus. Fear melted into anger, coursing under my skin. "You couldn't have tried a less deranged plan?"

"That's where we were going." He patted the pocket holding his knife. "But an accident would be easier to explain if something went wrong. Plus, I've rolled a car before." He smiled.

"If something went wrong—"

"Shhh. Keep your voice down." He surveyed the other patrons. "Nothing went wrong, as I planned, so ease up."

"But it could have. I could be dead."

"But you're not," he said sternly. He grabbed my shoulders and looked me in the eyes. "Can we get past this now?"

I slid to my end of the couch, arms crossed.

"Anyway, I came here and did everything to get to know you. Then the bookshelf fell on you and you walked away without a scratch, so I took a chance today and cranked the wheel."

"A little over the top, don't you think?"

"Got your attention, didn't it?"

I rolled my eyes, which received an unwelcome chuckle. "If I'm so indestructible, how come I can't do all your magic stuff then?"

"Have you ever tried?"

"Very funny. Of course not. But you said you were born with it. If I was born with it, don't you think I would have noticed by now?"

"Did you have a happy childhood?"

"What does that have to do with anything?"

"Man, you're stubborn. Answer the question, please."

"I guess so," I said.

"Well, I didn't. As a kid, I had rage problems, and when I got angry, strange things happened. Eventually, I started to notice that my anger and sudden random weather changes were linked somehow. If you didn't tend to 'lose it' emotionally, you probably didn't notice if or when you did do something ... err ... unique."

Unique. The word resonated. Why did it seem like a curse to me? I searched my brain straining to figure it out, then it hit me. Mrs. Abernathy. She called me *unique*. Maybe she was trying to tell me about this all along. "Are you sure this is all from your father?"

"Of course, I'm sure. I already explained all of that." He looked upset that I was questioning his theory, which he obviously whole-heartedly believed.

"You did. I was just thinking maybe there's some other explanation."

His voice rose. "No. I know what I'm saying."

A few people turned and stared at us.

"This is all from my father. Our father. Believe me."

"I'm trying," I hissed. "This is just a lot to take in. Maybe you believe all this so easily because you think it gives you the answers you're looking for."

His eyes darkened and his forehead turned red.

"And there is nothing wrong with that." I raised my hands in surrender. "If I was in your situation, I'd want answers too."

"But you are in my situation. Why can't you accept that? Nick did this to us. He made us who we are."

There was that name again. Why did he have to keep saying it? Nick, the guy Mom dated, possibly my father. It was a common name, but for Drew's dad to have the same one in the same map-dot town seemed too much of a coincidence.

Drew sulked and picked at the upholstery. His chocolate-brown locks and dark eyes were the same color as mine, at least when he wasn't angry. He had an angular face and mine was round, but the lone dimple on his left cheek matched the one I saw in the mirror every day. We differed in height, but other than that, the resemblance was unmistakable. How did I miss this before? Did I suddenly want it all to be true?

I shook my head and straightened up. There were at least six people in here that could resemble either of us. The girl from my history class reading a magazine by the door had the same poker straight hair and long eyelashes as me. The guy sitting at the back by the stairs had Drew's lanky arms and legs. We could be related to almost anyone in town. We didn't have to be related to each other. "How do you know all this stuff you've been told isn't just garbage?" I asked. "Maybe people around here just make things up. I'm not sure they even consider the consequences."

"Are we talking about me, or are we you talking about you now? Just because you're getting picked on at school about being a witch doesn't mean I'm wrong."

"How did you know about that?"

"Everyone's been talking about it since you got here. Did you really expect me not to know?" He smirked.

"How could you? You don't ever talk to anyone."

"Doesn't mean I don't listen."

"It's not true, by the way," I added.

"I never asked you if it was. Now can we get back to my story?" He leaned against the arm of the couch as if he were settling in for more storytelling.

"Fine." I sat back into the plush cushions again. "You said you'd explain, in detail, how you do what you do." I lowered my voice. "Your superpower thing."

He chuckled. "It's not a superpower, and I said I would explain it to you, but not here."

"Why not?"

"Too many witnesses."

I gulped.

"Don't freak out. I just can't go around starting fires and making it rain. It's not exactly normal, especially indoors."

"Really? Not normal, you say."

"Do you want me to show you what I can do or not?"

Apparently, he did not find my sarcasm funny. "Of course I do."

"How about tomorrow then? We can see what you have locked away in that brain of yours too."

"Sure." My skin burned. Excitement? Fear, maybe? "I'd like that."

"Any more questions?" He crossed his arms. "Questions I can answer here."

"How did you know about my birth certificate? And the blanket." I might not have magical powers locked away in my subconscious, but apparently, I had abandonment issues.

"When I asked around, a few people had old pictures of you with that ugly blanket from when you used to come visit your Grandma. The birth certificate was a wild-ass guess, though. I threw it in to sound more convincing."

"Oh." My throat tightened. So stupid. And I thought I wasn't letting him manipulate me. My anticipation crashed. "You mislead people a lot, don't you?"

"Only when I need to. It wasn't easy to get you to listen, so I did what I needed to do."

"Like calling the cops at Lily's party?'

"Guilty." He grinned.

"Wait ... the fire last night. Did you start it?"

He shrugged. "Maybe."

"Drew!"

"Easy now. It was a small brush fire. Nothing would've gotten damaged. I swear."

"Not the point."

"Sorry. I needed to get you alone, but you were always busy talking to people."

I narrowed my eyes. "Were you watching me?"

"Since you got here, but those friends of yours were always lurking around."

"Wait." I raised my hand as the thought hit me and then jabbed my finger at him. "You didn't cause the accident at the arena too, did you?"

"How wicked do you think I am? Besides, I saved you, remember?"

I looked away and out the window. Big fluffy snowflakes had started to fall.

"Look." He grabbed my arms and turned me to face him. "I know I'm asking a lot, but I want you to trust me. I need you to trust me. Give me a break. I promise I'll show you more tomorrow and then you can decide for yourself."

"Then no more lies, Drew."

"No lies. As long as you're listening, I don't need to lie anymore."

"Okay. You get one chance, but no guarantees that I'll believe you."

His face brightened as if he'd found a lucky penny, his lips bending into a smile. "I promise, you won't regret this."

"I think I already do," I muttered.

"Hey, no negativity."

"Fine," I replied as my mouth stretched into a yawn. "I should go home now. I need to process this and sleep."

"Sure, but one more thing. I need you to swear not to tell anyone about this. None of your friends, not your mother—"

"Oh crap!" I scrubbed my hands across my face and buried my fingers in my hair, pulling at the roots.

"What?"

"My mother. How am I going to explain all those scratches

on the car to her?" I pulled hands in my sleeves and my leg began to twitch, vibrating the entire couch.

"Right." Drew leaned back and picked at his fingernails, seemingly unconcerned with my impending Mom-inflicted torture. "Why don't you tell her you went to the show and someone vandalized it? I'm sure that happens all the time in the city."

"You think that'll work?" My foot twitching had reached warp speed.

He shrugged. "Do you have any better ideas?"

"No, but if it doesn't work, I'll be locked up 'til I'm fifty."

"It'll work. You're my sister. Didn't you tell me I have a talent for lying? Besides, you already lied to her once today about where you were going. What's one more lie?" He grinned.

"I never said I lied to my mother."

"But you never said you didn't." He jumped up from the couch and reached out his hand to help me up. "Now let's get you home."

THIRTEEN

The smell of incense stung the inside of his nostrils as he walked around the tiny shack. A strong distracting scent, heavy citrus with a spicy overtone, but better than the more pungent, earthy scents he'd encountered on his travels. No matter the continent, mystics sure loved their fragrances.

Maybe if they spent more time learning their craft than stinking up the world, he'd have the answers he needed by now. Every shaman, medicine man, and guru in every corner of the world was as useless as the last one he'd hunted down. Most were charlatans, only after money or celebrity, but with little knowledge. The authentic knew enough to be wary of him but could offer no legitimate help. The imposters he rewarded by burning their villages to the ground. So here he was, trying again, sweat pouring from his brow in the blistering heat.

Shelves around the room displayed skulls, candles, and various figures he didn't recognize. Brightly colored tapestries illustrated with primitive stick drawings and symbols covered every spare inch of wall. The show was likely for the tourists, although he doubted there were many tourists in this part of Haiti. The people around here were poor and starving, and they stared at him strolling through the ghetto as if he were the Reaper.

A young girl in braids and a thin white gown appeared from

behind a dark curtain on the opposite end of the room, then motioned for him to follow. He'd seen all manner of large burly handlers protecting their wise ones, but never a child. The girl waved again, and he followed.

Mambo Perpétue Danticat wore a bright-blue head scarf and a white gown matching the girl's. The skin on her cheeks fell limp against her bones, and her arms extended from her wide sleeves, frail and brittle like toothpicks. Years of survival smoldered in her eyes, a slow burn whispering that she was quite old and had been for a very long time. A tribesman in Africa told him that she was the most powerful Vodou Priestess on earth, but she looked as though she might shatter if he spoke too loudly.

Compared to the front of the shack, this room was stark, just the Mambo in her wicker chair and a few spent candles lining a platform behind her. The girl bowed before the Mambo and then disappeared behind the curtain again, the room strangely smaller with fewer people in it.

"*Eske ou pale kreyòl?*" the old woman asked in a low raspy voice.

He shook his head, understanding she'd asked if he spoke Creole, but not knowing the words to reply.

"No matter," she continued in English, but her lips did not move. The words she said but never spoke resounded in his head, echoing in his ears with perfect clarity. "You appear to be younger than I had imagined."

Fear and excitement sparked beneath his skin and he trembled. Never before had he been in the presence of someone truly powerful. "I have come—"

She raised a tremulous open hand into the air. "I know why you have come, child. You seek your salvation."

He stood silently, reluctant to be cut off again.

"But you are not of the mortal plane. Why should I help you?"

He stepped forward and the Mambo clenched her fist. An unseen force tore through his body and forced him to his knees before her. His heart pounded in his ears, and his breath hitched in his throat. For the first time in his human existence, he was afraid.

"I see darkness in you. You know great power and you poison the flesh of that body as it poisons you. Weakens you. You seek separation. To be released."

He nodded slowly. She rested her arm on her lap, palm up, and signaled for him to place his hand in hers. He obeyed, surprised by the softness of her thin, dark skin.

"The body and the soul are one entity, yet they are not. They work in unison, but only the soul can exist alone. When we die, the body ceases but the soul endures. Since you have corrupted this body, it does not age. It is cursed by your wickedness and you cannot be free until you release your hold on it."

"But I've tried," he blurted then stiffened, frightened she would strike out at him again. When she did not, he continued, "I've done everything I can to dispose of this body, but it will not die."

She retracted her hand and settled back in her chair, eyes closing slowly like the sun sinking into night. "Then the evil soul must find a new host."

FOURTEEN

Smoke burns the back of my throat. I cough. An empty room, flames licking the walls. No doors. No windows. No escape.

"You're finally here," a small voice says. A brown-haired boy sits cross-legged in the corner.

"How do we get out of here?" I ask.

He smirks. "We don't."

"Help!" I shout. I stomp my feet and pound the walls. "Help me!"

Pain knocks me to my knees. My hands shake as the blood sizzles in my veins. The skin on my knuckles splits. Yellow, bone-like claws slice their way out and replace my fingers.

I scream, staring down at my monster hands.

"No one can save us." The boy's hands are gone too. They've turned into twisted claws like mine. His smile fades and he scratches his claw hand across his face. Red lines run down his cheek. "I've been bad."

"No!"

I lunge forward. The boy disappears behind a wall of fire. I cough ... again ... and again ... and again. The room spins in circles. I'm going to die in here. I'm going to—

Bang!

My eyes snapped open and I jerked upright. I sat tangled in a mass of damp covers on the floor of my room, dripping with sweat. I scanned the room and exhaled with relief, my lungs still aching. No fire. No locked doors. No creepy little boy in the corner. It was just a dream. One messed-up dream.

I gathered up my comforter and sat down on the edge of the bed, rubbing my hands over my face, trying to erase the images in my brain. What was that all about? So many things since yesterday hadn't made any sense.

First off, what *was* Drew? He couldn't have put the car back together without something severely warped inside him, which led to the scarier question: was I really just like him? I'd never had much family—just me, Mom, and the occasional grand-mother—but based on the timeline, Drew could be my brother.

Maybe I wanted him to be my brother.

I gagged. What a sick thought. Was I deranged? But still ... a family. A real family.

Mom always had a way of making sense of things, but I promised Drew I wouldn't tell her about him. I didn't want to drive him away before I got a chance to know him. I dragged myself out of bed, trudged downstairs to the kitchen, and plopped into a chair. No sense in being held captive in my room by an overworked and seriously screwed-up brain.

Mom chopped red peppers on the counter. "Thought you decided to skip Sunday altogether."

I glanced at the clock. 11:45. "I didn't sleep well."

"Is something wrong?" She put down the knife, worry lines creasing her forehead.

"Just some crazy dreams, that's all."

"That's your mind trying to make sense of the world. When bad things happen, it tries to find an explanation." She resumed her cutting.

"Bad things?" My eyes widened. How did she know?

"Yeah, the car. I know you were probably scared, but I appreciate you telling me the truth. I can't imagine how awful you must've felt coming out of the mall and seeing the car destroyed like that. The city is getting rougher all the time."

I sighed in relief. With my overloaded thoughts, I'd forgotten about the car. "I guess it's a good thing we moved then."

"Yeah, sure is." She smiled to herself. "I'm still shocked no one reported someone spray-painting a car in a public parking lot. And did they really need to scratch it up, too?"

"Yeah." I peeked down at my hands and remembered Drew with his can of black spray paint, trying to save me once again. He said Mom wouldn't believe my vandalism story unless I truly committed to it, so I let him finish the job of trashing my car. He was dangerously good at being deceptive. "I guess some people are too afraid to tell the truth."

Mom dropped the knife and scurried over to the table, yanking me out of my seat and wrapping her arms around me. The scent of sweet red peppers and cucumber melon dish soap rolled off her skin. "It'll be okay."

She smoothed her hands down the back of my head and my stomach twisted. I'd gotten away with another lie—a big one— but instead of feeling relieved, my insides knotted with guilt.

"I just wish I could protect you from all the bad things out there in the world. All I want is for you to be safe." Her words drove a samurai sword of shame right through my abdomen.

My pants pocket vibrated. I pulled out of Mom's grip and grabbed my phone, hoping it was Drew. Mom frowned.

"It's Lily." I showed her the caller ID.

She huffed and shook her head as I crept into the living room.

"Hey." I glanced into the kitchen to make sure Mom wasn't listening. "What's up?"

"Some of us were going to catch a movie later. Wanna come?" Lily asked. "Trying to enjoy the last moments of freedom before the cops tell my parents about the party and they ground Ben and me for life."

A movie. In the dark. With Bennett. My cheeks burned. That would be perfect. "I can't. Sorry." Sorrier than she'd ever know, but I needed to talk to Drew today. I lowered my voice. "Family stuff."

"No worries. You forgot your jacket, by the way. I'll bring it to school for you."

"Thanks." The pain in my stomach bled into my chest. "I left when I heard the cops were coming."

"Smart. But all they did was clear everyone out," she said calmly, like this happened every weekend. "You didn't notice if Drew showed up, did you?"

"No," I blurted, regretting it instantly. Why did I have to lie to her? All I had to say was that I saw Drew at her place. She wouldn't automatically know he was my half-brother, or that he was, well ... whatever he was. How could I be so stupid? The lie prickled hot under my skin as if I were still in the burning dream room.

"Oh." She sounded discouraged. "He's more of a challenge than I thought."

"Sorry."

"It's okay. But if you change your mind about the movie, it starts at two.

I hung up and stared at the phone. I wanted to go. I really liked Lily and her friends, plus maybe I could sneak a few minutes with Bennett. But I couldn't go. I promised Drew I'd meet him, and I didn't want to miss the chance to ask him more questions. Maybe I could do both. I flipped to my phone keypad, then stopped. I didn't have Drew's number. *Grrr!*

I wandered back into the kitchen and curled my fingers into my sleeves, berating myself for being socially awkward.

"Lily's a friend from school?" Mom asked as she opened one drawer under the kitchen counter, then another.

"Yeah." If I hadn't blown already it. I sat down at the table, fidgeting with my phone. "What are you looking for?"

"Cheese grater. Have you seen it?" Mom rummaged through the cabinets. "I swear things just disappear around this place."

"Nope, sorry. Maybe there are ghosts living here."

"Or maybe it's not unpacked yet." She closed the cupboard door above the sink and turned toward me, seeming to ignore my humor. "Would you mind heading to the attic and checking if it's in the last few boxes up there?"

"There are more boxes? How much stuff do we have?" I mumbled and then trudged up the stairs.

More boxes. At least it gave me something to do besides wonder when Drew would show up. And it kept me out of Mom's sightline. Sooner or later she'd notice that I was wound up tight to the point of practically vibrating. Also, I'd passed up a chance to see Bennett, so it was best I kept busy for everyone's sake.

I dug through the stack of boxes until I found one labeled *Kitchen Miscellaneous*. Why it had ended up in the attic, I couldn't imagine. Instead of carrying the whole box downstairs, I found a utility knife and sliced through the tape. The cheese grater treasure was right on top. At least one thing went right.

Sunlight filtered through the attic window and glinted off the utility knife blade. I slid my finger across the angled tip. Sharp. Very sharp. A blade like this could easily draw blood, but

Drew said nothing could hurt me. Was it true? Maybe the car accident was just dumb luck.

I closed the attic door and sat on the floor, staring at the knife in my hand. What harm could it do? If Drew was wrong, I would need a Band-Aid. If he was right...

I shuddered.

I held my breath and ran the tip of the blade against the soft fleshy part of my palm. The metal tugged my skin, but it left no mark, and thankfully, drew no blood.

Okay. This still could go either way. Maybe I didn't push hard enough or just had tough skin. I looked away and winced as I pressed the blade firmly into my palm and slid it toward my wrist, biting my lip from the pain.

There was still nothing to see, not even a scratch.

Okay, this was getting freaky. I hadn't noticed my lifelong lack of injuries before, but suddenly it was all I could think about. As scenes from the past flickered in my mind, I couldn't remember ever being hurt before, never a drop of blood, not even a scratch. In my life. *Ever*. I always thought I was just lucky.

This can't be true.

One last test. I turned my head to the side and bit down on the top of my sweater sleeve. Cringing, I dug the tip of the utility knife into the center of my hand as hard as I could. Pain shot up my arm and into my head like I'd touched a bare electrical wire. A muffled scream rang in my ears. I dropped the knife and cradled my shaking hand in my lap, pain as bad as if I'd sliced off a finger. But the skin of my palm was still intact. Not even an indent from the blade marked my flesh.

This couldn't be happening! Another scream stuck in my throat. I could live with Drew not being normal, but not me too. I stared at my hand again in disbelief. I had to see Drew. Now. I had to know more.

Footsteps thudded below me. I gasped and tossed the knife into the corner, then grabbed the grater with my sore hand, flinching. Throwing open the attic door, I scrambled down the ladder and intercepted Mom at the bottom.

"Oh good, you did find it." She took the grater from me.

I snapped my stinging hand away.

"Wow, you're jumpy today. And you look really pale. Are you all right?" She placed her palm on my forehead.

I mentally tried to force color into my cheeks. "Yeah, I'm fine. Took a lot longer to find than I thought."

"Okay." She backed away, scrutinizing me. "I thought maybe you ran into one of those ghosts you talked about."

I laughed, but the sound came out strained and nervous.

"I think you need to lighten up," Mom said. She placed her arm over my shoulder and led me back downstairs.

The whole day passed without any word from Drew. I didn't have his number, but if he'd wanted mine I knew his stalker-like tendencies would've kicked in to find it. But, no call. No text. Nothing. Unless he'd changed his mind. Irritating minutes slipped into agonizing hours until bone-white moonlight sliced across the wooden slats of the living room floor. I pounded up the stairs to my room, leaving Mom on the couch, too engrossed in her book to notice.

I collapsed on the bed and counted the ugly little flowers on my curtains, hoping to settle the caustic disappointment bubbling in my blood. Where was Drew? I had questions—lots of questions—but he clearly didn't care. Holding my hand in the air above my face, I traced the lines on my palm—head, heart, fate—the tendons beneath my skin still stinging where I'd tried to cut them. I curled my fingers into a fist and punched my comforter. Stupid Drew. Why couldn't he do what I wanted him to do for once?

Pulling the diary out from under my mattress, I flipped to the next unread passage. My nightly bedtime story, complete with a princess, Prince Charming, and an evil queen.

December 12

I don't know what I am going to do. I took a test today and I'm pregnant. I knew something was wrong, but I never thought this could happen to me. I'm only seventeen.

I was supposed to be getting out of this stupid town and away from all these stupid people, and as soon as they find out I'm pregnant, I'll be the town slut. As if they don't already talk about me behind my back.

I can't do this. I can't raise a baby.

And when Mother finds out ... she hates Nick, and when she realizes it's his, I don't know what she'll do.

FIFTEEN

Tink, tink, tink.

I forced my eyes open and scanned through the darkness, refusing to lift my head from the pillow. Nothing. I shut my eyes again.

Tink, tink, tink.

Nope. Definitely something. Reluctantly, I sat up.

Thunk!

Something thudded onto the floor. I glanced over the side of the bed. The diary lay open on the carpet. I reached over and tucked it back under the mattress.

Tink, tink, tink.

The window, maybe? I rolled out of bed and peeked through the ugly cotton curtains to see Drew winding up for another toss. I jumped back as a chunk of ice hit the glass.

Tink!

I threw back the curtains and whipped open the window, hoping to get his attention before he launched another attack. "What are you doing?" I hissed, my cheeks hot against the cool night air.

"I thought you wanted some lessons?"

"I waited for you all day, and it's—" I grabbed my cell phone off my desk. "Two in the morning. Where've you been?"

"I said I'd come today. I didn't say when."

"Very funny. Today is over. It's tomorrow already. My mother would freak if she heard me creeping out the front door in the middle of the night."

"Come out the window then." He smiled under the street-lamp as though amused with himself.

"That wasn't the point."

"I know, but there are fewer witnesses around at this time of night—in case you aren't as in control as you seem to think you are."

"Don't worry about me. I have a lot more self-control than you do."

"Oh, so you're a chicken then. I see." He grinned wider and turned to walk away.

"Wait," I called.

It was a terrible idea. A completely awful, stupid, terrible idea. But instead of slamming the window shut and crawling back into my warm bed like my brain told me to do, I rummaged through my closet and pulled on several strategic layers of sweaters and an old pair of gym shoes that barely fit. Waiting for Drew had taken up too much of my day to go back to sleep. Besides, even if I fell climbing out the window, I wouldn't get hurt.

I pushed the corner of my desk closer to the window, climbed out onto the first-floor roof, and gently closed the window behind me. Taking a gulp of cold night air, I launched off into the snow bank below. I landed on my butt and a jolt ran through my spine, but no broken bones. I clambered to my feet.

"Nice look." Drew smirked as I approached the sidewalk. "You didn't jump that far. What's with the body armor? Couldn't just use bubble wrap instead?"

"I didn't have my coat. Would you rather I woke up my mom and told her I was going out?"

"Guess not." He plunged his hands deep into his pockets and proceeded down the sidewalk as I trailed behind, tripping in the fresh snow. Dark houses with empty windows watched us crunch down the sidewalk, shadows of naked trees stretching across our path.

I shivered underneath my four sweaters and rushed ahead of him. "I waited all day, you know. You said you were coming and you didn't show."

"Correction. I did show ... just not when you expected me to." He picked up speed.

"You could've told me you weren't coming until the middle of the night."

"Yeah, maybe." He shrugged and darted past me. "But you seem pretty amped to see me for someone who wasn't sure they believed my story yesterday."

"Well..." My palm twitched at my side, the center tingling where the box cutter should've sliced through to my knuckles. I struggled to keep up with Drew's determined gait. "I thought I should give you the benefit of the doubt."

"Really?" His left eyebrow rose as I caught up to him.

"But that's before you stood me up."

"Doesn't matter now. We're here."

I stopped short. Ahead of us stood a little park with a kidney-shaped manmade lake. "Where is here, exactly?"

"It's Henderson's Pond. You really should get to know this town a bit better. It's kind of pathetic."

"Thanks." I rolled my eyes. "I meant, what are we doing here? This is a pretty public place."

"No one is going to notice us here at this hour. Besides, they'll probably think we're doing drugs or something."

"Great. 'Cause that's so much better."

"Lighten up. We'll be fine."

"So what are we going to do out here, anyway?" I followed Drew deeper into the park.

"I thought maybe we'd start with water."

"Water?" The thought of water made me cold.

"Yes, Avery, the four elements—earth, air, fire, and water. Don't tell me we have to go over that again?"

"No." I slid my hands into my hoodie pocket. "I just don't see any water around here."

He chuckled. "There's tons of water here. Except it's frozen, that's all. Let's start with the basics."

He circled behind me and grabbed my biceps, pushing me onto a nearby bench. Coldness from the metal seeped through my jeans and froze my thighs. I tried to stand, but Drew glared at me and began pacing like a teacher lecturing his class.

"Now," he began. "The key to controlling the elements is tapping into your power—the power within—and willing it into your subject matter. It's kind of like turning on a light switch. The power is there, but you have to complete the electrical circuit by flipping the switch. If you don't turn the switch on, you'll never see the light. Get it?"

I raised my hand, caught up in his teacher-student dynamic. "You said all this happened to you randomly at first, so how could you control things without trying when you were angry?"

His gaze drifted to the sky. "I guess the anger acted like a power surge. An overload of the entire system."

I nodded.

He continued pacing. "Once you tap into the power, the other tricky part is to understand how the element works to make it do what you want. For example, wind and water are both similar because they both have a flow—a direction." He made wave-like motions with his arms. "Controlling that flow and making it obey you is the hard part. Water is the simplest of the two because you can see the flow, so it's much easier to focus."

Drew fumbled inside his coat and withdrew a small thermos. He poured some liquid into the lid and placed it on the bench beside me. "Now watch."

I kept my eyes on Drew. He moved a few feet back from the bench and met my gaze. He furrowed his brow and nodded toward the bench with his chin. "Pay attention."

The surface of the liquid began to ripple as though a wind blew across the top. Slowly, the liquid oozed up the sides until it cascaded over the top and down the outside, freezing on the bench.

I watched the whole trick unfold until the cup was empty, mesmerized like a kid at the carnival. It wasn't as impressive as putting a car back together, though.

"Pretty cool, huh?" Drew picked up the thermos again. "If you can tap into the flow of the water, you can make it move wherever you want."

"You just stare at it?"

"No. You focus on it. Two different things." He refilled the cup. "Your turn."

"I don't think I can." I tensed my shoulders. It didn't look hard, but I wasn't Drew.

"You never know until you try. Now c'mon." He stepped back and waved me toward him.

I sighed and dragged myself off the bench.

Drew stood behind me and whispered in my ear, "Now, look at the cup and think about the water inside. Think about how it moves."

I tried to force my brain to follow his instructions, but really, the whole situation was ridiculous.

"Now think about where you want it to go. Visualize it running up the sides of the cup and down the outside. Think about your outcome."

I squinted and focused on the water, running a video of flowing water over and over and in my head.

"Okay," he said. "Now flip the switch."

My eyes narrowed in concentration, so tight my vision blurred. Nothing happened.

Drew looked inside the cup.

"See I told you. Nothing." I gave up and relaxed.

"You're not trying hard enough."

I squinted again, contemplating what should happen. My arms and legs flexed, fingers and toes curled tight.

Drew looked down at the cup again and huffed.

"What?" I said, breaking concentration again. "I'm trying."

"Not hard enough. I know you can do this."

"No, you don't. You only hope I can. But I can't."

"Yes, you can. You're just too scared to admit it."

"This is stupid." What more did he want from me? It already creeped me out that I'd tried to cut a hole in my hand. It was perfectly fine if I couldn't be all magical too. "I'm not scared. It's just not working."

"Then prove it. Try again. Really try."

"No. I'm tired Drew, and I want to go home."

"Do it," he yelled.

"No."

He opened his mouth as if to argue, but slammed it shut. Then he marched over and grabbed my hand with a firm, stinging grip and dragged me toward the trees, huffing and puffing until steam circled his head. "Let me show you something."

I stared back as the view of town vanished under the treetops, lifeless wooden limbs stretching out above me and covering us from sight. Darker. Secluded. No one around to hear me scream. The last time Drew showed me something, I ended up trapped in a pile of mangled metal and shattered glass. My queasy stomach told me to leave, but he promised he'd never try to hurt me again.

If only I trusted his promises.

"Stand right here." He stopped under a particularly ominous willow tree and clamped his hands on my shoulders, his thumbs at the base of my neck. I squirmed, but he held tight, his fingertips digging through my layers of sweaters, positioning me into some unseen perfect spot.

Moonlight filtered through the trees, casting inky shadows across his face, his lips a hard line. "Don't move."

I shrank my neck into my sweater. He stomped in front of me and scooped up a handful of snow as I shifted my weight to my toes, ready to run. He packed the snow between his palms, his eyes fluttering closed. He grimaced as he pressed his hands together until his knuckles turned white against his cold-reddened fingers. "Now watch."

He fanned his hands open. Resting in the center was a flower. A peony or gardenia, or some other flower with delicate tiny petals, each one glistening in the moonlight as if it were made of tiny glass shards.

"Is that ice?" I reached out to touch it but stopped, lifting my eyes to meet his.

He nodded. "Take it."

I cupped my hands and he gently passed the flower to me. A chill ran across my skin as it landed on my palm. It really was made of ice. Amazing. Drew created this perfect, beautiful thing out of ice—just for me. I studied it closer. The petals looked white, but they were clear, as though my finger would float right through if I tried to touch them. The ghost of a flower that never existed.

"Blow on it." A crooked smile twisted Drew's face. "Like a birthday candle."

"Seriously?" I lowered my chin to my hands and softly exhaled. The flower exploded into a cloud of snowflakes. They whirled around my head, faster and heavier, making it impossible to see. My heart pounded as the cloud shrank around me.

Closer. Tighter. Then it shot into the air, spun high above my head, and disappeared.

"What was that?" I looked up at the sky.

Drew stared past me and pointed up. I turned around. The branches of the tree behind me were covered in thick hoarfrost. No, not frost—the fluffy heads of ice flowers. Each branch hung heavy with them as if in full bloom. Moonlight reflected off hundreds of petals casting a brilliant glow around the tree. It was sunshine and summertime, all in the middle of the night. For the first time since I arrived in this town, I almost felt warm.

"It's incredible," I whispered. "It's like nothing I've ever seen before. It's like—"

"Magic," Drew said with a grin I could hear in his voice. "Now, what do you say about giving the water thing another try?"

I sighed. "Sure."

We returned to the bench and I resumed my position. I stretched and shook out my arms. Maybe that would help get whatever it was flowing.

"This time, close your eyes." Drew stood behind me with his hands on my wrists, his voice low and calm. "Think about what you are trying to do. Can you do that?"

I nodded.

He placed his hands on my shoulders. "What are you thinking?"

I swallowed and tried to focus, but the image of flowers kept sneaking into my brain. I'd never be able to do something like that.

"Avery, what are you thinking?" He tightened his grip.

I stiffened under his touch and shook my head. *Focus, Avery.* "I'm thinking about the water overflowing the sides of the cup."

"Now tell it what you want it to do."

"Spill over the side of the cup," I whispered as if saying it too loud might make me sound completely insane.

"Repeat that in your head, but make sure you mean it. Feel what you're saying."

Spill over the side... spill over the side... Dizziness crashed over me as red lights sparked behind my eyelids in a pattern of dots and shadow. I quivered.

"Keep concentrating." Drew let me go, and a cool breeze brushed my face as he walked away.

Something ticklish rose in my throat as if someone were pulling a string up my esophagus and out through my mouth. Reflexively, I opened my lips to let it out, gagging as the invisible thread thickened. Then as quickly as it had come, it vanished.

"Open your eyes," Drew said.

Water pooled on the bench and ran over the sides.

Drew laughed, his eyes fixated on the water.

I did it!

"Well done." Drew applauded.

My cheeks burned and I shook. Waves of energy pulsed through me, but I couldn't move. An electricity circulated between the cup and me, still connected and fully charged, like I needed to finish what I'd started. The water kept flowing.

"Don't overdo it."

But I couldn't stop. A gush of water burst into the air and sprayed Drew as the cup flew off the bench and landed in a snow bank.

Drew jumped back. "Easy." He laughed again, wiping the water off his face with his sleeve.

I stumbled forward. The energy flooded out of my body and a deep chill settled into the now empty spaces in my muscles. All the magic gone.

"Wh-what happened?" I asked.

"You did it, that's what happened." Drew's face contorted

in an un-Drew-like way, wide-eyed and undisturbed by pretense or subtext, nothing but raw glee. "You made it move!"

He grabbed my arm and tugged me toward the bench, my feet almost lifting off the ground.

"But why did it explode?"

"Oh that. You got overwhelmed. It happens."

I gasped. "Overwhelmed?"

"Don't worry about it. Control takes practice." He parked me back on the cold bench and crouched down. "How do you feel? Are you okay?" His tone shifted from joy to concern as he intently stared up at me with his dark eyes.

"I'm okay," I said, reassuring him and myself. "I feel fine."

"Good." He flashed me his mischievous smile. "The first few times can be intense, but eventually that all fades away. Soon you'll be able to control the experience, instead of it controlling you."

"So it gets better?"

"Yes, much better." He handed me the half-empty thermos. "Drink this. It'll help."

Cold water rushed over my dry throat. Small aftershocks tingled through me as I drained the bottle and stared blankly ahead, my thoughts clear and confused all at once. Lightening flashed in parts of my brain I never knew existed, while my arms hung limp and tired by my sides. If I left now, I might get some quality sleep before sunrise. But could I really sleep after this?

"Had enough for one night?" Drew asked.

"No." I smirked. "I want to go again."

~

I repeated the water trick over and over until I finally managed to do it without losing control. I started to anticipate the shock to my body but still gagged when that strange feeling ran up the back of my throat. The trickiest part was trying to remain calm.

Drew seemed to go through a small transformation as well. No more sarcasm, threats, or insults. He actually seemed to be enjoying himself. Excited for me, and maybe excited for himself to finally find a kindred spirit in what must be a very lonely existence.

"The fun part about all this is that once you get the basics down, you can look for more creative ways to use the element. For instance, the beauty of Shady Creek is all this snow."

"I don't really find it beautiful. I just find it cold."

"Oh yeah?"

The powdery snow around my feet began to swirl, rising higher until a giant funnel cloud of snowflakes whirled around me. A human snow globe. I reached out and pushed my finger into the moving wall of snow, and it dropped into a pile on the ground. I stared at the fluffy flakes at my feet.

"Fun, huh?" Drew said. "Give it a go."

Moonlight cast a dreamy blue glow over the little park and made the snow sparkle. With so much white stuff to work with, I could easily create a Drew-sized snowman. Drew, stuck inside a pile of snowballs. I smirked and looked off toward the horizon, concentrating on the snowflakes. That familiar feeling rose in my throat, and a small perfect ball formed on the top of the snow bank. It rolled slowly, picking up volume as it moved toward Drew in lines, circles, and figure eights, coming to rest at his feet at the size of a generous watermelon.

"Impressive," he said. "I hope you didn't plan on hitting me with that."

I shrugged. "Maybe."

"I've been at this much longer than you. You'll never beat me."

"Is that a challenge?" I giggled.

"No." He dropped his chin and glowered at me.

I gulped. Intense Drew was back.

"Come here." At lightning speed, his stare down flipped into a smile, and he took off down a cleared path.

I followed him to the end of the frozen pond.

"The more stable an element, the harder it is to affect. It's a bit of a trade off," Drew said. "Unstable elements like wind and fire are easy to affect but harder to control. Stable elements like earth are easy to control, but harder to affect. Water is both, normally unstable, but stable as ice."

He squatted down at the edge of the pond and spread his hand wide, resting it palm down on the surface of the ice. "Physical contact strengthens the connection between you and an element and sucks less of your energy."

Crack!

I jumped, grabbing Drew's arm and knocking us both to the ground.

Drew laughed and pulled me back to a crouch beside him. "You really need to toughen up."

I glanced back at the pond. A huge crack cut across the surface of the ice. "Did you just split the pond in half?"

"I'm pretty sure you didn't do it from falling on the ground."

I jabbed him with my elbow.

"Now watch again, and try not to panic this time." He kneeled, placing his hand a few inches from his last blurry handprint. Another thundering crack and a small jagged line spread across the glossy surface of the pond. "Wanna try?"

"Okay." Still crouching, I waddled over to the edge of the pond and stretched out my hand. I flinched at the cold against my palm and concentrated on the ice. Energy shot through my chest, knocking the wind out of me and throwing me backward.

Drew caught me before I hit the ground. "Avery. Avery. Are you all right?"

I shook off the dizziness and sat up. "Yeah, I'm fine. Just lost my balance."

"I think we're done for tonight." Drew rose to his feet and held out his hand. "This thing, this power, it's like a muscle. You need to work it out to make it stronger, but you can't overdo it. This might be too much in one day."

"But I didn't finish. I can do this." I dismissed his offered hand and inched back over to the edge, quickly sliding my hand onto the ice. With a loud crack, a broad line skated alongside Drew's jagged ones.

"Are you happy now?" Drew crossed his arms. "You're going to hurt yourself."

"I'll be okay." I jumped up from the snowy ground, and the world spun in circles as if I were riding the Tilt-A-Whirl at the carnival—the one ride I always puked after.

"I'm not kidding. You'll make yourself sick." He put his arm around my waist, and I forced my knees to stay standing even though they screamed at me to let Drew hold me up.

"Don't worry about me." The words came out more chipper than intended. "We don't have to stop now."

"Actually, we do. In case you forgot, we both have to get to school, and I don't think your mother would be too pleased to find an empty bed."

"I guess not." Since when was I the reckless one and Drew the voice of reason?

Drew took both my wrists in one of his hands, his skin hot against mine. "Trust me, we'll do this again soon. I promise."

We walked slowly, silently, the few blocks to my house. Drew seemed to be taking in the early morning stillness, and I had too many thoughts and questions I didn't know how to verbalize.

"Dammit." I looked up at my second-story window. "I can't get back into my room. Do you think you could boost me up to the roof?"

"Avery, you have to start thinking differently. We're special, remember?" With that, he furrowed his brow and drifted into a vacant stare. The snow in the yard whirled into a mound underneath my window, conveniently peaking inches from the roof. A more rugged climb than a staircase, but it would work.

A slit of purple sky rose in the distance. Mom would be awake soon, but my feet didn't want to move. Going inside seemed final. As if I'd wake up and none of this would've ever happened. Back to plain, boring Avery.

"Thank you," I said quietly.

"For what?"

"For finding me. Without you, I would've never known about all this magic stuff." I stared at my feet as I kicked at the snow. "And I've kind of always wanted a brother or sister. A real family, not just me and Mom."

"No problem." His face glowed pale white under the streetlights, but red crept up his neck from the inside of his jacket collar.

Before I could stop myself, I wrapped my arms around him. He still scared me, but suddenly the thought of losing him scared me more. After all, we were family. We were blood.

Drew gave me a hesitant squeeze. "Thanks for believing me."

"You're welcome," I whispered. I started up the makeshift mountain and glanced back to see Drew smiling and shaking his head.

I slipped only once on the way up to the roof, then I removed my shoes and stealthily entered the unlocked window. Nothing appeared out of place and my door was still shut, calming the nerves in my stomach. I leaned out the window to wave at Drew, but he was already gone. I planted my feet firmly and grabbed the top of my desk for support, willing my snow ladder to scatter so Mom or our nosy neighbor wouldn't ask questions.

The dizziness came again and a dull throbbing pain grew at the base of my brain. I gripped the desk tighter. Maybe I did need to ease off for a bit. My body seemed to gain two hundred pounds as the adrenaline of excitement faded. Too heavy to bear for even one more second.

I fell on the mattress, mentally and physically spent. My eyes closed before my head slammed against the pillow.

Sixteen

I dragged myself into history class Monday morning, struggling to set one exhausted foot in front of the other. My limbs hated me for keeping them up all night, but blood buzzed through my veins, charged and ready for a new day, an electric smile splitting across my face so deeply that my cheeks hurt.

"Morning Taylor." I grinned harder as I slid into the desk beside her.

A scowl descended across her face. "I'd strongly consider changing desks."

"What?" I peeked behind me to see who she was talking to, but when I turned around again, Taylor's death stare bore straight through me.

"You're either very brave or very stupid to talk to me after what you did to Lily," she snapped.

As if on cue, Lily appeared in the doorway. She glanced at me, then rolled her eyes away and took a seat at the front of the class, far away from me.

I frowned and rubbed my forehead. "I don't get it. I didn't do anything to Lily."

Taylor snorted and moved to an empty desk beside Lily. As I stood up to follow her, Miss Bradley marched through the door.

"Okay everyone, I'm sure your weekend was wonderful, but it's time to get going," she announced with a sharp clap. "Sit down, Avery. Time to learn."

My cheeks flamed and I dropped back into my seat. Lily leaned over and whispered to Taylor, and they both turned to glare at me.

I stared at a creamy spot on the ugly, brown linoleum as Miss Bradley's voice faded into background noise. What the hell was going on? Things seemed fine on Friday night, and even when Lily called on Sunday. Was she mad that I didn't go to the movies with her? She didn't seem to care on the phone, and besides, would it really piss her off this much? Or—my heart pumped faster—maybe Taylor said something to her about me having a thing for Bennett. Maybe I should've told Lily.

Rumbling voices crept into my thoughts and I looked up. Everyone around me packed up their books and headed for the door. When did the bell ring?

I grabbed my stuff and pushed through the other students into the hallway.

"Lily!" I raced down the hallway after her. "Wait up. What's going on?"

"What's going on?" She spun around, nearly taking Taylor out. "Why don't you tell me, Avery?"

She strode toward me and my knees shook. I wasn't sure why she was mad, but I was going to pay for it.

"What are you talking about?"

"Oh, maybe that you're a liar and a backstabber."

"What?" I gasped. "I—"

"Save it, liar. I know about you and Drew."

"Me and Drew?" I pulled my history book tight to my chest and scanned the crowd around us. She couldn't mean she knew about the magic stuff, could she?

"I know Drew showed up at my party and you left with him. And Becky Browning saw you two all cozy at Java on Saturday."

Cozy with Drew? Not quite. I didn't even know who Becky

Browning was. "Lily, that's not what happened. There's nothing going on between Drew and me."

"Really?" She sounded unconvinced. "Then what exactly were you doing with him?"

"I was ... we were..." What was I supposed to say? He tried to kill me, then we had coffee and talked about our paranormal father?

"I thought so." She jutted out her chin. "Stuff like that might work in the city, but not around here. You're pretty stupid if you thought I wasn't going to find out."

My pulse thumped in my ears. "It's not like that."

She turned to walk away, then doubled back, shaking her French manicured finger in my face. "And what's worse is that you tried so hard to convince me to stay away from him and then went after him yourself. You're totally disgusting." She spat the last words with a venom I hadn't expected she was capable of.

"That's not true. I never—"

"Here comes your prince now. I hope you two are happy."

"Hey," Drew said as he came up behind us. Lily glared at him, made a righteous grumbling noise, and then marched off in the other direction. My eyes welled up and a brick settled in the bottom of my stomach.

"What's her problem?" Drew stared after Lily before turning to face me. "Whoa, what's with you?"

A tear broke past my lashes and trickled down my cheek.

"Let's get you out of here." Drew took my arm and whisked me outside to the school courtyard.

I tried to fight against the tears but a few more escaped, the winter wind freezing them to my face.

"What the hell, Avery?" Drew plunked me at a picnic table.

"Lily hates me." I choked back sobs.

Drew laughed. "That's why you're so upset? Who cares?"

"Someone saw us together and she thinks we're a thing now. I lied about seeing you at her place, and now she thinks I'm lying about you and me."

He laughed harder. "Lily thinks we're a couple. That's hilarious ... and disturbingly wrong."

I grinned and coughed on my tears. Dating my brother? Ridiculous! But of course, Lily didn't know that.

"But I lied to her. I shouldn't have lied. If I hadn't, maybe she would believe me that there's nothing going on."

"Why did you lie to her?" His lips pressed together.

"I-I ... I don't know." If I had told the truth, this wouldn't be happening. It wasn't as though she would've figured out our secret if I'd said Drew was there. It was more like my subconscious was trying to hide him or something.

Maybe I deserved to be hated.

"So what did you tell her? About us, I mean?" He crouched down in front of me, face to face, his hands flanking my legs on the wooden seat.

"Nothing. I never got a chance. I told her we weren't together but that was about it."

"Good," he said with a heavy sigh. "And you can't tell her anything. Nothing at all, you understand?"

"Why can't I tell her you're my brother? It'll get her off my back. I don't have to tell her about everything else. You know, the magic stuff."

"No, Avery. You can't say anything. This town is one streetlight bigger than a gas station, and if you tell anyone we're related, they'll start asking questions. They'll watch us even more closely. And what if they start digging? What if—" He leaned in closer and lowered his voice. "What if they find out what we are? Do you know what kind of trouble that would cause for us? They'd take us away and study us. You'd probably never see your mom again."

I swallowed. Hard. Never see Mom again? The thought burrowed in my chest and stung. I rubbed the sleeve of my sweater across my face. "But what am I supposed to tell her to make her stop hating me?"

"You're going to have to deal with it. Being what we are brings secrets to keep. Simple people like Lily in there won't understand." He nodded toward the school. "Stick to your story that we aren't together, but leave it at that."

I nodded and looked down, tugging on my sweater sleeves.

"We're better than them. We're special. And the sooner you realize that, the better off you'll be." Drew lifted my chin and looked me in the eyes. "Now promise me you won't tell Lily—or anyone—anything. All right?"

"Okay." I certainly didn't feel special, more like a complete disaster.

"Good." Drew nodded back sharply. "Now on to more important things. What are we going to teach you tonight?"

I practically fell into the house after school. It took the last ounce of strength I had to push the door open. My body hurt from being dragged around all day, and my eyes threatened to close any second. My cozy bed called from upstairs, tempting me to crawl under the comforter and forget this day ever happened, but the rumble in my stomach screamed louder. Almost as loud as the ringing echo of Lily's words. Besides, Mom would ask a million questions if she found me sleeping when she got home in a half hour.

Meow! Whiskers slunk around the corner from the kitchen.

"Hey, girl." I gave her a quick rub behind the ears. "I hope your day was better than mine."

She purred loudly and pushed her head into my hand.

"Hungry?" She followed me into the kitchen. "Yeah, me too."

I filled her dish in the corner and found pizza in the freezer. Perfect. Not exactly gourmet, but it required little effort. I yanked open the box, set the oven temperature, and popped in the pizzasicle.

Okay, now what? If I sat down, my face would slam against the tabletop before my butt hit the chair. I had to keep busy. I turned on the kitchen radio and bobbed along to the music, but the rhythm droned, making me drowsier. I ran outside and checked the mail. Nothing, but the cold wind perked me up a bit. I went back inside and surveyed the kitchen. I could do dishes. Wow. How pathetic was that? Washing the dishes to avoid my life.

I filled the sink, mesmerized by the rising soap bubbles. I caught myself drifting off several times, almost falling over. If coffee didn't taste so bad, the caffeine sure would've helped.

Once the sink was full, I slid the dishes into the water one by one. They splashed as they broke the surface. My mind drifted back to earlier that morning when I'd splashed Drew, and I smirked. I dried my hands and checked the front window to make sure Mom wasn't coming up the street and then flicked off the radio.

"Watch this, Whisky." I stepped back from the counter and closed my eyes, pushing through my tired fog. When the strange tickle started at the back of my throat, I slowly peeled my eyes open. A small stream of water ascended from the sink, shimmying and twisting higher in the air. An aqueous python dancing for its snake charming master. When it reached about eye level, I willed it to stop, and it obeyed.

Whiskers stared at the water hovering in the air and let out a sharp hiss.

"It's only water, silly." The cat bolted from the room. I

resumed my focus. Starting at the top, I slowly split the stream into two, like pulling apart two pieces of licorice. Dizziness rippled through me as the water forced itself back together and I squinted, concentrating harder to pull the water apart for a second time. At least I wasn't nauseous today. Drew was right. It was fun. Maybe it wasn't so bad being special.

"Avery?" The front door clicked shut.

Mom. As my brain switched into panic mode, the stream of water crashed back into the sink, splashing all over the floor. I grabbed a cloth and dropped to my knees, frantically drying the tile.

"What are you doing?" Mom asked as she walked into the kitchen.

"Dishes?"

"Next time try not to make such a mess, okay?" She gave me a warm smile. The oven timer beeped and she scurried toward the oven, pulled out the hot pizza, and slid it on the counter. "Went all out today, didn't you?"

"Thanks." I finished wiping up the water and tossed the dishcloth on the counter. "I tried, you know."

"Someone's cranky. I was just joking." Mom sliced and plated the pizza. "You know I appreciate it when you help out."

"I know." I gave her a quick hug. "It's been a long day."

I scooped up the plates, placed them on the table, and sat down.

"That makes two of us." She rubbed her forehead and joined me. "And sorry I'm late. We had an emergency at the end of my shift, and I had to take care of the paperwork."

"What? Did someone get a splinter?" I joked and took a big bite of my pizza.

"No, some kid fell through the ice at Henderson's Pond."

"Henderson's Pond?" Mom's words punched my breath away, and I choked on my food.

"Yes. Are you okay?"

I swallowed, and the pizza scalded my throat. "Yeah, I'm fine. What happened?"

"A little boy was playing on the pond and fell through the ice. Apparently, it's such a small body of water that it's long frozen by now, but for some reason, the ice was cracked all over. It's strange."

My hands trembled. I dropped the pizza and leaned back in my chair. "Is the kid okay?"

"I'm sure he'll be fine. He's pretty shaken up though. I'm surprised you're so concerned."

"It's sad, that's all." And it was all my fault.

"Okay. Aren't you going to eat?"

"I really don't feel well."

"You do look pretty pale. Are you sure everything's okay? Do you need to talk?" She put down her pizza and her eyebrows knit together.

"I'm fine." I forced a smile. "Just tired. I think I'll go to bed, if that's okay?"

"Sure, honey, get some rest." She rubbed my arm as I passed.

I headed upstairs and lay down on my bed. I'd almost hurt someone—a little kid— all because I'd been careless. Last night, the rush of all that power slamming through my body and the control I'd had over it had intoxicated me, set my blood on fire. But underneath, a lingering heaviness pulled tight on my ribs, even heavier now exposed in the daylight and faced with the consequences of what I'd done. The rush was gone, and now it terrified me.

I rolled onto my stomach and swallowed hard, my throat still itchy and raw from being scorched by mozzarella. In my nightmare, I'd been burned too. The stench of smoke and melting flesh. Monster claws protruding from my hands. I fluttered my fingers in front of my face. Still human. But maybe I would turn into something hideous one day. I shook my head as if that could wipe the image from my subconscious, but no luck. No matter what this power was, Drew and I had messed with the real world and could've hurt someone.

Tucking my arms underneath my pillow, I finally let my eyes close, but didn't feel the release I'd hoped for. What if someone hadn't been there to save that kid?

What if—

I pushed the thought from my mind. He was alive. That was all that mattered. The kid was still alive.

SEVENTEEN

"Where do you think the power comes from?" I flipped a beer bottle off the fence and sent it flying into the snow.

As promised, Drew showed up at one in the morning, ready for another round of freak training. After a few solid hours of sleep, I felt better, but still confused about my new reality.

He'd taken me to an old barn behind his family's property. The house stood large, square and solid, kind of like a fortress, but with more windows. The shutters needed paint, and cracks webbed up the gray stone walls. Some parts still whispered of a time when it would've been an impressive home, but it was mostly a decaying corpse. If Drew didn't live here, I would've thought it was abandoned. But the house seemed to fit him, dramatic and surprising with an edge of something slightly sinister inside.

Tonight's lesson was wind. We started slowly by sliding buckets across the empty barn floor and moved on to more delicate tasks, like knocking over one particular beer bottle in a line. Apparently, that was supposed to work on maintaining precision instead of ending up with an unplanned tornado. To me, it felt like target practice.

The shock I'd had when I first began using my power started to fade, and I wasn't blinded by red lights anymore, which helped me see what I was doing. Unfortunately, that peculiar feeling in the back of my throat still made me gag sometimes. I couldn't wait for that to go away, which Drew assured me it would.

Drew reset the bottle on the fence. "I've told you plenty of times, the power comes from somewhere within. I thought you said you could feel it."

"That's not what I meant. I'm talking about the source of it. You told me the mayor's son started using powers after he died. Where do you think those powers came from? Do you think the witch gave it to him—the one who brought him back to life?"

Drew grabbed the edge of the fence and stood motionless in the snow. "I don't know. Maybe he brought something back from the dead?"

"Like another person. Maybe another witch?"

"No. Darker. A demon maybe."

"A demon? Seriously?" I dug my hands into my pockets. How much did he expect me to believe?

"As if your explanation is any better," he scoffed and returned to aligning the bottles, moving them closer together.

"Do you think it's evil?"

"What?" He spun around to face me, his face scrunched up and sour.

"I asked if you thought it was evil. The power or the demon thing or whatever."

"What do you think?"

I stared down at my feet and kicked at tufts of snow. Evil might explain my bad dreams and the constant pinch in my stomach since Drew came along. Or maybe they came from the lies I'd told, the bad choices I'd made. Maybe I just wanted an excuse for the sudden undeserved downgrade in my social status. "I don't know yet. But I've been trying to figure that out."

"Does it matter?" Drew's eyebrows raised.

"I don't know that yet either. I just want to understand and make sure I'm not doing something wrong."

His gaze slid off me and into a faraway place beyond my shoulders, maybe processing my words and calculating his own or maybe just counting every star in the moonlit sky. Eventually, he blinked and snapped back into the moment. "Well, how does all this make you feel?"

"I don't like all the secrets and hiding from everyone."

"Is this about Lily again?" He rolled his eyes.

"No." Kind of. "I feel terrible lying to people."

"You didn't have any trouble lying before all of this. Hell, you've been lying to your mom on a daily basis since I met you."

"That doesn't mean I don't feel guilty about it, and besides, this is a bit more serious than sneaking out to a party. Maybe you could come over one time--in the daylight—and meet my mom. Maybe it would be better—"

"Oh no." He shook his head.

"We don't have to tell her anything yet. We can wait until you're comfortable, then maybe we can stop sneaking around in the middle of the night."

"Do you hear yourself?" he yelled.

I jumped.

"We can never tell anyone about this. What does this world do to people who are different? They wipe them out. They poke and prod at them and never leave them alone. They'd probably lock us up in some institution and study us somewhere, if not kill us outright. Think, Avery."

He stomped back and forth, shaking his head, his expression twisted and dark. His lips moved, but without sound, as if he was talking to himself.

"I'm sorry." I played with my coat sleeves and stepped back. "I'm having a hard time figuring this all out. Plus, I feel bad about this kid at Henderson's today."

"What kid?" He stopped pacing and stared at me.

I looked toward the lone bottle on the fence, refusing to meet his eyes. "My mom said there was this kid. A little boy playing on Henderson's Pond and the ice broke and he fell in."

"Did he live?"

"Yeah, but I keep thinking it's my fault. If we hadn't messed around with the ice, he wouldn't have fallen in." I fidgeted with my sleeves again. "If he died, it'd be our fault."

"How is it our fault if other people don't keep better tabs on their brats? What was he doing out there by himself, anyway?" He screwed his face into a frown. "I'd blame the parents."

"But—"

"But nothing," he interrupted again. "Is this where all the 'evil' talk is coming from?"

"I don't know. Maybe."

"Look, I don't think our powers are good or evil. They just exist. It depends how you use them."

I nodded, acknowledging his words, but not sure I fully agreed. His explanation was too simple, or maybe he didn't know the real answer.

"Now, how do you feel when you use your powers? When you're out here with me? No one watching. No judgments." He inched closer, his expression relaxing again.

"Good, I guess."

"You guess?" He raised an eyebrow.

"Really good." I tried to fight down a smile. "I feel strong. Like I could do anything."

"That's great. That's how it should feel. Free." He nodded. "Do you feel evil?"

I shook my head.

His lips turned up, flashing his perfect teeth. "Then no, I don't think your power is evil."

I reached out and pulled him into a hug. Again, his rigid arms silently screamed his hesitation, but he'd have to get used to it. Right now, I needed someone to hold me together before I completely fell apart, and he was the only person I had left.

"Thanks," I whispered. Then I let go.

He shook his head and cast his gaze to the ground, then swept back the lock of dark hair that flopped across his face, gripping it at his crown. An odd pinkish tinge faded quickly from his defined cheeks. "Okay, so remember, control is easy with no distractions, but it's a lot harder when your concentration is compromised. This time when you try to knock over the bottle, I'm going to do whatever I can to throw you off. All right?"

"Sure." I steadied my feet in the snow.

"Ready?" He crouched in a cat-like stance.

"How did you learn all this stuff?"

He sighed and straightened up again. "Someone sure is chatty today."

"I mean, you're teaching me everything you know, but who taught you? Are there others like us out there?"

"I haven't met any, so I figured it all out myself. Not everyone is as lucky as you are."

"That must've been really hard."

"Yes, it was. Now, can we please get back to work?"

"Fine." I took a deep breath and focused on the leftmost beer bottle. "I'm ready."

EIGHTEEN

THE NEXT MORNING WAS NOT GOOD. MY HEAD pounded from lack of sleep as I propelled myself down the icy sidewalk, slow and zombie-like, dreading what type of wrath Lily would rain down today. I scrunched down into my coat collar, trying to block the cold winter wind and trying to assure myself that things would get better.

I should've stayed home.

I crossed the road and approached the school. A car horn blasted at me. The sound pierced through my aching skull, and I leaped as the driver screeched to a stop inches from my leg. My heart pounded double time.

Nora shouted through the windshield of her pretty black car, but I couldn't hear what she said, and I had no energy to argue. I just got out of her way. The car sped into the parking lot, nearly clipping my heels as I stepped onto the safety of the sidewalk. But Nora wasn't anywhere in sight when I started to cross the road. Had she been waiting for me?

No. Thinking everyone was out to get me was just paranoid.

I stumbled into the school and through the hallway, dodging nasty stares—my first day all over again, with less curiosity and more hostility. Lily's network reached further than I'd thought. And then I reached my locker. The lock was missing and the door hung half open. I pulled it open farther. Completely empty. No books, no notes, not even my emergency hair elastic. I slammed the locker shut and rested my forehead against the cool metal door, staring at my feet. So this must be how things played out in the country. You mess with one and you get vengeance from them all.

After choking down the urge to scream, I noticed the garbage can to the left of the locker bank overflowing with paper. I pulled a sheet from the pile. Sure enough, crumpled pages torn from my notebooks filled the bin. I dug through a few layers of paper and found my chemistry textbook, fortunately still intact. I rescued the rest of my textbooks and piled them on the floor as laughter echoed behind me. Refusing to respond, I dug deeper to see if any of my notes were salvageable, but most were ripped and covered in someone's spaghetti lunch.

I shoved everything but my English textbook back into the locker and then raced off to class, tugging at my sweater sleeves and wishing I could hide in my shirt until the end of the day.

Sliding into a desk at the back of the class, I peeked at the empty spot where Drew normally sat. Maybe he'd decided to skip first period and get some sleep, or maybe he'd swagger in at the bell as usual. I folded over the desk and closed my eyes, begging my brain to stop hurting. Voices fluttered around the room as people arrived, but no one bothered me.

The classroom door clicked shut and the bell rang.

"This is completely unacceptable," Mrs. Sharp's high-pitched voice exclaimed.

I bolted upright in my chair, assuming my attempt at a nap had set her off.

Still no Drew.

"Who's responsible for this?" Mrs. Sharp asked, staring down at each of us with disgust.

In a large hasty scrawl, someone had written, *A Witch or Just a Bitch*, across the entire chalkboard.

Warm saliva built up in the back of my throat. A clear message directed at me, the taunting glances flying my way confirming it, in case I didn't already know. I wrapped my arms tight over my stomach and swallowed. Lily wasn't even in this class.

"When you're in this school, you are expected to treat each other with respect." Mrs. Sharp frantically wiped the defamatory message from the board. "I don't ever want to see this again. Whoever did this can expect a lengthy suspension."

The room stayed silent and Mrs. Sharp changed the subject to the themes of illusion and reality in *The Tempest*. A brutal combination of pain and humiliation stung my eyes. Any chance that the entire school was not on Lily's side disappeared into oblivion. The fear on my first day had finally come true. I was an outcast. I'd expected Lily to ignore me, or maybe make catty remarks, but this was all-out war. Stuck in hostile territory with no chance for escape, at least not until graduation. I shrank down in my chair wishing to disappear.

Drew never showed up to class, but I scanned the hall for him afterward with my fingers crossed. No luck. I trudged back to the lockers, counting floor tiles to avoid eye contact. I stopped in front of mine, looked up, and sighed at the open door. Pillaged again. I leaned back and checked the garbage can.

Yep. Déjà vu.

After loading up with my entire course load of textbooks—again—I maneuvered through the crowded hallway to class. Nora sat on top of her desk, deep in conversation with Taylor, but as I walked by, she glared at me.

"Like I said, Taylor," Nora continued, too loud not to be deliberate, "she just ran out in front of my car. She's a complete head case. You should've seen her."

An argument rose in my throat, but I pushed it down. Nora had already made up her mind about me anyway. I paraded across the room and sat as far from her as possible, and then I organized all my books in a neat pile beneath the desk as a collection of stares weighed on the back of my skull.

"What's she doing?" the guy beside me whispered to the random skater guy beside him.

I bit my cheek, counted to ten, and concentrated on not losing it on them both. Fists and teeth clenched, I agonized over every minute as the class ticked by, willing myself not to break down in front of everyone. My head throbbed harder.

When the bell rang, I took a deep, satisfying breath and relaxed slightly. Lunchtime. One full hour without being boxed in a room with these people. I quickly collected my stack of books and stumbled out the door.

Something slammed against my leg—a booted foot. I flew onto my knees. The jolt sent pain spidering through my head and my books scattering across the tile.

As people filled the hallway, snickering and threatening to trample me, I scrambled over the floor, shoving books against my chest and trying to keep my hands from getting crushed. A couple of cell phone lights flashed. Great. Now I'd be crawling on the Internet later. As I reached for my chemistry book, a green high top sent it sailing across the floor. The book stopped, balancing precariously on the edge of a staircase six feet away. At least it was out of traffic.

I struggled through the crowd, enduring a few more shots to the head as I tried to stand, and plunked down on the top step. I grabbed my chemistry book and caught my breath. Like the video game with the little frog and the racing cars, I'd survived. Barely. I tilted my head back to outsmart gravity and hold back the tears threatening to fall. Above the stairwell, the sign for the cafeteria spread across the wall in thick black letters. Lily said no one ever used the cafeteria. Perfect. I gathered up my books and snuck down the stairs.

As I swung open the double doors, the wonderful, stuffy

smell of underused space flooded over me. From the second of several long rows of standard cafeteria tables, five unfamiliar faces swiveled in unison and looked me over with irritated stares. After a few seconds, they looked away and put their heads together again, shutting me out. As long as they gave me my privacy, I had no problem giving them theirs.

I marched through a long hall of drab and windowless prison-like walls and picked a table on the opposite end of the room, close to another set of exit doors.

After dumping my books on the table, I rested my head on my crossed arms. Every muscle in my back released, easing my headache, but not getting rid of it entirely. What was I going to do when lunch was over? My head would explode before four o'clock if I had to deal with any more of Lily's revenge. Even if it were true that I'd poached Drew from her, why did she need to make such a big deal about it? And bullying me for being a witch was cruel, but ironically not far from the truth. If she really knew the things I could do, it would be so much worse.

It seemed Drew had a point about keeping our secret quiet.

A small tear trickled along the bridge of my nose and splashed on the tabletop. Alone and helpless, I was trapped in the box of secrets I'd built one small piece at a time. Why couldn't I still be back in Detroit with my friends? Away from small-town drama and screwed-up fairy tales. Back in my normal life where I belonged.

One tear became two, then another and another, until tears poured down my face, but I didn't care enough to wipe them away. I gasped, trying to choke back sobs and avoid drawing attention, but eventually gave up. No one down here likely cared.

"There you are." Drew straddled the bench beside me, shaking the table. I rolled my head to glare at my uninvited guest.

"You look terrible," Drew said, but his expression seemed unaffected by my misery.

I rubbed my face with my sweater sleeve. "Today hasn't been the best day. Everyone's out to get me."

"And just think, it's only lunchtime."

"Thanks for the sympathy," I muttered, crossing my arms and hugging them close to my body.

"For what? We're in high school. People here are like dirty rabid rats that feed on your weaknesses and insecurities. You expected anything less?" He thumbed through my textbooks as if we were discussing some TV show instead of my emotional breakdown.

"Have you always been this heartless?" I asked.

"It's not heartless. It's real. You don't see it because you have this fantasy that people are inherently good. Once you realize that everyone up there only cares about themselves"—he pointed toward the ceiling—"you'll understand what I mean."

I'd thought Drew and I were past all that bad boy loner stuff, but I guessed not. Maybe it wasn't really an act. At what point in his life did he start hating the world?

"Now, if we're done with this topic, I want to talk about last night."

"What about it?"

"You did well, but you seemed distracted."

"Okay. So?"

"I think you need to develop more strength before we move on to something new. Tonight, we should work on developing your focus, building up your strength, and really opening up your mind to your abilities."

"Does it have to be tonight?" I rested my face on the table-top. "I'm exhausted and my head is killing me. Can't I have a break for one night?"

"A break? We've barely started and you already want a

break? I thought you'd be a lot tougher than this." He leaned away from me and frowned.

"Yes, I need a break. I've been out every night with you, which is physically and mentally draining, then I come here. All this drama with Lily is sucking the rest of me dry. I feel raw."

Drew cocked his head and stared at me as if I were a weird animal at the zoo. I considered adding something to further my point, but the throbbing in my skull urged me to take advantage of his unexpected silence.

"Listen, Avery, you would really benefit from being a little less human."

"What? What does that even mean?"

"Look at you." He got up and circled to the other side of the table, across from me. "Sitting here whining about some stupid girl you've known for about five minutes. You're pathetic."

"That's not fair."

"Your head is full of all this worry and guilt and emotional garbage that keeps you from achieving greatness. If you could get rid of all that crap in your head, you could be much further along. I put up with this idiotic nonsense yesterday, but I'm not going to do it again today."

"You really are a jerk." I stared at him, resisting the urge to smash my fist into his jaw.

"Maybe so, but we are gods among these people, and they don't know how lucky they are that we don't squash them like ants on the sidewalk. If you want to be like them, weak and foolish, go ahead. But I thought you were better than that. I wouldn't have bothered confiding in you if I didn't."

How dare he just show up and talk to me like this? Drew was a semi-truck, and I was the unsuspecting cyclist in the wrong place at the wrong time, broken and bleeding along the highway. What did he expect of me? If being *less human* meant being close-minded and rude like him, it wouldn't happen. After all, as much Lily hurt me, I kind of started it.

"I think I need some sleep." I groaned and planted my face back on the table. Continuing this conversation was pointless. He'd probably twist my words against me anyway.

"Again with the whining." He tossed his hands in the air. "I'll leave you alone tonight, but only if you promise to get yourself together."

"I'll see what I can do," I snapped.

Drew headed toward the door. He threw it open harder than he needed to and turned toward me again. "Remember what I said. Lose the stupid human melodrama. You don't owe them anything." And then he disappeared.

I soaked up the Drew-free silence for a few seconds, my head pounding even worse than before. With trembling fingers, I checked the time on my cell phone. Five minutes left to hide in this dungeon before marching back into the mouth of hell. With sloth-like momentum, I peeled away from the table, battling between the need to go to class and the urge to stay put. The mysterious five from the far table had already left. Hopefully, they hadn't heard anything incriminating.

As I ascended the stairs from the basement, ground-level daylight hurt my eyes, and my hands began to shake more violently the nearer I came to the top.

Stay calm. Just bite down and muddle through the next few hours.

I turned the corner and halted. Ahead of me, Lily and Taylor chatted outside the door to the chemistry lab. The blood pumped faster in my veins and my stomach clenched. Forget this.

I hid behind a locker bank and pulled out my cell phone.

"Shady Creek General Emergency, how can I help you?" a familiar voice chimed.

"Mom, it's me."

"Oh hi, honey. What's going on?"

I lowered my voice and tried to sound as raspy as possible. "I'm feeling sick so I'm going home, okay?"

"I'll see if I can get away." Panic set into Mom's voice, her words ringing two octaves higher. "I'll be home in a half hour. Tops."

"No, Mom. I'll be okay. I just need to go to bed."

"Are you sure? I can get someone to cover me. Really."

"Stay at work. You'll be home in a few hours anyway."

"Okay." She sighed. "But if you feel worse, call me immediately."

"Sure. See you later."

I slipped the phone into my backpack as the bell clanged in the hall. Even the pain splitting through my skull seemed bearable now that I was going home.

I powered through the snow in a hazy struggle with all my books, anxious to close the gap between me and my warm bed. Mrs. Abernathy stood stoic in her front window as I stumbled past. I flashed her an overdone smile, and she retreated behind her dark curtains. Did she watch everyone, or just me?

So weird.

Finally, I burst through the door and headed straight upstairs, stripping off my scarf and mitts as I went. I dropped my textbooks on the floor and collapsed on the bed. Despite how tired I was, my brain wouldn't slow down enough to let me sleep. I slid my arm under the mattress and found the diary.

February 18

We have a plan. After the baby's born we're going to leave this place. Our little family. If Mother can't support us, then she's never going to get to be a grandmother. Nick says we'll run away where no one will find us. He'll get a job and we'll figure it all out together. Mother is still trying to keep us apart, but she doesn't get that it's not her choice. I love him. He even gave me a little gold heart necklace so when we can't be together, his heart will always be with me.

We're going to be happy, the three of us. I bet no one will even miss us when we're gone.

NINETEEN

THE SUN BEAT DOWN THROUGH THE WINDOW AND warmed the side of my face. I glanced at my cell phone on the floor. 8:10 AM. Only five minutes before the alarm—not enough time to fall back asleep. I forced myself out of bed and stood on shaky legs.

Even though I'd slept all afternoon and all night, I didn't feel any better. I staggered to the window and stared at the sky. The happy sunshine mocked my misery. How could everything look so cheerful when my world was falling apart? Lily had declared war, Drew was being his condescending self again, and I couldn't figure out how to deal with being a secret freak. I squinted against the blinding sun and willed the wind to deposit two clouds directly in the path of the light. Much better. Cloudy and dull, just how I felt.

There were no footprints in the snow outside, which meant Drew kept his word and left me alone—not that I would have heard him anyway.

My stomach grumbled. Skipping lunch and dinner yesterday had left me famished, so much that I thought I smelled food, but it was too early for that.

I quickly showered and dressed, and then pounded down the stairs to the unmistakable, almost drool-worthy, scent of maple syrup. A warm plate of pancakes waited for me on the table. Mom hadn't made me breakfast before school in a long time.

"Morning, sleepyhead. I thought you'd be hungry after

missing dinner." Mom placed a glass of orange juice beside my plate.

"Thanks, Mom." I gave her a quick hug. "Love you."

"I love you too." She chuckled and patted my arm. "Now eat up."

I sat down and shoveled each forkful in my mouth without even thinking to chew.

Mom sat down in the chair next to me. "Avery." She leaned in close, her eyebrows furrowed. "Are you okay?"

"Sure. I'm fine," I lied.

"Seriously, what's going on with you? You don't seem yourself lately, and to tell you the truth, you look pretty rough."

Her insult hit like a slap. I jerked my head back. "Thanks."

"I'm not trying to upset you. I'm just worried. You used to tell me everything, but since we moved here, I don't know what's going on. And it sure feels like something is going on."

I picked at the edge of my placemat, avoiding eye contact. What was I supposed to tell her? Everyone hates me because I'm trying to cover up the fact that I met my half-brother who takes me out every night to move things with my mind?

"Really, Mom, I'm fine. I'm probably getting a cold or maybe the flu." Another lie. They seemed to come hard and fast this morning.

"Are you sure?"

"Yes." I reached over and squeezed her rough, dry hand.

"Okay, but you can tell me anything. You know that, right?"

I nodded.

"And I was thinking, how about we hang out on Friday?"

"Hang out?" I scrunched up my face.

"Whatever you want to call it. You should probably be taking it easy anyway. We could order take-out, and if there's anything you want to talk about, we can do that too."

I gave her a warm smile. "Sure. Sounds good."

"Great. Now I'm off to work, but I'll be home right after school. Okay?" She stared at me in eerie silence, her eyes wide and questioning, probably waiting to see if I'd break down and tell her my deepest secrets. But that definitely wasn't happening. Eventually, she let out a heavy sigh, tucked a few stray hairs over her ear, and then headed out to the foyer. After a few minutes of rustling, the front door creaked open and then clicked shut.

I sighed. I'd have to be extra careful around Mom from now on. She clearly didn't know about my sneaking out at night or about Drew or even the disaster my social life was in. Otherwise, she would've kept pressing for details. But it didn't mean she wouldn't find out. And now, if she thought something was off, she'd be watching more closely. I'd be in worlds of trouble if she knew the truth.

I shook off the paranoia and dug my fork into the stack of sticky, fluffy goodness. *Mmm.* Pancakes.

Today will be a better day. I repeated the words for the hundredth time as I turned the corner onto the sidewalk. Maybe if I said it enough, it would be true.

Something flickered in my periphery. Mrs. Abernathy, peering out from behind her curtains again. I waved politely and she backed away. Maybe she was on Team Lily too. I kept walking and Mrs. Abernathy returned to her post. Why was she so interested in me? What did she want? Maybe she was just bored, cooped up in that house all day.

I made it all the way to the school and my locker without so much as a glance from anyone, but my reprieve stopped there. A crudely drawn picture of a witch burning at the stake was taped to my locker door. I ripped it off and tossed it into the same garbage can where I'd found my books the day before. I closed my eyes. *Don't get angry. It's going to be fine.* After three deep breaths, my anxiety settled. *That's it. I can do this.*

I organized my textbooks in my locker and snapped on the replacement lock I'd dug out of the junk drawer this morning.

"What did you do to my sister?"

I flinched and glanced up. Bennett leaned against the locker bank, watching me. I closed my locker and took another deep breath. Then I scanned his face, his gorgeous face, trying to figure out what he did and didn't know. No use volunteering a list of my alleged crimes. "She didn't tell you?"

"Of course she did, but I usually stop listening when she starts on one of her rants." He wore a crooked smirk that any other day would've made me blush, but today I knew better. He was probably here to hate on me too. I'd hoped he might have somehow climbed into a black hole and missed this whole mess, but maybe I had no luck left. I slid my gaze toward my locker, studying the lines of the vent and wishing he wouldn't see the humiliation in my eyes.

Then Bennett laughed—not a mean, check-out-the-freak kind of laugh, but a low, nervous chuckle that tumbled into the small space between us and lingered, waiting to be answered. I jerked my head back. He grinned and folded his arms loosely against his chest, leaning against the locker bank. Maybe he wasn't mad at me. Or at least, he didn't seem to be.

"I thought you might have a less dramatic version of the story for me."

"It's all a big misunderstanding." I twisted my fingers in the strap of my bag, choosing my next words carefully. I couldn't say "going out with" and "Drew" in the same sentence. Conjuring a mental picture of that crazy would ensure Bennett would never want to see me again. "I'm hoping I can get it straightened out."

"I figured." He ran his hand through his hair. "But I know how determined Lily can be when she's on the warpath. So if you ever need a friend, you can talk to me. If you want."

My heart sank. Like I thought—just friends.

"And I thought you might need this." He dug my jacket out of his backpack and handed it to me. "You left it at our place and Lily said she would bring it to you, but I'm guessing she decided to hold it hostage."

"Thanks. I was looking for that." I took the jacket and stashed it in my locker, discretely inhaling his subtle minty scent still lingering on the fabric.

"So ... uh ... do you have a habit of leaving your clothes lying around at other people's houses?"

"No." I whipped around and slammed the locker shut. What exactly *did* Lily tell him?

Bennett's face flamed and his eyes widened. "That didn't come out right, did it?" He rubbed the back of his neck and looked at his feet. "I didn't mean anything by it, I..."

"Don't worry about it." Oh. My. God.

"I tried to give your coat back after school yesterday, but I couldn't find you."

I adjusted my bag on my shoulder and shifted forward on my toes. "I wasn't feeling well, so I went home early."

"Are you okay?" He stared at the floor, but his voice sounded genuinely concerned.

My heart skipped, and I tried to force down a smile. "I'm fine, but I was hoping I would see you sometime this week too."

"Oh." It was his turn to smile. Awkwardly. He lifted his eyes and met my gaze, leaning in closer.

I swallowed hard and fought the urge to look away. "I wanted to talk to you about Friday night. I really—"

Nora and a girl whose name I couldn't remember charged up and slipped between Bennett and me, facing him.

"We don't think Lily would appreciate you talking to her, Bennett," the nameless girl said.

"You can tell Liliana that I can talk to whoever I want, and if she has a problem with that, she can talk to me herself." Bennett's face morphed from kind and friendly to hard as granite and twice as cold.

Maybe I actually had an ally.

Nora huffed at him.

I tapped my foot, hoping they'd go away, but both girls stood there like annoying statues. Bennett weaved right and attempted to sidestep Nora. She pivoted on her heel and planted her hands on her hips, keeping us separated.

"Seriously, Nora?" He scowled at her.

She shrugged but didn't back down. I peeked over her shoulder, and Bennett shook his head, rolling his stare to the ceiling.

"See you around, Avery." He gave me an apologetic wave and then walked away.

With Bennett out of sight, the two girls threw me matching sneers and pranced off in the opposite direction. Any hope I had that my penance was over was officially gone. My stomach churned as anxiety crept back into my body.

As if attracted to my misery, Lily appeared around the corner with an armload of paper and marched by, flashing me a bitchy scowl.

Why couldn't she leave me alone? I glared at her as she walked away with her obnoxious, perfect little strut. Fluid and weightless, as if she'd done nothing wrong. My cheeks burned and my nails dug into my tightly fisted palms. Why did she feel the need to be so cruel?

A whisper brushed my ear as a cool breeze stirred. It whizzed past me and toward Lily, scattering her papers like autumn leaves across the hall.

She dropped to the floor and scrambled to gather them up as everyone else plodded past.

My anger subsided. I grinned. It felt good to watch Lily suffer, even just a little.

And then the wind disappeared, faster than it had come.

I glanced back down the hall. Wind didn't blow indoors, at least not that strong. Unless all the outside doors were open or … unless I called it. I swallowed. This was my fault.

I ran to Lily and helped gather up the sheets of paper.

"Those are mine." She yanked the pages from my hands. "Haven't you learned not to steal things from me yet?"

"I was trying to help." I grabbed a few more pages.

She snapped her head toward me and snarled. "You're the one who's going to need help."

I tossed the pages in the air and backed away.

"Nice job," a voice whispered in my ear.

I whirled around to face Drew. He stood beside me, grin wide like a circus clown.

"What do you mean?" I asked.

"You know what I mean. You finally took my advice and stood up for yourself."

"But, I didn't feel anything. I always feel weird when I do magic things. Wait. Did you do this?"

"As much as I would like to take credit for messing with Lily, I just got here." He glanced around at the other people in the hallway and lowered his voice. "What were you thinking about before it happened?"

"I was wondering why Lily couldn't leave me alone."

"Were you angry?"

"Of course I was angry. She's making my life a total nightmare."

"Then that's your answer. Your anger allowed you to focus

and clear out all other distractions, so you didn't have all of the regular side effects."

"But I didn't focus on knocking around Lily's notes. This type of thing has never happened to me before."

"Because you never knew how before. If you've never done magic before, your brain doesn't know how. But once you've done something, the memory's always there to access anytime you want, and sometimes when you don't intend to."

"So I could make it rain by accident?"

He laughed. "No, you were amped up so your emotions set you off. If you keep calm, you'll be fine."

"And if I can't?"

"That's why you need to learn control. You can't just walk around randomly messing with the universe."

"I guess not."

"So how does it feel, the ability to make someone else suffer for a change?"

"I feel kind of guilty."

"Really?" He raised one of his thick eyebrows and glowered down at me. "Look at her over there."

Drew pointed across the hall where Lily stood, shuffling her pages back together. As he dropped his hand, she looked up and tossed me a hostile glance.

"Do you think she feels guilty about harassing you?" Drew asked. "Doesn't it make you feel a little bit better having finally hit her back, even if it was pretty weak?"

"Weak?" My mouth twitched.

"Aha." He pointed a finger in my face. "So you did enjoy it, didn't you?"

"Maybe a little." I pulled at my sweater sleeves.

"I knew it." His grin broadened. "What have I told you before? If you embraced your power, life could be so much simpler. So much better."

"Embrace my power? Seriously? Who talks like that?"

"We do. We are gods among these mortals. But only if you allow yourself to be."

"I don't have much else to lose."

"Does that mean you're in? Fully, completely?"

"Maybe."

He put his arm over my shoulders and guided me down the hallway. "Today is going to be a better day."

TWENTY

I DROPPED INTO A PLUSH BROWN CHAIR BY THE
window, still wondering why we had come to Java Nation at
lunchtime. When Drew appeared outside my history class and
announced that we were going on a field trip, I never thought
he'd bring me here. I'd boycotted this place all week to avoid
possible contact with Lily's army. Who knew if or when they'd
show up?

"Not that chair." Drew's face contorted into a disgruntled
glare. He pointed to two wooden chairs tucked in the corner.
"Over here."

I dragged myself out of the prime spot and moved across the
room.

For the last several days, Drew's ill-tempered alternate
personality had taken a vacation, leaving behind a happy Drew
who was sometimes almost pleasant. He'd even started showing
up earlier at night and seemed to try to get me home so I could
salvage a few hours of sleep before school. Still not enough, but
I didn't feel like the walking dead either. We'd finally hit a
rhythm we both could handle.

And I was getting stronger too. Drew said I wasn't ready to
learn the fire element yet, but I'd mastered the other three. Just
moving through space seemed different now. My limbs seemed
longer, more fluid. My reflexes snapped faster. It wasn't the god-
like feeling he'd promised, but at least it was a pleasant distraction from my lack of social life.

Lily had also toned down the torment. She still shot me the

occasional nasty stare, but generally left me alone. So did most of the student body.

Besides, Lily seemed preoccupied with her sudden unfortunate string of bad luck. For some strange reason, the sprinkler system went off whenever she or her crew entered a room. Last week her locker door lock needed replacing four times because it wouldn't open, almost as if someone had fused its metal insides together. My personal favorite, however, was when snow buried all the student cars in the parking lot, forcing everyone to dig out their vehicles— especially difficult and absolutely hilarious in the unprecedented wind that sprung up out of nowhere. For the first time in Lily's blessed existence, the world was working against her. And the best part was that she had no idea Drew and I orchestrated all her misery.

"What are we doing here?" I sat down in the wooden seat, already missing the plush armchair Drew evicted me from.

"You'll see." His grin glimmered with something unknown that seemed both exciting and treacherous. "Just eat up."

At least he bought lunch. I pulled the waxy paper off the sandwich and then politely wrapped it back up. Egg salad. Gross.

I sipped my hot chocolate slowly and leaned back in the chair as Drew devoured his sandwich. He had managed to get my drink right, so I had to give him credit for that.

The front door swung open and familiar voices drifted in. Of course, today would be the day they'd decide to come here. I cringed. Lily entered first with Taylor, chattering away as they headed to their usual table up front. Max came in next, hand in hand with Katie, followed by Justin, Nora, and Bennett. I glanced away, stupidly hoping that if I didn't look, they couldn't see me, but my gaze kept shifting back. Amazingly, Drew chose the one table with a perfect view of Lily's, likely his demented plan all along. But how had he known she was coming?

Justin gave Max a high five and sat down close to the window. Taylor joined Justin, who wrapped an arm across her chair. Bennett and Nora, however, hung back by the door, deep in conversation. They were uncomfortably close to me. I held my breath, hoping they would just sit down. I hadn't spoken to Bennett since we were interrupted at my locker, and I figured by now he couldn't have escaped the witch rumors flying around about me. As much as I didn't want to be hated by everyone, I really didn't want him to hate me.

Nora jostled Bennett with her elbow and they both laughed. She leaned close to his ear and her long dark hair blocked my view of their faces. When she pulled away, he was grinning. He put his arm over her shoulders and guided her off to the regular table.

What?

I struggled to exhale and my hands trembled. I slid them underneath my thighs so Drew wouldn't see. Tears stung my eyes, but I pushed them down. I couldn't cry. Not here. Not in front of Drew or all these other people. What I really wanted was to run out of the restaurant.

They couldn't be together. Could they? Taylor said they were a couple once. Maybe they got back together. But why would he even like her? She was so, so ... not right for him. She was too severe, too mean, too—

A hand waved slowly in front of my eyes. I snapped to attention.

"Where did you go?" Drew asked in a serious tone.

"Sorry. I was just thinking about something." I shook my head to erase my crazy thoughts, my cheeks still burning.

"Think on your own time." He smirked and rubbed his palms together. "We're here to have some fun."

"What do you mean?"

"Watch." Drew shifted his gaze toward Lily's table.

"You knew they were coming, didn't you?"

Drew shrugged. "I might have heard Nora mention something before history class."

I clenched my jaw. So much for the almost-pleasant Drew.

Nothing seemed out of the ordinary at Lily's table. They were all talking and laughing and just being them. My throat went dry watching, part of me still longing to be sitting there instead of here. Maybe if I was over there, my life would be easier. And maybe if I was sitting at that table right now, Nora wouldn't be touching Bennett's arm and ripping my heart into a million pieces with her perfectly manicured black nails.

Lily jolted forward in her seat and fidgeted with her silver cuff bracelet. She moved it farther up her arm, leaned back, and shifted it down to her wrist again. Then she bolted upright and yanked the bracelet off, chucking it across the tabletop.

The rest of the group turned to stare at her.

Taylor picked up the bracelet, examined it closely, then set it back down and shrugged.

Drew snickered.

"What did you do?" I asked.

"I heated up the metal in the bracelet. Must have hurt like hell." He leaned back in his chair.

"Really?" I raised an eyebrow at him.

"Oh c'mon, it's funny. And I cooled it down before Taylor touched it."

"Sure." I crossed my arms and slouched in my chair. Maybe another day I would've found Drew's idiotic pranks hilarious. Today, they irritated me. A lot of things in this room irritated me right now. Spending energy on Lily wasn't going to change things, wasn't going to set the world right, but if it made Drew feel powerful, he could go ahead. I wasn't interested in participating though.

Drew wobbled his head and mouthed a few mocking sounds, then returned his attention back to the other table. Katie's pencil rolled off her school books, across the table, and onto the floor. She reached over and placed it back on top of the books. Again, the pencil rolled off the table and onto the floor. She picked it up. It rolled again.

I kicked Drew's shin under the table. "This is stupid. Why are we doing this?"

"I thought you didn't want them bothering you anymore. I'm trying to show you how to have a little fun with your powers and not be a victim."

"Well, it's not fun. It's a complete waste of time."

"That's because you're not doing anything. How come you're in such a vile mood all of a sudden?"

"That's it. I'm leaving." I sprang up from my chair. "You can spend your time spinning pencils, but it's not proving anything. They all still hate me."

I turned on my heel and slammed directly into a mane of golden blonde hair and the subtle whiff of exotic flowers.

Lily.

"I'm so sorry," I mumbled.

Lily straightened her sweater and glared at me, then Drew, then back again. "I thought you'd be smart enough to go back to wherever it was you came from, but I guess not." She flipped her bottle-blonde hair over her shoulder and headed toward the basement stairs that led to the bathrooms.

I held my breath and bit my tongue, wishing that for once, I could bleed. Lily's opinion shouldn't matter to me anymore, but it did, and I hated her for that. I hated myself for that.

"And you would prefer to sit back and take that?" Drew nodded after Lily.

He was right—she was never going to stop. Watching her walk away, so self-absorbed, so arrogant, so ... so perfect. I dropped back into my chair as Lily took the first step down.

I couldn't help myself.

Yes! A voice hissed in my ears, slow and menacing, slithering through the hollow ventricles in my brain, trapped inside my skull.

Lily's balance wavered.

I saw the fall before I heard it. Her feet slipped and she tensed. Her arms flailed, clawing at the air. Then she flew forward and tumbled down the entire flight. A hollow smack echoed up the stairwell. She screamed from the bottom of the stairs and the entire restaurant ran toward the doorway to the basement.

It had been delicious to watch her fall, but the awful sound of impact and her scream echoed through me, resting heavy in the pit of my stomach. Drew and I stayed in our seats and watched as Bennett and Max helped Lily up the stairs. She rubbed the back of her head, her face twisted in what looked like pain, but she didn't cry. Spots of blood stained the arm of her white sweater.

"I didn't think you had it in you," Drew whispered with delight.

I pulled at the sleeves of my coat and clutched the cuffs tightly in my fists, refusing to look up. Seeing Lily would make it real. Before now, everything I'd done could be forgiven, but I'd hurt someone this time. Guilt pressed down on my ribs, ripping me apart with each breath. But I wasn't sure what I felt worst about—what I'd done, or that I'd wanted it to happen.

"You did this," Lily snapped as she passed, struggling against Max's grip.

I froze. How did she know?

"You just fell, Lily. Calm down." Bennett stepped in front

of her and held her back from charging our table.

"No. I was pushed, and she pushed me. I know it." Lily jerked her head toward me. Her face paled and she winced.

"Avery was all the way over here. She couldn't have pushed you." Bennett's voice dropped low, soft and reassuring. "I'll drive you home so you can sleep it off, okay?"

Lily leaned her head on Bennett's shoulder. As they started out the door, Bennett glanced back at me with an apologetic half-smile. I nodded and tried to smile back.

The restaurant cleared out, and the regular clatter of dishes and conversation resumed.

"Where did that come from?" Drew asked.

"I'm not sure. Lily made me angry and I wanted her to ... hurt." It sounded more insane when I said it out loud than it did reverberating in my head, but it was the truth. The scary, messed-up truth.

"How did you do it? I mean, I didn't feel any wind come through. Did you make a puddle for her to slip on?"

"I'm not sure. I didn't think about it that much. It just sort of happened."

"Intense." Drew nodded and smiled. "I would've expected your concentration to be more deliberate. Maybe you're a lot stronger than I thought."

I tugged at my sleeves again. "Doubtful. It was probably that emotional response thing you were talking about before."

"I guess. But it looks like we might need to ramp things up a bit."

"What does that mean, exactly?"

He pulled his hands in front of him and drummed his fingertips together like a villain in a superhero movie. "Wouldn't you like to know?"

I shook my head and something dark twisted in my chest. "I think it's time to head back to school."

TWENTY-ONE

"No more hurting people. That was a one-time thing." I pointed at Drew, my voice stern. "And I don't want to hear anything else about Lily either."

He'd been recapping Lily's fall play-by-play, like a scene in the latest horror flick. The sound of her head hitting the tile still stuck in my ears. I'd crossed some imaginary line this time. I knew it, and Drew reveled in it.

"Okay, okay." He raised his hands in surrender. "That wasn't what I had in mind anyway.

I exhaled deeply, and steam puffed around my head. I hoped I'd made my point, but Drew had been acting strange all night, giddy and weird, so who knew if he was even listening.

I turned my back to him and locked my sights on the swing set, willing the metal links to bend and break. Cars speeding along the highway hummed in the distance. It was early, definitely before midnight, and the thought of getting caught nagged at my brain. This rundown, graffiti-tagged playground probably wouldn't attract a crowd, but the change in schedule kept throwing me off.

Or maybe it was Drew's stare burrowing into the back of my head.

A cold wind whistled past, and the old merry-go-round screeched in the breeze. I cringed, then curled my hands into fists and focused harder. One of the links on the right-hand side of the swing snapped and the seat dangled on the remaining chain. I focused on the left side.

Drew stepped closer, his breath moving the hair on the back of my neck.

"What?" I spun around, and Drew jumped back. The swing seat crashed to the ground.

"Nothing." His eyes widened, almost as wide as his delightedly goofy smile. "What's your problem?"

"You're my problem. You've been skipping around here like a leprechaun and you won't tell me what's going on. So spill, or I'm going home." I frowned, crossing my arms.

"Fine. I thought of a fun thing we could do, but I wasn't sure if you'd be interested."

"Try me."

"Nora's house is past those woods over there." Drew pointed to a thick forest that wound up the hillside behind me. "And I figured you might want to have your way with that shiny car of hers."

"Seriously? What makes you think I would want to do that?"

"Because you hate her."

"She's not my favorite person..." Temptation and guilt bounced around my brain, slamming into each other and fighting for supremacy over my thoughts. "But I wouldn't say I hate her. I don't know her well enough to hate her."

"Why not? She hasn't exactly been nice to you. Didn't you say she tried to run you over?"

True. I probably disliked Nora as much as Lily right now.

"But don't you think messing with her car is a little extreme?" Less extreme than knocking someone down the stairs, but I swore I'd never do that again, even though something in my blood sparked at the thought of it. Something strange and powerful.

"Besides, I heard she's with that Ben guy you like."

"No!" I blurted, then clamped my hand over my mouth. I'd

seen them together earlier and tried to convince myself they were just friends. But all that laughing and touching fed the fire in my veins.

"'No' you don't like him, or 'no' you hadn't heard? You're always gawking at him like he's some sort of boy band loser, so I figured you were into him."

"I so don't gawk at him." I scowled. At least I didn't think I did. I'd have to be more careful.

"So you don't care?"

"No. Doesn't matter to me who he goes out with." I turned away from Drew, hoping he wouldn't see my face flaming bright crimson through the dark or the tears starting to well up in my eyes. He didn't need to know that his words had punched me in the stomach. Besides, he was never happy with me when I cried.

"You okay?" He rested a hand on my shoulder.

I shrugged him off. What harm could it do to make Nora feel less than perfect for once? Drew always said I needed to stick up for myself. Maybe he was right. I plastered a phony smile on my lips and spun back around. "What were you thinking?"

Drew didn't want to take the road in case someone saw us, so we had to go through the woods, making the trek much longer than I'd expected. Thick brush scratched at us as we walked, and filtered moonlight cast frightening shadows between the trees. My pulse raced. If a squirrel jumped out, I probably would've run screaming all the way home.

Finally, we reached a winding road. It led to a yard with a brown brick house, much larger than those in town—like a country estate in an old soap opera. Several windows lined the front, all framed with white shutters, and a mammoth triple-car garage jutted out from the side. Ornate light posts illuminated the sweeping arc of pavement connecting the house to the road and reflected off the chrome of the two sports cars parked in the driveway. What was inside the garage if expensive vehicles like those were left out in the cold?

Drew ducked down in the bushes close to the road but far enough away to remain hidden. He tugged my jacket and pulled me to a crouch beside him.

"How do you know when she'll be home?" I whispered.

"Easy. She was at school working on the yearbook, and the school's alarm system goes on at eleven o'clock, so everyone has to be out. Assuming she comes home right away, she should be here any minute." His teeth gleamed in the dark from his wide grin. "Unless she decides to go visit her boyfriend instead."

I cringed. Of course. Drew would plan every detail. He didn't do anything that wasn't calculated, just like his reminder about Nora and Bennett. One more dig to let me know I'd missed my chance with him.

I pushed up on my tiptoes and stared at the pavement. The plan was simple. Ice up the road and create a mini snowstorm to run Nora off into the ditch. It seemed foolproof, considering the steepness of the hill and the windiness of the road. I swallowed hard. It sounded less demented when he told me about it in the playground, but up here I wasn't so sure.

"Wouldn't it be simpler if we just threw a brick through her windshield?" I asked.

"No. If you did that, she'd come after you. The cops could get involved, and we'd get all kinds of unnecessary attention. This way, Nora can only blame herself for wrecking her car and you get to give her a scare in the process. I say win-win."

My stomach knotted, the thought of sitting in my own crashed car still too fresh. "Isn't this a little overdramatic?"

"Just feeding off you. If it was up to me, I would've pushed someone down the stairs weeks ago."

I scowled. "What if something goes wrong? I told you, I'm not hurting anyone again."

"There's no one around for miles. She's just going to skid off the road and smash her bumper. She's got airbags. She'll be fine." He patted me on the back, almost knocking me over.

We finished icing down the street as a set of familiar headlights started up the hill. I breathed deep and coughed on the cold night air.

"Shhh," Drew whispered, pressing his index finger to his lips. "She's coming."

The sleek black hood of her car reflected under the streetlights and a thump of indie rock music pounded through the evening stillness. Unmistakeably Nora.

I clenched my fists and prepared to attack.

Do it. A voice hissed in my ear.

I looked at Drew. His gaze was fixed on the oncoming car. "Be quiet," I barked.

"I never said anything. Quick."

Snow swirled and blew across the road in a thick fog that blocked the car from view. The howling wind blurred with the revving car engine as Nora's car struggled to climb the icy hill. Blinking four-way lights sliced through the white sheet as she inched farther and farther up the road.

"What is she doing?" Drew stood up. "More snow."

I obeyed and the snow blew harder, hiding Nora's lights in the haze. She reached the corner and managed to make the gradual turn without faltering. Her driving skills were actually pretty impressive.

"Screw this," Drew hissed.

A bright spark shot through the snow and an orange light

grew in the middle of my storm. Something wasn't right. I dropped the snowy curtain to find out.

The orange light rose from Nora's trunk. Omigod! Her car was on fire.

"What did you do?" I jumped to my feet and grabbed Drew by the collar.

Nora's engine revved and the car swerved on the ice. It fish-tailed into a spin. My breath hitched as the brakes squealed and the car started to drift off the road. Suddenly, it pitched, and headlights came speeding toward us.

Drew's jaw dropped and he grabbed my arm. "Run!"

The sound of smashing metal ripped through the night. I glanced back over my shoulder. The car's front end was crumpled like paper against a tree trunk. Headlights beamed off into the woods as flames crept up the side of the car with Nora slumped over the steering wheel.

I gasped. She was going to die. Drew's grip tightened around my wrist. I twisted and pulled. "Let me go. I have to help her."

"No. We have to get out of here." Drew turned his head as Nora's house lights flashed on. "Now."

Get out of the car, Nora. Get out of the car.

Drew dragged me back into the woods, struggling against him and staring into the flames.

Just get out of the car.

As if she heard me, Nora shook her head. She slammed her shoulder into the car door, but it wouldn't move.

Heavy footsteps pounded down the driveway behind us as Drew pulled us farther into the trees. I tugged my arm one last time and broke Drew's hold. As I darted back toward the road, the car door opened, and Nora fell into the snow, her screams echoing on the air.

A man burst through the bushes lining the end of Nora's

driveway and ran toward her, scooping her in his arms. A trail of blood fell on the white ground, then followed them away from the car.

"Let's go." Drew yanked my arm again.

We ran deeper into the bushes. I wanted to stop. I wanted to go back and make sure things were okay, but some inner force kept me moving forward. Nora would be okay. She had to be.

Boom!

The ground shook. Behind us, a cloud of smoke and fire erupted into the sky. My knees gave way.

Yes! The voice spoke again, breathy and menacing, as Drew pulled me back to my feet.

"Did you hear that?"

He continued ahead, pushing sharp pointy branches out of his way and trudging through the deep powder. "We don't have time for this."

Blood pounded in my head and my legs dragged as if they were blocks of ice. We wove through the trees, led only by the light of the moon. My lungs ached as I tried not to breathe in the smell of burnt plastic. I wasn't sure where we were going, but Drew seemed to know the way, so I pushed forward, following the backs of his shoes. Eventually, the woods thinned and we arrived back in the playground where we'd started.

Drew bent over, holding his thighs, then glanced back toward the woods. "I think that's far enough."

I collapsed onto my knees, struggling to catch my breath. "Are ... you ... sure?"

"She'll tell them she hit ice. No one will think to come looking."

We were safe. My shoulders relaxed and tears began to flow.

"You've got to be kidding." Drew shook his head and rolled his eyes.

"That wasn't supposed to happen." My sobs grew stronger.

Tears rolled off my chin down into my jacket, freezing against my neck.

"Keep it down." He pulled me to my feet. "Sometimes things don't happen the way you expect. Get over it."

"Get over it? You played me, didn't you?" I hammered my balled fists into his chest. "You planned all of that. Knowing when she would be home. Knowing exactly what you were going to do. You were going to kill her."

"Calm down. I never planned on killing her. The opportunity just presented itself." He shrugged.

"You're sick. You know that?" I staggered toward the tree-line, unable to look at him. "It's bad enough that you ... did what you did, but being so excited about it ... I don't think I will ever get that disgusting sound of my head."

"What are you talking about?"

"That sound. That low hissing sound you make when bad things happen. It's disturbing." I pulled my jacket tighter to my body and choked back the warm spit building up in my mouth.

Drew stepped in front of me, forcing me to stop. "I didn't do that. What did it sound like?

"You said things. Like 'do it,' but raspier than that." I shivered. "Like a hiss."

He smiled. "Have you heard the voice before? Does it always tell you to do things?"

"Thanks. You're not funny."

"What? I wasn't joking. Have you ever heard the voice before?"

"Only today." I wasn't sure where he was going, but he'd better not tell me I was crazy. If he did, I'd punch him right in the face.

"This is wonderful." He clapped his hands, and his lips perked up into an elated smile.

I squinted, still trying to find the joke.

"Really. It is wonderful. The voice is yours, or at least the demon part. You've finally tapped into that part of yourself. I've been trying to get you there since I first told you about your powers."

Demon parts? I had demon parts in me now. What happened to not knowing the source of the powers? All those stupid stories he told me that I fell for, over and over without question. I trusted Drew because he knew things about myself that I didn't. But everything he said was a lie.

Were we even really related?

"So this whole time you were trying to turn me into a demon?" I snapped.

"No, not turn you into a demon, just wake up your demon. It's always been there, just kind of muted. Sort of like walking around in sunglasses—you can see everything, but it isn't until you take them off that you get the full effect of the sun. You're running on full power now. Make sense?"

No. Nothing made sense. He'd hidden too much information from me for that. "Do you hear the voice?"

"All the time."

"This is completely cracked." I threw my arms in the air and turned around, walking farther into the shadows and away from Drew. "And you didn't think it was important to tell me that I will hear demonic voices in my head. Real nice."

"I didn't want to scare you."

"I'm pretty damn scared now."

"Keep your voice down." He rushed over, his hands up and his stare darting into the dark.

"Why now?" I asked. "Why not when all this started? Why am I only hearing the voice now?"

"Not sure. Maybe it has something to do with ambition."

"English, please." I stomped my foot.

"When you're being purposefully bad, the voice shows up."

"Great. Now I'm evil. This is all your fault."

"How is this my fault? You make your own choices. I haven't made you do anything."

"But you put all this stuff in my head. If I'd never met you, I would be in bed right now, worrying about things like getting into college. But no, now I have to worry that we almost killed someone back there."

"She wouldn't have died. You need a much harder impact for that."

I clenched my fists and growled.

"You didn't honestly think you would get all of this power and not have any negative side effects?"

"You're a negative side effect."

"Now, be nice. I understand this stuff is all new to you, but you've got to get a grip. Your soul is the same as mine, and there's some black in there. You're just taking longer to figure that out."

The cold wind brushed over my face. I wanted to say so many things, but nothing would express the depths of disgust I felt. I rubbed a gloved hand across my forehead and down my cheek. I was evil. Born of hell, serial-killer-type evil. And I knew it—the nightmares about Drew, the guilt that lingered in my gut after using magic, questions about the real source of my power. I'd sensed it so many times but never admitted that it could be true. I didn't want it to be true, and Drew had promised me that it wasn't.

Or maybe … I gasped and my knees shook. Maybe I liked it.

Drew reached his hand toward my face, but I jerked away. I wanted to turn and run but my feet wouldn't move.

"None of this matters now anyway. Now that you have activated your full demon powers, you can fulfill your destiny."

"My destiny?" My head swam. Too much information. Too much ridiculous information.

"Yes. I've had a plan for you all along. You don't know how long I have waited for this moment." He clamped his hands on my biceps and stared into my eyes with a devious, crooked smile.

His gaze bore into my skull, but I had trouble focusing on his black eyes. His grip tightened and my arms began to tingle. The sensation spread slowly through my shoulders and into my chest, tightening around my lungs.

"What are you doing?" I choked.

"Be quiet," he snapped.

A strange new feeling tore through my body and burrowed in my veins. An excruciating anguish, like every muscle was being ripped from bone, and my limbs writhed and twisted in torment. I tried to scream, but the sound caught in my throat and it hurt to breathe. My heart pounded in my ears. A sour metallic smell burned my nostrils.

What was happening? What was he doing to me?

Please stop ... please stop. The words were trapped in my mouth, refusing to pass my lips. The pain blitzed again, my mind slipping away. I couldn't take it much longer. My body was dying inside my skin. Finally, my legs buckled. Drew tightly held on, refusing to let me fall.

Stop! Stop! Stop! Then...

"Stop!" Every sensation tore through me again in reverse, draining out and pushing back against Drew's fingers dug deep in my skin.

Drew let out a pained yell, then tossed me to the ground and staggered backward.

The pain subsided, but every inch of my flesh that pressed against the ground still ached.

Drew shook and sputtered as if he'd been punched. "I told you to shut up." He stood over me as I cowered in the snow. "How did you stop me?"

"Wh-what happened?" Fresh tears poured.

"What can I possibly do with you now?" Drew paced, tearing at his hair and refusing to look at me.

"What did I do?"

"Nothing! Absolutely nothing. That's the problem." He kicked the ground, spraying snow all over me, and then sprinted off into the night.

My arms and legs twitched, but I couldn't stand up. It was as if my brain and bones were no longer connected. The freezing wind blew across my skin. I might have shivered, but I wasn't sure. An aftershock of pain hit me and everything went black.

TWENTY-TWO

ONE HUNDRED FORTY-SIX YEARS AGO

The old man cringed as he watched the boy come up the front steps. He considered not answering when the boy knocked, but he knew there was little point. The boy would let himself in anyway. In his younger days, the old man could keep unwanted visitors away with protection spells, but with age, both his body and his magic had weakened. Soon he'd have no power left at all.

He moved from the window and sat down in his chair. As expected, the boy stormed into the sitting room, mud and dirt smudging his dark slacks. A story likely came along with the mud, but the old man didn't care to hear it. No story involving this boy was ever good.

The boy's youthful face looked the same as it always did, dark with a hint of the devil. The old man's guilt had stayed fresh too, but sometimes old mistakes could not be fixed with apologies. Besides, the sight of the rogue only upset his ulcer.

"What can I do for you this time, Nicholas?" the old man calmly asked.

"You know what I want." The boy ran his hands through his hair and began to pace, his agitated gait making the small room feel smaller. Stifling.

"I've told you before. It cannot be done."

"And I told you to find a way. I'm tired of hiding, thinking someone might see me like this." He thumped his chest with his fist and pulled at the collar of his shirt. "Knowing I've never aged a day past seventeen."

"I'm sorry, I—"

"You're sorry?" The boy leaned over and balanced himself on the arms of the old man's chair, inches from his face. "Do you have any idea what it's like to be me? To go from being all-powerful and then reduced to simple parlor tricks by this inferior mortal body. You did this to me, you stupid fool. Now set me free."

The old man shuddered. He didn't like the boy to get so close. It was far too dangerous, and the rancid stink of stale booze lingering on the boy's breath made him gag. He was no longer a match for the boy, and his only option would be to try to diffuse him yet again. He swallowed hard. "I ripped a hole in the universe when I brought you here. That is not easily done, and there are ramifications to that kind of unnatural act."

The boy leaned closer, the fire of hatred burning in his eyes. "I don't care."

"I don't have that kind of power anymore. I would never survive doing that again."

"Then die trying." The boy spat and launched himself away from the chair, sending it into a vigorous rock.

The old man braced himself, rattled and nauseated, until the chair slowed to a moderate pace. He tried to slow his breathing too, but his racing heart made it difficult to keep from gasping. "It wouldn't do any good. I still wouldn't be able to harness that kind of power."

"Don't you have daughters? Three, I believe. Get them to fix your mistakes." The boy resumed pacing, and his brown eyes darkened to almost black. Next would come the rage. It always did when his irises darkened.

"Leave them alone. They are not like us. They don't have any of my powers," the old man lied.

"And why should I believe you?"

"Because every single day, I wish for a way to send you back to whatever realm you came from. Trust me, if there was a way, I would have found it by now." The old man closed his eyes and tried to draw whatever strength he had left. He might be guilty of lying, but he would never risk the lives of his girls, no matter how much he needed to rid the boy of his demon half.

The boy groaned and clenched his fists. The old man leaned back in his chair, expecting the boy to come flying at him again.

"This is not over." The boy stomped out of the sitting room and slammed the front door. The pictures on the wall shook.

The old man sighed. He had survived another visit, but his aging heart could not take many more. He saw the boy turn at the end of the front walk and stare back through the window, forehead lowered and hands clenched in tight fists at his sides.

The old man shivered, thankful for the pane of glass between them.

The boy's lips curled to a smile.

The harsh smell of smoke filled the old man's living room. He pushed himself up from his chair and hurried to the door, but the metal door knob wouldn't turn. Flames erupted all around, licking the walls, ravaging the furniture, coming for him. He collapsed against the door and sank to the ground. No point in fighting. He'd never win. At least in death, he might find peace.

Heat and smoke circled the old man's head as the flames ate through the floor toward him. He closed his eyes and pictured his daughters as the fire razed his little house to the ground.

Twenty-Three

Present Day

When I saw the small slip of paper taped to my locker, my stomach turned, dreading whatever torture awaited me. My mind was sore and shattered from the night before, and I still wasn't sure how long I'd lain passed out in the snow, alone and helpless. Fortunately, sleep erased the physical pain Drew had inflicted on me, save two unmarked spots on my upper arms where his fingers dug into my flesh. Normal people would have massive bruises, but freaks like me just had pain.

When I'd eventually awoken in the park, it had still been night and I'd been alone. Every part of me had ached as I'd struggled home, trying to figure out what had happened and whether Drew had really left me there to die. I felt raw and violated, but I'd survive.

I'd escaped far luckier than Nora did. Mom had updated me on her condition—conscious and stable—likely assuming we were friends. Except we never were.

I stared at the paper on my locker again. Probably another stupid drawing. I ripped it down, but it wasn't a picture at all. It was worse.

Avery,

I am very sorry about last night.
Can we please talk so I can explain?
I will look for you at lunch.

Forgive me,
Drew

My hands trembled as I held the note and examined the hallway. Drew was probably watching me. It was the type of messed-up thing he'd do. My gaze darted from person to person, but he wasn't around.

I slouched against the locker door and reread the note. Waves of nausea pelted my stomach like a tsunami. I couldn't handle seeing Drew today. Part of me wanted to scream and yell and throw things at him, while another more prominent part feared he'd try to hurt me again.

Neither scenario would end well.

I closed my eyes, urging myself not to cry.

Taking a deep breath, I grabbed my books and headed off to class, scanning every face to make sure I didn't bump into Drew. I turned the corner. Bennett stood at the far end of the hall, rooting through his locker. My stomach churned again. Nora. Did he know I'd sent his girlfriend to Emergency? By hurting her, had I hurt him too?

I wanted to apologize, but I couldn't do that without implicating myself. I could, however, ask how she was and offer support. After all, he was the only one who talked to me after Lily cut me out. I took a deep breath and headed toward him.

Wait. What was I doing? What was I going to say? What if he asked questions I wasn't prepared to answer? I turned and diverted to the other side of the hall, moving quickly until I'd passed him.

No. I halted, my brain arguing with my feet. I needed to do this. I needed to make some sort of amends for what I'd done. I really needed someone to listen. I spun around again and headed back toward Bennett's locker.

But too late. Lily was already standing beside him.

I ducked into a storage room doorway right before Bennett's locker bank and slunk back against the wall, worried I'd been seen, or worse, seen hiding. I'd almost killed someone but seeing Lily still reduced me to a scared mouse. If she came around the corner, she'd likely drag me through another round of hell.

Not everyone needed magic to be powerful.

Breathe, it's going to be all right.

I edged closer to the end of the wall. It was tough, but I could still make out their voices.

"You can't tell me you haven't noticed anything unusual going on since she's shown up here," Lily said.

I bit my lip and inched closer.

"Maybe, but it doesn't mean one caused the other. Sometimes weird stuff happens," Bennett replied. "Maybe you have it in for her."

"In for her?" She sounded offended or at least faked it well. "I was nothing but nice to her from the second she showed up. I did everything I could to ignore the rumors, and for a minute, I really thought we could be friends. But you can only disregard so much before you have to see what's been in front of your face the whole time."

"You don't honestly believe all of that witch garbage, do you?"

I winced.

"I didn't think I did, but it's pretty hard to ignore," she said.

"Why? Because the universe isn't giving you everything you want for a change? I don't think your sudden bad luck has anything to do with Avery. Maybe it's karma."

"What about her pushing me down the stairs? Or Nora's accident? Those aren't coincidences."

"Seriously, Lily, she didn't push you. I saw her sitting across the room the whole time. She wasn't even anywhere near you."

"But Nora says she saw something before she hit that tree."

"Nora has a concussion. Besides, it was probably a deer or maybe a fox."

"Look, I didn't believe it at first either, but you've heard all the stories, just like me. There's something odd going on with her family. People always talk about them, then there's nothing for a long time, and suddenly she shows up here and stuff starts happening again. It's not a fluke."

"That Drew guy showed up around the same time too, maybe it has to do with him. Ever think of that?"

"Drew and Avery are always together. If he has anything to do with this, I'm sure she's in on it."

"You're delusional. She doesn't come off as the evil psychopath type to me. She seems like a nice person."

"Nice person? Omigod. Bennett, do not tell me you have a thing for her." Lily's voice dripped with disgust.

"No, I don't." Bennett said, "Well maybe. I don't know. I think I did once, but it doesn't matter now."

I gasped, and the wind sailed out of me in a sharp, suffocating thrust, like holding my head under water. If only...

Lily's voice softened. "Honestly, you should let that one go. Drew doesn't seem to be going anywhere, and I'd hate for someone like her to mess you up."

I scrunched up my face, still drowning. Mess Bennett up? I'd never do that.

"Maybe, but only if you stop being paranoid. She's not out to get you."

"I can't. I just need proof and you'll see I am so right about this."

"I'm not helping you."

"That's fine. I'll figure it out on my own. But please, get her out of your head. You'll be better off."

"Fine. And if you don't find what you are looking for, call off your witch hunt, okay?"

"Deal. But you'll see. I'm going to prove it."

"Sure," he said flatly. "I have to get to class."

A locker slammed.

I darted from hiding, my pulse racing. The bell sounded, but I couldn't go to class. Lily's vendetta. Bennett's confession. Drew's mysterious plans. Their words swirled and plucked my emotions like out-of-tune piano keys, creating noise and chaos in my brain.

I pounded down the stairs toward the cafeteria, then spun around and ran back up. Drew would find me in about five seconds down there. I pulled out my cell phone and hovered my thumb over the screen, waiting for inspiration about who to call, but I couldn't tell anyone what happened, especially Mom. I glanced up. Everyone had gone to class, leaving me exposed in the empty hallway, sunlight streaming in from the windows as if trying to make my presence more obvious.

I needed to get out of here.

A red exit sign beamed at the end of the hall. Perfect. I raced toward it and thrust open the door. Cold air and the rank smell of rotting food from a nearby dumpster slapped my face. So maybe this wasn't the escape I'd hoped for. I'd have to keep moving.

To my right, lines of cars waited in the parking lot. To the left of the school sat a squat brown building with a sign above the doors that read *Public Library*. I'd noticed the building before but never paid much attention to it. But now it seemed like the exact place I needed to be. No one would think to look for me there.

I crept across the lot and opened the large glass door.

Behind the front counter, an elderly woman arranged books in orderly piles. She looked up at me with a scowl. "Shouldn't you be in class?"

"School project," I muttered and tapped my backpack.

"Fine." She thrust her finger toward a *No Cellphones* sign on the wall. "No exceptions."

"Of course." I nodded and shut my phone off, shoving it into the depths of my school bag.

The librarian sighed and resumed her sorting, and I made my way into the stacks. The building was virtually deserted— except for me and the hawk lady at the front. I found the farthest corner of the building and dropped to the floor, casting my bag to the side and putting my head in my hands.

How had things turned so bad so quickly? I had no idea where Drew was or what he'd done to me, and now I had to worry about Lily exposing me too. What if she found out about my powers? What would people think? What would Mom think? I'd hidden so much from everyone that I'd probably implode if everything were laid bare for all to see.

And I had a lot to answer for. Nora. Slumped over her steering wheel, seconds from incinerating along with her car. Lily. Falling down the stairs, and although seemingly fine, she could've cracked her head open. And Bennett. He was the only person around here who didn't seem to care what everyone else thought—a much better person than me—and I'd completely blown my chance with him.

I rubbed my temples and imagined ways to throw Lily off my trail, but every plan I considered would likely make her more suspicious. And for what? Drew had told me what he knew, but after yesterday, it could all be lies. I didn't even know what I had to protect.

As my thoughts tumbled, sunlight beamed through the skylights and chased shadows of the bookshelves across the floor. I had to move too. Maybe, if I knew what everyone else seemed to already know about me and my family, I could figure out what to do. I wiped my face with my sleeve and decided to do some digging of my own. I couldn't rely on anyone else to get me out of this, and I wasn't going down without a fight.

With renewed hope, I marched back to the woman at the front desk. "Excuse me."

She glared up at me over her bifocals. "Can I help you?"

"I was wondering if you happened to have old copies of the newspaper on file."

"Could you be a bit more specific? Which paper are you looking for?"

"The local one?" I said meekly.

"I assume you mean the *Chronicle*." She sighed, likely annoyed with my ignorance of civic institutions.

"How far back did you need?"

"As far back as you have."

Her eyes widened. "What exactly are you looking for?"

"Uh..." I glimpsed the children's section in the corner, decorated like a forest with paper leaves and acorn pillows. "Family tree project. Need to trace my history."

"Well, let's see..." She left her desk and entered the stacks.

I followed her.

"Fortunately for you, all articles are in a database, searchable by keywords. You have to pull the actual paper from the archives in the basement, but at least it'll tell you where to look." She sat down at a computer terminal. Her fingers flitted over the keyboard, clicking icons and entering passwords until she pulled up a generic search engine screen. "Good luck."

I took a seat, and the librarian headed off again leaving me to my work. Where to start?

I looked around to make sure I was alone and typed the word *witch* in the small box under the *Shady Creek Chronicle* banner at the top of the screen. After several seconds, the little spinning circle vanished, and pages of article titles appeared. I scanned the list and noted several movie reviews, a discussion of the 1983 high school production of *The Wizard of Oz*, and other articles that weren't what I wanted. My shoulders sank, but I guessed no newspaper would accuse someone of being a witch in print.

I clicked on the search box again and typed *Belmont*. The results came much faster. Only seven articles were found. Mom's birth announcement, a wedding announcement for my grandparents, and a few other items discussing craft sales and bridge club events. But no birth announcement or reference to me at all. Drew said he found me through my birth records, but maybe he didn't mean through the newspaper. Teenage mothers must be a big scandal around here. Nothing but ordinary, dull lives for the Belmont household.

Leaning back in my chair, I rubbed my hands over my face. Now what? I must have overlooked something. Then it hit me. Grandma's name. When Drew referred to her, he didn't use her married name, Wilomena Belmont. He used her maiden name, Wilomena Edwards. So had Taylor. Why would they do that? I entered *Edwards* into the search box and the computer whirled into action. It churned up several hundred records. The titles were vague, but they were meatier than any of my other searches.

After eliminating the same Belmont wedding announcement and anything else that looked like a dead end, I had jotted down about fifty references. Pleased that my search was improving, I headed down to the basement to pull files.

Fluorescent lights buzzed and cast an institutional glow over the stale, chilly room. The impeccable tidiness of the large space told me it probably wasn't used often. Large cream-colored filing cabinets lined the walls and a banquet-sized table filled the center of the room. A solitary blue upholstered chair sat at its head.

I chucked my bag on the table and started digging. The papers were well organized, but it still took a lot of time to flip through each issue to find a specific article. Much of what I found wasn't very useful. Apparently, a distant uncle once ran for city council, and another won some prize for gardening, but no notorious or suspicious behavior. In fact, most articles were very positive, highlighting how my relatives had saved a young woman from a three-story fall, been on a hunting expedition to take down a bear terrorizing the residents outside of town, or had delivered a lost child home to their parents. If anything, the Edwards had been assets to the community.

The only article that caught my attention came from the mid-1800s. An Edwards's family home was completely destroyed by fire. I paused for a moment and reread the article, but the fire didn't seem to be anything more than an accident, although arson hadn't been ruled out. I set the issue aside.

Hours later, my eyes were dry and tired from reading and the dust kicked up while rummaging through the filing cabinets. Not one thing supported Lily's theory about witches, so unfortunately, I was still as lost as ever.

I flipped through the final paper, another one from the 1800s, and found an article about a fishing accident. I scanned quickly, expecting another hazy recount of days gone by, and stopped in the middle of the page.

Nicholas Andrew Montgomery, 17, was pulled from Lake Manitawaga. Montgomery was presumed drowned, but made a miraculous turnaround and is expected to make a full recovery. Family friend Deagan Edwards visited the youth yesterday and commented, "Nicholas was in very bad condition, but by the grace of God has been returned to us. He is a very lucky young man."

Mayor Montgomery declined to make an official statement.

Residents are cautioned to avoid entering ice surfaces due to early spring thaw...

I stared at the page. It didn't imply anything strange or unusual about the Edwards family or about the Montgomery boy, but it showed there was a link between them. My great-great-great-great grandfather Deagan was there when my other great-great-great-great grandfather supposedly attained his powers. Did Deagan know what really happened, or could he be the witch that brought the Montgomery kid back?

So many new questions.

With a new focus, I collected my reserved articles and headed back upstairs to search for more information. I charged back to the computer terminal to find the articles about the Edwards still listed across the screen. I should have cleared the search results, but it was too late for that now. Frantically, I typed in *Nicholas Andrew Montgomery*, and a list of several news headlines appeared: "Mayor's Son Arrested in Connection with String of Arsons," "Montgomery Survives Drowning Twice," "Teen Suspected in Vandalism Incident over Long

Weekend," and several more with a similar theme. The dates spanned several decades.

Something was definitely wrong with Nicholas Montgomery.

As I scratched down the article references, a throat cleared. I jumped and dragged my pen across my notes.

The librarian stood in front of the desk. "Just a reminder, the library is closing in five minutes. Did you find what you needed?"

"I think so," I replied. "What time is it, anyway?"

"I'll take the papers." She ignored my question and reached to scoop the newspapers from the desk beside me.

"Wait!" I slammed my hand down on the pages. "Can I borrow these?"

She glared at me with her owl-sized bifocal eyes, her lips flattened into a thin line. "These are not to leave the library."

"Oh. Okay. Can I just take some pictures with my phone?" I dug the cell out of my bag and switched it on.

"If you hurry, there is a photocopier in the back corner over there." She pointed over my shoulder.

"Thanks. I'll use that." I smiled sweetly and shut down the search screen. Photocopies would be way easier to read.

"Five minutes." She held five fingers in the air.

I headed to the copier and glanced at my phone. 5:57. A silver half-moon rose over the dark skylights above my head. I'd been here all day and was ridiculously late getting home from school. I checked my call history. Eight from Mom already! She was going to be so mad. I copied the two articles, tucked them safely in my bag, and chucked the original papers on the front counter as I sped past. The librarian shook her head.

I raced out the door and crunched through the snow as fast as my legs would move, avoiding patches of ice. Head down, I charged forward, concentrating on every step. A pair of scuffed high tops stepped into my way. I skidded to a halt, almost falling into the snow bank beside me.

Drew.

"What's the hurry?" he asked.

I steadied myself and struggled to catch my breath. "I'm really late getting home." I slowly backed away from him. Memories from last night flooded back, and my quaking knees threatened to give out. I shivered, but not from the cold. He likely wouldn't try anything in the middle of the street, but my muscles burned remembering the pain he'd caused.

"Late? Late from where?" He raised his eyebrows. "I looked for you all day, but no one saw you anywhere."

He stepped toward me.

I stepped backward again.

Concern flashed across his face. Did he think I'd be happy to see him?

"You don't have to run away from me. I won't hurt you."

"But you did." I gritted my teeth and tried to hold his stare.

He extended his hand and I jerked my arm back.

He retracted. "And I'm sorry about that. I won't let it happen again. I promise." It almost sounded sincere.

"What did you do to me?" I tried to keep my voice level, but it threatened to crack.

"It's kind of hard to explain."

"Try," I growled from a black, broken place inside my chest.

"I will. I promise. But not here. Not now. Just trust that I am very, very sorry." He tried again to reach out to me, but I backed away.

"I can't trust you," I said. Did he think he could apologize and it would all be okay? The desire to hurt him grew stronger than the need to run away.

"Of course, you can trust me. You're all I have. The only

one I can tell about ... things. The only one who will understand. Please, say you'll forgive me."

The wind picked up and swirled between us. Strands of hair whipped at my cheeks, and I swiped them away from my face. Clearly, this wasn't natural, but I didn't know if it was my anger or his regret fueling the weather change.

"I don't know if I can."

"I'll make it up to you," he pleaded. "If you'll let me."

I rolled my eyes and planted my hands on my hips. No more falling for his lies.

"I promise, when I come by later, things will be different. We can do anything you want. You're in control. I swear. I—"

"Actually," I said, "I think we should slow things down a bit."

"What?" Darkness flooded his expression. "But we were finally making progress."

"I really need a break from all this, and people are starting to get suspicious."

He snarled. "What people?"

"Lily for one. She's looking for proof that you and I are behind all the strange things that've been happening."

"What's she going to do? There's no way to link us to anything." The pangs of conscience that seemed to plague him moments ago drifted away into the dusk.

"I'm not sure, but she's really determined. We should lay low until she gets bored and forgets about it." And hopefully, I could keep some distance from Drew until I figured out what to do next.

"No. I have plans and some biscuit is not going to ruin them for me."

What plan was he referring to? It didn't matter. Time to shut him down. "You aren't going to get far if she outs us to the entire town."

"Why don't we make her stop looking?" he asked.

I trembled, tempted to ask what he meant, but afraid to hear the answer. "Or we can lay off and wait," I said with measured calm. "You said you've waited years to meet me. Can't we pretend to be normal for a few weeks?"

"A few weeks?" he barked.

I shrugged, still trembling. "Or whatever. Let's get through this weekend, and we'll talk about it again on Monday. She might cool off after a few days away from school."

Drew's cheeks and forehead reached a new shade of red, and under the ominous flicker of the streetlight, he looked like he might explode.

I tensed. He might come out swinging.

"This is ridiculous," he snarled. "We shouldn't need to bow down to the humans."

The humans? Neither his anger nor his arrogance was persuasive. "We do if we don't want to be found out."

"Pathetic." He marched past me, knocking the bag off my shoulder.

I sighed and realized I'd been holding my breath. I watched him storm away and opened my mouth to call after him, but quickly shut it again. Nothing good would come from another confrontation. Besides, I was really, really late now. At least I might have bought myself a weekend free of him.

I ran the rest of the way home and opened the front door to find Mom standing in the foyer, phone in hand.

"Where have you been?" Her yell was shrill enough to beckon all the dogs in an eight-mile radius.

I closed and locked the door behind me, bracing for her wrath.

"The school called and said you'd been missing all day."

"I was working on a project." I lied for the second time today. "I'm really sorry."

"And you didn't think to call me?" She shook the phone in my face.

"I lost track of time."

"That's no excuse. I expect better from you, Avery Marie. Who knows what could have happened to you?"

"It's only six o'clock."

"Don't get smart with me. I was mere seconds from calling the cops. Now get in that kitchen, eat your dinner, and get to your room. You're grounded all weekend."

"What?" I threw my bag on the floor. "That's totally unfair. It was an accident."

"You'll be more conscientious in the future then, won't you?" She pointed toward the kitchen.

I marched past her like a little girl, refusing to meet her glare.

"I honestly don't know what's gotten into you," Mom said. "I don't even think I can trust you anymore."

I slumped into a chair. There was no point in fighting. She was probably right.

Twenty-Four

Our big old house shrank overnight and turned me into a prisoner. Walls closed in, and there was nowhere far enough away from Mom.

In the light of day, her threat of grounding stuck. I had never, ever, been grounded before, and the punishment was ridiculous. I insisted I desperately needed to go to the library to finish my fictional history project, but Mom argued that she could go and pick up whatever I needed, or even worse, come with me and help. I'd figured once she'd calmed down she'd let me off the hook, but not this time. Maybe she'd been turning in early to read parenting tips in those leather-bound books of hers.

Having lost that battle, I retreated to my room, considering how to get out of the house and back to the library. The Montgomerys must be intertwined with the Edwards, but how? Without those newspapers, I'd never find the truth.

I flipped on my archaic but functional computer and cruised onto the Internet. I typed every keyword I could think of into every search engine I knew, but I could not generate one hit on any history about Shady Creek. Apparently, the world outside the town border forgot it existed. I also searched for what Drew may have done to me two nights ago, but the best I found was information on possession. That didn't sound quite right. In the end, most sites recommended I contact a priest. That likely wouldn't help, but I wrote down a few names and numbers anyway. I turned the computer off and headed back downstairs. Having my mother look over my shoulder was still better than being cooped up and helpless. I found her in the living room, digging through her purse.

"I give up. If you want to babysit me at the library, let's go."

"Watch your attitude, missy," she snapped back, without looking up from her purse. Fortunately, she couldn't see me roll my eyes.

"And we will have to do it later," Mom continued. "I got called into work for a few hours. We'll go when I get back."

"But what about my project?"

"I said we can go when I get back." She pulled her keys from the bottom of her bag and headed toward the front door. "I'll be home by three."

Perfect. A few hours of freedom.

She pointed a rigid finger at me. "And don't even think of putting one toe outside this door."

I fought the snarl curling on my lips. "Why would I? I'm grounded, remember?"

"Exactly." She nodded. "That's why I will be calling you every hour and I have Mrs. Abernathy on alert. She'll tell me if she sees you leave. Have a good afternoon." She slammed the door and was gone.

Abernathy. Why did Mom have to get that nosy old lady involved? Mrs. Abernathy probably already told her something about me sneaking out for Lily's party. Might explain why she was so against me going out. *Grrr!*

So I paced in my room. I peeked out my curtains. The heat of the sun prickled on my skin, inviting me outside. I could sneak out through the window and through the backyard, but if I got caught, Mom would bolt the window shut from the outside. I dropped down to the floor and crossed my legs. Still trapped.

I needed to get ahead of Lily and see what was available for her to use against me. There wasn't much information about my family, but it wasn't hard to find that Drew's family wasn't exactly upstanding. All Lily needed to do was look. And Drew had betrayed me. No surprise. Most of his story checked out, but he'd overlooked some important details. Did he know the Edwardses were connected to our father? A door had opened in my mind that refused to shut until I made some sense of what I'd learned. I had to be overlooking something. A key to this puzzle.

I pulled the photocopied articles out of my schoolbag and laid them on the floor, then added Mom's diary to the group. There had to be something. I kneeled over the papers and started reading. Whiskers came into my room and walked back and forth across my lap, tail whacking me in the face with each pass.

"Get out of here," I barked.

She continued her parade.

I picked her up and tossed her into the hallway, then returned to my spot on the floor. She sat in the open doorway and meowed loudly. I clamped my hands over my ears and tried to concentrate on the words in front of me, but I couldn't focus. Couldn't that cat shut up for ten minutes?

"Whiskers," I shouted. "Be quiet!"

And she stopped.

My chest fell, heavy and sad. Did I just yell at a defenseless animal? I was such a wreck. Maybe I should get her a treat.

Whiskers still stood in the doorway with her mouth wide open, but no sound came out. Strange. Like watching the *Discovery Channel* with the mute button on. She shook her furry head and tried again. Her jaws opened. Silence. She stared at me intently, her back arched and tabby fur standing on end.

I'd done this to her and she knew it.

I reached out to pick her up. Her face scrunched up into what looked like a soundless hiss and she bolted.

What had I done? How could I make Whiskers lose her voice? She wasn't a rock or a bottle of water. She was a living, breathing thing. This didn't make any sense.

I searched through closets and looked under beds but couldn't find her. But even if I could, what would I do? Part of me wished I could talk to Drew, maybe he'd know what happened. Maybe he'd hidden this from me too.

Whiskers's empty pink bowl sat in the corner of the kitchen. My stomach knotted. That was why she'd been so annoying in the first place. Poor hungry kitty. I grabbed the bag of food from the pantry and filled her dish, hoping to at least do one thing right by her today. I rattled the food around, trying to coax her out, but no luck. She must've been terrified.

I looked behind the armchair, behind the television, and even inside the basket of magazines. Dropping to my knees, I peeked under the couch. Nothing but dust bunnies and an object in the far corner. I reached under until my fingertips caught on something cold and hard. I pulled it out. The metal bottom from the unusual ornament that fell off the tree and smashed a few weeks ago. That thing really got some distance. I ran my index finger along the outside. It had been so beautiful.

Ouch. My finger caught the edge of a piece of glass. Of course, only pain. No blood. I sucked on my finger until it felt better.

I took the ornament into the kitchen and chucked it in the garbage. Whiskers's bowl still sat untouched in the corner. I hung my head and pushed my hair away from my face. What had I done? And how was I supposed to explain this when Mom got home? Whiskers's voice just stopped working? Like anyone would believe that. Mom already had me under house arrest. She'd keep me locked up until I graduated if she suspected anything else. However, that might not be a bad thing.

The doorbell rang. I ran back into the living room and pulled back the curtains to see Mrs. Abernathy on the front steps. Dammit. I didn't have time for company, especially nosy company. But if I didn't answer, she'd rat me out to Mom. I took a deep breath and opened the door a few inches, barely enough to talk through.

"Hello, there. How are things going?" Mrs. Abernathy asked.

"Good. I'm doing homework. Thanks."

"Aren't you going to invite me in? I'm freezing my knickers off out here."

I backed up and opened the door wider, trying not to imagine this woman's *knickers*. I hoped she wouldn't stay long.

"I'm sure your mother already told you that she asked me to keep an eye on you today. She told me about your predicament."

I nodded. Great. Was I going to be neighborhood news now? Deviant Belmont girl gets grounded.

"I thought it might be nice if you came over for tea."

"Oh." That was the last thing I wanted to do right now. "That's very kind of you, but Mom told me I'm not allowed to leave the house. Maybe another time?"

She waved her wrinkled hand dismissively. "Don't worry. I've already called her and she thought it was a great idea. Said you were working on a history project. Maybe I can help."

"Then sure." I tried not to look disappointed, although I could feel my shoulders start to hunch.

Whiskers slunk into the foyer. Why couldn't she stay hidden a few more minutes?

"Nice kitty." Abernathy crouched down, rubbing her thumb and fingers together.

Whiskers slithered around me to Mrs. Abernathy, who pet her furry head. Whiskers leaned into her palm. Her mouth opened.

My hands trembled.

Meow.

I exhaled. She was okay. I hadn't ruined her. "Come here, silly." I picked her up and held her to my chest.

Whiskers purred and nuzzled into my sweater. Her voice was back. Had I imagined the whole thing?

"Now get your things, dear," said Mrs. Abernathy. "Time to go."

TWENTY-FIVE

THE SCENT OF CHAMOMILE AND FIREWOOD welcomed me as Mrs. Abernathy pushed open her front door. I'd envisioned a lot of macramé and even more cats, but to my surprise, I saw neither. The décor wasn't modern but it lacked the expected kitschiness. Everything was a beautiful polished wood with deep red and gold accents. Kind of a regal country look. Pictures of smiling children covered the walls and the crackling fireplace made it even cozier. Somewhere I wanted to curl up and dream about a normal life.

She ushered me into the kitchen and I sat at the ornate wooden table.

"How do you like our little town, Avery?" she asked over her shoulder as she filled the teacups from a shiny silver kettle.

"Good, I guess." I neatly crossed my hands on the table.

"You guess? That doesn't sound very encouraging. What's the matter?"

"It's just taking longer to adjust than I thought." A complete understatement.

"These things take time. I'm sure it will get better."

"Thanks." I tugged on the sleeves of my sweater and buried my fists in the fabric.

"I remember your mother at your age. She was such a handful." Mrs. Abernathy took two teacups and placed them on the table. They had chipped gold rims and red roses painted on the sides, so dainty and special-looking. She must really like her tea.

"Really?" I asked. "How come?"

"She and your grandmother were always arguing about one thing or another, plus I don't think she was too pleased about having a grandchild as young as she did."

"Oh."

"Not that she didn't love you," she added quickly. "In fact, you were the most important person in her life. She only wished she'd gotten to know you better."

"Me too. I feel like there's a lot I don't know about her." I spooned a few scoops of sugar into my cup and stirred the hot liquid. The steam warmed my fingertips. "Did you know my father too?"

"Not all that well, I'm afraid. He wasn't welcome around your place much, so I only saw him once or twice. Handsome young man." She smiled and sipped her tea. "You look a lot like him, you know."

I courteously smiled back, but couldn't help feeling thwarted. Clearly my father had lived in this town, but no one really knew him.

The fire popped in the other room. I wasn't sure what to say. I didn't know Mrs. Abernathy, and we'd only really talked when she'd brought over the casserole a few weeks ago. All we had in common to discuss was my grandmother, or maybe why she felt the need to watch me when I left my house. What else had she seen out her window? Maybe she knew more than I thought. Maybe I just needed to ask her the right questions.

"So I have something I've been meaning to ask you." I concentrated on dunking the tea bag in the china cup and avoiding eye contact. "When you said my grandmother was 'unique,' what did you mean by that exactly?"

She smiled. "I'm sure you already have your own ideas on that, otherwise you wouldn't have asked."

Not helping. "I don't really know," I lied. "But people sure like to talk around here."

"It's important to know where you come from. I tried to tell Wil that for years. We can never escape our past. We can only choose how we let it affect our lives going forward."

"So you're saying Wil ... I mean, my grandmother, didn't want me to know about my past?"

"You or your mother for that matter. Doesn't change anything though."

"Doesn't change what?" It sounded as though she was dancing around an important piece of information, but her demeanor remained as smooth as glass.

"Doesn't change who you are. Who you'll become."

I returned to dunking my tea bag as she quietly sipped at the other end of the table. This was going nowhere. She was too vague. I cleared my throat. "I've heard things about her."

"What kind of things, dear?"

I hesitated. I didn't know how to bring this up without sounding ludicrous. She might even toss me out and call my mom, but I'd run out of leads. "Some people say she was ... was..."

"A witch?" Mrs. Abernathy didn't even raise an eyebrow.

"Yeah." I let out a relieved breath. "How did you know what I was going to say?"

"Because she was a witch. I never referred to her that way, but some people are more comfortable using certain titles. Names like that are for people who don't understand. Can't blame them for their ignorance though. It's hard to deal with things that challenge the way you think about the world."

"So she was?" I asked, confused.

"Of course, dear."

Whoa. So it was true. Grandma was a witch. I'd already started to believe the whispers, but to hear someone say it out loud and without malice somehow made it real.

I returned to fidgeting with my unwanted tea. My mind

clouded with new questions. "What did you call her then?"

Mrs. Abernathy chuckled. "Wilomena, of course." She gently placed her cup down, and it tinkled against the painted saucer. "To me, she was always just my friend, but to others, she was a witch and sometimes worse. But if those fools ever needed help, she was the first person they turned to. And never once did she hold their prejudices against them. She was a kind soul, that woman." The lines around her eyes began to crinkle.

I shifted to the edge of my chair and wrapped my toes around the legs. "What kinds of things could she do? Move objects? Start fires?"

"Heavens no! You teenagers watch too many movies. She could only affect living things. The Edwards witches were known as great healers. They didn't cause things to happen, they caused the living conduit to do things. Heal themselves in a sense."

"Oh." That wasn't the answer I expected, but maybe it explained what happened to Whiskers. But what about the elemental stuff? Did this mean I was messed up from both sides of my family?

"Don't sound so disappointed, Avery. Your grandmother was a very powerful woman. Until you were born she did all kinds of amazing things."

"Until I was born? What happened then?"

"That's when she stopped practicing. Something happened that night. She had ferocious headaches for weeks and could barely get out of bed. When she recovered, she vowed to quit magic for good. She'd already driven away both your mother and your grandfather by keeping secrets. After losing everything, she kind of gave up."

I swallowed hard. It all sounded so tragic. I wished Grandma were still here so I could talk to her. "If my grandmother was a healer, why didn't she stop herself from dying?"

"I asked her that myself once, and she said she didn't have the strength anymore. The cancer made her weak. At some point, no one is immune to death, no matter how powerful they are." Her eyes went glassy, but she managed to hold back any tears.

"If she kept her magic a secret, why are you telling me now?"

"Over the years, she realized keeping her history from you and Elizabeth was wrong, but there was never a good time to tell you the truth. You girls visited less and less, and there was always so much tension." She pressed her tremulous hands on the table and rose from her chair. "But she did ask me to give you something when I thought you could handle it."

I followed Mrs. Abernathy into the living room. She took a glossy lacquered box off the fireplace mantle and wiped a thin layer of dust off the top.

"Here." She opened the lid. "She wanted you to have this."

Inside the box was a small gold key. My shoulders sank. Just a key? From her story, I expected some sort of amulet or magic charm. But no.

"This key is for Wilomena's trunk of journals. You should find it in her attic."

"Thanks." I took the key and clenched it in my fist. "What's in them?"

"I'm not sure, but I understand she wrote down everything about her abilities. They should answer any questions you might have." She closed the box and returned it to the mantle. "Now, would you like a cookie?"

"No thanks. I should probably get back to my history project." I stared at my closed hand. "But can I ask one more question?"

She nodded.

"What do you know about the Montgomerys?"

Mrs. Abernathy sharply exhaled. "I haven't heard that name in ages. Sad history, that family."

"Really?" I sat down in a nearby rocking chair and leaned forward.

"Long before my time." Her eyes rolled up toward the ceiling as if she were trying to tap into some lost memory. "A boy about your age nearly drowned out on the lake. Poor child suffered some sort of brain damage. His family was so ashamed they shipped him off to some mental health institution on the east coast. He never came back."

"Did the boy ever get better?"

"I don't really know. Most assumed he died." She tossed a small log on the fire. It snapped from the heat. "Mainly because of the ghost."

"What?" Now there were ghosts here too?

"For decades after the boy left, people claimed they saw him around town."

"Maybe he just came back."

"Maybe. But the story goes that he never looked any older than when he left, even when he should've been in his late nineties."

I shuddered, rocking the chair. "Did you ever see him?"

"I'm not that old, dear. Besides, it's all hogwash anyway. Something to scare the kiddies off the lake."

"Wow. That's weird."

She smiled. "That's Shady Creek."

"Well, thank you for the tea and the gift." I raised my hand with the key and then tucked it in my pocket for later. It was almost three. Mom would be home soon. I put on my coat and boots but hesitated before opening the door. "So you believe in witches, but you don't believe in ghosts?"

She shrugged. "I've seen witches before, but never once have I seen a ghost. You've got to draw a line somewhere."

TWENTY-SIX

I LAY ON MY BED AND RAN MY FINGERTIPS OVER THE tiny teeth of the key. Not only was I part elemental demon, I was also part witch. Or was I only one or the other and confusing the two? Either way, I was a total freak show. Maybe one day my nightmare would come true, and my skin would split open to reveal big yellow claws.

And how come Grandma never told me? I understand her wanting to protect me, but how did she know what I needed protection from? I'd gone my whole life thinking I knew exactly who I was, but I wasn't even close. Had anything in my life even been real until now? Hopefully, the journals would give me some answers—even if I hadn't quite figured out all the questions yet.

I peeked into the hallway. Pots and pans banged in the kitchen. Mom must be making dinner. Silently, I crept into the attic.

I wasn't sure where to begin with all the stuff stashed up there. I ripped through piles of old clothes and blankets and shuffled boxes around, trying to find the trunk. Mrs. Abernathy said it was about four feet tall with navy leather and gold buckles. A large piece like that should stand out.

I picked up an old lamp. Absolutely hideous, no wonder—

"What are you doing up here?"

My heart leaped into my throat and I spun around, almost dropping the lamp. Mom's head poked up through the attic hatch.

"Just looking around." I slid the gold key into my back pocket. "And make some noise next time you're going to sneak up on me. I almost had a heart attack."

"But I wouldn't really be sneaking then, now would I?" Mom continued up the stairs into the attic. "What are you looking for? Maybe I can help."

Dammit. Trapped.

"Well … I … nothing in particular. Really. I need some information on Grandma for my family history project, and I thought going through her old stuff might help. Is this everything she had left?"

"No. Some of her things were donated or went off to storage until I'm ready to deal with them. What do you want to know?" She picked up an old blanket I'd tossed on the floor and folded it over her arm.

"I'm not sure," I said. "What she liked to do. Maybe what she looked like when she was young. I just don't think I really knew her that well when she was alive."

"Yeah." Mom's eyebrows rose. "I get that feeling too sometimes."

I suppressed a laugh. If she knew what Grandma had hidden from her, this would be a very different conversation.

"So why come up here? Why didn't you ask me?" She stared, her eyes narrow but soft, and chucked the blanket on a nearby box.

"I … I…" *Think. Think.* "I knew you were having a hard time, so I didn't want to bother you."

Her face relaxed. "Never be afraid to ask me questions."

"Thanks." I smiled. "So what happened between Grandma and you? Why did you hate her so much?"

She shuddered and crossed her arms, her left hand splayed over her collarbone. "I didn't hate her. Besides, it's complicated."

"You just told me to ask questions, but you still won't answer them. That's fair."

Mom raised a finger and furrowed her brow, clearly intending to yell, then her shoulders slumped. "You're right."

She sat on the edge of a large box and stared blankly at the floor, tucking her hands in the gap between her thighs. She'd never looked so small before. Maybe I should've kept my mouth shut.

She inhaled deeply and then forced all the air out in an exaggerated sigh. "It all started when I was your age. Mom—my mom—never liked your father. No matter what I did, she never gave him a chance. When she found out I was pregnant, she was livid. I expected her to be upset, but it was almost as if she thought I was carrying the Antichrist. She always called you 'it.'"

It. That stung, but Grandma's judgment wasn't far off.

"The night you were born, she rushed me to the hospital and then left to call your father to come. She was gone for hours. When she returned, she told me he wasn't coming. He was never coming." Her eyes filled with tears, but she paused and managed to blink them away.

I sat cross-legged on the floor. "I still don't get it. If my dad left, why were you mad at Grandma?"

"Because she was the reason he left us."

"What?" I blinked several times in disbelief.

"I asked her if she'd done or said anything to him, and she never denied it. She never admitted it either, but she did keep saying, 'maybe it was for the best.' After I was released from the hospital and back on my feet, I took you and left for the city. For years, she begged me to move back here with you, but I couldn't deal with what she'd done. Especially since she could never tell me the truth."

"And how come you never told me?"

"At first, it was too painful, and you were too young to understand. Then as years went on, you never asked about him, so I never bothered."

"Did you ever try to look for him? Did he ever contact you?"

She grimaced, years of prolonged anguish flashing across her face. "I tried to find him. Many times. As soon as I was out of the hospital, I marched right over to his house. I even brought you with me, thinking if he saw his baby girl, whatever my mother had told him or paid him or whatever wouldn't matter. When I got to the door, a woman answered and said he didn't live there. It was like he had completely vanished. I kept looking for a few years after that, but with raising you and working all the time, it got to be too much. He was gone, but I needed to be there for you."

"Oh." I stood up and gave her a hug. Her arms shook as she pulled me tighter.

"What was he like, my dad?" I mumbled into her shoulder. "Can I see a picture of him?"

"I think I might have one somewhere. There weren't many. Besides, I never needed any pictures. Every day I look at you, and I see him. You have his eyes and his dark shiny hair, and his smile. That wicked little smile. You would have liked him." She let me go and swept a stray hair over my ear. Her eyes sparkled and a subtle curl of a smile graced her lips. After all this time, she still loved him. "I'll see if I can find something."

"Did you ever forgive Grandma?" I asked.

"Yes. Right before she died. She never admitted exactly what she'd done, but she said that anything she did was to protect me and that she loved both of us very much." Mom's tears started to flow as she took my hands in hers. "Don't worry about it though. You're a great kid without him. He may be your father, but he didn't make you the fabulous person that you are. You decide who you are, not anyone else, okay? It's his loss, not yours."

The tears poured down her cheeks and she took off down the ladder. I considered searching for the trunk again, but I really didn't feel like it anymore. Besides, it didn't look like the trunk was up here anyway. My ribs pulled tight around my lungs. I hated seeing Mom cry. I knew things were bad, but I didn't know how betrayed she still felt. Maybe scars can sting as bad as the cut sometimes.

I paused outside my bedroom door, listening to Mom weeping down the hall. I wanted to fix it, but I knew I couldn't. No amount of hugging would wash all that pain away. Hopefully, she wasn't mad I'd brought all this up.

Sighing, I tucked the key into a pencil cup on my desk. I'd look for the trunk again another time. After all, it couldn't have just disappeared.

I moved my desk chair to face the window and sat there motionless, staring into the sky. Dark, heavy clouds blocked out the last few rays of sunlight. It looked like it might even snow. Maybe the weather was just reacting to my lousy mood. Or Drew's, wherever he was.

Staring out into the gray, I slid the small gold heart around my neck back and forth along its chain. My family history kept getting weirder and weirder. Beyond all the insane supernatural stuff, there was this whole mess of other lies. It seemed no one in this family could manage to tell the truth—even me. Was there anything else I didn't know or had I finally reached the bottom of the deceit bucket?

Mom's story made two important things very clear—she had no idea my dad was part demon, and Grandma knew the whole time.

A soft knock on the door pulled me out of my thoughts. I tucked the necklace back into my shirt. "Come in."

Mom opened the door slowly. Her face was puffy and her eyes had faded, dull and distant. "It's not great, but I have this." She held out a small colored piece of paper, folded down the center.

It was a picture of a girl, no older than me, smiling at the camera. Her wavy, red-brown hair extended past the frame of the photo and I instantly recognized her soft gray eyes, even without the lines and the deep crease in her brow.

"This was you?" I asked, my gaze flitting from the photo to the real thing and back again.

"Uh-huh." Her breath hitched, still choked from crying, then she unfolded the other half of the photo. "And this is your father."

Devilish expresso eyes stared up at me from the photograph. I gasped. The same unruly hair, the same grin, the dimple—this guy looked exactly like Drew.

"Handsome, wasn't he?" She tried to lighten the mood, but the sorrow in her voice betrayed her.

I pulled her into a hug and squeezed her tight. I handed back the photo, but she waved me off.

"No, you keep it." Her eyes welled again. She kissed me on the forehead and slipped away, closing the door behind her.

I stared at the photo again. I couldn't deny that Drew and I and the man in the photo were family. We both looked so much like him, Drew most of all. Maybe it was a good thing he'd never met Mom. That probably would've given her a nervous breakdown.

I propped the picture against my nightstand lamp and pulled out the diary from underneath my mattress.

August 4

It's coming, I can feel it. I don't know why, but somewhere inside me I know this baby is coming soon. I don't know if I can do this. I'm scared I'll screw her up. I'm scared nothing will ever be okay again. I'm scared the baby won't want me. I'm scared of leaving too. I'm scared we won't make it and we'll end up coming back here as those dumb kids who thought they could raise a baby on their own and failed. Everything is happening so fast. Too fast.

I'm really scared.

TWENTY-SEVEN

Nora was back. She sat in her regular seat at her regular table in chemistry class, chirping to Lily as if she'd never been away. A warm sense of calm prickled my skin. At least this week was starting out all right. Nora was alive and well and back at school. No reason to feel guilty anymore. At least not as guilty.

I hurried past them, catching the scowl on Nora's face. It looked like she wasn't as relieved to see me as I was to see her.

My lab partner—Chris or Scott or something one syllable like that—already sat perched on his stool, book open and pencil sharp. No surprise. He was the kind of guy who'd win a Nobel Prize one day or at the very least get his head dunked in a toilet by every frat house at whatever Ivy League school he went to. And no wonder he was the only partner-less student when I arrived mid-semester. However, on the plus side, he didn't talk much.

"Hi," I said as I sat down and pulled out my books.

He raised his eyebrows then looked away, his usual antisocial version of "hello."

The bell rang and Mr. Jefferson closed the door. He began his lecture—something about titrations—but his words breezed past my ears and floated away. Instead, all the pieces of information I'd collected about my family swirled around my brain, smashing into each other, but none of them would fit together properly.

I glanced at my lab partner. His keener stare hung on Mr.

Jefferson's every word and completely ignored me. Good. I flipped to a clean page in my notebook.

What I know for sure:

1. *Drew and I are definitely related.*
2. *Our father is some sort of demon and Grandma knew it.*
3. *Grandma was a witch.*
4. *Mom is oblivious to points 1 through 3.*

I shook my head. My life was an enormity of screw-upped-ness, like some sort of monster-themed soap opera. But what did it all mean?

The weight of a stare fell on my shoulders, and I flinched. I covered my notebook with my arm and looked up to see my lab partner glaring at me.

"Are you planning on helping, or are you just going to sit there?"

Everyone else had scattered around the room, collecting their equipment for the experiment.

"Uh ... sorry." I flipped through my textbook to find the directions.

He rolled his eyes and slid his open textbook toward me.

"Thanks." My face warmed. At least I didn't feel terrible about not bothering to remember his name anymore.

He grabbed a beaker and thrust it at me. "Why don't you go fill this with water? Think you can handle that?"

I opened my mouth to argue but quickly shut it again. The only way I'd catch up now would be if he told me what to do. Smiling my best fake smile, I took the beaker.

I stood in line at the sink, thankful for a few more minutes to get my brain focused on school again. School seemed pointless compared to my escalating family drama, but I had to go to avoid calling attention to myself. Maybe I could get away with skipping next period.

An elbow slammed hard into my arm. I jumped and the beaker slipped. I snapped my hand out, barely catching the lip of the glass. Whew.

"Why are you always in my way?" Lily's mouth stretched into a snarl and she shoved me again.

I gripped the beaker tighter but refused to move.

Flipping her hair, Lily mumbled under her breath and marched back to her workstation.

Yep. Definitely skipping next class.

I filled the beaker and carefully walked back to my table, holding it in both hands, my elbows tucked close to my sides in case someone else wanted to knock me around. As I set the beaker on the tabletop, an ominous shadow darkened the classroom door sidelight. I looked closer. Drew stood in the hallway, waving at me.

I looked away, pretending I hadn't seen him. I needed to get my head straight before dealing with his kind of crazy. Maybe if I ignored him, he'd go away.

"Are you ready yet?" my lab partner asked with his you-are-a-waste-of-skin attitude.

I nodded as he turned on the gas and lit the Bunsen burner. I listened to his instructions, welcoming the excuse to avoid eye contact with Drew. It bothered me that he was lurking out there watching me and bothered me even more that I cared.

I wrote down measurements as my partner performed the experiment by himself, adamant not to let me touch anything important. Probably for the best. Liquid bubbled in the elaborate setup of test tubes and beakers and irritating thoughts of Drew bubbled in my brain, distracting me.

"Mr. Jefferson! Help!"

Ahead of me, Lily flapped around like a well-dressed bird, her Bunsen burner flaming halfway to the ceiling.

"Mr. Jefferson!" Lily shrieked again.

Nora shut off the gas but the flame kept burning bright. She tossed her hands in the air, palms open to the roof, and shook her head.

Mr. Jefferson ran over and a crowd gathered as Lily ripped the gas line from the valve, but the flame shot a few inches higher.

How was there a fire with no fuel?

I glanced out the sidelight. Drew stood laughing through his demented smile—all guilt, no shame. *Of course.* I raced toward the classroom door. A soft crackling noise clicked behind me and I skidded to a stop, finally realizing the end game.

I spun around and gasped. Flames engulfed the beaker and crept higher.

I focused on the glass. *Stay still.*

Too late. With a crack, the beaker shattered, blasting pieces of hot glass through the air like missiles. Everyone jumped back. Lily screamed, clutching the side of her face. I focused on the boiling liquid, forcing it to stay in place. It obeyed and I released my mental hold, letting it rain down softly onto the workstation.

I closed my eyes and sighed.

A blast of heat pricked my face. My eyes snapped open as the entire workstation exploded in flames. Lily screamed again. The sleeve of her cardigan flared and flames ate the fabric. Nora ripped the sweater off Lily's shoulders as blood ran off Lily's hand, creating dark red splotches on the white linoleum floor. Nora stomped on the sweater.

"Everyone clear out," Mr. Jefferson ordered. He aimed a fire extinguisher at the remaining blaze. A cloud of white foam erupted and people scrambled toward the door.

Nora led Lily out of the room, wailing. Blood oozed from her wound through her tightly clamped fingers.

I joined the crowd. My nails bit into the skin of my palms— not like it mattered, they couldn't bleed. But I wished Drew could. I'd love to see him hurt right now.

As soon as I cleared the classroom doorway, Drew grabbed me and tried to pull me away from the other students.

I yanked away from his grip. "Leave me alone."

"C'mon," he whispered. "Don't make a scene. Just come over here so we can talk."

"No."

"I will pick you up and drag you off if you'd prefer," he said calmly and headed off down the hall.

I followed with rage bubbling through me and my teeth so tightly clenched that they threatened to shatter. If he touched me again, I'd probably throw up.

We turned a corner and I flailed my arms toward the chemistry lab. "I thought I told you to lay off. What the hell was that in there?" I yelled.

"Keep your voice down." Drew waved his open hands at me, head jerking around, surveying the empty hall. "I told you I didn't think that 'laying off' was a good idea. I did what I thought was best."

"What you thought was best? That's the problem, Drew, you don't think. This is my life you're messing with, not yours. And in this case, it might've been someone else's life you ruined. Lily might be really hurt."

"Accidents happen. How is it my fault some airhead can't follow simple directions?" He shrugged as if he really believed the nonsense he was spewing. "Besides, worst case is disfigurement. It isn't like she would've died or anything."

I covered my eyes with my hand. "Do you seriously not have any remorse for the things you do?"

"Why? Remorse is for those who feel regret. I don't regret the things I do."

"You don't regret anything you've done to me? You don't regret hurting me and then leaving me passed out in the middle of a field?"

"It was a necessary evil." His cheeks tinged pink and his typical stare down didn't have the same wicked menace. "Besides, I should ask you the same question. You were the one who almost killed Nora, you were the one who lied to Lily in the first place and made her hate you, and you are the one who has alienated yourself from everyone who has ever been remotely nice to you here. I'm sick of listening to you whine about how much you're suffering. You brought all this on yourself and then dare to lecture me. Hypocrite."

"Do you know how much pain you put me in? I could barely move my feet to walk home. Like my entire body was ripped into pieces. Like I might die. What did you do to me?"

"It's difficult to explain," he said calmly. "It won't happen again. Forget about it already."

"Just forget about it? I will not forget about it." I vibrated with anger. "I expect you to give me an answer, and I want it now."

I could kill him.

I wiped my sleeve across my face to catch the tears rolling down my cheeks. Didn't he know the reason I had to lie was because of him? Since he'd come into my life, I'd become a different person and not one I was proud of.

"You're weak," Drew spoke softly and grabbed my hand. "You're not a good person, Avery, but you won't let yourself accept it. Don't fight who you are."

I jerked my hand away. "Who I am? You don't have a clue about who I am."

"I know a whole lot more than you think. Probably more than you know yourself."

"I doubt that." I crossed my arms and stepped back against a locker, letting my head bang against the metal. "Leave me alone."

"I know you have a power deep inside that you can't even fathom, and I can help you reach it. You just need to stop being so bloody scared. Besides, I can't leave you alone. I still haven't taught you all you need to know. We haven't covered fire yet."

"I don't care. I can figure it out myself."

"So you're a master now?" He laughed and bared his teeth. "A few weeks ago you didn't even know about your powers, but now you think you're a pro?"

"I'll manage just fine."

"Doubtful. Besides, you saw how dangerous things can get when fire gets out of control. You need me."

"I don't trust you."

He rubbed his hands over his face and let out a deep sigh. "How about this—I'll teach you fire and complete your training, then you can decide what you want to do. I'll be on my best behavior. Promise."

Tempting. Very tempting. There was still so much I didn't know. But it was too much right now. He was too much right now. The revelation shot through my brain and out my mouth. "I'm done," I whispered.

He glanced up and down the hall, as though I might be speaking to anyone else, then stepped toward me. "What did you say?"

"I said I'm done. I've had enough."

"You can't be done, Avery. It's not like you can switch your power off." His face scrunched up in confusion, or maybe disgust.

"I know that, but I think what I'm saying is that I'm done with you. I can't deal with you. Stay away from me."

He stood there with a completely incomprehensible, twisted expression. Not moving. Not speaking. His lack of fight unsettling.

I held my breath.

He tilted his head and stared at me, eyes wide. "Is that really how you feel? You don't want me around?"

I nodded.

"But you're the only real family I have."

"Maybe one day we could try again." My throat tightened. Pain gathered in my chest as the gravity of what I was leaving behind pressed down on me. I didn't want to lose my brother, but I was making the right decision. I couldn't let myself be like him. "But right now, I need you to leave me alone."

"No. No." His voice wavered and he shook his head. He reached for my arm, but I jerked away.

"Don't touch me."

"I won't hurt you, I promise, I—" Drew scowled and shifted his gaze over my shoulder, his hard exterior slipping back into place. "What are you looking at?" he barked.

I turned. Bennett stood at the end of the hallway. His stare darted from me to Drew and back again. "Are you okay, Avery?"

"I'm fine." I rubbed my face with my sleeve and plastered on a smile.

Drew tapped his foot and glared at Bennett. "Do you mind? Private conversation here."

"Are you sure you're okay?" Bennett stepped closer.

I wanted to tell him. I wanted to run over and let Bennett take me away, anywhere but here. Somewhere we could hole up and scream and cry and throw things until all this insanity fell away. "Yeah. I'm sure. Everything's fine."

Bennett lingered for a moment, still scanning me over.

I forced another smile. "Really, it's okay. We're done here anyway."

He shrugged, walked past us, and rounded the corner.

I watched him walk away and took a deep breath. "I'm serious, Drew." I spun around, a new surge of courage washing over me.

But Drew was gone.

TWENTY-EIGHT

A CHILL SEEPED INTO MY BONES AND RIPPLED DOWN my back. The day was warmer than usual, and the hot sun melted enough snow to give the world a damp sticky feeling. Kind of like spring, but not quite. I loved feeling the heat on my face, finally, even if the humidity gave me the shivers.

The pathways between stone crosses and markers were well packed and easy to walk on. Even though I rarely saw anyone here, the fresh flowers and even fresher footsteps in the snow proved it was well visited. I snickered at some old joke about people "just dying to get in." It was odd the things you remember when you really shouldn't.

It didn't take long to find the right spot. Even with a few layers of snow, the upturned ground helped me to pick out Grandma's somewhat recent grave. The headstone wouldn't be in place until next April—something about concrete and frozen ground not mixing well—so until then, she'd be unmarked and unknown.

Someone had visited recently. A bouquet of half-dead roses stood straight out of the snow as if they'd been planted there. A few petals had fallen, shriveled purplish blobs on crisp white snow. They looked sad.

I took a breath and focused. The heads of the roses straightened and brightened to a rich blood red. Much better. I couldn't do anything for the fallen petals, though. Sometimes dead things had to stay dead.

I spread a thick blanket on the snow, sat down, and looked

around. No one else here. Perfect. Not that it mattered if anyone saw me, considering I still hadn't figured out why I'd come anyway. I'd felt drawn here, compelled maybe, the urge growing stronger every day. Or maybe I was just lonely.

Days had passed in a blur. I still couldn't find Grandma's journals, but I'd spent some time doing research, time I probably should have used to study, but I couldn't concentrate on textbooks anyway. The Internet had loads of information about witchcraft, except I couldn't tell what was real and what was somebody's sick joke. What kind of witch was I, anyway? Other than my tie to living things, I wasn't sure.

Drew disappeared after trying to maim Lily in chemistry. He wasn't in class and no one seemed to miss him. Or at least I didn't. Sometimes, in the school parking lot or in a crowd of people on my way home, I'd think I saw his face. Sharp pain would slice through my chest, but as soon as I looked again, he'd vanished like a ghost, if he was ever there at all. Drew wouldn't stay away forever, but hopefully, on the day he resurfaced, I'd be strong enough to face him.

I crossed my legs and breathed deeply. Even though I'd been sleeping normal hours again, my nerves surged with restlessness most of the time. I glanced around. Still alone.

"So ... how's it going?" I asked the pile of snow-covered dirt in front of me.

Nothing. Only a light breeze whistling through the memorials.

"I didn't really have anyone to talk to, so I thought if you couldn't be here you might want to listen. Lots has happened since you've been gone. Turns out I'm part demon. Did you know that?" Heat rose up my neck, but the words kept flowing. "I think you probably did. One of the many secrets you kept from me, it turns out."

I pushed to my feet and started pacing in front of the grave.

"And the whole witch thing too. Why didn't you tell me? I'm a lot tougher than I look. Really, I am. You'd be amazed at the things I can do now. I can control the elements. Start fires, tornadoes, move bricks and stuff. That's been pretty cool. I can make plants grow. Make people laugh, make them cry. It's spectacular."

I rubbed my hands over my face and grabbed onto the back of my neck. My skin felt hot through my mitts.

"And it sucks. You know that. It really sucks. I can't tell anyone. It's like I'm trapped in this damn town, its secrets choking me in my sleep. I can make people do whatever I want, except I can't make them talk to me. Can't make them get past all their stupid drama to give me a chance. And Drew. I have a brother. Did you know that too? He's a complete train wreck, just like me. He's an elemental too."

My legs sped up. Shorter strides, harder steps.

"I think these powers might be poison. They sink into our brains and make us crazy. All of us. Me, Drew, you, my dad—whoever he is. I feel it under my skin, etching me. I don't want to be crazy, but I don't know how to stop it. Maybe I could have stopped it. Maybe if I knew."

I spun toward the grave again and screamed, "Why didn't you tell me?"

A dense cloud of breath formed as I gasped for air, and my last words disappeared into the empty sky. A crow flew off a nearby treetop.

I swallowed and shook my finger at the ground. "But you know what? I'm not going to let it ruin my life anymore. You'll see. I'll show you all."

Drained from vomiting my thoughts in a string of words and haggard breaths, I sat back down on the blanket and pulled my knees to my chest. Had it made things better or worse? I rested my temple on my kneecap and sighed. Maybe it was too late. I was already crazy.

"Mom misses you," I whispered into the stillness. "She's stopped crying, but she still holes herself up in her room every night. She hasn't been the same since we got here, since you ... we don't talk much anymore."

Big fluffy snowflakes drifted silently through the air. They melted against my flaming cheek and rolled down across my face, dripping into my lap. I watched them fall for a few minutes, inhaling the faint smell of wet earth still hanging on the cold bite of winter. Beyond the cemetery fence, the sun had already started to slip into evening. It'd be dark soon.

I wiped my face and rose on unsteady legs. Time to go home. I shook out the blanket and folded it over my arm. Facing the grave again, I closed my eyes, my cold wet lashes matting together.

"I'm sorry. I wish you were here."

Twenty-Nine

I finally did it. This morning a bird flew into our living room window. It hopped around the front yard with a broken wing, falling every few steps. Its chirp was so sad, almost like a cry. The poor thing looked so small. So weak. I picked it up and wrapped my fingers around its body. The sleek soft feathers brushed against my skin, and the bird's hyper-fast heartbeat thumped against my palm. And in my mind, I could see it pumping, hard and strong, my own pulse picking up to match its pace. A single staccato rhythm. A link. A connection. I closed my hands tighter. One quick move and it'd be dead. A squawk and then it fluttered. I opened my hands and the bird spread its wings and flew away.

I actually healed it.

IN THE COMFORTING DEPTHS OF THE SCHOOL cafeteria, I scribbled the details of my latest achievement in a small coil-bound notebook. It seemed a rite of passage for the

Belmont women to record their lives in journals, and I finally understood the appeal. It grabbed all the thoughts whizzing inside my head and pinned them down.

Healing was Grandma's trademark and until today, I'd never managed to pull it off. At least not on something made of flesh and blood. Maybe my powers could be positive after all.

The cafeteria door banged closed and I jumped, slamming the journal shut and sliding it into my binder. I glanced up. Bennett lingered in the doorway, his gaze darting around the room until it finally rested on me. He smiled his light, lazy smile, and goosebumps rippled down my arms. If only things were better and I could smile back at him that way.

I hadn't seen him since I said goodbye to Drew in the hallway, and we hadn't really talked since he returned my coat. That whole conversation seemed lifetimes away now.

"Hey," I said as he sat across the table from me. "Looking for someone?"

"Yeah." His eyebrow arched. "You."

My leg vibrated under the table and I grabbed my thigh to make it stop. Lily must've found out something—or she sent him to investigate me. Either way, his visit meant trouble.

"I wanted to know if you're okay." He stared at his hands, folded on the table. "I mean, is everything all right?

After the last few nightmarish weeks, I wasn't sure I was exactly human anymore—but I couldn't tell him that. "I guess so. Why wouldn't I be?"

He quickly glanced up, then looked back down again, clearing his throat.

I leaned forward. "Are you all right, Bennett?"

"I want to tell you something, but I'm not sure if I should." His voice dropped to a whisper. "It's about your boyfriend."

"My boyfriend?" I choked. It was the first time I'd heard

someone say the B word—and from the last set of lips I wanted to hear it from.

"Yeah. I'm kind of worried about you and Drew." He glanced around as though someone in this empty room might hear him, or care if they did.

"I don't—"

"That day I saw you two fighting in the hall, it looked really intense, like he might try to hurt you or something."

"It's not—"

"I mean, when he's around, he seems like he's always telling you what to do, and I've heard bad things about him. If that's what you're into, then fine, but I think you deserve to be treated better, and I don't want you to ... well ... change for him." His shoulders dropped, relaxing as he caught his breath. Then he stared. Straight at me.

Locking eyes with his, especially all wide and intense and the deepest evergreen, scrambled my brain. And this time, no one was around to interrupt. I tilted my gaze down. Watching his chest rise and fall beneath his thin gray t-shirt didn't help. My heart pounded against my ribs, a drumbeat so loud that if Bennett couldn't hear it, he was likely the only one for miles.

He might still like me.

I inhaled through my nose and held my breath. Anything to keep my voice level. "Drew isn't my boyfriend."

"No?" Bennett leaned back. "But I thought both of you ... and Lily said ... and..."

"Nope, not my boyfriend. Trust me, there's no chance of that happening."

"Sorry." He pushed himself away from the table and slowly edged backward toward the door. "I should've stayed out of it."

I scooped up my books and followed. "It's not a big deal. Besides, it's kind of nice that you were looking out for me."

He stopped.

"If you haven't noticed, people around here don't really like me. They think they know me but most of them don't. If you ever want to know anything, just ask. I'll tell you." I bit down on my cheek. I'd basically just admitted I was a social outcast. Could I be any more pathetic? But he wasn't leaving. Shouldn't he be running away by now?

"I do have one question." He stepped closer.

I gulped. I should've kept my mouth shut. I didn't want to end up lying to him too.

"Want to go to the winter fair with me tonight?"

"Of course," I blurted. Then my stomach clenched. "Who else is coming?"

His brow furrowed. "No one."

I didn't want to ask, but I already had a boyfriend-stealer reputation. I couldn't take another blow. "What about Nora?"

Confusion swept across Bennett's face.

"Never mind. I heard you two—"

"Definitely not. Who told you that?"

"No one really. Forget I said anything."

"Sure. I guess we're even." He grinned. "To tell you the truth, she kind of drives me nuts."

I giggled, fighting the urge to agree with him out loud. Who knew when my words might come back to bite me?

"So you'll come? Even if it's just me?"

I nodded.

"Good." He smiled and backed toward the door. "It's a great way to start winter break. I'll see you at seven."

"Wait a second," I called after him. "Did you plan on asking me this whole time?"

He shrugged. "Maybe."

"But when you came down here, you thought I was with Drew."

His cheeks pulsed a telltale red. "I told you, I don't think he's the right guy for you."

"And you are?"

"I guess we'll find out." He laughed and disappeared through the door.

The latch barely clicked closed when a heavy, icky feeling crept up from behind. Things were about to get bad. I should've known. Any time I had a chance to talk to Bennett, the universe knocked me back down—this time all the way to hell.

My hands balled into fists. "What do you want?"

"Wow, someone's a little tense."

I sighed and turned around. Drew stood right where I'd envisioned him, flashing me a smug smile.

"I came by to see if you're done needing your space and all that."

"For some reason, I don't think you're all that worried about me," I said. "So tell me what you want and go away."

His jaw dropped in an overly dramatic sort of way and he slapped his hand to his chest. "Sis, I'm hurt and appalled that you would think so little of your family."

"We may share blood, but you're not my family," I hissed. "Family doesn't try to kill each other."

"Whatever you want to believe." He launched himself onto a nearby table, his black high tops dangling inches from the floor. "Anyway, I'm here to get you back on track. I'm sure you've been struggling without me."

"Actually, I'm just fine. I think I might even be better than when I met you."

"So that's why you're hiding down here in the dungeon? Yeah, I can totally see your improved quality of life."

"You're a psychopath." I headed for the door.

"You know what you need? Some heavy-duty practice. Wipe off those cobwebs."

"Don't worry about me." I kept walking. "I've been getting plenty of practice."

Drew jumped down from the table and followed me. "Oh c'mon. I'll teach you whatever you want to know, and I'll even try to be nice. It'll be fun. Besides, you wouldn't want to have an accident and hurt someone, would you?" He tilted his head and smirked as if he knew he was pulling my strings.

"Just go away. Besides, I have plans that don't involve you."

He raised an eyebrow. "Plans? But I'm the only one who'll even talk to you."

"Thanks. But I have a date." I scowled and pulled my books to my chest. "Why can't you let me be normal?"

"Because you aren't normal. Can't you see that? Why waste your time drooling over one of these losers when you can embrace your destiny?"

"First off, Bennett is not a loser."

"Bennett?" He scowled. "Man, you have lousy taste. There's no way I'm going to let you go out with him."

"That is so not your call."

"We are better than these people. You are better than these people. Think of what you can do that they can't." He brushed the back of his hand against my cheek.

My stomach churned and I snapped my head away. Whatever little game he intended to play, it was time to shut him up. Anger coursed through my veins and my fists clenched.

Shut up, shut up.

I focused every last ounce of energy on Drew and snapped my eyes closed.

All noise fell away and a smile burst onto my face. I snapped my eyes open to enjoy the fallout.

Drew glared at me in sheer terror, his left hand clutched at his throat.

"So how do you like that? That's something new I've been working on." I marched back and forth in front of him, head held high. He needed to see he couldn't control me anymore. "One little thing I forgot to mention. Remember that rumor about my grandmother? Well, it's true. It's all true. Not only am I half ... whatever it is you are ... I'm also half witch. Now, unless you want to see me do some things you'd wish you hadn't, you better listen up. I don't care what your so-called 'destiny' is for me. I will do what I want and without your permission, and you are not going to say or do anything about it. Are we clear?"

Drew's mouth flapped open and closed, soundless like a ventriloquist dummy with no master. Finally, he lowered his eyes and nodded.

"Stay away from me, or I will unleash my new powers on you. I don't want to see you, hear from you, or find out that you've been hanging around anyone I know. You're twisted and messed up, and I don't want you here. Go back to your boarding school and get out of my life."

I spun around to leave, but he lunged forward and pressed his fingers hard into my flesh. I wriggled out of his grip and focused on his feet.

"Stay," I commanded while backing away.

Drew tried to follow, but his feet stuck to the floor. Wide-eyed terror returned to his face. He tugged on his legs, unable to move them.

"Don't worry. I'm sure it'll fade in time." Just like Whiskers's muteness.

He let out a muffled scream, his voice still fixed deep in his throat, as I pushed through the double doors and headed up the stairway.

Sunlight poured in through the main floor windows, and

the hallway glowed warm and golden. With a deep breath, I emerged from the basement and slipped into the stream of students in the hall, disappearing into the comforting dullness of normal life. And I was okay. I didn't feel the need to run or hide. Maybe things were finally starting to get better. Or maybe not. Either way, my escape from Drew was long overdue.

THIRTY

"WHAT DO YOU MEAN YOU'RE FORBIDDING ME TO GO? You can't do that," I yelled and stomped my foot so hard that the Christmas tree ornaments quivered on their branches.

"Oh yes, I can." Mom thrust her hands on her hips and glared at me, her eyes narrowed almost to the point of closing. "The way you've been acting lately, you're just going to get yourself into more trouble. The last thing you need is some boy ruining your life."

I bit my tongue with enough force that I'd be sucking down a mouthful of blood if I could bleed. I wasn't her. I wasn't going to come home pregnant at seventeen. "You haven't even met Bennett. How can you hate him already?"

"I don't hate him, but you're getting on my last nerve lately. You've skipped school, your attitude stinks, and I know you've been keeping something from me. I feel it. You're better than this, Avery."

She sounded like Drew, the boy she should really be concerned about ruining my life. If she'd thrown in the word "destiny" and looked a little more homicidal, I would've thought they were the same person. Why did the people in my life not want me to be happy?

"And what about the way you've been acting?" My brain face-palmed as the words tumbled out of my mouth, but I couldn't take them back. "You're always locked in your room or face down in some ratty old book. How do you know what I need if you don't ever talk to me? Why can't you tell me what's really going on?"

"Because you wouldn't understand," she snapped. "You—"

Ding dong.

The doorbell echoed through the house and we both jerked our heads to stare at the door. I peeked at my phone: 6:59. Right on time.

Mom turned back to me, her lips pursed. "Don't even think about it."

The right thing to do was to listen to her. Head upstairs, blare some angry music and forget Bennett had ever bothered to talk to me. But tonight, as anger bubbled hot under my skin, I didn't care about doing the right thing.

I marched past Mom, whipped open the door, and raced down the front steps, almost bulldozing Bennett into the shrubs. "Let's go."

Bennett steadied himself and lingered on the front step. He nodded at the open door.

"Good evening, Ms. Belmont," Bennett said in an ultra-polite voice.

I doubted Mom cared. She glared at us and slammed the front door with a loud *thunk*. I cringed and hurried away from the house before she changed her mind and came barreling out after me.

"Where are you going, Avery? The car's over here," Bennett said.

I skidded to a stop, nearly bailing on the sidewalk. My feet had moved faster than my brain. I exhaled and the muscles in my body relaxed slightly. Putting on my best smile, I spun around and headed back to where Bennett held open the passenger door. He'd really put in some effort tonight. His jeans fit far too perfect to be accidental, and his hair was freshly styled into soft, haphazard spikes. Over his typical hoodie, he wore an expensive-looking leather racing jacket accented in a dark green that matched the mossy color of his eyes. He looked exactly like the kind of guy I'd love to get in trouble with. Maybe Mom *should* worry.

"You okay?" He looked at me quizzically as I slid into the car seat. "Maybe I should go."

"No, it's fine. I'm fine."

He closed the car door, waved at Mom, who now stood in the window, and proceeded to climb into the driver's seat.

Deep breaths. Just get it together and everything will be okay.

"What was that about?" Bennett pulled the car into the street, the house and Mom disappearing behind us.

"She's a bit overprotective and it drives me nuts." I closed my eyes and breathed in, concentrating on my lungs filling up with air and letting the tension drain out of my body. "Sorry about that."

"Are you sure you still want to do this? We could go out another night."

I opened my eyes and peeked over at him. I'd spent too much time hoping for this exact moment to happen to give it up now. "No. It's fine. She'll get over it."

"We could always run off to Mexico or something."

"Mexico would be nice. Warm and very far away."

He laughed, still concentrating on the road. I decided not to tell him that I wasn't joking.

Bennett pulled into a busy parking lot, stopping and starting as people darted around the cars.

Bass thumped outside my window, and two large white tents glowed in the darkness at the far end of the park. I opened the car door, letting the intoxicating, salty-sweet smell of popcorn and cotton candy flood in. Nice. Definitely potential for fun.

Bennett leaned against the car, waiting for me to get out. "I figured we could go skating."

My knees quivered. Me and skating was not a good idea. Me and anything requiring athleticism and balance was not a good idea. "Sounds fun, but I don't have any skates."

"Don't worry. I stole Lily's for you. I also brought extra socks in case her monster feet are too big." He popped open the trunk and produced a well-worn pair of black hockey skates and pristine pair of pink figure skates. Of course, Lily's skates would be pink.

He tied the skate laces together and draped them over my shoulder. I forced a smile. He smiled back and grabbed his own pair by the blades, closing the trunk with a thud.

"Are you sure about this?" I asked. "I mean, Lily kind of hates me right now. If she finds out I'm using her stuff, she might be mad."

"Don't worry about Lil. She's great with the drama but weak at holding a grudge."

I bit down on my cheek to stop myself from laughing out loud.

"Try talking to her. I'm sure she'll understand once she's cooled off."

"We'll see." *If she doesn't kill me in my sleep first.*

We found a spot on a long bench beside the rink. Shoes and boots snaked in crooked lines behind us. It amazed me how people in small towns left their things lying around, fully expecting them to be there when they came back. In a way, it was kind of sweet.

I loosened the laces on the skates and reluctantly pulled my left foot out of its soft, warm boot and into the cold air. Instantly shivering, I slid it into the hard skate.

"Here." Already in his skates, Bennett crouched in front of me and took the laces from my hands. "It's important to tie them tight so you don't twist an ankle. Don't want you to end up in the emergency room."

He worked fast, tightening each row of sparkly laces and finishing with a rough tug on the final bow. My foot tingled and started to go numb, but I didn't mind. I watched as he tied the right foot with long, thin fingers weaving and pulling the laces in short, sharp movements. Halfway done, he glanced up through a thick fringe of dark eyelashes and quickly looked down again. My left foot twitched. Maybe he would be trouble for me, but I couldn't wait to find out.

"Perfect." He rose to his feet and offered me a hand. "Now let's see what you can do."

My legs wobbled, but I did manage to stand up without crashing back down. The last time I remembered being on blades was in elementary gym class, and I'd hoped I wouldn't ever need to do it again. After all, it involved two of my least favorite things—being cold and making an idiot of myself.

I slid out a few feet as Bennett glided backward, as natural as walking. My ankles threatened to give out, much weaker than I'd remembered, but I fought the urge to complain, smiling at Bennett instead. I drew in a deep breath and pushed off with my left foot. To my surprise, I didn't fall over. Bennett's smile widened.

My first few strides were rough, but soon I glided along like a pro—or at least like someone who wasn't going to fall and take out a bunch of people at any given moment. Not sure if I'd be able to stop, though.

"You're not as bad as you make yourself out to be," Bennett said, still skating backward in front of me.

"Thanks, but it's still early." I stumbled as the toe pick caught the ice but managed to steady myself. "By the way, could you stop doing that? That backward thing. You're making me nervous."

"And here I thought you were making me nervous." He grinned and glided to my side so we moved in the same direction.

"Why would I make you nervous? Scared I might fall and break my neck?" It was a real possibility, after all. "Or are you second guessing being seen with me in public?" The words stung as they tumbled out of my mouth. I bit my tongue.

"Why would I care about that?" He skated backward in front of me again. The intense closeness of being face to face fueling my humiliation.

"Why wouldn't you? I'm not exactly welcome around here."

"Because the same thing happened to me. A few years before you got here, I was the one hiding in the cafeteria."

"People thought you were a witch too?" But of course, I really was one, not that I planned on telling him. "Or are you a goblin or vampire or something?"

"No. A standard choice-cut loser, I think. Whatever it was, someone decided I wasn't worth it, so they made my life a living hell." He laughed. "Or maybe they thought I was a freak show."

Freak show. Wonderful. I gritted my teeth. "You seem to be fine now. How did you get over it?"

"Lily, actually. She told me to stop worrying about what other people thought, and eventually, they'd get over whatever problem they had."

"That really worked?"

"It was hard, but yeah. People only have power over you if you react the way they expect. Change your reaction and they have to try something else or give up."

"Good advice. I might need to try that."

A little girl whizzed by my feet, banging me behind the knees. I stumbled forward, but Bennett caught my arms before I hit the ground.

"Careful." He laughed as he helped me to my feet again.

"Thanks."

He grabbed my hand.

I held my breath.

He turned and smiled, a mischievous twinkle in his eyes, brighter than any star. "So you don't fall."

The last signs of evening faded into full-on night. Strands of white lights lit the trunks of trees surrounding the skating circle, and the sky shimmered with stars as if someone had climbed up and strung lights up there too. The nearly full moon hung low, and even the wind seemed to have died off. It couldn't have been more perfect.

Once I stopped tripping on my words—and my own feet— I relaxed. We skated. We talked. School. Music. Movies. My old friends in the city. His fledgling indie band. Our plans for winter break. It was good. It was normal.

"And no one figured out why there was a donkey in a Boston Red Sox t-shirt on the golf course?" I laughed.

"Nope." Bennett shook his head and a few stray snowflakes came loose and fluttered through the air. He flashed a sly grin as we both watched them fall.

I liked watching Bennett smile. The lopsided way his lips curled up. The way his eyes narrowed so you could only see a small strip of green peering out. There was something effortless about being with him that made me forget all the heavy things in my life. It made me want to be happier.

I let the frosty air fill my lungs. As I breathed out, a familiar silhouette slipped through the crowd surrounding the rink. Drew?

My shoulders plummeted, and I blinked. No. I must have been seeing things.

Edging Bennett closer to the outside of the rink, I scanned the crowd again. Perched regally on a nearby bench, arms draped effortlessly across the back, was Drew, staring right at us.

Oh no.

Even with his forehead down and the distance between us, his eyes burned through me. People flitted around him but he never broke his stare. He raised his hand and wagged a finger back and forth.

Uh oh. Trouble.

I held tight to Bennett's hand and pulled him back into the crowd on the ice. "Maybe we could take a break." I glanced back over my shoulder. The bench sat empty. My pulse raced. At least when I could see him, he couldn't surprise me.

I searched face after face as the other skaters continued their rounds. And then my feet began to slide. Everything was moving. Colors swirled—streaks of blues, reds, and greens. Voices rumbled louder, deafening, drowning out the ringing of my heart hammering in my ears. I gasped, my hand pulling from Bennett's, the unmistakable lightness of floating as my feet left ground.

I bit my lip as I crashed down onto the ice. *Ouch!* All pain, no blood. The world stopped spinning and moved at regular pace again.

"Had enough?" Bennett crouched in front of me, resting his arms on his knees.

"Yeah, I think so."

He helped me to my feet. "Let's get some hot chocolate. But only if you promise to drink it, not wear it this time."

Like at the hockey game. Could've been years ago. "I forgot about that."

"I didn't. My car smelled like chocolate for a week."

"Sorry."

He leaned close and ran his index finger underneath my chin. "Don't be. It reminded me of you."

I swallowed. Heat grew in my frozen cheeks. "Oh."

Bennett touched his forehead against mine. The smell of soap and peppermint. His lips so close. I closed my eyes.

"I can't wait to get these skates off," he said, and the heat of him disappeared.

I opened my eyes again. He was already sitting on a bench untying his laces. Dammit.

Sitting down beside him, I pulled my arms into my body, trying to avoid brushing against him and sending my wishful thinking into overdrive again. Instead, anxious thoughts resurfaced about Drew lurking around. Fear rose in my chest as my gaze swept over the fairgrounds. I couldn't see Drew anywhere, but that didn't mean he couldn't see me.

"Why don't we go to Java for a drink instead?" I suggested. "It's starting to get cold."

"No worries. The tents are heated. It'll be warm once we get inside."

"Isn't it getting late?"

He pulled back his sleeve and checked his watch. He frowned. "It's still early. Only 9:15. Unless you want to go home."

"Of course not. Never mind." Why couldn't Bennett get the hint that we needed to get away?

As I loosened each row of laces on my skates, a relaxing tingle shot up my legs. If I hurried and drank fast, maybe we could still get out of here before Drew found us. Or maybe anxiety was messing with my brain, and I'd only thought I saw Drew. Maybe I imagined him.

I moaned quietly as I slid my feet out of the hard skates and into my comfy boots, my skin prickling in my socks and my brain still whirling with rationalizations.

Bennett scooped up the skates in one hand. "I'll run these back to the car, so we don't have to lug them around."

"It's fine. I can carry them. Just stay here."

I searched the crowd. I couldn't risk being alone with Drew potentially on the loose.

"I'll only be a second." Then Bennett was gone.

My stomach clenched.

A snowball nailed me in the side of the head. Cold, wet snow dripped down my face. I wiped my cheek and sighed. "How did you find me?"

Drew plopped down on the bench. It wobbled. "It wasn't hard. I thought about the lamest thing I could possibly do tonight, and here you are."

"Okay. You've seen me. Now get gone before Bennett comes back."

"Sis, are you ashamed of me?" He spread his fingers open on his chest, feigning shock.

"Ashamed. Disgusted. Terrified. Probably other 'ed' words."

"Terrified? Bad play. You should never let anyone know your weaknesses."

"Did you seriously come here for a lecture?" I turned away and crossed my arms. "Lesson learned. Leave now."

"Actually, I came to discuss that little magic act you pulled on me today. Where have you been hiding that set of skills?"

"Drew, get out of here."

He dug his fingers into my bicep and leaned toward me, his breath sharp with liquor. "Listen very carefully. I don't plan on leaving. Not unless you come with me."

"That is so not happening." I tried to pull away, but he held tight.

"I said listen," he snapped, spit landing and freezing on the side of my face.

I wiped it off with my sleeve, disgusted.

"You have thirty minutes to ditch the boy, or I'll make sure he never speaks to you again."

I stiffened. "And what are you going to do?"

"Wouldn't you like to know?"

"You can't threaten me. I'm just as powerful as you, you know. You can't boss me around anymore."

Drew leaned close and whispered in my ear. "Really? What are you going to do about that here with all these people watching? I've been playing at this for a lot longer than you. Don't fool yourself into thinking you can outsmart me."

He locked eyes with me and licked his lips.

"Hey." The greeting came from behind me. It wasn't friendly.

I turned. Bennett stood at my back, glaring at Drew.

I slid to the far end of the bench. "Drew came by to say hello. But he's leaving now. Right, Drew?" I imitated his forehead-down evil stare, hoping he'd get the hint.

"No hurry." Drew stood up, brushing imaginary dirt off his thighs, then locked stares with Bennett. "I was surprised to see you here, considering Avery is so pathetically clumsy. Graceful as a three-legged dog, that girl."

"She did fine." Bennett stepped in front of me and closer to Drew, using the few inches he had on him to their maximum potential. "Maybe you don't know as much as you think you do."

I held my breath.

"Surprising. She was just telling me about how much she hates everyone in this"—he flexed his fingers in air quotes—"stupid town. But I guess you must be the one exception. Unless of course, you're only a distraction to pass the time."

I jumped up and wedged myself between them. "Enough, Drew."

"Isn't that adorable? You found someone who can tolerate you. Must be magic or something." He glared at me, with an evil sneer.

I kicked him in the shin.

"I'll see you both inside," Drew said. "You should hurry though. I'm only going to be around for another thirty minutes or so." He sidestepped around me and walked past Bennett, patting him on the shoulder. "Good luck, buddy."

Bennett watched him walk down the snowy path toward the main tent. "Nice guy."

I scrubbed my hands over my face, gulping in a mouthful of frosty air. What was I supposed to do now? Thirty minutes. Why did Drew have to be so vicious? All I wanted was one night. One night. Why couldn't I have that? And what about Bennett? Could I trust Drew to keep his word about leaving him alone?

I looked up. "You know he was making all that up, right? Trying to be a jerk."

"Sure." Bennett nodded, but the scowl on his face didn't seem to agree. "He doesn't bother me. Let's go get that drink and forget about it, okay?"

I nodded and followed him down the pathway.

Drew skulked somewhere inside the tent like a hateful gargoyle waiting to rain down contempt on my life. I couldn't let that happen. Walking into the tent would be just like handing Drew a gun and hoping he wouldn't pull the trigger. Who would he shoot first—me or Bennett?

But any public place made us accessible to Drew and his demented plans. Going to my place wasn't an option with Mom there, and we couldn't go to Bennett's because Lily would make things miserable.

Or we could run to Bennett's car, lock the doors, and just drive off somewhere. Anywhere but here. But how would I explain that? *I know it's our first date, but would you mind going rogue with me for the rest of my life?*

Then a thought descended on my brain like an impending storm cloud, darkening and twisting as it grew into a full realization. There was only one real possibility left. I had to end things with Bennett—at least until Drew got bored with me or I found a way to get rid of him for good.

I balled my hands into fists, picturing the various methods of torture I wanted to subject Drew to. Cruel, wicked, things. The ground rumbled beneath my feet. People stopped moving, confused looks on their faces. Bennett teetered in front of me but regained his footing as his head swiveled back and forth, scanning the fairgrounds. He glanced back over his shoulder and shrugged.

Drew was right. I couldn't do anything with so many witnesses around. Stupid Drew. I breathed deep and exhaled.

Get it together. You're scaring the locals.

I grabbed Bennett's arm and tugged him away from the tent. "Come with me."

After one last glance to make sure Drew didn't follow, I led Bennett toward a small cluster of trees at the far end of the park. It wasn't perfect, but we could hide out for a few more minutes, and the walk would give me time to figure out what to say.

"Did you feel that back there? The ground shaking? Like some mini earthquake or something," Bennett said as we tramped out toward the trees.

"Yeah," was all I could come up with.

The lights and music fell away as we marched deeper through the snow. Would this be how I would have to deal with everything in my world—walking away? My chest tightened. I thought these powers were supposed to make me stronger, not a pathetic coward.

We finally reached the shelter of trees, far away from the crowd. I stopped under the cloak of a pine tree and leaned to the side, making sure we weren't followed. Nothing out here but us and the moonlight. The dim light spilled over Bennett's face and I sighed. Now-or-never time. "I need to tell you—"

His lips pressed against mine. The warmth of his skin. The shock of mint on my tongue. Hot and cold in perfect balance, making me dizzy. Too soon, he let me go, breathless.

"You were saying something?" he whispered, his mouth still so close to mine that my knees shook.

I lunged forward. Face first. Bennett stumbled, but I wrapped my arms around his neck and he regained balance. And kissed me back. He held my jaw and tangled his fingers in my hair. Tightening my grip, I pushed my lips harder against his, falling into his rhythm. A shiver rippled down my spine. Goosebumps.

The wind picked up, whipping my hair against my face. I pushed the strands back over my ear as the ground beneath our feet trembled. But this time, it wasn't me.

"What's going on?" Bennett pulled me closer.

"I don't know. Nothing good." We'd been found. I peeled myself from his arms and searched the darkness around us.

A creak thundered and echoed through the clearing. Then, a menacing growl.

"Look out!" I pulled Bennett's arm as the shadow of a pine tree descended over us. Too late. His pained scream echoed in my ears as the giant tree struck us to the ground.

THIRTY-ONE

"Bennett."

Why wasn't he answering? The weight of his body crushed against my ribs, and my breath stuck in my chest, but I couldn't see him. All I could see were stars.

"Bennett."

The world shifted in and out of focus and the strong scent of pine needles filled my nose. Still no response.

I forced my head up. A flood of dizziness cast a black cloud over my vision and turned my stomach. I kept still until my sight returned, and I could make out Bennett's head resting inches from my face. He wasn't moving.

Pain shot down my spine as I pushed myself into a seated position. Every muscle burned. If being indestructible hurt this bad, Bennett might be—no! I wouldn't let that happen.

Burrowing my hand into his collar, I pressed two trembling fingers against his throat. I fumbled around until I found it— the rhythmic beat of his heart. He was alive. Unconscious, but alive.

I slid my hands under his arms and pulled his limp body toward me, but he wouldn't move. His leg was stuck beneath the tree trunk. Putting my head in my hands, I fought the urge to cry. How could I help him? What was I going to do? How could this night have gone so horribly wrong? Bennett was going to hate me. Mom was going to kill me. And if there was any part of me left after that, Drew and Lily would take turns finishing me off.

Footsteps crunched in the snow. I looked up. A dark silhouette approached from between the trees.

"Hello," I pleaded. "I need help. Please. Someone's really hurt."

The crunching rushed toward us. A sliver of moonlight flashed across the stranger's face.

Drew.

I shivered.

"Don't come any closer!" I raised one hand and cradled Bennett's head in my lap with the other—as if that would protect him.

"Didn't you call for help? I'm just doing what you asked." Drew shrugged and took another step toward us.

"You don't care about me. You don't care what I want."

Drew cocked his head. "That's not true. I gave you thirty minutes to get rid of the boy. It's not my fault you chose to make out the whole time." He crept closer. "Disgusting, by the way."

"Go away. I need to get him to the hospital." I stood up, woozy and staggering.

"No. I need to talk to you. Now." He stomped his foot and growled through gritted teeth.

"And you figured if you pinned me under a tree, I might be more open to discussion?"

"No. Not exactly."

I turned and pushed against the tree trunk that imprisoned Bennett, but it wouldn't budge. Each push made me weaker. "I'm tired of you making all the rules."

"This isn't about rules. It's about following through. I promised he'd never speak to you again if you didn't meet my deadline, and I keep my promises. I guess I wasn't clear on the 'never speak again' part." Drew smiled at me and then lunged at Bennett.

"Get back." I swiped my hand through the air and wind ripped Drew across the field.

He staggered to his feet and tore back toward us. I struck again and slammed him into a tree.

Crouching beside Bennett, I called the wind again, and the fallen tree trunk rolled off his leg.

"Impressive," Drew shouted as he stood again and held his arms open to the sky. "That's the fight I've been waiting to see from you. Too late though."

The ground rumbled beneath me. Snow swirled and pelted my face, making it almost impossible to see. The wind picked up again and tossed me backward, arms flailing. I fell to the ground halfway across the bluff and a sharp jolt ricocheted through my spine.

With a wavering balance, I scrambled to my feet and took a deep breath that hurt all the way down to my kidneys. Bennett still lay on the ground about twenty-five feet to my right, Drew just as far away to my left. A perfect triangle—each point an equal distance from destroying each other.

Drew glared at me in the moonlight, then bolted toward Bennett, his sadistic laugh ringing on the frigid air.

"Stop!" I shouted.

Five strides in, Drew halted, his feet stuck to the ground. He tugged at his legs for a moment then smirked. He jerked his head to the left. Wind slammed against me, ripping against my legs and forcing them back. I dug my heels into the snow. If I lost focus, Drew would get free. The wind blew harder, stretching my frozen skin back against my bones and whipping strands of my hair so hard it felt as though they might rip from my scalp. I tumbled backward and my hold on Drew faltered.

Free again, Drew charged for Bennett. I pushed myself from the ground as he sprinted past. Fury blasted from my chest into my head and I screamed. "I said get back."

Heat barreled from me through the bluff, threatening to knock me over. Trees burst into flame like matchsticks igniting at my command. Pain tore through the top of my head, and I screamed again.

"What are you doing? Are you trying to get found out?" Drew yelled. He skidded to a stop about eight feet from Bennett.

Pressing my palms to my temples, I yelled, "I don't care. I won't let you hurt him."

Drew glanced from me to Bennett's limp body. "Idiot." He took off toward the fair and disappeared into the dark.

The flames rose higher and higher. Sheets of smoke hung in the air and burned the back of my throat. I struggled to run, my feet barely coming off the ground as I dragged my tired legs through the snow.

Finally, I made it back to Bennett. who was still lying face-down in the snow. I crawled beside him and rolled him over into my lap again, his skin warming my numb fingers. A faint cloud of breath came from his lips. He still might make it.

I grabbed his head in my hands. "Wake up, Bennett. You need to wake up."

The pain in my head throbbed again, and the world swirled with smoke. He didn't move. I coughed, and tears carved paths down my frozen face. "Please, Bennett, wake up."

Power rippled through me and I lurched forward, feeling Bennet's pulse beat in time with mine. He groaned and leaned his cheek against my palm. I concentrated harder, picturing his heart pumping hard to keep him alive, the blood coursing through his veins. Sharp agony stabbed my eyes, and I struggled to hang on. Darkness descended over the images of Bennett until they faded and disappeared. I crumpled and let go, my power drained. Bennett's body jerked and stiffened in my lap. Fighting Drew had worn me down too much to save him.

Flames caught the fallen tree trunk beside me and ate their way closer. Behind us, the circle of fire grew bigger, towering over our heads, blocking out the night. Smoke closed in around us and stung my lungs. I coughed. Why wasn't anyone coming? What if no one did?

I rose to my knees. One more thing to try. Grabbing Bennett's jacket, I sat him up and his head dropped limp to his chest.

Just hang on a little longer.

I propped him against my shoulder and wrapped an arm around his waist, then pushed my sweaty hand down on the ground, snow cold against my flesh, and forced us both to our feet. His weight bore down on me. I stumbled through the snow, struggling to move each foot forward as biting numbness spread through my limbs. Everything blurred—the smoke, the flames, the trees, the sky.

Voices came toward us, and a thin line of shadows ran through the smoke.

The shadows began to spin. My heart thumped in my ears, drowning out the night. Pain. Exhaustion. The taste of ash. I breathed in one last time as we tumbled to the ground—again.

THIRTY-TWO

A LARGE MAN IN A GRAY COAT PEELED BENNETT OFF me and carried his limp body away. As I raised my head to shout, "Wait," the world spun again. I coughed from the smell of smoke on my skin. Sirens blared in the distance, screaming their way closer. Someone lifted me up and carried me at a run toward the main fairground. The jarring motion stung my spine. As we whisked past a blur of worried faces, I searched for the man in the gray coat, but he was gone.

An ambulance waited in the parking lot, and a young EMT took my hand. "It's going to be okay."

I pushed up on my elbows. "Where's Bennett?"

He placed his hands on my shoulder and gently eased me back down. "You need to relax."

"You don't understand. He's not safe." I struggled against his arm across my chest.

"Everything will be okay," he repeated in a calm voice. "You're okay."

My arms shook, threatening to give out, so I lay down. But it wasn't okay. It was definitely not okay.

~

"You're a very lucky girl. Not one bruise, bump, or scratch." A white-coated Dr. Jackson, who insisted I call him Dr. J., replaced the stethoscope around his neck and patted me on the head as if I were a toddler. He smiled with a shocked, wide-eyed gaze, and the crinkles in his forehead edged down toward the bridge of his nose.

"Must be luck." I tried to act surprised, but my head swam with too many other thoughts.

I didn't feel lucky. I felt doomed. But of course, how was a doctor supposed to know that? I'd been crushed by a tree and didn't have a scratch—a miracle for most people. Except for some dizziness, which apparently was not a concussion, I was completely fine.

"Now hang tight, little lady. I'll be right back." The doctor winked and headed toward the door.

"Dr. Jack—I mean Dr. J.?"

He stopped at the doorway and turned toward me.

I put on my best smile. "Is Bennett Price all right?"

"Not sure. But don't worry about that right now. Okay?" He disappeared into the hall.

It wasn't okay. What if Bennett hadn't even made it to the hospital? What had I done? If I would've just listened to Drew, I could've saved him. My stomach knotted.

Dangling my legs over the side of the bed, I looked around the sterile room for a distraction. Nothing. Minutes ticked by. I checked my cell phone. No reception. No messages. I kicked my feet. What was taking so long? Maybe if I found Bennett myself, I could try healing him again. Assuming Drew hadn't gotten to him first.

I hopped off the bed. Still woozy, I grabbed my coat and bounded toward the door.

Drew sauntered into the doorway, blocking my exit. "Trying to escape?"

"Leave me alone."

"Aw, you don't want to see me?" He faked a pout.

I tried to dart around him, but he volleyed back and forth in front of my every step. I dodged him until the room spun, and then retreated to the bed.

"I came here to see how you're feeling after that nasty accident, and you can't even be polite. If this is how you treated poor Bennett, I wouldn't expect a second date."

I scowled. "What were you doing at the park, Drew?"

"It's a public place."

"Cut the crap."

"Fine. I needed to talk to you." He plunked down on the end of the bed, and I shoved him off. He scowled, but backed down, grabbing the back of a nearby chair and leaning coolly against it. "You say you're done with me. I say you're not, so we're at a bit of an impasse. I wanted to sort that out."

"There isn't anything to sort out. This isn't an impasse. This is you stalking me." I jabbed my index finger at him.

"Not stalking you, protecting you." He began to pace.

Great, he was in a lecturing mood. "Protecting me from what?"

"From yourself. I don't think you quite realize the ramifications of your mongrel birthright."

I raised an eyebrow. "Excuse me?"

"Part demon, part witch, part human. You're a total mess." He stopped in front of me and smirked with that ominous twinkle in his eye again. "But I'm willing to put up with you."

"I hate you." The words came out naturally and uninhibited from the bottom of my gut.

"No, you don't. You're mad at yourself for letting this happen."

"Seriously?" I recoiled as if he'd reached over and smacked me in the face. "I let this happen? I don't think so. This is all your fault."

Drew fidgeted with the various medical implements attached to the wall. "Ah, that's where you're wrong. I warned you, and you chose not to listen. Life is full of choices, Avery, and sometimes you make bad ones. His death is on you."

His death?

I gasped. Bennett was dead? But when I saw him ... back at the fair ... he was still breathing ... wasn't he? I touched my cheek, his breath still on my skin, his face still warm in my hands. It couldn't be. Tears welled up and trickled out. "He's dead?"

Velcro ripped and Drew attached a blood pressure cuff to his arm. "Hell if I know. That's not my problem."

"Get out," I growled.

"You don't mean that." He started pumping the small ball to inflate the cuff. "Besides, we need to chat about this whole witchy thing."

My jaw clenched. I leaned over and hit the red call button near my bed. "Out."

"All right, all right, I'm gone." He removed the cuff and let it slam against the wall on its stretchy cord. He pointed at me sternly. "But we will talk."

He slipped out the door.

I wiped my face with my sleeve and jumped down from the bed just as a stocky middle-aged woman with pink and purple scrubs walked in with the name "Loretta" in block letters on her security tag.

She frowned at the blood pressure equipment still swinging near the floor. "Did you need something?"

"Yeah—I—" The words caught in my throat. "Is Bennett Price okay?"

The woman rolled her eyes. "Are you immediate family?"

I shook my head.

"Then I can't release that information."

"But is he alive?"

"Of course he's alive. Now you need to sit back down."

The nurse roughly guided me by the shoulders back to bed. She crossed her arms and tapped her foot until I climbed back onto the mattress.

"Is that all?"

"I guess." I didn't want to be trapped in here, but at least I knew Bennett was safe.

The nurse scooped up the blood pressure cuff and placed it into its plastic holder on the wall. "And these are not toys." She scowled at me and marched back into the hall.

Seconds later, Mom burst into the room, still wearing plaid pajama pants, her hair matted and messy. "There you are." She wrapped me in a constricting hug, rocking me from side to side and refusing to let go.

I squeezed back and pressed my face into her shoulder. "Hey, Mom." The words sounded muffled against her coat.

"Are you okay?" She stepped back and scanned me over, worried furrows tugging at her ashen skin and the small lines around her eyes.

My throat tightened again. I nodded. "I'm okay."

"Thank God." She hugged me again with a little less force. "When the hospital called, I was so worried. I kept thinking such terrible things on the way over."

"But I'm all right."

"I know, sweetie." She smoothed my hair back behind my ears. "I talked to the doctor and he said you can go home."

"I can't yet. I need to know how Bennett is first."

"No, you need to get home and get some rest." She lowered her eyes and glared at me in her motherly way. "Besides, he's still in surgery."

"He's in surgery?" I pressed my palms down on the mattress and attempted to jump off the bed, but she grabbed my forearms before my toes could hit the floor.

"He'll be fine, but we need to get you out of here. You shouldn't be sitting around a hospital waiting room all night."

"But—"

She sandwiched my cheeks in her palms. "I'll get Debbie at the front desk to call if there's any news, okay?"

I reluctantly nodded.

As I followed Mom through the maze of stark-white hallways, I peeked in every room for Bennett and in every dark corner for Drew. Eventually, Mom linked her arm with mine and yanked me the rest of the way to the nearly empty waiting room.

In the far corner by the vending machines, Lily stared at a television set on the wall. I lowered my head, hoping she wouldn't see me. The mental image of her jumping over the magazine rack, hands aimed for my throat flashed before my eyes. I blinked to make it stop.

To her left sat a couple dressed rather fashionably for a hospital. They must be Lily's parents. Her mother leaned against her father's suited shoulder. He had one arm around her and the other in his lap, fingers laced in hers. Their suffering was my fault. I needed to do something.

"Hold on." I slid my arm out of Mom's grasp and marched over to the corner. I was compelled to talk to them, I needed to know it would all be okay, that they would be okay.

Lily's stare nearly bore a hole through my head, but I ignored her and focused on her parents.

"Excuse me," I said meekly. "Is Bennett going to be okay?"

Mr. and Mrs. Price looked at each other. Then Mrs. Price rose and her lips twitched as if trying to smile, but unable to overpower her worry.

"You must be Avery." She extended her hand.

I took it and nodded. The man gave me a weak smile of acknowledgment.

"They say he'll be all right." Mrs. Price's voice seemed more optimistic than her expression.

"I'm very sorry for what happened." My face flushed. She had no idea how sorry.

"It's not your fault. Accidents happen. It's just a good thing you're safe and sound. You're a very lucky young lady."

Lily's nostrils flared and her eyes narrowed.

"Thanks." My cheeks burned hotter and I stared at the floor.

"We'll let him know you asked about him," Mr. Price said from his chair.

"I'd like that."

We all stared awkwardly at each other with parted lips and silent tongues. There were so many things I wanted to say, but what could I say? I could never really explain what had happened. Instead, I nodded and took a step toward the exit.

"Oh, Avery." Lily leaped from her chair, nearly plowing me over. She wrapped her arms around me and I stiffened. Awkwardly, I hugged her back, confused but pleased. Maybe my exile was finally over.

And then she squeezed me tighter until my ribs ached. "I'll destroy you for this," she hissed in my ear.

I winced as though I'd been punched in the stomach. She smiled sweetly and returned to her seat. Her father reached over and clasped her hand.

Suddenly desperate for fresh air, I bolted for the door, tripping over chairs and tables. Outside, I leaned against the hospital's rough brick wall and bent over, gripping my knees, gasping for air, unsure whether I was more terrified or furious.

"Are you okay?" Mom put her hand on my shoulder.

"Just a little dizzy."

"I parked over here." She took my arm and peeled me from

the wall, sliding her arm around my shoulders. "Everything is going to work out. You'll see."

The car sat under a streetlight, the cloudy yellow glow accenting the scratches and missing trim still not repaired since the crash. Did everything need to remind me how much I'd screwed up? As if I hadn't gotten the message already.

"I told you going out tonight was a bad idea," Mom mumbled as she yanked open the driver's side door.

"Really?" I hung my head, exhausted, and fell into the passenger's seat. When she climbed into the driver's seat, I said, "You really want to go there?"

She shrugged, turned over the ignition, and drove off down the street.

THIRTY-THREE

Okay, you can do this.

I repeated the words under my breath as I paced in the hallway outside Bennett's room. Peering from the corner of the door frame, it didn't seem like there were any visitors. All I could see were Bennett's toes peeking out of the stark-white cast at the end of the bed. I smiled. He had nice toes.

Debbie, from the front desk, had followed through and called last night with an update. They'd put a pin in Bennett's lower leg. The surgery went well and he'd be all right. Even with good news, I slept horribly, bad dreams plaguing me all night. As I watched the sun rise through my bedroom window, I decided not to be hopeless. Magic got me into this, but it could also get me out. Part of me was destructive, however, another part was a healer. It still took all my courage to return to the hospital and face him, but I had to make things right.

Guilt built up in the back of my throat, stuck like a piece of dry bread. Again, I was tempted to get gone before anyone saw me. But no. I had to do this.

I tiptoed into the room. The dull roar of a television strapped to the ceiling helped muffle my footsteps. Bennett was propped up by pillows with an IV in his arm, his head flopped toward the window. Apart from the cast extending from his toes to just over his knee, I couldn't see any other injuries. No gauze or bandages.

His eyes were closed, dark lashes fanned against his ashen skin. His jaw clenched, making pained shapes in his cheeks.

Hopefully, it was only physical discomfort, not a bad memory. At least I could help with that.

Slowly, carefully, I inched my hand along the itchy hospital sheets and up the side of the cast until my hand rested gently on his calf. He didn't move. If I did this right, at least he wouldn't feel any pain—assuming I could fuse the bone back together. Taking his pain away was only a start in making things up to him. It was the least I could do.

"Avery."

I jumped and snatched my hand away from the cast and clasped it to my chest. "Bennett! You scared me."

"Really? 'Cause I was the one who woke up with someone standing over me." He laughed, but I took a step back, digging my fingers into my cuffs. He groaned as he sat up. He blinked. Red puffy skin circled his eyes and his eyelids drooped. "How long have you been here?"

"Not long," I lied, finally gathering the courage to look at him. "I wanted to see if you were okay, but I can go."

"Can't you stay? I was hoping you'd come."

I shifted my gaze to the chipped beige floor tiles, wishing he hadn't said that. Wishing I could feel flattered. Wishing I was normal. Instead, guilt sliced through my chest like a thousand box cutters to the heart.

"I'm so sorry, Bennett. This wasn't supposed to happen." The watery haze of my welling tears distorted his face. "I did everything I could to help you ... but ... I thought you were dead." I wiped my tears with my sleeve. "I should be the one lying here, not you."

"Hey, hey." His voice was soft, calm. "You didn't know what was going to happen. Besides, there are worse ways to die." His lips curled into a sleepy grin.

"Not funny." I smacked my hand down on the mattress, and he flinched. "Sorry."

"Stop apologizing. I was worried about you too." He took my hand. "Now, how are you? No permanent injuries?"

"I'm okay. How are you feeling?"

"All right. My leg feels like someone took a chainsaw to it and the doctors think I might have a concussion. But they say I can go home today."

"There were definitely no chainsaws, if that makes you feel better."

"Good to know. Everything is kind of a blur."

"What exactly do you remember about what happened?"

He rubbed the back of his head and his eyebrows furrowed. "Not much really. Last thing I remember was you shouting at me to move, then the ceiling of the ambulance, and then here."

"Are you sure, that's all?"

"I think so. Except the smell of smoke. I remember smoke." His nose scrunched up. "Maybe I can remember more if I try."

I thrust out my hands. "No, no. Don't push yourself. You didn't miss anything. The most important thing is that you're safe now."

He laced his fingers through one of my flailing hands and ran his thumb over my knuckles. "Are all your dates that hardcore?"

"Not typically."

"Good." He smiled. "But maybe next time we should go to the movies or something. Indoors. Not a lot of movement."

"Next time?" He must've hit his head harder than I thought. A tiny glimmer of anticipation sparked in my stomach, but reality quickly snuffed it out. As much as I wanted to see Bennett again, it wasn't going to happen until I'd dealt with Drew. I was so sick of everyone else dictating what I could and couldn't do.

"I—"

"Who was stupid enough to let you in here?" Lily charged

into the room, several shades of angry red, and stood on the other side of the bed with her arms crossed and her hip jutting out to the side.

I yanked my hand away from Bennett.

"Get out." Lily pointed at the open door.

"Ease up, Lily," Bennett said. "This is my room, remember?"

"And you wouldn't be here if it wasn't for her." She flipped her hand in my direction. "Remember?" she scoffed.

Bennett rolled his eyes. "You're impossible."

"I'll just go," I said.

"Good." Lily huffed. The red mark on her cheek from the chem class explosion stretched longer as she scowled.

I winced, remembering her scream.

"There's no reason to leave." Bennett glowered at his sister, then grinned hopefully at me. "I want you to stay."

"Well, I don't." Lily turned her back to me.

"That's not your decision," Bennett said.

"You hit your head," Lily said. "What do you know?"

"I'm fine, Lil."

"Clearly, you aren't, because you can't see what a disaster she is. I warned you, but you won't listen. She's not normal, Ben."

That hurt. Everything she said was true. Bennett got hurt because of me, and I couldn't guarantee he wouldn't get hurt again. I wasn't normal, and strangely, Lily was the only one who could see it. The weight of her truths twinged behind the bridge of my nose, but I managed to keep the tears away. I refused to let her see me as a sobbing mess. She'd enjoy that too much.

"You know what, Lily?" I stared at the back of her head, but not too hard, consciously avoiding the desire to make it explode. "I'm standing right here. You've done everything possible to make my life miserable. I'm sick of it. I'm sick of your back-handed crap. I might not be who you expect, and you may not like me, but I'm done letting you knock me down. I really like Bennett, and as long as he still wants me around, I'm staying. I know I'm a good person—or at least I'm trying to be—so maybe you can stop being so nasty to me and back off." My chest heaved, every last breath devoured by my speech.

Lily whirled around. We shot each other malevolent stares, enough fire and fury between us to raze the entire town.

"Enough," Bennett snapped. He glared at Lily. "Maybe *you* should leave."

Without taking her eyes off me, Lily headed to the door.

Bennett and I looked at each other, wide-eyed. She actually listened.

The on-call nurse rushed into the room. The unhelpful Loretta from last night, only different colored scrubs.

"You again?" she scoffed, her bitter expression proving she remembered me too.

Lily followed the nurse and sneered, pointing a finger at me. "She's not family. I want her removed. My poor brother needs his rest."

I hit the hallway in two quick strides, picturing the look of triumph on Lily's smug face.

"Avery," Bennett called, but it didn't matter.

Walking out was better than being dragged away. Lily had more than enough ammunition to poison Bennett against me, and she clearly wasn't interested in calling a truce.

Would I ever be able to live a normal life, or would my secrets keep haunting me forever? My lungs tightened with pain as I struggled to inhale. The weight of my emotions was suffocating.

The second I opened the front door, chill outdoor air hit my face and frustrated tears fell. I wasn't going to give up on Bennett, but I had to figure out how to convince Lily to be reasonable. How could I ever make peace with someone who hated me so much?

I tore up the sidewalk and glanced back at the hospital entrance. Good. Lily hadn't followed me. Neither had anyone else.

And then, wham! I slammed into someone and fell backward to the ground. I looked up, and Drew stared down.

"What the hell are you doing here?" I slithered away from him on my butt and then scrambled to my feet.

"The same as you, I'm guessing." Drew smiled snidely. "To visit a hurt friend. Are you okay? You look rough."

"Rough? What did you expect?" I barked. "You could've killed him or me. Is that what you want?"

"Of course not." He put his hand on my shoulder.

I jerked away.

"Now calm down, will you? Besides, I did warn you."

"Warn me? You threatened me. And I told you to leave me alone. I—"

He raised his hand. "Enough," he said sternly. "Frankly, I'm tired of your little game here. We will resume practice and your insubordination will be forgiven. I think you've learned your lesson."

"Me? Insubordination? You aren't my teacher. I told you to stay away from me and my life and you definitely didn't listen to that."

"You may think you're tough because you've got a few new tricks, but don't think for a second I can't take you on." His face hardened and his voice dropped to a hiss. "Trust me, I don't lose. Ever."

He leaned closer, rising onto his toes and towering over me. A pitch-black shadow swallowed his brown eyes, rings of sinister red bleeding around the irises.

I gasped and clutched my stomach, his new level of fury freezing me to the core.

"If you insist on disobeying me again," he said calmly, "I'll make sure you visit that boyfriend of yours in the morgue instead of the hospital. And forget magic. I'll take him down the old-fashioned way." He pulled out his pocketknife and held it discreetly next to his leg. He grinned and flipped out the blade. "I've killed far better men than him, and I don't think he'll put up much of a fight. Can't run too fast with a broken leg."

"You wouldn't," I said.

"Do you really want to see if I will?"

I shook my head.

"Because if I do, I'll find someone else to hurt too, just to get my point across. Maybe your mother, or one of your other friends. Oh wait, you don't have any other friends." He cackled. He tucked his knife into his back pocket, and his laughter faded. "So what's it going to be?"

I muttered expletives under my breath.

"What's that?"

"Fine." I snarled. "Just leave everyone else out of this."

"Great! I'll let you know where to go when I'm ready."

Drew strode forward, but I stepped in front of him. "I said, leave everyone else alone."

"Easy now." He shrugged. "I don't know why you don't trust me. Besides, I know where he lives, where he goes, what he does. Do you really think you could stop me?" He turned and walked away from the hospital.

Hate vibrated through me as he sauntered down the icy sidewalk and disappeared around the corner.

Thirty-Four

I PLUNGED MY HANDS DEEPER INTO MY JACKET pockets and held my arms tight against my body, wishing I was anywhere but here. The winter night was still, but frigid. It burned my nostrils as I breathed in, and formed dense clouds around my head as I breathed out.

Drew paced under the dull glow of a nearby lamppost—the same spot he'd taught me about my powers. The same bench where I'd manipulated a cup of water for the first time and first realized that life was never going to be the same. That night held so much promise. Exciting new powers and a new half-brother to share them with.

Now magic burdened me, and the sight of Drew, even in the distance, turned my stomach. This would be the last time I'd see him. It had to be. I couldn't spin in this cycle anymore, me running away, Drew making threats, and me crawling back again. No more living in fear of what he might do to me or someone else. No more feeling helpless. If he didn't agree to leave me alone this time—and really mean it—I'd tell everyone our secret.

If only I'd had the courage to do it sooner.

I took one last deep breath and crunched the rest of the way over the crusty snow, halting a few feet behind Drew. He stopped pacing and whirled around. Light from the lamppost filtered across his red blotchy face as he slid a hand through his wild and downright sloppy hair, gripping it at his crown. His normally razor-sharp stare seemed unfocused, distant, and devilishly menacing, as though recalling a pleasantly vicious memory from another time.

I shuddered. The last time I'd seen this look, I'd picked myself up off the ground after he'd tried to kill me. I dug my heels into the snow, refusing to come any closer. The longer he stared in my direction, the more confidence trickled out through my trembling knees.

"Thought you might've gone back on your word." He flashed me a dimpled smile, more sinister than sweet.

"I didn't really have a choice, did I?"

"Oh, Avery, there's always a choice. It's whether or not you can deal with the consequences of making it."

"Whatever. What do you want?"

"Always so grouchy."

"You have that effect on me." My eyes narrowed as he walked toward me. Then he stopped, a good ten feet away, wisely keeping his distance. "If you don't mind, let's skip your melodrama. We have important things to discuss."

"You're right. We do." I mentally reviewed my prepared exit speech.

"I'll go first." He took another cautious step forward. "I've been doing a lot of thinking about your little hybrid gene pool, and I think it could have some really great side effects."

I crossed my arms.

"You have the ability to affect living things. Your grandmother healed people. I thought if you could make someone better, then maybe you could make them worse as well."

"You think I can make people sick."

"Not sick. More like dead."

"What?" My head snapped forward. "Have you lost your mind?"

"Think about it. You can control the destructive force of

fire, and you can manipulate people's will. Why couldn't you combine those powers to kill things?"

"You want me to stare at people and set them on fire?"

"Not the person exactly, but their essence. Their soul."

Laughter burst from my diaphragm, a full-out belly laugh.

He tilted his head.

"That's absolutely ridiculous," I said.

"You have two different forms of magic flowing through you—elemental and life force or quintessence. I've never heard of anyone possessing both before, only you." Drew's tone was almost giddy like he'd found a lost treasure.

"Maybe you just haven't come across it. Not too many witches and demons in Michigan."

"I'm talking worldwide and throughout history. I've been researching this stuff a lot longer than you know. You're unique."

I stopped laughing. "Unique." I hated that word. "Even if it's true, what makes you think I'm going to wish people dead?"

"Why not?" He shrugged.

And that was the problem—Drew didn't care if anyone lived or died. He had no consideration for human life.

"This is messed up, even for you." I turned to walk away before he could rope me into anything else.

But Drew jumped in front of me and pressed his hand to my chest, right below my throat. "Where do you think you're going?" His eyes burned down into mine, inky shadows with fire-red rings. Angry Drew was back.

"I held up my side of the deal. I showed up. Now let me leave. Nothing's going to happen here." I swallowed thickly, hoping my fear didn't show.

"I'm not so sure of that." He gave me a villainous grin, teeth bared, and then sped past me to the giant tree near the pond.

My brain told me to run, but my legs stayed put. Was it fear, or worse, sick curiosity?

Drew returned with a cardboard box. Still sporting a disturbing smile, he placed the box on the bench beside us. It wiggled around and made scuffling noises. He unfolded the top flaps and pulled out a cat.

Whiskers.

I froze and my mouth fell open.

Whiskers hissed and batted at Drew's forearm with her front paws. He gently petted her head.

"I didn't think you would sign on to kill an actual person right away, so I figured we could start small."

"Not a chance," I blurted in disgust.

Drew pushed Whiskers back in the box, her paws flailing, claws catching on the flaps.

"No, Drew," I shouted. "I'm not a killer."

"Of course you are," he replied calmly. "Blood runs wicked through your veins, just like mine, but I choose not to fight it. It's who we are. You need to let go and accept it."

"I'm nothing like you."

Drew laughed, a little too hard and a little too loud to be normal. Then he dove behind me, twisting my left arm and pinning it tight against my back. The cold chill of his sharp blade pressed against the flesh of my neck.

I swallowed. He couldn't cut me, but I braced for the pain he would inflict by trying.

"Now listen to me." His hot breath brushed my ear. "You need to learn to do what you're told. Just imagine the sheer power you have. The ability to take a life at will. To know you have absolute control over another living thing. You decide who lives and dies. I could rule this place like I've always dreamed, with you as my ruthless assassin."

"I won't do it. I don't want any of this." Everything

tumbled out of focus and into a heavy new reality that stung my eyes. Keeping the holding pattern between me and Drew made my limbs ache, but I couldn't give in.

"The first kill is hard, but it gets easier as you go. Eventually, you won't even care." Drew's vise-like grip tightened.

I shuddered as his words needled in my brain, dragging out enough tears to drown the world. "No, Drew. I'm done with you."

He laughed again. His chest heaved against my back, pushing me closer to the blade.

"I'm serious. I'm going to tell everyone about us, my mom, even your mom—"

"Good luck with that." He clucked in my ear as he tightened his grip on the knife handle.

"Then get out of my life. Just go and leave me alone. I'll keep quiet." I closed my eyes, half expecting him to cut me for being so demanding. "Otherwise, I swear I'll tell. I can't take the secrets and the threats anymore."

"It's because you're weak," he whispered against my hair. "I loathe that about you. Your pathetic human weakness."

"Then kill me." The words tumbled out of my mouth without thought or reason. Did I really want to die?

He tugged my arm tighter against my back as choking sobs stole my breath. "You know I can't hurt you." He tossed me to the ground.

I clambered back to my feet, but Drew had already made his next move. He grabbed Whiskers harshly by the scruff of her neck.

"Now." The smoldering circles of fire in his eyes stoked bright again. "I might not be able to hurt you, but this cat is not so lucky."

He slid his knife across Whiskers's front leg, and her fur darkened. Drops of thick red blood dripped onto the clean white snow. She squirmed furiously, and a fire-alarm squeal rose from her throat.

"Stop it," I screamed and lunged toward her.

Drew held the knife out to me. "No, you stop it. Put the poor animal out of its misery."

"No. This is enough."

"Toughen up. It's only going to get harder from here on."

I grabbed fistfuls of my hair and pulled, sending a blast of wind that pushed Drew onto his back, Whiskers still clutched in his hand. Icicles rained down from the surrounding trees, stabbing Drew's arms and head and then shattering on the ground. He fought against the attack and rolled into a crouch, pushing the wind back toward me and knocking me on my butt.

"Insolent girl," he shouted. "If you won't get me out of this inferior body, the least you can do is listen when I tell you something."

What was he talking about?

He raised the knife to Whiskers again. Whiskers thrashed against his grip and slashed her paw across Drew's cheek. The faint pink stripes faded faster than they appeared.

I'd seen this scene before—in my nightmare. The disturbed little boy in the burning room clawing his cheek. Except this time, I couldn't wake up to make him disappear.

"Dirty beast," Drew yelled and tossed Whiskers in the air. "No more mercy."

Whiskers landed in the snow bank with a piercing cry. Drew fixed his eyes on me and snapped his fingers. Flames sparked on the snow, morphing Whiskers from fur ball to fireball. She yowled. I leaped toward her but Drew stepped in front of me. I blinked and smothered the flames in snow. Whiskers rolled on the ground, her cries screeching higher and sharper, cutting my heart into slivers.

I slammed the heels of my hands into Drew's shoulder and pushed him off balance. Sulfur and copper stained the air, and bile-laced vomit oozed up my throat. I swallowed it back and rushed toward Whiskers. As my fingertips grazed her ravaged skin, an arm slammed across my stomach and yanked me back.

"No, you don't." Drew dragged me to my feet and locked his arm across my chest, trapping my arms.

"Let me go." I elbowed Drew in the ribs, but he only pulled me tighter. I had to touch Whiskers to heal her. I'd never pulled it off any other way. I concentrated hard between the tears pouring down my face. "Come here, Whiskers."

She rose on shaky legs and crumpled back down, wailing pitifully, writhing.

"She's dying, Avery," Drew barked in my ear. The tip of his knife dug against my back. "Roasting alive in her own skin. Every nerve sizzling and screaming. The cold snow against her raw flesh, freezing and burning at the same time. She's suffering, but you can stop it. You can take her pain away."

"I can't," I said, suffocating on my own tears.

"It'll take her a long time to die, Avery. Even when she stops howling, it will hurt. If she's lucky, the pain will kill her before the burns do."

I dug my fingers into Drew's leg and twisted.

He flinched but didn't give any slack.

"I can heal her, Drew. Let me. Please. Make it stop."

"You know what to do to make it stop. You're the one with the choice. Watch her suffer or set her free."

"Don't make me do this. I won't."

"Maybe you need a little more motivation." Drew ripped the cold blade across my back, slicing me from spine to side, and pain seared through my kidneys. My tortured scream merged with Whiskers's and my knees gave out, but Drew wouldn't let go. He clamped his arm tight over my chest and stabbed the knife into my hip, sending agony up my torso. "I can do this forever," he said. "You'll never bleed a drop."

He twisted the knife tip against my flesh, each turn tossing a match on the inferno blazing in my gut. I closed my eyes and focused on Whiskers. I wanted her pain to stop, my pain to stop, neither of us safe until I gave in.

Kill, the demon voice hissed in my ears, and I trembled. Black shadows oozed down the inside of my eyelids, blocking out all light. Cold spread through my veins, turning blood to ice and stiffening my limbs, yet my heart still thumped in my ears. Breath caught in my throat, and my lungs ached for oxygen. I grasped at my throat with frozen fingers, trying to remove what felt like two hands gripping my neck, but no hands were there to fight.

Whiskers's howling stopped.

As quickly as it had come, the iciness and tightness lifted. Drew relaxed his hold and I lurched forward, gulping the crisp air, choking from my gluttony.

Whiskers's body lay limp on the snow, a floppy mass of skin and chunks of fur.

"What've you done?" I croaked, my throat raw. I ran to Whiskers and laid my hands on her body. As red stained my fingertips, I held my breath.

Whiskers, wake up... Whiskers, wake up...

I closed my eyes and tried to see Whiskers's pain, tried to tunnel through her body with my mind to fix her, but I couldn't see anything. I clenched my eyes tighter, wet lashes matting together, but nothing. No connection. No magic flowing through me, just Whiskers's body cooling in my bloody hands. I shook my head. "No!"

"It's too late. You can heal. You can't raise the dead." Drew chuckled. "Or you could, but we both know how well that works out."

Tears came harder, soaking my jacket. I pet the mangled fur on her back, over and over, a hole burrowing deep in my chest. "I'm sorry. I'm so, so, sorry."

"Your first kill. I knew you had it in you." Drew put his hand on my shoulder.

I pushed his hand off and stared at the blood on my fingers.

"You felt it, didn't you? You felt death."

And I did. Whiskers's death flowed out of me, cold and hollow.

I killed her.

I was a killer.

I lurched forward and vomited on the snow.

"You'll get used to it," Drew said. "I have big plans for us."

"I'll never help you. You're a monster." I sobbed, wiping my mouth with my sleeve.

"And now, so are you."

The reality of Drew's words stabbed deeper than his knife. I really was no better than him. I killed a living thing.

I ran.

"You'll change your mind," Drew yelled. His laughter echoed across the night sky.

I ran blindly for blocks, too numb, too overwhelmed to think.

I am not a killer.

I am not a killer.

I repeated the phrase like a mantra as if saying it out loud would make it true. But it wasn't. I killed Whiskers. I killed her, and I couldn't take it back.

Thoughts spun in my head. Drew. Whiskers. Bennett. Blood. Lies. Death. And the most frightening thing of all—me. What other terrifying things was I capable of? Were other people even safe around me anymore?

By the time my thoughts slowed down, pink light crept

along the horizon. Dawn. I found my street and headed home. Hands shaking and lightheaded, I managed to slip in through my bedroom window. As I slid it closed behind me, I froze. The air was different. Heavy.

I wasn't alone.

A shadow shifted beside my bed.

Through the darkness came one word. "Sit."

Thirty-Five

"WHAT ON EARTH DID YOU THINK YOU WERE DOING?"
It was the fifteenth time Mom had asked that question, but I
couldn't respond. Instead, I fiddled with the loose threads in my
hoodie pocket, my bloody hands burning, threatening to
expose the despicable, broken thing I'd become.

She paced in front of my bed for a while and then returned
to the same spot, looming above me, and continued to yell for
an answer. Still, my words wouldn't come.

Truth was, I didn't know what I was doing. Not anymore.
Everything I thought I knew about myself and my life was a lie.
My entire family had kept secrets from me. Deadly secrets.
Could I even trust myself?

"You are damn lucky. You have your history exam in..."
Mom squinted at her watch in the faint morning light. "Thirty
minutes. Now clean yourself up and get in the car. You reek."

She stomped out of my room, slamming the door behind
her. The dull throb in the back of my head pulsed in response. I
rose from the desk chair, and my knees nearly buckled from all
the crying and running I'd done. I glanced out the window, half
expecting Drew to be there, but there were only snow banks.
Sliding my hands out of my sleeves, I played with the window
latch and considered taking off, but I didn't have anywhere to
go. Besides, sneaking out was how I got into this mess in the
first place. I had to get moving. Mom would slaughter me if I
didn't.

I'd forgotten about the exam, and I wasn't ready. I couldn't think about history when my future hung on the edge of Drew's knife. At least I had a future. Whiskers didn't, and it was all my fault.

Tears streamed. I rubbed my eyes with my sleeve, gagging from the acidic smell of my own puke. I ripped off my sweater and fell to the floor, holding my head in my hands. My mind was flooded with her death. The sight, sound, and feel of it.

Crying harder made it impossible to breathe. I gasped for air as I said a silent prayer—to who or what, I didn't know. Faith wasn't something I knew about, or at this point deserved. It just felt like the right thing to do. But who would listen to the prayers of a demon?

And Drew wasn't done with me. Now that he knew what I could do, he wouldn't stop until I was exactly like him. Depraved and disconnected. Next time would be worse. Next time he'd take away someone else I loved. Next time would be a human life.

Honk!

Mom was waiting. After slipping on a clean hoodie and scrubbing my hands and face, I stumbled down the stairs and out the front door.

Honk!

I winced and covered the sides of my head with my arms. Probably another way Mom had chosen to torture me. I wished sneaking out was the only thing I'd done to deserve how lousy I felt.

I slid into the passenger seat and Mom gave me another angry glare and then sped off, spinning the tires on the ice.

"I don't know whether I'm more angry or disappointed," she finally said as she parked outside the school.

I hung my head and stared at the dried blood still dark under my fingernails.

"Why won't you talk to me?" Mom slammed her palm against the steering wheel.

"Because you wouldn't believe me anyway."

She pivoted to face me. "And why would you say that? Have I ever not listened to you?"

"Only every day since we moved here."

"That's not true." Her face contorted as if she was trying to recall some lost information. "Respect is not an entitlement. It's earned and you haven't exactly been worthy of it lately."

"Yep." Pulling my hands into my sleeves, I eased out of the car and slammed the door behind me.

Mom got out too and charged toward the entrance.

"What are you doing?" I leaned against the car.

"Walking you to class. I'm not sure if I trust you to make it there yourself."

She marched off.

I caught up and led the way through the hallway, empty for winter break, my head lowered. I wanted to be angry, but she was right. The second she turned the corner, I would've run the other way. "This is it." I reached for the classroom door, but she grabbed my arm and turned me to face her.

"I don't know what's gotten into you, but it needs to stop. I know there's a good kid in there somewhere. You just have to find her again. You're better than this. I know it."

Lunging forward, I wrapped my arms around her. "I love you, Mom."

She squeezed me back. The hard edge of her voice softened. "Now get in there, and go straight home after."

I nodded and she tore off down the hallway.

With seconds to spare, I slid into a desk in the empty classroom.

"Nice of you to join me, Miss Belmont. I thought you'd

decided to forget about your exam." Miss Bradley offered a pleasant smile that didn't quite carry to her eyes.

Was that a joke or an insult? Either way, I didn't really care.

She placed the exam on my desk. "You may begin."

Flipping through the pages was pointless. I wouldn't know the answers, and even if I did, I couldn't concentrate long enough to read the questions. At least it was multiple choice.

I absentmindedly circled letters as I considered my future choices. I could run. Pack up me and Mom and get out of town. Tell her I was still unhappy and couldn't take it here anymore. Or did I dare to tell her the truth? But Drew would never let us leave. He'd find me. I knew it.

But I couldn't give him what he wanted. I couldn't kill people. Drew already told me what it would do to me, the darkness I'd be letting in. And I could already feel it pumping through my veins. A drop of poison destroying me from the inside. Who knew how many people Drew would have me execute.

I turned the page. An essay question. "Choose a famous battle and describe the..."

I kept trying to read the first line, but the words jumbled and I couldn't concentrate. My head throbbed and I pulled at the hair near the base of my skull. Forget this.

I gathered up my papers and tossed the unfinished exam on Miss Bradley's desk. Her mouth opened but I sped out the door before she spoke. I had the only answer I needed.

I had to kill Drew.

~

I ripped open drawers and threw clothes on the bed. Socks, t-shirts, pants, underwear—all piled high in the middle of Mom's comforter. I might not get everything she needed, but at least I'd have the basics.

I had a plan.

Step one: Get Mom out of town. She worked until four, and I'd have her packed and ready to go when she came home. She'd be furious, but she couldn't be here when I went after Drew. It'd be tricky, but even if I had to beg, bribe, or blackmail her, I'd do it. If I failed, Drew would go after her. Fortunately, the people I cared about made up a short list.

Step two: Call Lily. She was the only person who'd believe me quickly enough to get Bennett somewhere safe. Having to confirm all the horrible things she already thought about me would be painful, especially since she'd tell Bennett and I'd never see him again, but at least he'd be alive to hate me later.

Step three: Take care of Drew. Still fuzzy on that one, but my head should clear once Mom and Bennett were gone. Details needed to be meticulous if I hoped to succeed. Acting on emotion hadn't gotten me far. This would take strategy.

I threw open Mom's closet doors and stretched to reach the suitcase on the top shelf, but I was inches too short, even on tiptoes. I jumped and grabbed the handle, falling forward into the closet and smashing my knee on something hard as the suitcase crashed to the floor.

Rubbing my leg, I pulled back the clothes to find a large, dark navy faux leather trunk at the back of the closet. It was so worn that the leather pulled away at the corners. Two wide straps ran around the outside and were held together by large gold buckles with small gold padlocks. Just like the chest Mrs. Abernathy had described, the one that had belonged to Grandma.

It couldn't be. Could it?

I bolted to my room and poured my pencil cup across the desk. In the mess of pens and pencils, I found the key Mrs.

Abernathy had given me and slid it into the first padlock. Closing my eyes, I gently turned the key.

With a faint metal click, the lock sprang open. I opened the other one. After tossing the locks aside and clicking open the buckles, I held my breath and lifted the lid. The bottom of the trunk was lined with ratty unmarked leather-bound books, spines facing up. One lay open and face down on top of the others.

I picked up the journal and thumbed through the pages. The thin sheets of paper were covered with inky scrawls and line drawings of symbols and creatures I didn't recognize. I reached back into the trunk and grabbed another volume, this one with larger pages. Weren't these the same ratty books I'd seen Mom reading before?

I flipped through the other journals too. Dozens of them, filled with writing. Everything was so detailed, they must've taken Grandma years to compile. Some passages recounted past experiences, others offered instructions like recipes and how-tos. As I flicked through the pages, a drawing caught my attention. I flipped backward until I found it again. Across half a page spread, a circle with long, finger-like swirls wrapped around the top and bottom. It seemed familiar. Tracing the picture with my finger, I searched my memory for the image.

Nothing.

Underneath the drawing was a note written in loopy scrawl.

Entrapment Spell

August 19th: The Entrapment Spell was a success. The crippling pain I feel in my head and my limbs is worth the sacrifice for not having to feel the pain in my heart when he would have taken her from me. Our family would not have survived him. If I die now, it will have been worth the fight. But I must survive to keep the vessel safe.

Black is the heart that worships evil. Dark is the soul that power corrupts. Light alone endures. Protego. Admoderor. Defende.

What was she talking about? Dark is the soul that power corrupts. No doubt. I knew that—almost too well. But what did it all mean? I turned the page, but it was blank. This was the last entry. I read the words under the "Entrapment Spell" heading several times—*protego, admoderor, defende*—but nothing became clearer. And the date. August nineteenth.

My birthday. What year was it written?

The pain in my head throbbed again. I squinted one last time at the drawing. I knew I'd seen it before, but where? Maybe if I could dull my headache, I could figure it out. I grabbed an ibuprofen from the kitchen cupboard and pounded back a glass of water, the promise of relief enough for the pain to back off a bit. I wiped my mouth, but the glass slipped from my hand, shattering on the tile floor. I went for the broom and stepped on a shard of glass. A sharp pain shot up my leg. Not again. Just like when I smashed the …

… the ornament.

The picture in the journal—it was the ornament!

But it wasn't a Christmas ornament at all. It was some magical object of Grandma's. The excitement from solving the puzzle faded to dread. The ornament was broken. What had I done? What did I let out?

I picked the glass out of my foot and headed for the stairs. As I passed the kitchen table, I skidded to a halt. There was a note.

Avery,

I think you need to learn how to treat family.

I have your mother at the old barn.

Meet me or I will kill her.

Tell anyone and I will kill her.

I would hurry if I were you.

Drew

I was out of time. Drew already made the first move, and he didn't plan on losing.

THIRTY-SIX

Clouds draped the sky, low and thick, blocking out the sun. A wet earthy smell hung in the air. Anyone else would have thought a storm was coming, but I knew it was much worse. The ominous darkness sent a message. Drew was angry. Very angry.

I stood at the gate of the Montgomery house and studied the tracks through the snow leading to the old barn. Only one set of footprints. That meant Drew carried Mom or hid her somewhere else. Knowing him, it might be a trick and Mom was safe at work. Or maybe he'd already—

No! I pushed that thought from my mind.

I stumbled through cold powder, trying to follow Drew's footprints through knee-high snow banks. The wind howled and pushed, but I forced myself to keep moving. The frustration from moving so slowly only fueled my fear.

As I got closer to the barn, the snow was packed hard and easier to walk on. I bent over to catch my breath. Now that I'd finally arrived, what was I going to do? The few details of my developing plan had fallen away as soon as I read Drew's note. Why could he never let me have the upper hand? Just once. But Drew was too calculating, too cunning, to make things simple.

Voices carried from the barn. I peeked through a small crack between the doors. Drew faced the back wall, talking wildly and waving his hands. I couldn't make out the words. As he paced left, I saw Mom sitting on the ground behind him. Her arms were raised above her head and tied to a supporting wall beam. I still had a chance. If I could get through Drew.

I leaned against the door and tried to think.

I wasn't ready to face Drew, but if I didn't, he would kill Mom. If I went to the police and he was cornered, he would kill her. The only other choice was to wait him out and see if he'd give up and go look for me. But there'd be a punishment for not listening to his demands. There always was. Too risky.

There was only one way out of this.

I mumbled a little prayer. Any help I could get at this point would be crucial.

At least I had the element of surprise. I took a deep breath and reached for the door handle. A gust of wind burst the barn doors open from the inside and knocked me to the ground. Drew stood before me, smiling with delight. "Took you long enough."

So much for surprise. I scrambled to my feet.

"Lizzie and I were just catching up," he said.

Lizzie?

Mom craned her neck and caught my gaze, her eyes wide and glassy. She looked scared but didn't seem to be injured.

I planted my feet in a wide stance and clenched my hands into fists. "Let her go."

Drew threw his head back and laughed—amped, wild, and absolutely deranged. "Did you really think I'd make it that easy? Besides, you're always pushing for her to meet me. Don't want to cut our visit short."

"Just tell me what you want." I gritted my teeth. Everything was a game to him. A dangerous game of twisting my words and using them against me for terrible ends.

He started pacing again. "I have a proposition for you."

His words jumbled together in my brain. Something was going on here. Something beyond Drew and his threats. This was my fight, but I felt as if I'd interrupted someone else's conversation.

Mom followed Drew's every motion. Every step, every turn, every flick of his wrist. But it wasn't fear. The intensity in her eyes was something else. A sadness I couldn't understand. But she'd never seen Drew before.

Or maybe she had.

Drew's dark features. His dimpled smile. The longer hair. He looked like my dad. To Mom, he probably looked exactly like the love of her life—just as she remembered him. Like seeing a ghost. A ghost who'd never aged, like in Mrs. Abernathy's story.

Drew's face, his eyes, exactly the same as the boy in the photo. And all of Drew's comments about humanity and being confined that didn't seem to make any sense. But maybe they actually did. Maybe those newspaper articles about the mayor's son, the damage he caused, weren't just stories. Maybe...

Why hadn't I seen this before?

"You're him, aren't you?" The words spilled out before the idea had fully taken shape. I clapped my hand over my mouth.

He stopped laughing and leaned forward on the balls of his feet. "What was that?"

"Your name's not Drew. You're that kid. The one who drowned. You're Nicholas."

A glimmer of amusement spread across his face. "And you're far more perceptive than I thought."

"Then that means you aren't my brother either."

He shook his head.

"You're my dad."

THIRTY-SEVEN

"Now that we're all up to speed, there's business to discuss."

His voice faded into a faraway whisper. He was my father. My stomach churned and warm spit pooled in my mouth. I might throw up. If he were my brother, I could separate myself from his depravity, but as my father, his evil violated me. It seeped through my pores, staining my soul. He was the reason for the inhuman parts of me. All the wicked parts.

He cursed me.

"You've been lying to me this entire time." I flailed my arms toward him, unable to put words to the more important things I wanted to say. The questions I wasn't sure I wanted the answers to.

"Not really lying," Drew said. "Just not telling the complete truth. Besides, did you tell your mother the truth about what happened to your car? Or about all those times you snuck out in the middle of the night? Or that you almost killed a classmate? Bad girl."

Mom winced and her mouth dropped open.

I caught her devastated gaze, willing her not to listen, not to let Drew in, but she lowered her head and shrank against the wall.

"This isn't some joke. Do you know how sick and twisted you are?" Drew's betrayal welled inside, seething just under my skin. It tore through my veins and burst from my flesh into the ground below. I groaned as the earth rumbled. A few old planks from the roof shook loose and fell, missing his head by inches and splintering on the ground.

"Calm down," he ordered, but I refused to stop. He raised a hand in front of him and the large double doors behind me slammed shut.

I jumped.

"Now it's time for you to make a choice."

"You tried to kill me, didn't you?"

"Well, first I tried to steal your body and then kill you, but it didn't work. How was I supposed to know you would turn out to be some sort of demon-witch cross breed?" He savagely swung his arms above his head, and his nostrils flared.

"Maybe I can't be killed."

"Sure, you can. I just haven't figured out how yet."

"Stop it!" Mom yelled. Her face was flooded with tears. "If you try to hurt her, I'll—"

Drew whipped around. "You'll do nothing!" You can't stop me. I've been poisoning her mind for weeks, and you did nothing."

The wind picked up, mimicking Drew's increasing agitation. Ice pellets banged against the roof like bullets. His resumed pacing, faster and faster, pulling at his hair, coming undone before our eyes.

Who knew what horrors that would bring? But I still had questions. "Where've you been for seventeen years?"

"Trapped." Spit flew from Drew's mouth. "Locked away for so long. Do you know what it's like to be so close to having everything you want and then to have some witch take it all away?"

Mom rose on her knees and leaned forward, her arms wrenched behind her. "That's why she hated you."

Drew shrugged. "Maybe."

A witch. Someone desperate enough to challenge Drew, and powerful enough to win.

The pieces flew together. "Grandma put you in that ornament, didn't she? She knew what you were."

"It's a good thing she's dead. It's better than what I'd planned for her."

"She protected us," I said.

"Shut up!" he screamed, his cheeks nearly purple. He slammed his palms against the side of his head. "I've had enough of your talking. You're always talking."

With his hands balled into fists, he continued hot laps across the floor.

I glanced over at Mom again, tracks of tears streamed down her cheeks and her body slumped against the wall—completely shattered. But she didn't look at me. She stared at Drew as if she was hanging onto his every word, likely more confused than I was. I scanned the back wall of the barn, trying to find a way to set her free, but from this distance I couldn't see how. I needed to get closer.

I inched farther into the barn, away from Drew but closer to the back wall. He mumbled to himself, pacing in jagged lines.

I crept forward again.

Drew shook his head and looked up. His eyes, narrowed to slits, burned through me. "When I came into this terrible world, my intention was to dominate the human species, but this stupid fleshy body holds me back. I can't do it alone, but we can do it together."

"I will never help you."

"What else are you good for? You can bring on someone's death simply by thinking about it. That's a gift that needs to be exploited."

"I won't kill anyone. Not for you."

"You will and you already have. That fascination. That

excitement in your eyes when you realized you had the power to choose whether something lives or dies. You're dead inside. Your demon will feed on your darkness until it overwhelms you and releases the trappings of your human side. The guilt, the sadness—all of it will melt away. You will finally be able to fulfill your destiny. With your skills and my vision, we could have these humans begging on their knees by the end of the month. Politicians, religious leaders, they'd bow down to us and we would rise against them all. We would be unstoppable."

"No." I pointed at him and gritted my teeth. "I'll never be like you."

"You just haven't accepted it, but you will. Stop fighting it."

"Never."

I clenched my fists and wind burst toward Drew, lifting him into the air and tossing him back onto the ground.

Mom yelped and backed away from him. Then she threw me a wide-eyed glance.

He quickly rose to his feet. "Don't waste your energy. It's already been decided."

"What's my other option?"

"There is no other option. You will be my ultimate weapon."

"You said I had a choice. What is my other option?"

He shrugged. "I'll kill your mother, then your boyfriend, and then anyone I can get my hands on until you agree to my first option."

Mom stared at me, trembling as tears poured down her cheeks, and she mouthed, "I'm sorry." As if everything were her fault.

Drew crossed his arms and anxiously tapped his foot, awaiting my response. He didn't offer me a choice. Either way, I'd become an executioner.

"So if I join you, you'll let her go?" I nodded toward Mom.

"No, Avery. Don't!" she yelled. She forced herself up on her knees and pulled at her restraints. "It's not worth it."

"Do we have a deal?" I had to get Mom out of here alive. I could plan my own escape later.

Drew stared at me, then her, then me again. "She would only keep you human. Keep you weak."

"I hate you."

I concentrated my disgust on Drew, throwing him into the air and slamming him against the back wall. The whole building shook. He clambered to his feet, and I threw him back down again. Then again.

He rolled onto his stomach and propped himself up on his elbows. "Kill me."

Kill me?

I stopped, breathless. "What?"

"Put me out of my misery. I can't die. I've tried. If you could kill me, I could get out of this body." He looked at me and excitement gleamed in his eyes. He hauled himself to his feet. "I will rip your world apart with or without you."

Kill him? It was tempting. Very tempting. The idea so simple. So perfect. Killing him would make everything better. After all, wasn't that exactly what I wanted?

The black film started to cover my eyes and ice prickled through my arms as if my body had made the decision before my head pulled the trigger. I let the sensation take me, strange and dark, my hate for him resonating as the invisible hands squeezed tighter on my neck. I didn't care how much it hurt, this was for a higher cause.

Killer, the familiar voice hissed in my ear.

Not a killer, I argued with the demon. *I'm saving the people I love.*

Killer, it mocked again.

My chest burned from a lack of oxygen and my body swayed. A haze formed over my thoughts.

"It's working." Drew's voice filtered through the haze. "Daddy's little killer."

But I wasn't. I didn't want to be.

The hands gripping my neck loosened and I could breathe again. The cold chill started to retreat.

If I killed him now, he'd win. He'd be set free and destroy me in the process. Maybe it was my destiny. Or maybe there was still time to decide for myself.

Killer. Killer. Killer. It echoed through my brain. *Killer.*

"No!" A scream escaped my throat and bounced around the peaked barn roof. The hands around my throat fell away, and I plunged back into the present.

"What the hell?" Drew scowled. "Just do it."

"I won't let you use me to get what you want. I'm not like you."

"Maybe you need a little motivation."

He reached into his pocket, flipped open his knife, and then tore off toward Mom.

Still woozy, I forced him back through the air. The knife slipped from his hand as he flew, and he crashed into a pile of crates.

"That's the spirit," he shouted, an elated grin breaking across his face. "Kill me."

"I can't."

"I guess you've made your choice. I knew I'd kill you both eventually anyway." He stood and took a battle stance—solid, aggressive, ready to fight.

A pair of rusty garden shears flew through the air. They sliced through my pants and scraped my skin. I howled and dropped to the ground, gripping my leg. Sharp pain shot through my calf. A shovel came at me, but I cast it away, wincing.

I scrambled to my feet before he could attack again. I needed to focus, but he wouldn't spare me a single second. I needed him to stay still. I needed him to freeze.

I planted my feet firmly and clenched my fists at my sides. A thick layer of ice started to crawl up over each of his legs and down his arms. He struggled to step forward, but the ice locked him to the ground. As the shiny surface spread upwards and encased his chest, his eyes bulged big and round like cue balls.

"Very clever." He cackled as the ice began to envelop his head.

It wouldn't hold him long, but it might give me enough time to think. I had to find a way to immobilize him long enough for us to get out of here.

The Entrapment Spell. Grandma made it work once. Maybe I could make it work again.

I stopped freezing Drew and started the spell.

"Protego, admoderor, defende. Protego, admoderor, defende..."

Wind swirled around the room, circling Drew's frozen body. Pain built at the back of my head, but I continued chanting. As its fury grew, the wind picked up momentum and churned into a deeper gray.

Suddenly, a burst of flame shot up from the center of the funnel cloud. The cloud dropped, freeing Drew as the ice melted.

"Nice try," he said. The delight drained from his face, replaced by a scowl of pure disgust. He held out his arms, palms up, and two streaks of orange flame shot out and ignited the wooden door frame behind me.

I bit down on my lip so hard that it stung, and I narrowed my gaze until the wind picked up again. The flames behind me roared higher. I tried not to panic and closed my eyes, blasting Drew with everything I had. Just as I regained control, a hard object socked me in the stomach, stealing my breath and sending me backward onto the ground. I opened my eyes. Rocks pelted from every direction. I raised my arms as a shield and redirected what I could, but they came harder and faster, pounding me into the dirt floor.

Then the beating stopped. I peered out from beneath my throbbing forearms. Drew lay face down on the ground. As he pushed himself up, Mom stared at him then blinked, biting her lip, and Drew dropped back down on his stomach. He grunted angrily, struggling to get upright. She blinked again, and Drew's arms collapsed as he crashed down.

"Enough," he screamed and raised his hand in her direction. A gust of wind knocked her off her knees and against the wall. He charged toward her and smacked her across the face. The undeniable sound of skin on skin rang off the rafters. Before I could run over and rip him apart, Mom grimaced, and Drew flew backward onto the ground again. As he pulled himself to his feet, she turned to me and nodded. Somehow, I knew this was the chance I needed.

I closed my eyes, trying to block out the chaos. I focused hard, drawing strength from conviction. Flashing images of Grandma, Mom, Bennett, and even Lily, urged me to keep going. I felt lighter and lighter until I couldn't feel the ground beneath my feet. I reached into my coat and wrapped my hand around the heart necklace, yanking the chain loose from my neck.

My eyes snapped open. Drew stared at the pendant dangling from my fist. A bubble of pure agony floated up the back of my spine and I knew it was time. "*Protego, admoderor, defende...*"

Wind kicked up dirt from the ground, engulfing Drew in a

dusty haze. As the air churned faster, pain ripped up my spine to the top of my head. The windy haze darkened until a dark black column twisted and writhed before me.

As Grandma's ancient magic flowed through me, the necklace swung viciously in my hand, and the metal links burned the flesh of my palm. A frantic pulse strobed in my ears and a bitter taste soured my tongue. I had to hold on.

Smoke filled the room as the fire reached the roof. A flaming beam crashed down on my right. Pain jolted through my skull and throbbed behind my left eye, turning the barn into a dizzy blur. My knees wavered as my breathing slowed.

I wasn't going to make it.

The chain whipped harder against my fist, and the dark funnel hurtled toward it, knocking me on my back. The darkness burrowed into the small pendant, nearly wrenching it from my hand.

"No!" Drew's voice shrieked from the vanishing funnel. The pendant stilled in my grasp.

Slowly, I inched my way to the back of the barn on quaking knees and grabbed the rope binding Mom's hands. I pulled and twisted at the knots, but they wouldn't give.

"Just go." Tears poured down Mom's cheeks. "Save yourself."

I sagged against the wall. I couldn't leave her. If she died here, so would I.

I wrapped my arms around her and buried my head in her shoulder. She smelled like Mom. Laundry soap and vanilla and that sweet something I could never place but could recognize anywhere. I wanted to apologize for everything I'd done. For getting us both into this and not being strong enough to get us out. No words seemed right. She could always find the words to make things better, but maybe I only inherited bad things.

I squeezed her as tightly as my sore arms could manage. "I love you."

"I love you too, baby." She nuzzled my hair.

Tears came fast, but I didn't want to let go to wipe them away. Through my wet eyes, the flames blurred. A burning timber crashed behind me and my head jerked back. A piece of metal on the floor glinted in the light. I blinked. Drew's knife.

I tried to stand, but my legs were too numb to respond. I reached forward, grabbed the knife handle, and collapsed against the wall, gasping for air. Then I crawled toward Mom. Clumsily, I slit the ropes, and Mom wrapped my arm over her shoulders, struggling to help me stand.

The smoke thickened. Flames moved toward the back of the building. Mom hauled me out through the barn doors. I pulled her arm from my shoulder and collapsed like a doll onto the snow. We were still too close to the fire, but safer than we were inside.

"What are you doing? We need to get out of here." Mom tried to hoist me up again.

"No. This needs to end."

I propped myself up on one arm and leaned forward, every muscle quivering under the weight. I swung the pendant in front of my face, the chain tightly clenched in my fist. A small gray spot bled out from the center of the heart, growing, consuming the warm gold plating until the entire necklace shone a cool silver in the moonlight.

I focused on the snowy ground in front of me and pictured deep layers of earth and rock shifting below. The ground opened with a thunderous crack, ripping a small chasm through the barn. Pain tore through my head and I screamed.

I dropped the necklace into the crack and willed the ground to seal itself.

It swallowed my father.

I screamed again as my trembling arm gave out and I slammed onto the ground. My head smacked so hard against the packed snow that I swore it burst open. Through my hazy vision, yellow and orange flames danced in the evening sky above. Was I still alive, or had I gone straight to hell?

THIRTY-EIGHT

AN ANTISEPTIC SMELL—STRONG, CHEMICAL—SET MY nostrils afire, as a rectangular block of white light swayed in and out of focus. Closer, brighter. Then finally it settled in place among the speckled ceiling tiles.

Telephones shrieked over the murmur of muffled voices. The buzz of hushed words, somewhere near, but too far away to comprehend. Ahead of me, a wall-mounted television solidified, dark and heavy in the blurry haze.

Yep. Still here.

I pushed down on the lumpy hospital mattress, arching my shoulders off the bed and sliding up to a seated position. Fireworks exploded behind my eyes, red and blue starbursts pulsing in time to the searing pain shooting out the top of my head.

Still not better yet either.

Resting back on the pillow, I carefully angled my head toward the window. My fists clenched as the last waves of ache rippled through my brain and started to subside. Last night passed in panic. Flashes of hallway lights as they wheeled me to my room. Frantic faces asking too many questions, met with garbled responses. Everything seemed so far away from the stillness of this morning—or afternoon. Who knew how long I'd slept?

Mom slumped near my shoulder on a mint-green chair with her eyes closed and one of Grandma's journals spread open on her thigh. Bands of sunlight streamed through the window and across her face, intensifying the creases of her skin that, even in sleep, pinched tight with worry. She knew the truth now, or at least most of it, and who knew how long she'd rest uneasy because of that.

I laced my fingers with hers and traced my thumb over her scratched knuckles, fear tightly gripping my sore chest. I'd almost lost her because of Drew. I'd almost lost myself.

Mom let out a soft groan, then slowly shifted.

Smack!

The journal tumbled from her lap and crashed on the dingy linoleum floor. She jerked upright, ripping her hand from mine, her eyes wide and bloodshot.

"Hey, you're awake." She let out a deep breath, then stretched her arms over her head and yawned, suspending her pointed toes just above the floor. "How'd you sleep?"

"All right, I guess. Had a lot to think about." I turned my head toward the ceiling again. "A lot to feel awful about."

"You too, huh?" Mom grumbled. "I just kept thinking that if I'd done things differently ... if I'd paid more attention to you, then maybe I could've done something sooner. Could've saved you from him."

"It's okay, Mom. It's my fault too. I should've told you what was going on."

"But he was my mistake. And there is so much I never knew." Her voice wavered, and she rubbed her palms up and down my arm. "I've made so many mistakes. I'm really sorry, Avery."

I placed my left hand on top of hers and squeezed.

She squeezed back tighter, her grip lingering, whispering to me in the silence.

I let go and rolled onto my right side, stiffness percolating in my shoulders. Mom settled back into her chair, swooping her arm down and snatching the fallen journal from the floor. She tucked it into her purse.

"So ... how long have you known that we were ... well, you know ... witches?" I asked, still unsure where to start this conversation. It seemed to come so easily to Mom when she grilled me last night about what I knew, but we'd hidden so much from each other that learning the whole truth would be a long process.

"Since Detroit. Since Grandma passed away." Mom crossed her legs and pulled her arms tight into her sides. "She told me about the magic when she was in the hospital, and shortly after we moved to Shady Creek, her executor sent me a sealed letter with a key to the trunk of journals and instructions on how to find it. I've been trying to make sense of everything ever since."

"But why didn't you tell me?"

She turned her head towards the window. "Because I didn't know what it all meant, and I didn't want you to get hurt. I thought I was protecting you until you were old enough to understand. Besides, everything was new for you here. I didn't want to pile on another challenge."

I crept closer to the edge of the bed. "I would've been okay."

"I know that now," she said with a shaky voice. "But I never knew about Nick. What really happened to him. Why he—that's one secret she managed to take with her."

She exhaled and turned toward the bed again, a thick line of tears glistening in her eyes. "I guess no matter how hard I tried not to be my mother, I turned out exactly like her. With the same terrible results."

"It's not all your fault."

"Maybe not, but it sure feels like it is." She forced a grin and wiped her eyes with her sleeve. "There will be plenty of time to talk about this once we get home. It's officially Christmas break, and I expect nothing but sitting on the couch and watching every obnoxiously happy Christmas movie ever made. How about that? Just you and me and Whisk—" Her face scrunched up, tears building again.

"I'm so sorry, Mom." I wrapped the itchy hospital sheets around my hands and tucked them into my fists, guilt clutching tight around my throat.

"I know," she whispered. "It was a difficult choice. You did what you had to do."

"I didn't want to hurt her. She was just in so much pain, and I couldn't stop it. I tried, I swear I did, but I—"

"Enough." She tented her hands together over her nose and mouth and huffed, then shook her head. "I'm not quite ready to deal with all of this yet."

"How's my favorite patient feeling today?" Dr. J. appeared around the corner, still wearing the same clothes as last night, a shadow of stubble spread across his jaw. Looked like he didn't get much sleep either.

"She's doing much better." Mom leaped up and wiped her hands over her face, then stood at the foot of the bed and tugged down the hem of her shirt. "Thank you for all your help."

Dr. J. flashed a line of perfectly straight teeth. He grabbed my chart from the slot on the wall and scanned the pages. "Everything looks good, Avery. Keep it up, and you'll be out of here by tomorrow."

"Tomorrow? But I really want to go home. You even said that you couldn't find anything wrong with me, no scratches, bruises, nothing from when I—"

"Fell down the stairs," Mom quickly added and flashed me a hard stare.

Dr. J. put the chart back on the wall. "Yes, I understand that, but you still came in here barely conscious. Plus, your headaches and severe exhaustion are not things to ignore."

"But I'm feeling better." I sat up and forced a smile. The

room swirled and distorted as the pain in my head surged back. "Honest."

"I'm glad to hear that, but since this is your second trip to the ER in under four days, I'm inclined to keep you here a little longer."

"Do you really think that's necessary?" Mom asked. "I can keep a close eye on her, and I'm sure Avery would rest better in her own bed."

Dr. J. cupped his chin, running his index finger down the side of his cheek, his questioning stare darting between Mom and me. "I don't know."

Mom tucked her hair behind her ear and stepped closer, her head seeming to tilt slightly to the side. She mumbled, "Please, Patrick?"

Patrick? Where did that come from?

He sighed, his gaze dropping to the floor while his lips lifted upward into a warm smile. "Fine. But if anything happens you need to call me immediately. Okay?"

Mom nodded. "Thank you for being so understanding. It means a lot."

Dr. J.'s smile shone in his eyes.

Mom twisted her fingers together behind her back, her cheeks turning from pink to red. "And would you mind writing up a note for Avery's teachers? I don't want a small health issue to affect her exam marks. Especially with college next year."

"Of course. Now, Avery," he said, still looking at Mom. "Make sure you rest and drink plenty of fluids. If your headache gets worse or you have any other problems, come straight back to the hospital."

"Thanks." Relief flooded through me. Going home. It was finally over.

Dr. J. reached into the pocket of his white coat and handed

me a lemon-yellow sucker. "Now take care of your Mom and be good, all right?"

~

My only goal for winter vacation was to do absolutely nothing and so far, I was right on track. Curled up on the couch in a flannel blanket cocoon, I stared at the twinkling tree lights reflecting in the window as a Christmas Eve movie marathon blared from the television in the corner. The ache in my head had finally subsided that morning, but I was still weak and far from my old self, if I remembered what my old self was like.

"Are you coming?" Mom poked her head around the foyer corner with a festive green, crocheted beanie on her head.

"Can't we just stay home? You promised. Just me, you, and television this year." I rolled onto my stomach and smooshed my face into the couch cushions. My left arm flopped down to the hardwood. I'd never been more grateful for only Mom and me celebrating the holidays together.

I'd seen enough of my other family for a lifetime.

"And it will be just us ... after the Christmas tree lighting in town square. It's a Shady Creek tradition. We have to go." She yanked on her gloves and scrutinized herself in the foyer mirror. "Besides, you need to get out of this house once in a while. You're starting to smell."

I tucked my nose into my sweater and took a whiff. "I don't smell. I totally showered this morning."

"Get up, Avery. You're going. End of story."

"Fine." I peeled back the layers of blanket and gritted my teeth. The brisk air of reality brushed my skin as I shuffled across the living room. This whole Christmas tree lighting thing sounded hokey, but right now, I could handle hokey. Plain, boring, or even cheesy would even be all right, but why couldn't it be indoors? I needed to start making things up to Mom, just not with frostbitten fingers.

"Hurry up, we're going to be late," she urged as I pulled my boots on.

I slipped on my coat and raced out the door after her but stopped short on the front step. On the sidewalk at the end of the yard, Bennett stood leaning over a set of silver crutches.

Bennett? At my house? Now?

Mom rushed past me and down the front walkway toward him.

Warmth rushed my cheeks as I smoothed my couch potato hair and checked my breath against my palm. It appeared that Mom still planned to keep some secrets from me, but ones like these were definitely okay.

"Thanks for inviting me, Ms. Belmont," Bennett said.

"You're welcome." She extended her hand, and he shifted his crutches to balance on his good leg, then awkwardly took her hand, almost falling into the snowbank. "I'm glad you could make it."

She turned and gave me stern look, softened by a smile. "I'll see you in the square. Don't take too long or I will come back for you."

I nodded and made my way down the front steps as she scurried down the street. Bennett's cast glowed with brightly-colored well wishes and scribbles. He'd been busy over the last week.

"Hey," I said, my voice uneasy.

"I heard you were in the hospital again. How are you feeling?" He smiled, his green eyes studying my face in that knee-quivering, heart-fluttering way I thought I'd never see again.

"Good, I guess. Still a bit shaky. You?"

"I'm fine, but who knew you were such a weakling?" He laughed. "Exhaustion? Really? Maybe you just need a nap."

"Hey, that's not fair." I playfully punched him in the shoulder.

He wobbled backward, his left crutch slipping out to the side. I grabbed his arm and held him upright, our bodies suddenly so close his breath rustled the hair dangling by my ear.

"No need to be so violent." He steadied himself and laughed again. Light and easy. Happy.

I stepped back and wrenched my jacket sleeves into my fists. "I'm actually surprised to see you here. After what Lily said, I figured you'd want nothing to do with me."

"I haven't listened to my sister before. Why would I start now?" Bennett shrugged. "She's overprotective, that's all. It's a twin thing. Plus, she's been having a rough couple of weeks and probably just took it out on you."

"Maybe. But hiding from her for the next six months might still be a good idea," I joked, but honestly, I didn't care what she thought anymore. There wasn't anything Lily could do that would be worse than Drew had subjected me to.

"I hope not." Bennett tugged at my sleeve and took my hand. "She'll have to get used to having you around. That is, if you want to be around?"

I glanced down at his fingers wrapped around mine and grinned. "I'd really like that."

"Good." He nodded and then his expression hardened. "So now there's only one thing left to deal with."

My chest tightened. What now?

"I was hoping for a second chance at that first kiss."

I breathed again. "Are you sure? Might be a bit danger—"

Bennett's lips pressed against my mouth as I swallowed the rest of my sentence, and mentally agreed to never speak again if he promised not to stop. I closed my eyes and kissed him back, knowing for once there was no Drew, no Lily, or anyone else to spoil it. It was what I wanted every kiss for the rest of my life to be like. Sweet, uncomplicated, and absolutely perfect.

He rested his forehead against mine and his words fell warm on my lips. "Much better."

I opened my eyes.

"No casualties this time," I said, half-joking, half-relieved.

His smile widened and his cheeks flushed. Maybe it was the cool evening breeze, or maybe his heartbeat raced as fast as mine. Too soon, he pulled away and situated his crutches. "Better go. Don't want your mom wondering where we are."

The second we entered the small courtyard in the middle of town, Mom waved her arms to flag us down. We zig-zagged through the crowd. Couples holding hands, kids laughing as they pelted each other with snowballs, and some people just standing there, staring up at the dark tree towering into the night sky, faces alight with anticipation for the first shining spark of the holiday. For the first time in a long while, things felt like there were going to be all right. They felt ... well ... normal.

We found a spot next to Mom near the front, just as the tree lights flicked on. Applause thundered and a chorus of "oohing" and "aahing" rose from the crowd as a bright, multi-colored glow washed over us. It reflected off buildings and snowbanks and happy wide-eyed gazes that were glued to the tree.

You could kill them all.

My mouth dropped open and a petrifying chill blasted through my veins.

That voice. It couldn't be. It couldn't be Drew. I'd made sure of that.

I frantically searched through the crowd.

They're weak. Do it.

The world spun into streaks of red and green. Laughter, loud and menacing, distorted around me. The noxious scent of people smothered my senses. All these people.

Do it! the voice demanded, clear and in command. The demon voice. The sick, demented version of my own voice that I'd inherited from my sick, demented father. I grabbed the sides of my head and tried to rip the thoughts from my brain, afraid everyone else could hear the terrible things I was thinking.

It would be so easy. Think of the power you have over them.

Black dripped behind my eyes and slowly seeped across my vision. I struggled to force it back, shaking and gasping for air. The crowd of smiling faces around me looked surreal as if I was standing outside a frosted window staring in. Watching them.

Not watching. Stalking.

I rubbed my temples and stared at the ground trying to focus. No, no, no. This was over. Drew was gone. I wasn't that person anymore.

Something fell on my shoulders. I pushed it away. "Get off."

Bennett pulled his arm back. "Whoa. Are you okay?"

"I'm fine," I blurted. I stared at the snow-covered ground, trying to find my breath. The whirling slowly settled as my stomach teetered like a spinner about to topple. I looked up. The world moved at normal pace again. It was all over.

I glanced at Bennett. Shock still stained his face.

"Are you sure, Avery? You look like it's the end of the world or something."

I chuckled, the sound broken and awkward through my clenched jaw. "Of course."

Bennett put his arm around me and I settled in closer to him.

He gave me a quick kiss on the cheek. "Because everything seems pretty great right now."

I smiled, while my stomach tied itself into knots. I listened for the voice, but nothing. Just the cheery sing-song voices of everyone around me.

"There is one thing that would make this better though," I said. "A little snow."

I raised my face toward the sky, concentrating until wet drops of snow melted on my cheeks and big fluffy flakes cascaded gently all around us. My own private snow globe.

I closed my eyes and tried to lock this scene away in my memory. A time when, for the moment, everything was okay. Drew was gone, Mom and Bennett were safe, and I finally knew exactly who I was. Being descended from evil didn't make me wicked. I knew that now. It was all a choice. My choice. Not my father's. Not the voices in my head. Mine. And I was choosing to be good. To control myself and my powers.

I had to. The world depended on it.

ABOUT THE AUTHOR

Born and raised in Northern Manitoba, Scarlett Kol grew up reading books and writing stories about creatures that make you want to sleep with the lights on. She believed that the treasures in her mother's jewelry box were magic amulets that would give her immeasurable power and old books could transport her to secret worlds. As an adult, not much has changed. Connect with Scarlett on social media or on her website www.scarlettkol.com.

facebook.com/scarlettkolauthor

instagram.com/scarlettkol

bookbub.com/profile/scarlett-kol

tiktok.com/@scarlettkol